→

→

PRAISE FOR *WALL OF BRASS* AND ROBERT DALEY

→

"HIGHLY UNCONVENTIONAL, AND RICHLY REWARDING SLEUTHING. . . . Mr. Daley emerged in the 1970s as the leading chronicler of unsavory activities behind closed doors at the city's station houses and Police Headquarters. Now he's back in his element, using the whodunit frame for an often absorbing exploration of renegade police work and ugly departmental politics."
—*New York Times Book Review*

"CAPTIVATES. . . . Robert Daley knows all the angles and how to tell a story. There's no pat solution to this mystery, either. The resolution is a stunner."
—*Cleveland Plain Dealer*

"FIRST RATE! TIGHT AND TAUTLY TOLD . . . AN ABSORBING CHARACTER STUDY . . . it's built around a character that readers will care about. . . . As in his best work, moreover, the author displays his bone-deep knowledge of New York cops and criminals."
—*Publishers Weekly* (starred review)

"THE WRITING IS CRISP, THE INSIGHTS CERTAIN. . . . In the New York Police Department, Daley has found an institution that does not budge. That makes *WALL OF BRASS* not only a great whodunit but also a fine novel of manners."
—*Washington Post Book World*

→

more . . .

→

"A SHARPLY ETCHED PORTRAIT OF A COMPLEX INSTITUTION AND THE FALLIBILITY AND DEVIOUSNESS OF THE PEOPLE CHARGED WITH RUNNING IT. . . . Daley has always been at his best in the higher reaches of the department, and it's gratifying to have him back where he belongs with *WALL OF BRASS*. He is a knowing topographer of the corridors of power. . . . A well-turned mystery . . . *WALL OF BRASS* plays to all his strengths and hard-earned insights."

—*Philadelphia Inquirer*

"A SCORCHING PROCEDURAL THRILLER. . . . A DANDY DETECTIVE STORY, WITH A STINGER AT THE END. But it's even better as a character study. . . . No one writes more knowingly or entertainingly about the New York Police Department than Robert Daley . . . HE IS A CONSUMMATE STORYTELLER."

—*Buffalo News*

"MR. DALEY HAS MADE THE NEW YORK POLICE THRILLER HIS SPECIAL PROVINCE, AND THIS ONE IS ESPECIALLY GOOD."

—*Dallas Morning News*

→

→

"ENTHRALLING. . . . Daley's sparse descriptions approach poetry. [He] is a master of character portrayal and his work transcends the label of police thriller. Chief of Detectives Bert Farber is an immensely appealing character."
—*Stamford Advocate & Greenwich Time*

"A POWERFUL PORTRAIT OF A BULLDOG COP WHO DOESN'T EVEN KNOW HIMSELF WHY HE WON'T LET GO."
—*Kirkus Reviews*

"DALEY KNOWS WHEREOF HE WRITES."
—*Pittsburgh Press*

"MR. DALEY TAKES ME INTO MORE CORNERS OF NEW YORK CITY THAN I KNEW EXISTED." —James A. Michener

"DALEY KNOWS THE COP WORLD. . . . He writes excellently about New York's racial and sexual politics. One of his best talents is displaying people in power jockeying for position, A CALCULUS OF WHICH HE IS A MASTER."
—*Mystery News*

→

ROBERT DALEY

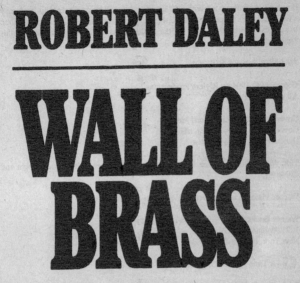

WALL OF BRASS

WARNER VISION BOOKS

A Time Warner Company

WARNER BOOKS EDITION

Copyright © 1994 by Riviera Productions Ltd.
All rights reserved.

Cover design by Jackie Merri Meyer
Cover illustration by Marvin Mattieson
Hand lettering by Tony Russo

This Warner Books edition is published by arrangement with Little, Brown and Company.

Warner Vision is a trademark of Warner Books, Inc.

Warner Books, Inc
1271 Avenue of the Americas
New York, NY 10020

A Time Warner Company

Printed in the United States of America

First Warner Books Printing: December, 1995
10 9 8 7 6 5 4 3 2 1

Let this be your wall of brass: to have nothing on your conscience, no guilt to make your face turn pale.

Horce *Epistles* 1.i.60

WALL OF
BRASS

∎1∎

THE PHONE rang.

The man had been heavily asleep, deep into the last dream of the night. Lunging for the phone in the dark, he knocked the bedside clock to the floor, and nearly the phone as well, but caught it. It was the hour when, if the phone rang at all, a man braced himself for bad news. A stroke or heart attack. A car crash. A distraught relative's voice. At this time of night, what else could it be?

But this man, as he brought the phone to his ear, was not alarmed, only confused by sleep. He was trying to orient himself. Men who worked for him, whenever certain events occurred, had orders to wake him up, and often did. Almost certainly a tragedy was about to be described, but it would not be personal to him.

Speaking softly because his wife beside him might still be asleep, he said his name and rank into the phone:

"Chief Farber."

At the same time he swung his legs out, groping for the clock on the rug.

"Something's happened. How soon can you get here?"

It was cold in the room—the window gaped like a yawn. The Farbers had been sleeping under an eiderdown, and it was still dark outside. Six-thirty, he saw, bringing the clock to his face. Almost time to get up anyway.

Bert P. Farber was chief of detectives, New York Police Department. He was in direct command of three thousand men.

"We're at Seventy-seventh and Columbus."

It was the voice of First Deputy Commissioner Priestly, who, from the traffic noises in the background, must be standing in a phone booth. What had brought him out so early? What had caused the slight tremor in his voice? Farber judged that it was grave, whatever it was.

"What's happened?"

"Just get here," said Priestly.

The first dep was an administrator, not a street cop. He managed the police bureaucracy, and shouldn't be on the street at all. What was he doing out there at six-thirty in the morning?

Priestly hadn't bothered to identify himself. Apparently he considered his voice and authority so well known that he didn't have to. Peremptory commands were enough.

Police headquarters seethed with ambitious men, of whom Bert P. Farber was one. All of them had learned to be exceedingly respectful in the presence of higher rank. If you wished to get ahead in the department there was no other way.

And Priestly was a man who seemed to like subservience from his subordinates. He seemed to like obsequiousness even better. But there were times when the chief of detectives stood up to him, and this was one of them. Having been awakened out of a sound sleep, Farber was in no mood to be pushed around. "Who is this?" he demanded.

"At this hour you're about ten minutes away."

"My car is in the garage and my driver is asleep."

"I'm sending a radio car for you. It's probably already out front."

"I have time to take a piss?"

The first dep had a way of projecting self-importance. "Do you know who this is?" he said menacingly.

"Now I do," Chief Farber said. "Be there in ten minutes."

When he had hung up he punched new numbers into the phone: his duty sergeant at headquarters. "Call my driver," he ordered. "I'll be at Seventy-seventh and Columbus. Have him meet me there."

Madge Farber had sat up and put on the bedside lamp.

"Would you mind telling me what that was all about?"

"Guy didn't say." He went over and closed the window.

"You know something?" said Madge. "I'm getting a little

tired of asking you questions and never getting a straight answer."

Her husband looked at her. "You want to argue, we can argue later."

He went out of the room knotting his necktie, and on the way down the hall grabbed his coat out of the hall closet and his attaché case off the floor. Then he was out of the apartment and bounding down the service steps without waiting for the elevator.

He came out through the glass doors and found that it was snowing. There was snow on the bushes and trees in front, and on the roofs of the parked cars along the curb.

The blue and white was waiting double-parked. One of the cops jumped out and held open the rear door.

The car had a cage across the backrest, and no interior door handles. The chief of detectives had no intention of riding as a prisoner to whatever awaited him.

"You," he said to the cop. "You ride back there, see how you like it," and he jumped into the front. After a moment the cop got in behind him and the door slammed.

"Seventy-seventh and Columbus," he told the cop at the wheel. "Put the roof light on. Run the traffic signals. Use the siren if you need to. Let's go."

The wheels fishtailed in the snow, whined, bit, and they were off. Once out on Third Avenue, the cop floored it. They went up the middle of the avenue at eighty miles an hour. Along the sidewalks snow drifted down through cones of light. The street looked wet and slick, and at each intersection the cop at the wheel slowed only slightly. Racing to crime scenes was the most dangerous work cops did, Chief Farber well knew, and he steeled himself for the collision that could come anytime. Although there were few cars moving, just one would be enough. But because he had no intention of showing these two cops—any cop—that he was afraid, he said nothing, but opened his attaché case instead. Reaching in past his gun, his sap, his handcuffs, his flashlight, a box of bullets, and some case folders, he withdrew his cordless shaver. He pulled the sun visor down to expose the vanity mirror. As nonchalantly as he could under the circumstances he began to shave.

By 60th Street the snow had turned to rain, which was a little less dangerous, not much, and he had finished shaving. Smoothing his face with his hand he said to the driver: "Anything come over the radio?"

"Not a thing, Chief."

This was curious in itself. Whatever had caused him to be summoned in what amounted to the middle of the night was not general knowledge as yet. A fire or explosion or some other catastrophe would have brought calls for units from elsewhere in the city. These cops would have heard it over the emergency band.

"It's been real quiet," said the cop in the back, his face so close to the grill that Chief Farber could feel his breath on his neck.

The two of them must have wondered what they were rushing toward, but they were only cops, and he was chief of detectives, so they did not ask him.

At 72nd Street the car knifed into the park. There was snow on the grass to either side, but the rain was coming down harder.

Once across the park, they raced up Central Park West and turned onto 77th along the face of the museum, moving slowly now because there were two radio cars parked broadside halfway down the street, and a taxi and another car were making U-turns, having been turned back. Steering through the gap between the police cars, they saw that the street beyond was snarled with other police vehicles.

Chief Farber threw the door open and stepped out into the rain and slush.

"Want us to wait for you, Chief?"

When you hitched a ride in a radio car the two cops always wanted to wait for you. A crime that drew the presence of the chief of detectives was an important crime. The city got plenty of those, but individual cops got two or three in a career. These cops here wanted to be part of this thing, see what the headquarters brass was going to do with it. At the very least, find out what it was.

"You fellows go back on patrol," Chief Farber told them. "Thanks for the ride."

Ignoring their disappointment he strode forward, hands in

his pockets, shoulders hunched, coat collar turned up, the rain beating at his hair. It was a cold rain and it was coming down pretty hard.

At the corner about thirty people milled around. Some captains in uniform. Some detectives in trench coats and snap-brim hats. Many patrol cops, including two big-assed women. The women had their hair tucked under their caps. They stood in the rain trying to twirl their nightsticks like veterans.

His first instinct was to think like a commander: nobody was doing anything. They were just standing around. Who was in charge here?

He was looking for First Deputy Commissioner Priestly, and he was looking for the body—he had always assumed there would be a body. Perhaps several.

The first dep was in a doorway, standing with John Kincaid, who was commander of Manhattan North detectives.

Chief Farber could see the body now. It was on the corner diagonally across Columbus Avenue, mostly on the sidewalk but with its arms outflung and its face in the gutter. Rainwater moved past its nose toward the sewer.

There was no one over there. Just the body. If there was only the one that was good, he wouldn't have to cope with a massacre, but also bad—to draw a crowd like this, it was somebody prominent. He peered up and down the street. There could be other bodies hidden by the parked cars, but it didn't look like it.

Columbus Avenue had been blocked off two streets up, he saw—more radio cars parked sideways, roof lights turning. Cops up there were diverting traffic onto 79th Street. The few pedestrians at this hour were being turned back as well.

Impressions were rushing at him fast and he was trying to coordinate them.

The doorway in which the first dep stood belonged, he saw, to a restaurant called Isabella's, and he stepped up into it. It was nice to be out of the rain for a moment. The other two men made room for him—grudgingly, he thought—and he studied what he could see of the body across the street.

"Who got killed?" he said.

"Go see," said First Deputy Commissioner Priestly.

"I get it," said Chief Farber. "You think it's someone I'll recognize."

"You'll recognize him."

"My brother-in-law. Somebody finally got the prick."

Kincaid snickered, but the first dep did not.

"Let me guess. The governor? Everybody would like to drill that guy. No, from your face I can tell it's not the governor. An actor maybe? That new comedian who's not too funny?"

The first dep stared at him until he allowed himself to be stared down.

"If the guy's so important, why is he still lying there?"

"We're waiting for the medical examiner," said Kincaid.

"I hope he gets here soon," said Chief Farber. "In thirty minutes there'll be five thousand people moving past this corner."

Leaving the doorway he crossed the empty intersection. No need to watch for a break in the traffic. Nothing moving in any direction. In a city as busy as New York this felt exceedingly strange.

The body was wearing sneakers, a designer jogging suit, a muffler around its neck, and a stocking cap pulled low over the ears. The muffler had fallen across the guy's head, or else some cop had laid it there as if to afford the corpse some privacy.

The chief of detectives bent down, lifted the muffler away, recognized the dead face, and immediately stood up and peered into the rain. It coursed down his face and felt like tears. Although he had spent much of his adult life looking down on bodies on sidewalks, nothing in those years had prepared him for this. After a moment he knelt down and put his hand on the corpse's shoulder.

A car was coming up Columbus Avenue, he saw, coming the wrong way on the one-way street. It stopped a few feet away and one of the assistant medical examiners, a Korean named Chang, got out carrying his bag.

"Somebody you know?" asked Chang as he approached. "You look like it's your brother."

"It's the police commissioner," Bert Farber said. He stood up, put his hand to his face, and wiped off some of the moisture.

"Jesus," said Chang.

"Yeah."

"Well," said Chang, "let's get him out of the water." He bent down on the other side of the body. "Help me with him."

They rolled the corpse over. As the face came up the eyes were staring. The rain struck them and they did not blink. It made Chief Farber look away for a moment. When he looked back Chang had closed them.

"How long has he been dead, Doc?"

Raising the corpse's arm, Chang let it drop, and it fell backward into the gutter, where the water was an inch or so deep. There was a watch on the wrist. That went into the water too. If the watch was not waterproof, it would be ruined, and Farber wanted to remove it from the water, though why? Its owner was dead.

"No rigor yet, right," Chang said. He lifted and dropped the arm, splash, a second time. "Thirty minutes, forty."

Chang had begun an exterior examination of the corpse's clothing. "Police Commissioner Chapman. Imagine that," he said. "So what do you suppose killed him?"

Farber said: "I hope you're going to tell me natural causes."

"A man this young? I doubt it."

The chief of detectives doubted it too. So did all the men across the street, he assumed. Otherwise, they wouldn't be there.

Chang unzipped the corpse's jacket, peeled up the sweater and T-shirt underneath, and a wound appeared, and he pointed to it. "That's what did the job, I imagine."

Chief Farber had seen dozens of bullet wounds, perhaps hundreds. He did not have to be told what he was looking at. He said: "I was hoping it was a heart attack—some goddam thing."

"Heart attack," said Chang. "Yeah. That's what it was, when you come right down to it."

The hole was from a fairly big caliber gun, a .38 perhaps. It was in the V of the chest, and puckered, like the mouth of a doll. A little blood had seeped out, not much. When the bullet hits the pump, Bert Farber reflected, the faucet runs dry.

It was easier to focus on the technical aspects of this than on the man who was dead.

"The back might be worse, if it went through," Chang said.

The morgue wagon had come into the street. The attendants were lifting their stretcher out of the back.

"Who could have done it?" Chang inquired, still studying the corpse.

This was what the chief of detectives had begun asking himself. It could be anyone. He said: "You tell me, Doc."

"Harry Chapman," murmured Chang. "I wouldn't have expected it. Would you?"

He's not affected by this at all, Bert Farber thought. He's more professional than I am.

They watched the attendants roll the stretcher up and throw back the rubberized wings of the body bag.

"I'll know more when I get him back to the shop," Chang said. "I'll call you."

"As soon as possible, Doc."

The attendants lifted the corpse. When they dropped the police commissioner on top of the bag he seemed to shiver, as if they had hurt him, which made Bert Farber bite down on his lip.

The attendants arranged the dead man and began folding over the flaps and zipping them up. The body bag looked long and heavy. As a patrolman, Harry had been a tall, thin young man. Of course dead men were always heavy.

Chang set off for his car even as a second car came onto the street and stopped, and the chief of the department, who was the highest uniformed officer and the man to whom Chief Farber reported, got out and strode forward. He had braid on the peak of his hat, four stars on each epaulette of his overcoat, and he was fuming.

He said to Farber: "They wake me up with this cryptic message to report—what the hell is going on here?" He gestured at the body bag. "Who's in there?"

"The police commissioner," Bert Farber said.

"The PC?"

"Somebody shot him," Bert Farber said.

"Who shot him?"

"Good question."

"Harry Chapman? Oh, Jesus."

The chief of the department, whose name was Terrence Sternhagen, was a big blustery man, but there was no bluster in him now. He spun around to face the opposite sidewalk, and his jaw seemed to be working. He said: "What are all those officers doing over there?"

"Waiting for somebody to tell them what to do."

"Well tell them then. That's your job."

Bert Farber said: "I just got here myself, Chief."

"A crime scene needs to be established. An investigation started." When Sternhagen stopped talking his jaw continued to work.

"I better see him," he said after a moment.

The chief of detectives nodded to the morgue attendants, who unfolded their flaps, and Harry Chapman was exposed to the rain a second time.

The first dep had come across from the opposite sidewalk. He stopped beside Sternhagen and they gazed down on the corpse for what seemed to Bert Farber like several minutes.

There's just the three of us now at the top of the department, Farber reflected, watching them. The mayor will have to appoint a new police commissioner, and it will have to be one of us, because he won't have much time to look around.

The law gave the mayor only ten days.

Which one of us will it be? Farber asked himself. He looked down on the corpse and then away. The first dep and the chief of the department had rank and seniority on him. Did he himself have a chance at the job? If he could crack this case quickly, yes. Otherwise probably not. He would be considered too young, too controversial.

The body of Harry Chapman lay on top of the body bag on top of the stretcher, and the attendants waited for orders to zip him up and move him.

"What was he doing out in weather like this?" said Sternhagen.

"Jogging," said Chief Farber. He saw that the plastic cover over Sternhagen's uniform cap was beaded with rain. "Supposedly he jogged three miles every morning."

"Harry Chapman was a fanatic about fitness," added the first dep.

As if trying to come to terms with what had happened, Sternhagen kept shaking his head. "But the weather," he said.

Chief Farber glanced up into the dark sky. "It was snowing earlier. It wasn't so bad."

"He was headed for the park," the first dep said. "Gonna run in the park, wouldn't you say, Bert?"

"You can't assume anything, Commissioner. At this stage you can't assume a goddam thing."

"So where do you start, Bert?" said Sternhagen.

In his head the chief of detectives had already started. The PC lived in Greenwich Village. He lived nowhere near this street corner. So what was he doing here at six o'clock in the morning? Could he have run all this way? Unlikely. If not, how did he get here?

He thought that these questions might occur to the other two men as well. So far, apparently, they had not.

First Deputy Commissioner Priestly was peering down at the late Harry Chapman. "How do you see the case, Bert?"

The tremor was back in his voice. Unquestionably this had shaken him—and not only the shock of Chapman's death. Probably he had wanted to run the police department all his adult life. Now, at least until a new commissioner was appointed, he would have to do it.

"You got a plan?" the first dep asked Farber. Priestly, who was near retirement age, had never been a detective. Neither had Chief Sternhagen. For once they were dependent on Bert P. Farber.

It was a moment before he answered. Priestly was obviously a shaken man, but it wouldn't last. Unless you keep him off balance, Farber told himself, he is going to lean on you night and day.

"I see it as your typical easy case," he decided to say. "No witnesses, no motive, no handle of any kind. How do you see it?"

"I want to know what you think," said Priestly.

"I think it was somebody who didn't like him."

First Deputy Commissioner Priestly did not grin back.

"An assassination?" said the chief of detectives rhetorically. "If so, which group? Black revolutionaries? Croatians? Islamic militants? The Medellín cartel? Puerto Ricans? The Mafia?"

"The Mafia never shoots cops."

"Maybe today they made an exception."

"You don't believe that."

"If some group takes credit, we may know a little better what we're looking for. Watch your local newspaper."

"I said I want to know what you think."

"It was a drug deal gone wrong," said Bert Farber. "The PC was secretly a drug dealer."

Be careful, he warned himself, when the first dep did not smile. Don't do or say anything to alienate this man. He might well be the next PC.

"Or it could have been someone he sent to jail in the past," he said, and paused. There was a good reason why cops kept their phone numbers unlisted. "Or maybe somebody tried to rob him. Stuck a gun in his chest and he resisted. Or he jogged up on some other crime in progress and tried to intervene. Possibly it was a personal settling of accounts. A jealous husband. A homosexual lover. Someone he cheated in a business deal or owed money to."

"A jealous husband?" said Sternhagen. "He wasn't that kind of man, was he?"

"People have secret lives that other people don't know about. That's because they keep them secret. Or so I've found. You've been a cop a long time. Is that what you've found?"

Sternhagen did not answer. Neither did the first dep.

"Or it could have been some freelance nut out on the street at six o'clock in the morning. Some weirdo who either knew who he was or didn't. Or a stray shot. Picture some drunken guy up in one of those kitchens up there." He gestured all around. "He's aiming at his wife, who screwed up the fried eggs again, and the shot comes out the window and kills Harry Chapman, who happens to be jogging by at that precise moment, and who also happens to be the police commissioner. You ask me what I think. I don't think anything. The possibilities at this stage are endless. I'm trying to keep an open mind. You should do the same."

Still and all, he had some ideas he was not mentioning yet.

"The first call I made," the first dep said, "I phoned the mayor."

The corpse on its stretcher was still at their feet. The scene was illuminated by the morgue wagon's headlights.

"Woke him up," the first dep said. "He was shocked."

Chief Farber watched spears of rain falling through spears of light.

"Then I phoned you men."

When one of the morgue attendants moved in front of the headlights the rain disappeared momentarily. Then it was falling again.

"So who tells his wife?" Chief Farber said.

Priestly and Sternhagen glanced at each other, and it was clear neither wanted to do it.

"Never mind," Farber said. "I'll go."

The first dep said: "I should be the one. I'm the one moves into his office."

"You'll be acting commissioner," said Sternhagen petulantly, "until the mayor appoints someone."

Good, thought Chief Farber, let the two of them fight about it.

He said: "I've known her so long it will be easier for her coming from me." He had known her longer than her dead husband and, for a time, better.

"That shouldn't be the criterion here," said the first dep.

"I have to talk to her anyway, trace his movements and so forth."

"I don't know," said the first dep.

"All right, Commissioner," said Chief Farber calmly, "you come with me." But when he saw how worried Sternhagen now looked, afraid someone might get half a step ahead of him, he added: "We can all three go if you like."

He saw both men considering what to do.

"Mrs. Chapman can make us breakfast," he said. He did not want the other two there. "Unless she's crying too much."

This remark decided it. "I don't think I can spare the time," said First Deputy Commissioner Priestly. "I now have the entire department to run. Express my condolences."

Chief Sternhagen said: "I'd best get back to headquarters

myself. There will be lots to do, as you can imagine. Tell her I'll stop by later."

"Just let me give out some instructions before I leave," said the chief of detectives. He recrossed the street and stepped up into the doorway beside John Kincaid.

Kincaid was a much older man and had been a detective commander longer, but Harry Chapman, upon becoming commissioner, had promoted Bert Farber over him. In group meetings Kincaid had been obliged to address Farber as "chief," but most times the word had seemed to stick in his throat. Most of the time Kincaid called him nothing.

"Who found him?" Chief Farber asked now.

"Two cops in a radio car." Kincaid got his notebook out. "You want their names?"

"Later. No witnesses, I assume."

"It was practically the middle of the night, and snowing. The cops said there was no one on the street."

Farber said: "Did anyone find his gun?" When a cop got killed, this was almost the first question. The presence or absence of the cop's gun posed additional questions, but sometimes answered some of them. If it was still in its holster, then the cop had been surprised. If it had been fired you scoured the hospitals for a wounded perpetrator. If it was missing altogether you were perhaps looking for revolutionaries.

"No gun, and nothing in his pockets. No ID, nothing."

"Beautiful."

"The first dep and I both live near here," said Kincaid. "We got here almost immediately,"

Because Chief Farber had looked down on so many corpses, the shock of this one was wearing off. Besides, he had work to do. Only two apartment buildings, he noted, looked directly down on the corner where Priestly and Sternhagen still stood over the body. A third building, the one above his head, was diagonally across the quiet broad street. Nothing else was close at all, for the other two corners were totally unoccupied. One was a school yard, and the other was the fenced-in grounds of the museum.

Kincaid gestured at the buildings around them. "I've

already sent men to canvass these buildings. I doubt they'll find anything."

The buildings were low and would contain few apartments facing the front.

"Did you send men into the park to talk to joggers?"

"A morning like this, I doubt there are any."

"Do it anyway."

Kincaid bristled. "I think I know what to do."

"Do it every morning for a week." The chief of detectives' car, he saw, had come into the street. His driver had stepped out and was waving to attract his attention. "You get lucky, you find someone noticed the PC jogging there," Farber said. "Some guy only runs two days a week, today and Saturdays, you won't find him until Saturday, but find him."

"I don't need to be told how to do my job."

"People forget things."

"I been doing it for some years now," said Kincaid huffily.

Kincaid had white hair. A contemporary of the first dep, he too was near retirement age. There were no promotions in his future. This realization had made him surly and inclined to talk back, something he would never have dared do earlier in his career. Bert Farber, who had never liked him, made no attempt to mollify him. "Canvass every building and store for ten blocks around," he ordered. "And look for bullets, too." On a corner as wide open as this one there was no telling where one or more stray bullets might have ended up.

It would take a lot of men. Normally, when a cop got killed, everyone wanted to help. Off-duty detectives poured in from all over. Pretty soon you had more men than you could use. But that might not happen this time. In general, cops detested headquarters brass. They might consider the PC not a cop at all, though he had been one. They might consider him a politician, or a rich lawyer from Washington. He had been those things too.

"Another thing. Where's his car? Where's his driver, who is also supposed to be his bodyguard. He had two drivers. One of them dropped him off someplace last night. One of them is supposed to pick him up someplace this morning. Locate them. I want to know what they have to say."

"I sent for them thirty minutes ago."

The traffic light on the corner turned from green to red, imparting a red sheen to the surface of this street on which no traffic moved.

"It's your territory, it's your case," Chief Farber said. A lie and they both knew it. It was Farber's case. "You report to me, and to me only. You don't say a word to anyone else."

"If Sternhagen or the first dep—"

"Tell them to see me."

"Anything else?" said Kincaid stiffly.

"Yeah. What was the police commissioner doing at this hour this far uptown?"

"I'll try to find out."

"Do that."

Bert Farber gazed across at the crime scene. It was a crowded sidewalk over there—not much room even to die. The glass-enclosed terrace of the Museum Cafe came halfway to the curb, as did the terrace of the Mexican restaurant next door. The curb was lined with parking meters and parked cars. On the corner were a fire alarm box, a mailbox, a wire trash basket, two public telephones, and a lamppost. Chained to the lamppost were two newspaper vending machines. On the sidewalk between the parked cars and the restaurants stood several full garbage cans and near them some discarded Christmas trees that lay on their sides waiting until the Sanitation Department got around to picking them up.

Across the street the stretcher under its burden was still there on the pavement, body bag still open. Harry Chapman was still getting his face washed. The first dep and Sternhagen stood over him talking—about what, Bert Farber had no idea—while the morgue attendants waited nearby.

■ 2 ■

AT ROLL CALL Patrolman Bert P. Farber was informed that he had a new partner, probationary patrolman Harry Chapman.

The platoon was lined up in two rows in the muster room. Bert, who was twenty-five years old, a young man with dark curly hair and a somewhat crooked grin, peered along the line, and the sergeant pointed Chapman out by putting his hand on the kid's shoulder. Bert nodded. A skinny kid with a narrow face, blue eyes, and sandy hair. He was about Bert's height, but much less muscular.

When roll call ended Bert drew the sergeant aside. "Where's Leo?"

"Out sick."

Leo was his partner. Bert thought of their car as Leo's car, not his own. Leo had been riding in it since the fifties, Bert only the last three years. Most of what Bert knew he had learned from Leo.

The sergeant said: "So take care of the new kid. Teach him how to be a cop."

"Sure," said Bert.

This was in the old station house on 68th Street—the present one hadn't been built yet. It was a tall, thin building. Like many station houses all over the city, it dated from the end of the last century. It had random width flooring that was so worn it was splintery, and this tour's platoon, twenty cops, clomped across the boards and out the door and down the steps to the cars. The precinct was patrolled by ten cars. At that time there were still thirty-two thousand cops overall, the most there had ever been or would ever be, the city's fiscal crisis and the layoffs it engendered being still a year or two in the future. There would be periods later on where the precinct's manpower would stretch no further than six cars.

As Bert started the engine, Chapman in the passenger seat reached across to shake hands.

"Harry Chapman," the kid said.

"Bert Farber."

"Farber," inquired Chapman. "Hmm. Are you Jewish?"

"What kind of question is that?"

"I just thought you might be Jewish."

"What difference does it make?"

"Believe me, I have no prejudice against any race or creed."

"How old are you, kid?"

"Twenty-two."

The kid's uniform was perfectly creased, brand-new. The kid was brand-new. "How long you been out of the academy?"

Harry said nothing.

"Let me give you a word of advice. There are times you can ask such a question, and times you can't. This is one of the times you can't."

"I wasn't trying to insult you."

Bert put the car in gear.

"I just like to know what's what," the kid said defensively.

Bert gave him a look. Eight hours in a car with this jerk. Eight hours every day until Leo came back. But he suspected how sick Leo was, and wondered if he would come back at all.

"So tell me about the precinct," the kid said. "I want to learn."

"Learn your sector, then worry about the precinct." In silence Bert drove up one street and down another.

They had been assigned to sector E, which extended in length from 72nd to 79th Streets, and from Central Park across to Broadway. It included the corner at 77th and Columbus on which Harry Chapman would later be found shot to death.

"Well," said Harry into Bert's silence, "then tell me about our sector."

"We are now passing the museum known as the Museum of Natural History."

"I know," Harry said, and he tried for a smile that would warm his partner up. "My grandmother used to take me there when I was little."

"That park on your left is called Central Park. It's very historic."

Harry's mouth began to tighten.

"This street here is called Broadway. Also known as the Great White Way. A very well known street. You may have heard of it."

The silence that followed this remark lasted twenty minutes during which Bert, driving, eyeballed every pedestrian, studied every storefront, and totally ignored his new partner.

The first job came over the radio.

"Two-Oh Edward. K," called central's voice.

"That's you," said Bert. "Answer him."

Harry's first official act as a cop, so to speak: to pick up the telephone mike and speak. But he sat frozen in his seat, unable to move, and finally Bert reached across him and grabbed the mike.

"Two-Oh Edward. K."

"Report of a ten-twenty-one, 115 Central Park West. See doorman. K."

"Two-Oh Edward," said Bert in acknowledgment. "Ten-four."

"What's a signal ten-twenty-one?" said Harry.

"A past burglary," said Bert, making a U-turn on 72nd Street. "Jesus, didn't they teach you anything?"

"You don't put the siren on?"

Making a left turn at the corner, Bert started up Central Park West. "No you don't put the siren on. 'Past' means the burglar isn't there anymore. Sirens scare people, and they cause car crashes. An address like that, it was probably the maid anyway."

The doorman sent them up to the twenty-eighth floor, where the complainant, who waited in the open doorway, led them inside. There were modern paintings on the wall, some sculptures on pedestals, and huge overstuffed furniture upholstered in white satin. They saw at once that the apartment had been ransacked, for drawers and their contents were all over the floor. They recognized also that the complainant's wife, who was in tears, was a famous actress.

Harry Chapman, Bert observed, couldn't take his eyes off her.

If he wants to stare at her, Bert thought, then he can be the one to fill out the sixty-one.

The room's sofa was the biggest Bert had ever seen, and he sat Harry down on it beside the actress, handed him the complaint form and a pen, and got him started on the interview, while he himself went over to the window and gazed down on Central Park. It was a winter evening, a cold, hard dusk, and the lights were winking on all over the city.

"You over there," the husband called.

Bert turned from the window. "Were you addressing me, sir?"

"Don't just stand there," the husband ordered. "Our apartment gets robbed and you cops stand around with your finger up your ass."

"What would you suggest I do?" Bert said. "Sir."

"Take fingerprints, look for clues, do whatever you're supposed to do. What am I paying you for?"

Even back then only the most egregious burglaries were investigated. There were too many burglaries and not enough manpower. Patrolmen took down the particulars, and that was the end of it. Usually detectives were not sent out. The department would not have admitted it, but that was the situation.

"The detectives will follow up on this," responded Bert. "Sir."

"Where the fuck are they then?"

Bert came over to the sofa and glanced down at the complaint form Harry Chapman was working on. There was a section marked "Reconstruct Occurrence." Harry had already filled it in, and this was what Bert read first. A cleaning woman had come into the apartment yesterday, had found the place a shambles, and had phoned the actress and her husband in Los Angeles. Los Angeles was the site of one of their homes—

they evidently had others—and they had flown to New York immediately.

The burglar or burglars had damaged nothing and stolen relatively little, Bert saw from the complaint form, a fur coat and some silverware—nothing that a rich actress could not replace. To be burglarized at all was bad, but these people had got off lightly. Sometimes all the furniture was slashed, the paintings were slashed. Or somebody had defecated in the middle of the bed—who would ever be able to explain why? Or sleep in the bed again either. Human beings were capable of grotesque behavior, as cops saw every day. Some of it was scarcely imaginable. Cops were in constant contact with the absolute limit of what people would do. Many cops became hooked on this, and were unable ever to move away from it, and one such, Bert had begun to believe, was Bert P. Farber.

"Where are the detectives you speak of?" shouted the husband. "I want them here instantly."

Would detectives investigate this particular burglary? Bert doubted it. The loss would probably not be considered substantial enough. Of course if the victim was prominent, as this woman was, it sometimes made a difference. The detectives might respond to the scene just to look her over.

He handed the complaint form to the husband. "If you'd just sign that, sir—"

"I sign it and you put it in a drawer somewhere, is that it?"

"Of course not, sir."

The husband knocked the form out of his hand. "I don't want paperwork. I want action. Go out and find the guy. Do something."

Bert was not going to wreck his career over this rude piece of shit. Bending down, he picked up the form and held it out a second time. It was always the rich victims who became abusive. The poor ones were in tears, and sometimes Bert would sit with them for as long as he dared, commiserating with them, making promises he knew would not be fulfilled. What they had lost could not be replaced, not by them, not ever, and he hoped his lies helped get them over the worst time, the first few days.

"You fucken cops. You think you're such hot shit." It was the beginning of a long, ugly speech.

"Martin," the actress said once, but this did not stop her husband, and after that she let him rant. At first as he listened the kid had a stricken expression on his face, but this soon changed to wonderment, Bert saw, and he rather liked him for it.

When he could take no more himself he put the form down on an end table. "Why don't I wait outside in the corridor," he said evenly. "Harry, see that he signs the complaint."

A little later Harry came out of the apartment. "I didn't know they had to sign the complaint."

"They don't. I just wanted to make the sonuva bitch do something he didn't want to do."

"Well, I got them both to sign it," Harry said. "And I got her autograph as well."

Bert almost laughed at him. He was such a kid.

In a way Harry had just been blooded for the first time, Bert himself had been blooded still again, they had been blooded together so that, as they got back into their car, the experienced cop was feeling more congenial toward the rookie, and he began for the first time really to show him the precinct.

The 20th at that time was a B precinct, some of it good, some very bad. It was long and thin like most Manhattan precincts, and was bordered on one side by Central Park and on the other by the Hudson River. It contained the Colosseum and its industrial shows, the Lincoln Center concert halls and theaters, and two major museums; meaning in police terms that thousands upon thousands of visitors were attracted into the precinct every day, people who did not live there and who were sometimes preyed upon by people who did. There were luxury apartments overlooking the park on one edge of the precinct, and along Riverside Drive on the other edge, but in between the white faces seemed to peter out, and in places the language became Spanish.

The three shopping avenues, Broadway, Amsterdam, and Columbus, Bert informed his new partner, were all right below 72nd Street. Above was another story. Their own sector, E, for Edward, was above the line. People from below wouldn't cross into it unless they had to.

"The Mason-Dixon line, eh?" said Harry with a grin.

"More like the Smith and Wesson line," muttered Bert.

In later years all of this was to change. The upper West Side was in the process of being gentrified even then, the buildings turning co-op, the yuppies moving in, Bert's Smith & Wesson line moving north block by block. By the time Harry Chapman was killed the line was up to 86th Street or even beyond.

"Now this street here," Bert said as he steered into it, "car thieves love this street. They grab two or three cars out of this street every week."

Harry craned his neck to read the sign on the lamppost on the corner.

And a little later, pointing, Bert said: "Major, major drug deals go down in that bar there."

Bert, as he continued to drive and talk, noticed that Harry was taking it all down in a notebook. "That doorway there is reinforced," Bert said, again pointing. "A bottle club. Caters to blacks. You can buy anything in there, women, booze, drugs. You can get killed in there too."

"Why don't we close it then?"

"We need hard evidence before we can close it, and they don't let people like you and me in there. We do close such places from time to time. They reopen somewhere else, and we have to start all over again with the surveillances, the warrants, the whole bit."

Harry was again making note of the location. Bert said: "You're a great little student, aren't you?"

"I don't want to forget any of this."

Bert said: "Hmm."

During the next hour they handled a cardiac arrest and a domestic dispute. The cardiac case was an old man lying on the sidewalk at Broadway and 74th. The night had got even colder, and Bert took off his coat and covered him with it. He knelt there with his hand on the old man's shoulder until the ambulance came. When he and Harry got back in the car, Bert made out the aided card. After that they resumed patrol.

The domestic dispute was over before they got there. One

of the neighbors must have phoned it in. The third floor of a brownstone that had deteriorated into a tenement. The enormously fat black woman who answered their ring would not let them enter. "You was misinformed," she told them.

Bert kept trying to peer past her, but she kept shifting her bulk to block his vision. "Everything all right in there?" he called out finally.

A white-haired black man shambled into view behind her. "No problem, officer."

"So fuck off," the fat woman said, and slammed the door on them.

At the end of the hall one of the other doors opened a crack, and when they turned a woman whispered: "They was screaming at each other a while back."

The two police officers could see only a slice of this woman's face, and she was whispering so softly they could barely hear her. "I thought they was going to kill one another," the woman whispered.

"You did right," Bert told her. "You hear any more screaming, you call us again."

"I ain't the one called you," the woman said. "It wadn't me. No sir. I don't know who mighta been the one called you. No sir, it wadn't me."

Going down the stairs Harry said: "Do you think it was really her called it in?"

"Jesus," said Bert.

At nine-thirty they were five and a half hours into their tour and it became their turn for meal period. Bert, who was still driving, reached across and grabbed the telephone mike.

"Car Two-Oh Edward to Central. K."

"Two-Oh Edward," responded central.

"Car Two-Oh Edward out of service for meal period at this time. K."

"Car Two-Oh Edward. Ten-four."

Replacing the phone in its cradle, Bert told Harry he knew a place where they could buy sandwiches to eat in the car. He didn't want to sit in a diner, he said. He didn't like to be stared at. People tended to stare at cops like they were film stars, and very often they came forward to interrupt your meal with their problems.

Bert double-parked in front of a deli on Broadway.

"I already got mine in the back," said Harry. Earlier he had tossed a rather bulky package into the rear seat.

"Okay," said Bert, and he went into the deli.

In a few minutes he returned and settled in behind the wheel. "This is a pretty good precinct for meal period," he said as he drove away. "Some precincts you can't eat at all. The cops have to go two precincts over to find something that's safe."

He drove the car through the open gate of the school yard at Columbus and 77th, parked, and turned the engine off and the interior light on. He got the hero sandwich and a container of coffee out of the bag in his lap, and sat munching and sipping.

Apparently Harry had finished his own sandwich while Bert was in the deli. The kid sat now with a book on his lap. "You always eat in the car?" he asked Bert.

The book was closed, but it was bulky there on his lap, and Bert was conscious that the kid wanted to get back to it. "Most nights. Why?"

"I was counting on being alone half an hour so I could study."

"Then study," said Bert. "Study anything you fucking care to. I won't say a fucking word."

"I didn't mean to offend you."

In the face of Bert's silence the kid felt obliged to explain. He was in law school, it seemed, and had to study. But Bert refused to talk to him and eventually the kid fell silent.

When they had resumed patrol the kid began again to explain. It was very important that he get through at the top of his class and quickly.

"Quickly?" said Bert.

"It's a three-year course. I have to get through in two."

The police department was only a way station for him, he said. Politics was where he was headed, and he wanted to move fast. "I hope to be elected president before I'm forty-five."

He said this so seriously that it was impossible to laugh at him, although laughter was what such a statement deserved.

Bert growled: "You'll be lucky to make sergeant by the time you're forty-five."

"On the contrary, I've scheduled it out."

Over the next two hours Bert got most of his life story. He was the son of a political columnist, and had lived some years in Washington. As a small boy the president had come to dinner to his parents' house. The president was Eisenhower then, or maybe Kennedy. The story wasn't clear and Bert didn't ask him—what difference did it make? Senators were always coming to dinner. He knew more politicians than Bert did cops. The idea that he could become president had been in his head a long time. All it took, he said, was hard work and the right resume.

He had been working on this resume since adolescence. He had quit college after two years to join the Marine Corps, where he volunteered for Vietnam immediately, asking for combat duty. Which of course was given to him. He achieved a minor wound—a bullet went through the fatty part of his left arm.

"I guess that made you a hero," said Bert sarcastically.

"A hero? A purple heart?" said Harry. "Not really."

By staying in college and then joining the police department, Bert had avoided military service altogether.

After a moment Harry added: "The captain did put me in for the Bronze Star as well. But I asked him to do it, you see. So I wasn't really a hero."

"A Bronze Star."

"Right now people are against that war," said Harry. "But in time, believe me, being a Vietnam vet will pay off politically."

"I see," said Bert, who was so amazed at what this kid was saying that he could hardly speak.

"Lucky for me I enlisted when I did," Harry said seriously. "The war's about over now. If I had waited I wouldn't have had it on my resume."

"I guess the police department is for your resume too."

"Absolutely." The big issue with today's voters, Harry explained, was crime in the streets. That he had been a cop would be a terrific asset when he began running for public office.

"So how long have you accorded us of your precious time?" said Bert.

"I completed junior and senior years in college in eleven months. Law school in under two years is completely feasible. When I pass the bar, I'm out of here."

"What's the next stop after that?"

"Assistant district attorney. They're dying for ex-cops over there."

"And of course you'll prosecute only the biggest cases."

"The commitment to the DA's office is three years."

"And when that's up?"

"Washington. The Justice Department."

"I see."

"Say, three more years. I'll be thirty years old, and I quit and come back here and run for Congress."

"That's interesting," said Bert. "Really interesting. Which district?"

"This one," said Harry. "I'll run on a crime-in-the-streets theme. Elect a man who has actually patrolled your streets, fighting crime at ground level. Right here on the West Side."

"Sounds good," said Bert, who felt an increasing need to burst into laughter. "Now you're a congressman. How many terms?"

"Say, three terms."

"And then?"

"Depends who's mayor. If I were offered the job of police commissioner, I'd take it."

"You'd take it?"

"It's a high-exposure job. Plenty of ink. It could translate into millions of votes later."

"Police commissioner, eh. I'll probably still be in the department. What job will you give me?"

"Assuming you meet the legal qualifications, whatever you want."

"Chief of detectives," said Bert. "That's the one I want."

"You got it," said Harry.

"Thank you, I really appreciate this," said Bert, and for a moment he thought he saw a glimmer of a smile on Harry's face, as if the humor of the situation was apparent to him too.

But then he realized there was no smile. Harry didn't see any humor at all. He was absolutely serious.

"You understand," he said, "we're talking fifteen years, twenty years from now, so I can't be held to an absolute timetable."

"You won't stay long as commissioner, I gather," said Bert.

"Two years maximum, and then a run for the governorship or the Senate, whichever is open."

"I get the picture," said Bert. "Governor for another two years and then—" He paused dramatically. "—And then the White House."

"It's been done before, you know."

In fact it had been. Theodore Roosevelt was police commissioner, then governor, then president at forty-three. PCs ever since had sat behind Teddy's big desk and stared across at his portrait on the wall.

"Well," said Bert, "Teddy Roosevelt was in another century."

"The principle is more valid today than ever."

All this time Bert continued to circulate, to eyeball the sidewalks, to peer into the parked cars as they passed, to study people's body language, particularly those who seemed to be only standing around, and particularly in the sidestreets, which were usually without stores at street level, and therefore darker, emptier than the avenues.

"What are you looking for?" said Harry once.

"Guys with a limp who might have a shotgun up their pants leg," said Bert. "Guys pretending to be drunk staggering into parked cars at the door handle. How the hell do I know what I'm looking for?"

But Harry had already lost interest in his question, and in Bert's answer. He was much more interested in giving forth his earnest drivel, trying to convince Bert of something, he didn't know what. Maybe he was trying to convince himself. He was so concentrated on Bert's reactions to him and his plans for the future that he scarcely even looked out the windows to see what was going on out in the streets.

"Want to make your first collar?" Bert suddenly asked.

"Collar?"

The kid sounded as if his mouth had gone dry, and Bert gave him a look, then said: "The guy on the corner there? Describe him?"

"Male Negro, about twenty-five, six feet tall, about one hundred sixty pounds. Wearing sneakers, jeans, an unbelted tan raincoat."

The man was peering into a shop window. "What else?" demanded Bert.

"He's watching us in the glass."

"Very good," said Bert. "Anything else?"

They were abreast of the man, then past him. Harry had turned around and was staring out the back. "Well, he's got a fur coat over his arm."

"I know a woman has a coat like that. Cost her about four thousand bucks."

"So?"

"Does he look like a man who would own such a coat?"

"Just because he's a member of a minority—"

"Don't give me that Supreme Court shit. The answer is no. Do you think he's armed?"

"No way of telling."

"He's got a gun in the right-hand pocket of his raincoat."

"How can you tell?"

Bert did not answer.

"Go around again," said Harry.

"I've already been by twice."

"I didn't notice."

"You don't notice much, I find."

After a pause Bert said. "The first pass, he went rigid when he saw me. It caught my eye. The second time he ignored me altogether. That's unnatural too. He was studying the sky. Must be interested in the stars."

They crossed to Amsterdam, went up to 76th Street, then came back down again. "I'll tell you once more, and for the last time. Cops are like film stars. If a cop is around, people watch him. People are never not conscious of where he is, what he's doing. Anyone pretends to be, like this guy, he's most likely dirty."

When they came to the corner of Columbus and 74th the

man was still there, the coat still over his arm. He never looked at them.

"He knows we've spotted him," said Bert.

The man was studying his watch.

"He wants to know what time it is," said Bert. "Take a look at his raincoat. Does it seem to hang heavier on the right than on the left?"

"That doesn't mean he has a gun in his pocket."

"It's either a gun or the tire iron he used to mug the woman he stole that coat from."

The man walked back to the building line and leaned nonchalantly against the wall. His body faced the street, but his head was averted, looking elsewhere.

"A stop is an exercise in pure power," said Harry. "The courts are right to look sternly upon a stop."

"You're talking about an illegal search and seizure, not a stop. And this is not the academy anymore, this is the street."

Ahead was a space beside a bus stop. Bert turned into it and doused the lights but left the engine running and they peered out the back window.

They waited there ten minutes while the radio crackled beneath the dashboard. Central handed out assignments, and cops in radio cars responded.

"What are we waiting for?" said Harry.

"What is he waiting for, that's the question," responded Bert.

All this time traffic coursed by them in the street. A bus pulled into the stop, some passengers got on board, and it pulled out again. The lights on the avenue turned red, and for a few moments nothing went by. When the lights turned green again there was a flood of cars and then, like an animal limping along behind the herd, a single car, which turned in toward the corner as if its driver intended to mount the curb. As the car slowed down, the man with the coat came toward it from the wall.

But with a sudden burst of speed the car veered out into the center of the avenue, the driver flooring it. The car went past them flying. At the next corner, although the light had turned red again, the driver went through without even slowing down.

"The buyer," Bert said. "He saw us."

"He went through a red light," said Harry. "Let's go after him."

"A summons for speeding is not what we want," said Bert, "and in this old crate we'd never catch him anyway. What we want is back there." And he gestured over his shoulder. "Want to make your first arrest?"

When Harry said nothing, Bert added: "When you grab him, watch out for his gun."

"Shouldn't we call for backup?"

"For something like this? They'd laugh you out of the station house."

"It won't stand up in court."

"It may."

"We don't have probable cause."

"Fuck probable cause. At the very least you take a gun off the street and you return a valuable coat to its owner."

With Harry still showing no desire to get out of the car, Bert felt contempt coming on strong. He wanted to see Harry show commitment to the hard and potentially dangerous job of being a New York cop, but it wasn't happening. He wanted to know where he himself stood with his new partner: could he count on him in a crisis or not?

Harry said: "I don't want to do it."

"If you're afraid he might shoot you, sit in the car, I'll do it."

"I'm the one who's been shot before, not you," muttered Harry. "I'm not afraid of getting shot." And then: "It's something else."

Bert stared at him.

Harry said: "I—well—I can't be up all night processing a prisoner. I've got an important exam tomorrow. I've got to get a good night's sleep."

An excuse like this was new in Bert's experience and he was trying to make it move through his head.

"You make the collar," Harry pleaded. "I'll back you up."

Without another word, Bert got out of the car. Behind him he heard Harry get out also, but because he never took his eyes off the man with the coat, he had no idea what Harry did then. Was he following? Had he planted himself behind what he imagined to be cover, the door for instance. Bullets went through car doors as easily as they went through people.

He wanted Harry close enough to hear what was said so he could testify about it later in court, if it got to court. He wanted him close enough to intimidate the suspect with his presence, close enough to help subdue the guy, if it came to that.

Bert was not a bit comfortable with the idea of Harry as backup, and he slid his thumb down into his holster. Police guns cannot fall out of their holsters, or easily be jerked out either, for there is a ridge of leather in there that catches on the edge of the cylinder and prevents this. Bert's thumb freed the gun, he hiked it up half an inch, and he also arranged his tunic so the grip protruded.

The man with the coat was gazing into the distance, trying to give the impression that he was unaware of Bert's approach.

"Good evening," Bert said. "How you doing? Nice night, isn't it?"

The man gave an exaggerated start of surprise. "I didn't see you there, officer."

Up close he was older than Bert had thought, about forty, and going bald. The streetlight was not far off. His forehead was six inches high, and now a single drop of sweat popped out on his scalp and began its slow roll down the slope to his nose. Not until it passed between his eyebrows did the man wipe it off.

"Nice coat you got there," Bert said.

"Yes sir."

"Mink, isn't it?"

"Could be."

"Worth a lot of money?"

"I don't know how much it worth."

"Where would one buy a coat like that?"

"Why you ask?"

"Maybe I'll buy one for my wife for Christmas." Bert at this time was unmarried.

"Maybe you take this one."

"You want to give it to me? Why would you want to give it to me?"

"Take it off my hands."

"We're not allowed to do that while we're on duty."

Another drop of sweat was rolling down the man's forehead. A single drop. Bert thought this amazing.

"This coat my mother's," the man said.

"Your mother's."

"She give it to me."

"Could I see it?"

"You want to see it?"

"Just to see if it's the kind of coat my wife might like."

The man handed it over.

Now came the difficult part. Bert had the coat in his left hand so as to keep his gun hand free. He was trying to manipulate the coat one-handed to see if it bore identifying marks, but it was a heavy coat, and the scene was illuminated by relatively little light that came from only one nearby street-lamp. He was trying to make the coat fall open to the lining and he was unable to observe what he was doing because he was watching the suspect at the same time, alert to any sudden movements he might make. A little help from Harry would have been appreciated, but Harry neither spoke nor moved. Bert had no idea even where he was.

Usually coats this expensive had a monogram, or even a name, stitched into the lining above the pocket. If this one did not, he did not know what his next move should be.

But the name was there. His eyes darted to it, then back to the suspect, then back to the name. He did this several times, trying to make the light fall on the name so he could read it. At last the letters took shape: Julia Petroski.

There were Negroes with Irish, Spanish, African names, Islamic names, even Negroes called Farber. But he had never met one with a name from central Europe.

"Is this your mother's coat?"

"My mother's coat."

"What's her name."

"I forget her name."

"Is it Julia Petroski?"

"Yes sir, that's it."

This would be funny, Bert thought, if it weren't so goddam dangerous. He said: "And what's your name?"

Bert, who was still holding the heavy coat, had the suspect

pegged as only a burglar or maybe only a fence. There was still the problem of the probable gun in his raincoat pocket, but he did not seem a violent type.

A small crowd had gathered to watch, four or five people walking home from restaurants or the movies. Some of them had probably got between Bert and Harry, which Harry should never have let happen. No one seemed alarmed by this jerk. Bert was distracted, and his guard was down somewhat.

"You got any ID?"

"I just get some out of my pocket," the suspect said, and his hand snaked downward.

Bert threw the fur coat at him, even as his own hand went for his gun.

But the suspect had had any man's instinctive reaction. He had caught what was thrown at him. Caught the thrown coat with both hands, and at least for the moment the danger was over.

"I got a better idea," said Bert, his hand still on the protruding grip of his gun. "Why don't you just slip out of that raincoat first. Drop the fur coat on the sidewalk. Good. Now the raincoat. Do it very slowly, please."

The raincoat landed with an audible metallic clunk.

"Now I'll look at your ID, if I may," said Bert.

The suspect stood now in a torn cardigan. The front of it looked ready to unravel completely. His billfold was in the cardigan pocket and he offered it to Bert.

"No, just the ID, please."

Bert peered down at a New York State driver's license that he was obliged to turn this way and that in the light.

"Are you Claude Green?"

"Claude Green, yes sir."

"Something about your raincoat bothers me, Claude," said Bert. "Did you hear the noise it made when it landed? Something's in that raincoat pocket." He nudged the coat with his foot. "What do you suppose it could be?"

"Whatever it is, it ain't mine. That coat is my brother's coat."

"Do you mind if I look to see what it is?"

"How can I mind when it's my brother's coat?"

Bert was being as careful as he could. In court the lawyers

could twist anything. He wanted to be able to argue if necessary that not only had he had probable cause to search the suspect's raincoat, but had even had his permission.

"Why don't you go over there and stand with my partner while I look to see what it could be."

The onlookers parted to let the suspect approach Harry, who stood, Bert now saw, leaning nonchalantly against the lamppost.

Bert crouched, slid his hand into the raincoat pocket, and brought forth a nickel-plated revolver. Saturday night special, he thought derisively. If you pulled the trigger it probably wouldn't even fire.

But it might.

Looking at it again he saw that two of the chambers had been fired, and that it smelled of gunpowder. He felt sweat pop out on his brow.

Bert flashed the gun at Harry, who had the sense to spread-eagle Claude over the hood of the car, toss him for additional weapons, read him his rights, handcuff him, and throw him into the backseat. Bert meanwhile took down the names and addresses of the now reluctant bystanders, who might be called to testify to the stop, search, and arrest of Claude Green, all of it done properly and according to law.

After driving back to the station house, and locking Claude into the downstairs cells, Bert went upstairs to the squad room like the detective he hoped one day to be, where he made phone calls about his prisoner. Harry, meanwhile, changed back into civilian clothes and signed out.

Bert was sitting at some absent detective's desk, his tunic undone, looking and feeling bemused, when Harry came back up, poking his head into the squad room to congratulate his new partner once again on arresting the burglar and recovering the coat, and to bid him good night before heading on home.

"You can't go home," Bert told him, "I'm sorry."

"Can't go home?"

"Julia Petroski was a real person."

"Was?"

"I found out where she lived. There aren't that many Petroskis in the phone book. She's dead. Her apartment is full of detectives. They figure she surprised a burglar and he shot her."

"Claude?"

"If you ask him, he may say it was his mother."

Harry came all the way into the squad room and slumped into the chair across the desk from Bert. After seeing him in uniform for eight straight hours, it was a surprise to Bert to see him in crepe sole shoes, chinos, and a leather jacket. As if he weren't a cop anymore. As if he were a civilian, same as everybody else.

"So it's not a burglary," Bert said, "it's a homicide. We've got to take him downtown. I'm sorry. Better go put your uniform back on."

Harry nodded glumly. He had his schoolbooks in his hands and he went out of the squad room and Bert heard him clomping up the stairs toward the locker room.

By the time Harry Chapman was killed the system had been improved. The station houses had been connected to the DA's office by closed-circuit television, allowing discussions about the evidence and the charge. After that a van would pass by each station house collecting all of the night's prisoners, transporting them en masse to arraignment court.

But on this particular night, Harry Chapman's first night on the job, the old system was still in force. At the 20th Precinct station house and all the others, arresting officers were obliged for the second time that night to throw their prisoners into the back of their radio cars, or detective squad cars, and to transport them personally to court, there to wait their turn to be called. Some nights the courtroom was so crowded they couldn't even get into it but were obliged to wait with their prisoners on benches outside in the hall. Usually they waited half asleep for the rest of the night. Their cars were out of service all this time and the officers themselves were not only out of service but also being paid overtime.

Upon reaching the courthouse, Bert nearly got into a fistfight with the assistant DA who had caught the case. The guy was younger than Bert. He looked even younger than Harry, though he couldn't have been, and he didn't want to arraign Claude Green on the felony murder of Julia Petroski. He said there wasn't enough evidence to support such a charge. He would ask for a charge of possession of stolen goods.

"If the ballistics test comes back positive we can rearraign him," he promised.

"He'll be out on bail by then," Bert said. "You'll never find him again." He kept insisting on a charge of felony murder, until finally he was screaming at the guy.

Bert got a docket number, he handcuffed Claude Green to a bench in the corridor, and they began to wait. Claude fell sound asleep, a sure sign he was guilty.

"I mean," said Bert to Harry, "could you fall asleep if you were about to be arraigned for a murder you didn't do?"

Sitting up for hour after hour Bert P. Farber dozed fitfully while Harry Chapman, never once giving in to the crushing fatigue he must have been feeling, pored over his law books, glancing over at Claude only occasionally to make sure he was still attached to the bench. It was six-forty-five in the morning before their docket number was called, and when the arraignment judge asked what the charge was to be, and the young assistant DA opened his mouth to answer, Bert beat him to it, crying out "felony murder"—which of course he was not supposed to do.

The young ADA decided not to object, the arraignment ran its course to the end, Claude was remanded to Rikers Island to be held without bail, and Bert left arraignment court glowing.

"You want to get a coffee somewhere?" he said to Harry in the street. They stood amid public buildings: nearby were the state and federal courthouses, both of which looked like Greek temples, and the towering municipal building, and City Hall in its small park. The light was just coming up, a cold, raw dawn. The air was very clear, it even smelled clean. Above their heads floated a few widely separated pillows of clouds, and the sky itself was beginning to turn blue.

"I can't," said Harry. "I got this exam this morning in my first course block."

They drove back to the station house, where Harry changed hurriedly into civilian clothes, jumped into his car, and was gone. Finding a diner already open on Broadway, Bert drank his coffee alone, no one else there to share his triumph with.

He went home to bed—he was still living with his mother

in a little apartment near Yankee Stadium. His father, a tailor, had been dead for some years.

Harry too went home, where he showered, changed his clothes still again, ate a bowl of cereal, then left for law school, where on no sleep at all he achieved a perfect score in the scheduled exam, torts or some goddam thing.

By four P.M. both young men were back in the station house for that day's tour. All the guys came by to shake Bert's hand and congratulate him on his great arrest, even guys he hardly knew. It wasn't often that a patrolman made an arrest for murder, and the precinct commander, Captain Priestly, who by the time Harry was killed would be serving as first deputy commissioner, came over and told Bert in front of everybody that he was putting him in for a meritorious.

Up until then Patrolman Farber had not spoken ten words to Captain Priestly. To the young cops in the precinct, Bert among them, Priestly was a remote, unapproachable figure. First of all he was very old, over forty at least, and he had what was to them tremendous rank. They never saw him toadying up to men with more rank than himself, nor did they watch him seeking to advance his own name and career at every opportunity.

Priestly said he was putting Harry Chapman in for an excellent police duty as well.

There was enough glory to go around, and Bert didn't mind, even though Harry hadn't done anything except wait with him all night in court; he assumed Priestly didn't realize this. In fact the precinct commander knew it very well; he knew also that decorated cops reflected credit on their commanders, and two decorated cops reflected more credit than one.

So Harry had a decoration coming that he had not really earned, and it made him apologetic. Bert had made the case one hundred percent by himself, and should have had exclusive recognition for it, he said. Although pleased, Bert did not want this to show, and so made a joke. The excellent police duty would look good on Harry's resume, he said. Looking troubled, Harry glumly admitted that this was probably true.

It was that same week, one night during meal period when he sat staring out over the steering wheel, that Bert formed the notion that a cop could be great at his job the way a musician could be great, or a painter. That a cop could be an artist of a kind. Art was the expression of insights and understanding that more ordinary people simply did not have, and would never have, was it not?

Bert sat munching his sandwich in silence while in equal silence Harry beside him pored over law books under the flexible light. A great cop, Bert reasoned, could take his insights and his understanding of the streets and of people, and he could express them. For instance, the moment he spotted Claude Green he had understood everything he needed to know. He did not have to be told, he just somehow knew, and then he had acted. It was as if he had received a message from the Almighty, and it was not the first time in his three years on the job that this had happened to him.

Bert did not believe in the Almighty, had no religious upbringing at all, but he did not know how else to describe the ideas he was trying to put into order. His understanding of crime and criminals was instinctive. He had no idea where it came from, and if this did not make him a kind of artist, then he did not know what art was.

Such a notion was new and he was unwilling at first to claim too much for it. It was not something he would ever speak of in the station house for fear the guys would rib him about it. But for him it was true, he could read and understand whatever police situation confronted him, know what had just happened, what was about to happen, who was who, and what his choices were. Know what to do next. He had a feel for the city and the job that most cops, Harry Chapman for instance, did not have, and furthermore he knew how to express it. You could almost say he knew how to let it flow out of his fingers.

Harry Chapman's own first arrest came a week later. It was not a good one.

He was off duty at the time. In the wake of all the praise Bert had received, and continued to receive over the next several days as men came back on duty after days off, or after being in court testifying, Harry Chapman seemed almost to withdraw into himself. His smile got thin and he seemed to brood a lot.

Bert recognized this. He told Harry to relax and not to press, he'd make a good collar soon.

But Harry decided to try to make something happen. Furthermore, not wanting to share any glory with Bert, he decided to make this try alone.

He had the time because his exams were over and he had a three-day break. In addition, Harry and Bert were working midnight tours this week. This left Harry free in the hours just prior to midnight when most criminals were most active.

At that time Harry lived in an apartment over his parents' garage in Englewood, New Jersey, so he drove into the city early, arriving just after eight P.M.

There was the bar on Columbus Avenue and 76th Street that Bert had pointed out to him as a drug mart, and Harry parked a block north of it. From the police academy he knew that ninety percent of drug arrests were sales to undercover cops, and he had decided to go in there and try to make an arrest he could build into a major case.

For two hours he sat in his car watching the bar. People went in and came out again. The trouble was he couldn't see much from so far away, he still had no idea what he would find inside, and he was no longer sure this was such a great idea. He began to wish he had his books with him and had spent his time studying.

Finally he got out of the car and for a time walked up and down the sidewalk, sometimes on the same side of the street as the bar, sometimes on the other, usually pretending as he passed in front that his attention was elsewhere.

This was boring too, and it seemed to lead to nothing.

About thirty minutes before he was due to go on duty he went into the bar, stepped up to the rail, ordered a beer, and stared into it, afraid that if he looked around too much he would give himself away as a cop.

The other patrons were mostly Hispanics, though there were some Negroes as well, and the principal language of the place seemed to be Spanish, which he did not speak. The only white face in the bar was his own, and there was no illegal activity that he could discern.

There had been a rather loud silence as he entered. He was aware of this, and also that all activity had seemed to stop. But it resumed quickly enough.

The bar was dim and run-down. He had the impression that the floor was unswept, the glasses smudged, the undersides of the chairs caked with gum. He could almost hear the cockroaches under the duckboards behind the bar, clickety-clack. He himself took showers every day, even twice a day if he was going out on a date, and a place like this was an offense to him. He could barely make himself swallow his beer.

A girl came into the bar.

He was aware of her immediately, how could he not be. She was young, she was white, and therefore, in his eyes, was on no legitimate errand. She was tiny, no more than five two, maybe a hundred pounds, and she was sniveling and looked wasted. She may have been Harry's age, or perhaps younger. The drug of choice at that time was heroin; the cocaine epidemic was still many years in the future. In Vietnam Harry had seen heroin addicts, and this girl fit that same picture. She must have come in to buy drugs—what other explanation could there be?—and he watched her surreptitiously, using the sides of his eyes and the mirror behind the bar.

She too had given a start of surprise to see a man at the bar who obviously did not belong there. She too decided immediately to ignore him, and she asked for a man named Chucho.

"Chucho around?"

The bartender pointed toward the back, and the girl went down the length of the bar behind Harry. There was a door back there. She went through it into a back room and was gone about ten minutes. As he waited for her to come out Harry began to worry about being late for work.

He heard her voice from behind the door. It was loud but muffled. He thought he heard her shout "Get your fucken hands off me."

The door opened, and she came back down along the bar. Now her clothing looked in disarray, she was breathing somewhat hard, and she was stuffing what looked to Harry like glassine envelopes into her purse. She passed behind him and went out the front door into the street.

Having already paid for his beer, Harry scooped up his change and as nonchalantly as possible followed her out.

She was half a block away, walking fast. To catch up he was almost running. He had seen the glassine bags, meaning he had enough already to lock her up for possession. But if he could get her for sales it would make a stronger case, so he decided to act as he imagined Bert Farber would have acted in his place. After some preliminary conversation, he would lead her off the street into an alley, make the buy and then the arrest. Once she knew she was in trouble, she would be willing to testify against this Chucho and probably a number of others.

He came up even with her and said: "How you doing? Mind if I walk along with you?"

She said: "Who the fuck are you?"

He wasn't used to hearing girls use language like this. He remembered his mother when he was a little boy threatening to wash his mouth out with soap. He said: "I saw you in that bar and I thought—"

"Get the fuck out of my way."

"I thought you might sell me something," said Harry. He did not feel very sure of himself. Bert Farber would have likened him to a girl who was determined to lose her virginity but not sure how to go about it.

"You thought shit."

Somebody should wash this girl's mouth out with soap. He said: "I went in there to buy a few bags but they don't know me the way they know you. They wouldn't sell to me."

"I don't know what the fuck you're talking about."

They were walking very fast. Traffic went by in the street. Pedestrians approached and went by to either side. The girl seemed to be looking back over her shoulder rather a lot, as if looking for someone.

Harry affected the whining tone he imagined New York junkies used. "I gotta have something," he whined. "You gotta sell me something. I need a fix. I'm in a bad way."

"Fuck off."

For another ten paces Harry continued to whine and beg.

"I said fuck off."

Harry gave up on the idea of getting her for sales. Possession would have to do, and he grabbed her and dragged her off the sidewalk into an alley they happened to be passing. She was surprisingly light. He had her around the throat and she was kicking him and giving out muffled screams.

"I'm being ripped off," she cried throatily, as loudly as she could, though there was no one present to hear her. "Get this ape off me. Where the fuck are you guys?"

"I'm a police officer," Harry announced formally, even as he grappled with her. "You're under arrest."

The next thing he knew he was on the alley floor, his head being thumped up and down, being beaten. Two men were doing it, and he saw they both had guns. His clothes were being ruined, he was worried about getting his nose broken or teeth knocked out, he was worried about being killed. It did not immediately occur to him who these men might be. He connected them to the girl easily enough, but took them for pimps or druglords.

The girl meanwhile was trying to pry them off him, beating at them, screaming at them, and finally, despite his dazed state he was able to make out what she was saying: "Stop, for crissake, stop. He may be on the job."

They stepped back, enabling him to get to his feet. "I'm a police officer," he croaked. And then, even though it was three against one: "You're all under arrest."

The older of the two men, he looked about forty, began to laugh. "You silly shit," he said.

"Let me see your shield," said the other.

"It took you two guys long enough to get here," said the girl angrily.

"We were tailing you down the street. We were close the whole time."

"You heard my transmissions. You knew I had a problem."

"You were never in any danger."

"He could have strangled me."

It was dawning on Harry that he had just made a serious fool of himself.

When he produced his shield the guns disappeared, but not the animosity. "You fucking moron," said the older of the two men. "You just stuck your nose into an undercover operation we've had going two months."

"If you haven't blown it on us, it will be a miracle," said the other. "Two months down the shitter."

"You're all on the job?" said Harry. He pointed toward the girl. "Even her?"

"Show him your shield, Kathy."

"I can't, it's attached to my underpants."

Suddenly she began to laugh. All three of them began to laugh, but not Harry Chapman.

He went to work that night with scrapes on his face and hands, one eye rapidly turning black, and the news swept through the station house. Harry Chapman had made his first collar, a five-foot-two-inch policewoman. He had tried to lock up an undercover cop.

In the days that followed there were many jokes, some of which were amusing, and some were harmless jibes, but some others were cruel. Hardened police officers effected girlish falsettos and employed punch lines that did not vary much: "Don't arrest me, I'm a policewoman."

In the locker room an entire squad would be putting on or taking off uniforms, and the place would rock with laughter.

Only Bert P. Farber stood up for Harry. "Leave the kid alone," Bert said more than once.

"They're all shitheads," he said to Harry. "Just ignore them."

The jokes stopped forever the week after that.

It was Harry's third week in the precinct. He and Bert were working days. They got off at four P.M., and Harry hurried around to the post office on Broadway with a package his mother had given him to mail. He was in civilian clothes, wearing his leather jacket, a stocking cap, and gloves.

He walked into the post office and into the middle of a stickup. Two men, possibly three. He had his mother's package under his arm, and the new off-duty gun he had just bought, five shots, riding inside his belt in the small of his back. The leather jacket just covered it.

Today that post office is armored like a bank, but it wasn't then.

There were five patrons inside. Harry made six. There was

a male Negro holding a gun on them. He waved Harry over to join the crowd. He had wild eyes, so that Harry imagined he was on something, maybe angel dust. At the police academy Harry had been taught the names of the various illicit drugs, but apart from marijuana, which he had tried, and heroin, which he had seen in Vietnam, he had had no practical exposure to any of them.

At the front of the post office was a counter. Behind it stood a second gunman and three frightened clerks, two of them females, with their hands in the air. This gunman, also a male Negro, had the same wild eyes as his colleagues. These guys are either crazy or stoned, Harry thought. They're liable to start shooting on no provocation. There are innocent people here whom I am sworn to protect.

He was going to have to take action. It was a relief to him that these people could not be mistaken for undercover cops.

The correct police academy procedure as Harry understood it was that he should identify himself and show his shield all around, and only then find and draw the five-shot revolver in the small of his back. This was what he believed he had been taught.

But behind the counter, busily dumping the contents of the cash drawers into a laundry bag, was still another individual who might have been a fourth clerk, under orders and worried about getting shot. Or else he might have been another of the stickup men. At first Harry couldn't tell. He was confused because this man was white.

What to do?

At the police academy he had been taught not to take action until he knew how many men he was up against.

Just then an elderly woman entered the post office. One glance at the gunman holding six patrons hostage was sufficient. She attempted to back out the door, but the gunman ran over and grabbed her, trying to pull and shove her into the group with the others. The woman went instantly stiff as a tree. She was not so much resisting as terrified.

Judging that this was the best moment he would have, Harry got his shield case out of his right-hand pants pocket, transferred it to his left hand, and attempted to flip it open with fingers unaccustomed to such work, even as he hollered "Police officer. Freeze."

The gunman near the door pushed the woman aside and fired shots at Harry Chapman. Harry had been shot at before of course, and one bullet had got him his purple heart, but that was the only one that had come close. Whereas these bullets were so close to his ears that he heard the wind as they went by.

He got his off-duty gun clear of his belt, did not drop it, brought it to bear on the gunman's head, and pulled the trigger.

Until this moment he had considered himself exceptionally calm and clearheaded, given the circumstances, but it takes a few seconds for a man to go down, and Harry kept firing until this one did.

He then whirled to face the counter. It seemed a miracle no one had shot him in the back, but the other gunman was gone, and so was the white man who had been rifling the drawers. There was no one there except the three clerks, their hands still in the air.

"You people get down," Harry shouted to them, and also to the former hostages behind him. "Everybody on the floor." And he ran toward the counter, for it seemed clear to him that the other two gunmen—he was sure now that the white man was one of them—were crouched behind it. It was only as he ran that the echo of his own shots began to play in his head and he tried to count them.

How many had he already fired?

He did not know, three at least, and maybe more. There could be only two bullets left in his puny little gun, or one, or none, and there were still two of them armed and hidden from him by that counter.

He had five loose bullets in his jacket pocket, but he was more afraid of being caught trying to reload than of trying to bluff it out.

His intention was to jump up onto the counter, but his leap didn't carry him high enough. His shoe caught the lip of it and he plunged forward, barking his shin and sprawling on top of the counter on his chest. He got his face and his gun over the edge pointing downward and he screamed: "Drop your weapons and place your hands on your heads."

They were both there all right, one of them with his gun pointed practically in Harry's face. It went off, the bullet went past his ear, and the force of the explosion, or the shock of the flame and noise, sent him backward onto the floor.

There he lay semi-stunned as the two men behind the counter rose to their feet and sprinted for the door. The white guy was faster than any black basketball player Harry had ever seen. He was a flash going by, and in an instant he was out the door and gone. The Negro on the other hand came around the counter shooting. He had what looked to Harry like a .9 mm automatic with a full clip in it, an endless supply of bullets for a confrontation of this kind, many more than Harry. He got off two more shots as he cleared the corner of the counter, and then he stopped halfway to the door, turned back, took careful aim at Harry, and began to empty the clip.

Again Harry listened to the awful noise, watched the barrel buck in the man's hand as it spit forth flame, and he brought up his own revolver. He had made expert in the Marine Corps. The police department may have been new to him, but not guns. Given the time to hold his breath and gently squeeze off a round he was a deadly shot. But those were not the conditions here. Nonetheless, he was able to remember his training, boot camp and the academy both, and he forced himself (as he later told the investigating detectives) to take all the time he needed. It was only a few milliseconds, but it was enough. You probably have only one bullet left, he told himself. If you miss you are a dead man. Furthermore you better aim for his head. A fatal wound is not enough. You have to stop him instantly, absolutely, or you are also dead.

Harry took aim, took a breath and held it, squeezed off his final round, and hit the man in the middle of his left eyebrow. End of shoot-out.

Harry ran over and kicked the guy's gun away. "Call 911," he shouted to the clerks behind the counter. "Tell them it's a ten-thirteen, assist patrolman." He ran to the first man he had shot and kicked that gun away too. Then he ran to the door and looked both ways. The white guy was not in sight. He ejected all his spent cartridges on the stoop, reloaded, and then bent over and vomited up his lunch. Meal period had come late that day. Two ham sandwiches and a cream soda. He thought the retching would never stop.

Wiping his mouth on his handkerchief, he went back inside. "Nobody leaves," he shouted, for this, too, he had been taught in the academy. And then to the still frightened clerks: "Get the names and addresses of all witnesses."

He knelt down beside the first gunman and began going through his clothes for identification.

"A doctor," the man muttered to him. "Need a doctor."

Harry nodded. "I'll have to ask you for some information first," he said conversationally, and from here on he knew exactly what to do. It was as if he had watched this scene in a movie, or read it in a book, or overheard cops in the locker room.

He had extracted a driver's licence from the wallet, and he peered at it. "You Elroy? You're in bad shape, Elroy. You need a doctor fast, and I'll get you one as soon as you answer some questions. The white guy put you up to this, didn't he?"

"I'm gutshot, man."

Harry could hear the first distant sirens. "What's the white guy's name?"

"I need a doctor."

"All in good time, my man."

"Don't let me die."

"I want the name of that white guy."

"Call an ambulance."

"And where to find him."

"I never saw no white guy."

"Well, I'm afraid you'll have to die then."

"Help me."

"Die, you prick."

Two uniformed cops burst into the post office, guns drawn. They stood back to back, eyes and guns darting around. Within a few seconds they were pushed forward by more cops, whose guns were also drawn.

Crouched over the wounded gunman, Harry ignored them. "The white guy," he demanded.

"I'm dying."

"He wasn't even a brother, so why not give me his name? What are you protecting him for?"

The paramedics arrived next. "Wait over there," Harry told them. "This guy wants to tell me something first. Don't you, pal?"

The wounded man began to cough up frothy blood.

"Without treatment you won't last another ten minutes," said Harry. "So long."

The man began to mumble something. Harry had his notebook out and his ear close. "Can you spell that name?" he said, but when he looked the man was dead.

Harry got to his feet. As he peered down at the dead man, he began to shake. The first detectives came through the door. Harry knew them only by sight, not their names—he was that new in the precinct. He couldn't stop shaking, but he gave them what he had.

"The name's probably phony," commented one of the detectives.

"The address too," said his partner.

Harry's teeth were chattering. "Send somebody up there right away," he stuttered.

"We'll take care of it." They looked at him sharply. "You all right, kid?"

"I'm cold."

They sat him down behind the counter wrapped in a blanket out of their car and tried to get more of the story out of him, but he no longer seemed to understand the questions and his teeth were chattering so badly that he could not be understood.

"It looks pretty good, kid," a voice said to him. It was Captain Priestly standing over him. "We got two people ready to testify you identified yourself properly, and fired only when fired upon."

Priestly wasn't worried about Harry but about himself. To have one of his cops accused of misuse of firearm was every commander's nightmare; there would be mountains of paperwork, and Priestly himself would look very bad. He was smiling because the witnesses' testimony so far was excellent: a valid shooting. And there would be another decoration to hand out, that would further enhance his prestige.

Harry wasn't worried about misuse of firearm. Harry's head was nowhere. Priestly had stepped back, allowing the detectives to continue the interrogation, but Harry's answers were incoherent, and the detectives soon gave up, left him, and went to question the other witnesses.

More and more men kept arriving, one of them Bert P. Farber, who was in civilian clothes. He found Harry alone, wrapped in his blanket but shivering as much as before, and he sat down and tried to talk to him, at times holding his hand. There must have been fifty people in the post office by this time, perhaps more. Some were uniformed patrolmen from all over the division, who had responded to the emergency call at great speed and risk. They milled aimlessly around, waiting to be told what to do. The medical examiner came and went. More detectives came, and once on the scene they worked in relays. The original clerks and customers, who would not be permitted to leave for hours, were interrogated over and over again. Also present was the morgue wagon crew, who waited for permission to remove the bodies, and many forensic detectives busy with their tape measures, their cameras, their tools for digging bullets out of walls, and their plastic bags for bagging the dead men's hands. The street outside bulged with police vehicles, traffic was backed up for blocks, and those inside listened to a cacophony of cater-wauling horns.

Superior officers kept flooding in, most of them trying to look important. Harry had just killed two citizens, that's what they were worried about. He better have been right or he and the department were in trouble. As time passed their numbers only swelled, as did their rank, and they stood over Harry in groups and pounded him with questions he seemed unable to answer, until finally Bert shouted at them: "Will you leave the guy alone, for crissake. He can't answer you." Bert had never raised his voice to superior officers before, and he was both amazed at himself and frightened. "He'll answer you tomorrow," Bert added lamely.

The next time Bert looked up he recognized the man standing over him as the chief of detectives. His name was Summers, a gruff-voiced man, fifty-five years old with permanent five o'clock shadow. He said: "How long you two fucken guys been partners?"

"Not long."

"You two're a fucken one-man police department." Summers liked to talk like the street cop he once had been. He added: "There's a place for you in the bureau, Farber, if you want it."

Bert said: "What about him?"

"When he grows up, maybe."

Bert said: "Hmm."

"You're the natural detective. He's only a hero. Natural detectives're rarer."

They were talking about Harry as if he were unconscious, or not there at all, which in a sense was the case. "Fucken heroes're a pain in the ass," said Summers. "They always want to be a hero again. They get in trouble. You gotta watch them like a hawk."

"He needs someone to teach him the job," said Bert, meaning he could not leave Harry just yet.

They gazed at each other. Summers did not have to be told about a partner's devotion to his partner. It was a kind of love, it was—even cops themselves couldn't explain what it was. Was it real, or only something to believe in, like a belief in God?

"I'm on the list for sergeant," said Bert. "It shouldn't be long. As soon as I get made, if the offer's still open—"

"You got it."

"He should be in the hospital," said Bert.

"So take him to Roosevelt. My car's outside. Tell my driver not to forget to come back. I'll be here awhile getting this fucken thing documented."

Harry was put in a semi-private room and given a shot that put him to sleep. Bert went out and wandered around, looking in shop windows. He phoned his mother and said he wouldn't be home for dinner, then went into a pizza parlor and ate a sausage pizza and drank a beer.

When he got back to the hospital Harry was awake and sitting up.

"You okay?" Bert said.

"Yeah."

Bert sat down in the chair beside the bed. "You don't have to come to work tomorrow, if you don't want to."

Bert watched him closely.

"I got classes tomorrow," Harry said, "and if I want to go to school I got to go to work."

Bert watched him.

Harry's eyes began to fill up with tears. "Jesus," he said. "Jesus, but I could have done without today." He began sobbing. "Jesus, two guys."

Bert walked to the window and looked out at the city at night. When the sobbing stopped he returned to the bed and patted Harry's hand. "It can't be the first time for you," he said consolingly. "You must have killed guys in Vietnam."

"I sprayed bullets into jungles in Vietnam. If I killed anybody I never saw him. But the two guys today, they were lying there dead."

"Self-defense," said Bert. "Them or you."

"I know, I know." And then, after a pause: "Did you ever shoot anyone, Bert?"

"No." Bert had never fired his gun on duty. He had no idea how he would have reacted in Harry's spot, and to his surprise this realization was galling. In some measure Harry had just got so far ahead of him he knew he would never catch up. Harry had walked on water, on clouds, had seen the other side of the moon. Bert, though older and more experienced, had not.

Harry's emotion now turned 180 degrees. "It's good in one way, isn't it?" he said. "A guy from the *Times* called while you were out. How he found me I don't know. He's coming up for an interview. I imagine there'll be television too. That's good for the future, don't you think?"

When the reporter and photographer came in Bert excused himself. He didn't want to stay for any interview. "You'll be all right now," he said, "and I need to get home."

When Harry reported for duty the following day, most of the men coming off or going on stopped by to talk to him. There were no boisterous jokes. They spoke to him quietly. Most of them, before turning away, patted his shoulder or his sleeve. It was this touching that was the surprising thing. There was nothing as overt as back-slapping or a handshake, just the brief, almost surreptitious physical contact. It was an expression of support, of course, but something more as well. There were 250 men in that precinct, of whom only one other had ever been in a shoot-out. All the rest handled guns every day—cleaning, reloading—and wondered how they themselves would behave if called upon actually to pull the trigger. Heroically, all hoped and perhaps believed. If the situation ever arose. A situation that most of them wished for, but which was, however, rare. A chance to prove themselves to themselves, and to the guys in the precinct as well. Prove their honor, loyalty, manhood, worth. Most realized such a day would never come, but it had come for Harry, and for him, question time was over. All his cosmic doubts about himself had been resolved.

The ragging of Harry Chapman ceased from that day.

In the car Harry's demeanor hardly changed. He remained terribly earnest, straightforward, blunt, an extremely serious young man, rather naive, and without much sense of humor. The awful events that occurred day by day in the precinct, usually to people who were already dreadfully poor, continued to surprise him—the space heaters that caught fire, the bathtub scaldings, the roach poison left lying around and ingested by toddlers. The crimes that people perpetrated on each other surprised him just as much, the same ones over and over again, the whippings and burnings, the wives savagely beaten, the stabbings, the shootings.

The injured children, the old and the sick brought out nothing special from him. To people in distress he showed compassion, but it seemed learned rather than natural, something he brought forth because it was required, rather than because it was the only possible human reaction. On the other hand he was never a macho type, never stood on authority or forced confrontations, as many cops did. He was not eager to arrest people, and would do it only as a last recourse. He was always polite to people, even those who abused him, and he tended to overexplain, like a lawyer only pretending to be a cop on patrol.

And there were times when he looked haggard, despite his youth, because of too little sleep. He always studied during meal period, and Bert, sitting beside him, learned to eat his own meal in silence. Afterward, as they rode, he would sometimes mumble to himself, the same phrases over and over, committing to memory what he had just learned. It drove Bert crazy, but Harry passed the next examination as he had passed the last one, with a perfect score.

He never went out with the guys after work. Bert would stand for hours with cops in bars, drinking beer, listening to the war stories, laughing at the mordant cop humor. It was at such times, and in times of great danger, that a man felt most truly a cop. One of the brotherhood, part of this one tribe, different from all other men.

Sometimes in bars Bert would be asked about his partner, and he would answer:

"Strange."

In the car Harry's conversation was usually about the internal politics of the department, or else about politics in Washington. He never talked about girls, which was one of Bert's principal topics at that time. Harry had no girlfriend, or at least never spoke of one. For the moment he was busy, was in a hurry, didn't have much time. He said this firmly. He said it like an old man who has much to do and not enough time left in which to do it.

Leo, Bert's ex-partner, never returned to work. Bert rode with Harry Chapman for six months, until his promotion to sergeant came through and he was sent to the police academy for additional training. When he came out he asked for the detective division, and got it.

In the 20th Precinct Harry Chapman was assigned a new partner, with whom he continued to patrol the same streets as before.

IN HIS CAR headed downtown Chief of Detectives Bert P. Farber tried to decide what he was going to tell Mary Alice Chapman, and how. Would she go to pieces on him? How soon could he begin to interrogate her?

"So somebody bumped off the PC?" said his driver beside him. "Who do you think done it, Chief?"

The driver's name was Hughie O'Malley. "I think you done it," said Bert, "and I'm going to charge you if you don't shut up."

The question had interrupted his brooding. It had changed his focus too: from Mary Alice to the mayor.

The city had no police commissioner. The mayor would have to appoint someone quickly, and if Bert wanted to be considered he had best get to him fast, before anyone else did. Mary Alice, despite all he had once felt for her, would have to wait.

"Turn around," Bert ordered. "Take me to Gracie Mansion."

The mayor should still be at the mansion, he would not have left for City Hall this early. Bert would brief him, present himself as an ally in the difficult days ahead.

Get the mayor thinking about him.

Harry's murder might not be solved for a long time. Cases like it—no witnesses and no apparent motive—were notoriously difficult. Some remained open for years, until the paperwork literally disintegrated in the folders. Bert could not afford to base his chances solely on solving the Harry Chapman case.

The mayoral residence was a big Federalist house surrounded by a high wrought iron fence. Set in a park, it overlooked the East River. To Bert it was a place of dark paintings, creaky floors, and boring conferences. He went up the steps two at a time, crossed the porch, and rang the bell.

A servant answered and led him downstairs into a basement exercise room where the mayor, a small, bald man in his sixties wearing a gray sweatsuit and sneakers, was riding a treadmill.

"You caught me at a bad time," the mayor said. His pate was beaded with sweat. He did not offer to shake hands.

The room was full of exercise machines, but only the treadmill was in motion. "You gotta keep going until it hurts," the mayor said. "I go thirty minutes every morning, most of it uphill." He was walking fast but staying in place. "I feel terrific. So why're you here?"

The mayor seemed displeased. Bert had not been invited, and he had interrupted the mayor's routine.

"I thought you would appreciate knowing what we have so far."

"No, you want his job. That's why you're here."

The mayor could be a suave politician, or he could be blunt. Unprepared for the bluntness, Bert fell silent.

"You had any breakfast?" the mayor said.

Bert shook his head.

"You'll forgive me if I don't offer you coffee and doughnuts personally," the mayor said. "This thing is programmed. I don't stop until it does. If you go upstairs, the man will give you something."

Bert again shook his head. "I'll tell you whatever you want to know, then go. I've got other stops to make."

He had expected to find this man eager for information. He had hoped that the conversation would then turn naturally from the murder of Harry Chapman to the subject of who was to succeed him.

The mayor said: "Great machine, this one, don't you think?"

Chief of Detectives Farber stepped closer and pretended to

examine the treadmill. It had a dashboard with more electronic dials and adjustments than a car.

"It's great for the blood pressure," the mayor said. He then added, without missing a beat: "So what are the facts so far?"

"He was out jogging, he was shot through the heart, he's dead."

"That's it?"

"That's about it."

"You got a theory?"

"We have to wait for some facts to turn up. At the beginning of every investigation you spend most of your time waiting."

"A bullet through the heart?"

"Yes."

"A single shot?"

"It seems so."

"Somebody's a helluva marksman, wouldn't you say?"

"Or lucky," Bert said.

"Maybe unlucky," the mayor said. "Somebody draws a gun on Harry Chapman trying to scare him, and the gun goes off by mistake."

"It's possible."

"You must have some ideas."

Bert ran down the list: a terrorist group, a mugging, a stray shot from somewhere else. "He was a politician before you appointed him PC," he added, "so there's one other possibility."

"Which is?"

"That he was shot by a disgruntled constituent." Bert's grin broadened. "It's the risk you guys take when you piss off the voters."

"Very funny," said the mayor, who was watching his dials. "A disgruntled cop, more likely."

This idea had occurred to Bert too. It was so horrible to contemplate that he had mentioned it to no one.

"A cop or a woman," the mayor said.

If it turned out to be a cop, Bert thought, it would destroy whatever confidence people had left in the department. A woman would be slightly better, not much. A woman would make for the juiciest headlines the city had ever seen.

"Of the two, I'd bet on a cop," the mayor said. "Look into it."

"I will."

"A lot of them must have wanted to get him."

"Not to that extent, perhaps."

"Motive and opportunity. They all have guns."

Bert remained silent.

"Think about it," said the mayor. "He wasn't PC long. How many cops did he fire in that time?"

"The department needed shaking up," Bert said. "You said so yourself when you appointed him."

"Shaking up? You call what he did a shaking up?"

Bert again fell silent. High-level police officials had no tenure at all. Bert—any commander—could be dismissed for almost any reason by almost any superior, especially this man here who seemed to be according him ten percent of his concentration while the rest went to his stupid machine. And a high-ranking cop was not like a baseball manager. He lived in a league with only the one team. If a police official got fired from the department there was no other he could move into. Ambitious officers lived a nervous life. They had to project competence and a certain servility both. At all times. They walked a very fine line.

Bert decided to say "Harry Chapman was an inspired choice by you, I thought at the time."

"So did I. But it didn't work out, did it?"

"I'm not sure I know what you mean."

The mayor's arms gripped the handlebars. His legs strode remorselessly forward. He was huffing a bit now. "Shaking up is one thing, upheaval is another. He had the department in constant upheaval."

"Yes," said Bert. "I assumed that was what you wanted."

"Not on that scale, I didn't."

The mayor marched steadily up his steep, nonexistent hill. "He was the worst mistake of my administration. When I make one it's a beauty. He was a disaster."

What was Bert supposed to say now?

"He managed to get himself more publicity than any police commissioner in history," the mayor said. "More than any mayor in history. Getting his name in the papers was all he cared about."

"Well," said Bert, "one can't control how the press will play things."

"Don't shit me. He laid it on on purpose, the same way he laid on those police escorts for himself everywhere he went in the city. You would have thought he was the mayor, not me."

"Well," said Bert, who was at a loss what to respond, "he may have overdone it at times."

"I don't know what he thought he was running for, but he was running for something."

Bert knew what Harry Chapman was running for, and assumed the mayor did too. And he wondered how much allegiance he owed Harry now. The answer was none. Harry was dead. Bert's allegiance was to himself.

"Seven minutes more and I can get off this thing," the mayor said. He was breathing hard, his pate glistened, and he let go with one hand to rub sweat out of his eyes. "Whoever shot him did me a favor. I was trying to think of a way to get rid of him."

"I didn't know that."

The mayor eyed him. "You didn't know much, did you?"

Bert said nothing.

"It's hard to get rid of someone the press is mentioning as a possible presidential candidate."

"Well," said Bert, "I better get going." The mayor had him completely off balance.

"What about the funeral?"

"I don't know."

"I want it in St. Patrick's Cathedral," the mayor said. "I'll clear my calendar for it."

"The family may prefer Washington. That's where they lived until Harry took this job."

"St. Patrick's," said the mayor decisively. "That's your job. Change their minds."

"I don't know if I can do that."

"You're a friend of the family, I was told."

"Not exactly, no."

"He made you chief of detectives, didn't he?"

"I was in line for the job anyway," said Bert defensively.

"It's settled then. St. Patrick's. I'll arrange it with the cardinal."

"They were married there," Bert said. "His wife may go for it."

"Make all those important fuckers from Washington come up here for the funeral," said the mayor. "Tell his wife I'll give the eulogy."

Bert looked at him.

"I get through with him," the mayor said, "he'll sound like Jesus Christ."

Bert nodded.

"Always speak well of the dead," the mayor said. "The first law of politics. He was the greatest PC the city ever had. I'm terrific at funerals."

"I'll talk to her," Bert said. "I'm going to see her next anyway."

"A two-day wake, then the funeral. Is two days enough for you?"

"I don't understand."

"To dig up any dirt on the guy. I don't want to be up there eulogizing him, and we find out he was up to his elbows in shit."

A bell rang inside the machine. The mayor sprang off and began wiping his face with a towel. In places his sweatsuit was soaked through. He stood there taking deep breaths.

"I'll call you, keep you informed throughout the day," Bert said, edging toward the door.

Throwing the towel over the handlebars, the mayor led the way upstairs. "So who should I appoint to replace him," he asked over his shoulder. "In your opinion?"

Bert said carefully: "There are a number of qualified men at the top of the department."

"Horseshit. That department breeds followers, not leaders."

Bert said nothing.

"So give me some names." They had reached the front door, but the mayor made no move to open it.

Bert decided to say: "First Deputy Commissioner Priestly

has been in that job under a number of commissioners for eight or nine years."

"The perfect subordinate."

"He would be the obvious choice."

"Is that how I seem to you, obvious?"

"Anything but."

This drew a smile from the mayor, and Bert was encouraged.

"He's too old," the mayor said. "Retirement right around the corner."

So much for the first dep, thought Bert, who was still thinking in terms of the three obvious choices. The first dep is not going to be the next PC. One down, two to go: Sternhagen or me.

But then the mayor surprised him. "Mind you, I'm not ruling him out, just thinking out loud for a moment."

"Right," said Bert, "you shouldn't rule him out."

They stood at the front door. Bert was on edge, whereas the mayor was having a casual conversation—was perhaps even toying with him.

"Chief Sternhagen would be an acceptable choice," Bert said, watching the mayor closely. "He's chief of the department, and the highest-ranking uniformed officer. The city would accept Sternhagen."

The mayor was nodding at him.

"Of course," Bert said carefully, "you could choose to go outside the department."

"Send out another search committee, you mean?. Takes too long, and I don't trust what they bring back. The last one brought me back Harry Chapman."

In that case, it seemed to Bert, there were only the three possible choices, the first dep, or Sternhagen, or himself. With himself no longer such a distant third.

"The law gives you only ten days, I believe," Bert reminded him. The mayor too was subject to higher authority. He might toy with his chief of detectives, if he so chose, but the law had to be obeyed, even by mayors.

"That leaves who?" said the mayor. "You?"

Bert had only a moment to decide how to react. Modesty? Obsequiousness?

He opted for charm. "I thought you'd never ask," he said with a smile.

"Find out who bumped off your friend," the mayor said, "and we'll talk about it."

Was the mayor announcing the conditions of employment? Or toying with him again.

"We'll have a joint press conference," Bert said. "I'll announce the arrest. You announce the name of the new PC."

"You got more balls than those other two guys," the mayor said, "I'll grant you that much." And he held open the front door of the mansion.

The rain had changed back to snow. Much sobered, the chief of detectives got into his car and they started downtown through the thickening snow. After a time his thoughts left the mayor, and whatever he might or might not have been promising, and fixed on the woman who waited for him ahead but didn't know it. The new widow.

The PC had lived in a town house on Waverly Place. When his driver had parked in front Bert sat unmoving while the windshield began to cover over with snow, for he found himself unwilling to get out of the car. "This is not going to be fun," he muttered aloud, then pushed open the door, stepped onto the snow-covered sidewalk, hurried carefully up the eight marble steps, and rang the bell.

He had to ring several times before he heard footsteps inside. He heard the peephole open, then close, and the door was pulled back.

"Oh, Bert," Mary Alice Chapman said, "it's you."

"Can I come in?" said Bert gruffly, and he marched past her down the hall and into the kitchen. He could hear her following, and at the stove he turned and faced her. Why did I lead her into the kitchen, he asked himself. Why not the front room? She studied him with a half smile on her face, mystified, no doubt, and not a bit ready for what was coming.

She said: "To what do I owe this honor?"

The ringing bell had got her out of bed, obviously. She had jumped up and put a bathrobe on. It was blue, and of some quilted material that made her bosom look bigger than he knew it to be. She had managed to drag a comb through her dark hair—probably only once, judging from how disarrayed it was. But the bell had been insistent and she hadn't had time to do more.

So she looked the way she looked. To him she looked very nice, but then she always had. She had high cheekbones and nice white teeth and a pointed little chin. She had dark eyes and a direct gaze that seemed to see more deeply into people than perhaps it did. Her hair was much shorter now, and parted on one side. She used to wear her hair halfway down her back. That was when he first knew her: a girl with long long hair.

He looked at her wearing the quilted bathrobe and no makeup and the half smile. People had two sides, the side they showed the world and the intimate one. This was what she had looked like every morning to the man who woke up beside her, namely Harry Chapman.

Who was dead.

"If you had a breakfast appointment with Harry, he's forgotten it," she said. Then she frowned, and he found himself studying the pleats in her brow and wondering what they signified. "Or else he'll walk in any moment," she said. "With Harry you can't always tell."

He stood with her in her kitchen in an intimacy he was no longer ready for. Not a sexual intimacy. More a family intimacy. Admit it, he told himself, you feel a sexual intimacy too, same as always. He didn't imagine she felt it, though.

He was still not ready for what he had to do next.

"If Harry were here he'd offer you a cup of coffee." She smiled at him. "So I'll offer you one." And she got the coffee can out of the cupboard above the stove.

He was tense, but perhaps she was too, for she was coming on a little too girlish.

He hadn't seen her much in recent years, and never alone. Official functions mostly, once when Harry was first running for Congress, several times after he became PC. He hadn't been alone with her since she was a college dropout and would-be actress working as a waitress and he was a sergeant who liked to play with her long long hair. In later years he would watch her on a dais, or talking to people at a reception—would find himself staring. The classic human reaction, he thought. A man always wants what he can no longer have, and a permanent rejection only made him want it more.

As a young man Bert had been a romantic. He had believed in romantic love. Loving a girl—this girl, anyway—made him feel like a god. He had thought being a detective was romantic too. And despite the nature of his profession he had stayed a romantic to this day, though he perhaps didn't realize it, and would have denied it if asked.

On another level he had become with maturity more practical. For instance, he had learned how to get ahead in his career. You did it not by breaking cases, which was what he had first thought, but by making the right political move—which mostly meant kissing ass. He had learned this as a sergeant and had refined it ever since. Of course, you were still required to break a case once in a while. And he had given up the idea of Mary Alice Riggs the day she and Harry Chapman got married. Or so he had imagined.

The intimacy he was experiencing so strongly at this moment had to do with standing alone with her in a room for the first time in such a long time. He did not know what emotions she felt, if any, but in him there was this residual sexual tension, and there was the worse tension of the job he had come here to do.

He said: "What time does Harry leave the house usually?"

"What time is it now?" she asked, and she glanced at the clock over the kitchen door. "About this time," she said.

"To go jogging?"

She was spooning coffee from the can into the coffeemaker, concentrating on the coffee, not him. "He runs to the river and out onto the pier and back. He varies it. Sometimes he runs over to Washington Square and around the park."

"How do you know where he runs?"

"I run with him, some mornings," she said, and she gave him another smile. "Nice mornings. Mornings I might be feeling particularly energetic." She went to the stove, turned on the burner, and put the coffeemaker down on top of it.

"Not this morning, though," said Bert.

He saw that she was beginning to look perplexed. "No, not this morning." She brushed a strand of hair out of her eyes.

"What time did he run this morning?"

"I don't know. He wasn't here this morning."

"Where was he?"

"He's in Washington. He's been there all weekend."

No he hasn't, thought Bert. "Where does he stay when he's in Washington?"

"What's this all about, Bert?"

He looked out the window into a courtyard. The snow was coming down hard. "How are the boys?" Bert asked.

She had twin sons. They were freshmen at Harvard and were on the swimming team. He had once overheard her joke that she had completed her family cheaper and quicker than other young women: only the one pregnancy, only the one set of hospital bills.

"The boys are fine. Come on, Bert." She got cups out of the cabinet, then turned to face him again, still unsuspecting but beginning to be slightly annoyed. What was he doing here so early? What was the mystery this was building up into?

He found he could not bear to do what he had come to do, and so put it off a moment longer. Besides which, she might be in possession of information that would help the investigation. He had to try to get that out of her first, didn't he? "When did you talk to him last?"

Again the frown. He had seen a lot of that frown at one time.

"It's none of your business when I talked to him last. Why are you here, Bert?"

That he had decided to do this job himself was a mistake. He should have let the first dep or Sternhagen do it. Stalling did not make it easier, not for himself, not for her. Be as brutal as possible, he advised himself. Get it over with quickly.

"Harry's been shot and he's dead."

She stiffened. There was no other visible reaction. After a moment she moved to the window and stared out at the falling snow.

He stepped up behind her. "There's a shoulder here, if you need it to cry on."

"I'm not going to break down."

He gazed over her shoulder out on the courtyard. The snow fell. The flakes looked bigger than before, wetter. "Do you have anyone who can stay with you?" he asked her. "Someone you want to call."

"No."

Her mother had recently died, he remembered. "Your sisters, maybe? Your sister-in-law?"

When she shook her head, he put his hands on her shoulders. She didn't shrug him off. She didn't do anything, just stood there without moving, while behind him the coffee began bubbling in the pot.

"I can have the Cambridge police pick the twins up and drive them to the airport," he offered.

She nodded, so he went to the wall phone and dialed it.

"What's their address?"

She opened an address book to a page and handed it to him, and when his duty sergeant came on the line, Bert instructed him what to do.

"There," he said, hanging up. "The boys will be on the plane within the hour."

"Are you so sure?"

He wanted to say something about the police brotherhood, to which she herself, especially at a time like this, still belonged. The one thing all cops knew about was death; every one of them in every city would be understanding, eager to help. The police brotherhood did exist, he wanted to tell her, and for you, now, could be counted on absolutely. But compared to her shock, her grief, and whatever else she was feeling, such an announcement probably would sound trite. So he said nothing, merely turned off the gas under the coffee and poured out two cups. He got milk out of the fridge and added it.

"When?" Mary Alice asked him. "How?"

He told her what he knew. He described Harry's jogging suit, his sneakers, the rain coming down, the way the traffic lights glistened red on the wet empty street, but tried to keep her from seeing the other more terrible details: rainwater running into Harry's nose in the gutter, or the small puckered doll's mouth in his chest.

"You've got to have someone to stay with you," Bert said. It seemed to him he could not leave her alone, but at the same time he could not stay himself, for there was too much to do.

"I'll get Madge to come over and stay with you," Bert said. His wife and Mary Alice were not really friends, but they had known each other a long time.

"No."

"Just till the twins get here."

He picked up the phone, considered a moment, then dialed not Madge but his duty sergeant again, ordering him to inform Madge and then send a radio car to pick her up and bring her here.

While waiting he sat down at the kitchen table, sipped his coffee, and watched Mary Alice Chapman, who only continued to stare out the window.

But finally she said in a low voice: "What time do the shuttles from Washington start running?"

"Not this early."

She nodded.

He said: "He must have come back last night."

Though he observed her closely, he noted no reaction to this statement.

He needed to know what Harry was doing in Washington, what she knew about his movements, where he might have spent the night. But how strong was she? Could he begin to interrogate her now or not?

He said: "Is there anything you'd like to tell me?"

When she did not answer, he added: "About Harry. About anything."

"No."

He thought she had hesitated briefly, but whatever she might have said remained unspoken.

He was not surprised. The wives of law enforcement personnel learned to keep their mouths shut. Their husbands lived close to crime, close to investigations, sometimes too close. Often the husbands got investigated themselves. Wives came to know this. Whatever the wife left unsaid could not later incriminate her husband.

Mary Alice Chapman might have much to tell him, but only after she had considered carefully. There was little chance, he saw, that she would tell him anything now.

"The department will want him to lie in state at headquarters," Bert said. He was not at all sure of this. The department was now in the hands of First Deputy Commissioner Priestly, who might not want any such thing. In the past Priestly had seemed to fear hasty decisions, indeed decisions of any kind. He would want to study regulations, tradition, precedent, but there was no precedent for a slain police commissioner. He would want to weigh positives and negatives, call one or several conferences.

Still, Bert thought he could force it through and that Mary Alice would appreciate him for it. He added: "And I think the funeral should be at the cathedral."

When she made no response he said: "I'll arrange it. Is there anything else you'd like me to do?"

"When we lived in Washington he used to say Arlington was where he wanted to be buried when the time came."

For the first time he saw tears in her eyes.

"Isn't that silly?" she said. "He wasn't counting on it this year, was he?"

"He was an ex-Marine," Bert said. "He was a former congressman, a former deputy attorney general as well. Arlington can be arranged. I'll take care of that too."

When she started to weep he embraced her, felt her body quivering in his arms. In the old days when he had embraced her she had sometimes quivered too, though from a different cause. He breathed in the scent of her hair.

She broke the embrace, went to the sink, and wiped her eyes on a dish towel.

"Madge will be here any minute," he said. "And your sons will be here."

They went out to the front room to watch for Madge. It took some time. Mary Alice stood at the window staring out at the falling snow. Bert was impatient to go. Finally the police car drove up and they saw Madge come up the steps.

"Madge will stay with you until the boys come," Bert said. "And I'll come back later."

The doorbell rang. They were in the hall and he was putting on his coat. "We'll catch whoever did this," he promised. He didn't know how the words sounded to her. They sounded fatuous to him and he wished he hadn't said them. Mary Alice knew as well as he did that most cases did not get solved.

He opened the door to Madge. "Take care of her," he instructed his wife.

"Can I speak to you a minute?" Madge said, following him out onto the stoop. "Why me?" She was whispering, though Mary Alice was too far back to hear. "We're not exactly close friends."

Bert had no answer to this question. People under stress reacted in strange ways. Under stress he had had his office call Madge, and no longer knew why. "She's in pretty bad shape," he said.

"Wait a minute," said Madge. "How will I get home?"

"Take a taxi."

"When will I see you?"

"I don't know," he said over his shoulder. He was halfway down the steps by then. When he heard the door close behind him he stopped on the sidewalk under one of those scraggly Greenwich Village trees without any leaves on it and looked up into the snow. He let it sting him, let it melt on his face.

Then he crossed the sidewalk and got back into his car.

His driver put the car in gear. "Where to, Chief?"

■4■

DETECTIVE SERGEANT Bert P. Farber met a girl. Patrolman Harry Chapman met her too.

Bert had been assigned to fourth district robbery-assault, working out of the Two-Four, one precinct up from the Two-Oh, and now that he was earning sergeant's money he rented an apartment on the top floor of a brownstone on 89th Street, half a block from Broadway. It was a walkup of course, four floors, but he was young enough not to mind that. It was also dirty and run-down. He bought gallons of white paint and on his days off painted it. After that the only problem was roaches. He sprayed, he bought traps, and at least you didn't see them so much anymore. The rent was twice what his mother was paying, with his help, on her apartment three times as big up in the Bronx.

He bought some not bad secondhand furniture and moved in, sort of. That is, he slept there nights that he worked late, or had an early court appearance, or had a date that might or might not lead to something. The rest of the time he trekked up to the Bronx as before and let his mother fuss over him. He had established his first home, but he was getting his mother used to the idea slowly.

He was one of two sergeants working under a lieutenant and supervising eighteen detectives. The fourth district, which encompassed four precincts, was not the busiest in the city but was busy enough, and there were more crimes than men to handle them. It became a matter of allocating manpower, and it fell to Bert to decide which cases to concentrate on, how many men to send out, and also which ones. In this way he worked on more than his share of cases, some of which became celebrated ones, and he made sure that by the time even the least of them got presented to the district attorney's office for prosecution, every detail was in place.

He was as often in the Two-Oh as in any of the district's other three precincts, and he would run into Harry Chapman from time to time. Harry had a new partner of course, a black cop. He had asked for him specifically, he said. The big issue in this country was going to be minorities. He was leaning out the window of his radio car explaining himself to Bert, who stood on the curb. In a few years he would run for office. Let his opponents in their speeches brag that "some of my best friends are black." He would be able to state, "My partner was black; we kicked in doors together, we arrested criminals together." Arguments like that would blow his opponents away. "You'll see," he said.

Bert and Harry met the girl the same night, though it was Harry who spoke to her first.

This was at a crime scene, which was where Bert met most of the girls he knew at this time. Crime scenes were good. A detective was a glamorous figure anyway, and people who had just been robbed were unnerved, particularly females.

A restaurant had been stuck up. It was a new one and it had opened only the week before on the corner of 77th and Columbus—the same corner where Harry would one day be killed.

It was in a storefront that had been boarded up for years. One day the boards, which by then were plastered with layers of scaling posters, were torn off and workmen began to install the restaurant. The gentrification of Columbus Avenue, which had been under way since the opening of Lincoln Center in the mid-sixties, gradually moving uptown, had at last reached 77th Street.

The robbers—there were three of them in ski masks—had burst into the place just before nine P.M. Since the restaurant was newly opened only six tables were occupied, twenty-one diners in all. Present also were the manager, the barman, four waitresses, and the cooks downstairs.

Using the sides of their guns, the robbers clubbed the manager to the floor. They did this immediately, presumably to show they meant business. The manager lay there bleeding. Forks froze halfway to lips.

The robbers upended the cash drawer on the bar, but there was not much in it, credit card receipts mostly, so they herded the patrons, the barman, and the waitresses downstairs into the tiny kitchen, a space crammed with hot stoves and built to hold at the most four cooks. Thirty-one people were stuffed in there, some of whom cried out as they were pressed against the stoves. They were ordered to empty their pockets and purses into a laundry bag held by one of the robbers on the stairs. The other two stood above him holding guns.

They cleaned out the place and left. Very professional.

The first radio car on the scene was Harry Chapman's. He called for an ambulance for the manager, and he notified fourth district robbery.

To Bert, who was on duty at that hour, this sounded like a crime that would make noise, so he decided to respond personally to the scene. And because there were going to be many witnesses to interview, he took three detectives with him.

He got there only a few minutes after Harry, but already five radio cars were parked outside—parked every which way, some with the red lights turning on top, some with doors agape. A crime scene always drew lots of cops. The attraction was almost sexual, the police equivalent of a free look at something forbidden. So Bert's first job was to chase most of the cops back on patrol, though not Harry, who, as the responding officer, had forms to fill out, and in addition would have to be interviewed.

Bert's second job was to get the victims calmed down, for as soon as he was seen to be in charge all had clustered around him. All were talking at once. He told them to return to their tables, that he would have detectives begin taking their statements in a moment. They were angry, nervous, and most were unable to sit still, but a few managed to continue eating their now cold food. Some called out for strong drinks, which the barman quickly supplied.

The girl was one of the waitresses, and Bert noticed her at

once. He noticed all the girls, for the waitresses in that restaurant were made to wear short skirts, fishnet stockings, and high heels, and they were standing now in a group against the wall.

The one who had caught his attention had dark hair that hung to the middle of her back. She had dark eyes and big white teeth and lovely legs. Bert considered himself a leg man. She was also very young. She and the others stood as close together as schoolgirls, as if they had broken some rule and expected to be disciplined.

Harry had noticed her too. As Bert turned to speak to his three detectives, Harry went over and separated her out from the others.

Having instructed his men to divide up the patrons and begin taking statements, Bert called Harry over.

"I'd rather you didn't disturb the witnesses," he said to him. "In fact, it would be best if you resumed patrol." As he spoke, Bert was gazing across at the girl, who, realizing she had caught his eye, began studying the floor.

"I thought that the first cop on the scene was supposed to stick around."

"As soon as you get the sixty-one filled out you can go."

He noted that Harry too was gazing at the girl.

"Good looking, isn't she?" asked Harry. When she looked up furtively he grinned at her, which caused her eyes to drop once more. "She's not really a waitress," Harry said. "She's trying to become an actress."

"Is that so?"

"So she told me. Her name is Mary Alice Riggs."

"Well," Farber lied, watching her, "I'm only interested in her insofar as she was witness to a crime."

After Harry left, Bert sat at a table in the corner and took statements, the barman first, then the cooks, leaving the waitresses for last. He was interrupted constantly because superior officers began to arrive. Singly and in small groups they kept entering and demanding to be briefed. The door opened and closed so often that the restaurant began to get cold. The superiors were like the cops earlier. A fresh crime scene aroused something in each of them. It was their turn for the free look.

Finally he had interviewed all the employees except the girls. "Which of you wants to go first?" Bert asked, and he bent to study the notes he had made. When he heard the chair pulled back he looked up and saw the girl sit down opposite him, the one whose big eyes and long legs had so attracted him from across the room.

She seemed nervous, so he said to her: "There's nothing to be nervous about."

"I'm not nervous." She sounded as earnest as Harry Chapman tended to sound. "It's just that I've never been in a holdup before."

"Welcome to New York," said Bert.

"I was born here."

"Not very long ago, though."

She did not answer.

"You're an actress, I believe."

She looked around her. "Who told you that?"

"I'm a detective, right? I detected it. So what have you acted in?"

"A few things."

"Anything I've seen?"

"Do you go to the theater?"

"Sure," said Bert. "So tell me about yourself." He put his ballpoint down and looked at her.

"What's that got to do with the holdup?"

He picked up his pen again.

"Name?"

She told him.

"You live alone?"

"Excuse me?" She had sensed that his interest was not entirely professional, and was immediately on her guard.

"Do you live alone?" said Bert. "You never know what details will turn out to be important."

"I live with two other girls."

"Address?"

She gave it, but no more.

"My place is only two blocks away." Again Bert put down his pen. "I'm surprised we haven't run into each other in the street."

She shrugged.

"Your father helps with the rent?"

"Not really."

"What does he do?"

"He's on Wall Street."

"And he lives—"

"In Scarsdale."

"Is this your first waitressing job?"

"Yes."

"Do you like the work?"

"It's okay. Look—"

"What have you acted in?"

"Small things."

"Broadway?"

"In school. And off Broadway."

Most robbery victims reached for whatever point of stability they could find. A detective could soothe them. He could ask personal questions and they would answer them. A detective could move in very close very fast. But with this girl it wasn't working.

"A friend of mine hollered 'Waitress' in a place like this, and no one responded," said Bert with a grin. "He hollered 'Actress' and guess what happened?"

"Very funny."

"I didn't finish the joke yet."

"They all came running. I heard it before."

"How could you have heard it before. It's a true story."

"Hilarious."

"All right, where were you when the robbers came through the door?"

"Halfway up the stairs from the kitchen, carrying a tray of four hot dinners. I took one look at the ski masks and the guns and went right back down again and into the ladies' room and locked the door."

"Quick thinking," said Bert.

She eyed him, but did not speak.

"Locked in the john the whole time?"

"Yes."

"With the robbers robbing people just outside the door."

"Yes."

"And you worried about them finding you in there."

"I'm locked in this minuscule cubicle with four steaming dinners. The vapor is coming up through the holes in the covers into my mouth, into my eyes, all these different odors. I started to gag. I was afraid they would hear me. I was afraid I would start to vomit and make a lot of noise and they would start firing shots through the door."

"Well," said Bert with sympathy, "you got away with it."

"Yes."

"Congratulations."

"They might have found me."

"I think they were too busy."

She made no response.

"Would you be able to identify any of them?"

"No."

"What was your impression of their voices?"

"They were voices."

"And nothing of yours was stolen?"

"No, nothing. If that's all you want to know from me, the other girls are waiting." And she glanced meaningfully over toward them.

Bert made a show of studying his notes.

"Ever been arrested?"

"Of course not."

"What's your date of birth?"

She looked at him and did not answer.

"I need it to see if you have a B number. Maybe you're a known criminal. Maybe this is an inside job, and you're the one fingered it." He smiled broadly at his own wit.

She gave her date of birth.

She was almost twenty-one. Bert was twenty-six by then, one of the youngest sergeants in the department.

She said: "Can I go home now?"

"I have a few more questions."

"Like what?"

"What's your phone number?"

She folded her arms across her chest, her lips came together, and she stared off to the side.

"Honey, you're a suspect in a robbery."

"I'm meeting them in the Bronx in ten minutes to divide the swag. How did you guess? And don't call me 'Honey.'"

"I have to know how to get in touch with you."

"Why?"

"If we catch these guys, I may have to call you in to make an identification."

"I told you I didn't even see them."

"You never know," said Bert.

"The other girls are waiting."

"If you don't give me your phone number you're impeding the investigation. I'll have to lock you up."

"Lock me up?"

"Did you ever hear of the crime of obstruction of justice?"

He looked at her, and at last a smile began to come on. "Are all detectives like you?" she said.

Bert pushed a piece of paper across the table. "Here, write it down. I won't even look at it unless I have to."

She laughed and wrote it down.

She lived in what had once been a studio. At some point the landlord had chopped it up into compartments so he could call it a two-bedroom apartment and charge a bigger rent. Mary Alice shared one of the bedrooms with one of the other girls. They had bunk beds, and hers was the one on top. Since the room was not much wider or longer than the beds, it had no space for any other furniture. It was, of course, windowless.

The first night he took Mary Alice out she never let him see it. He was not used to girls being on time, but this one met him practically in the hall and pulled the door closed immediately. He never saw the inside until weeks later when he brought her flowers because she had the flu and was too sick to go out. Her "living room" was about as wide as a bowling alley, and it contained the only window. He asked what the rent was but she didn't want to tell him. When she finally did he cursed softly. "I'd like to lock that landlord up," he said, "because he's a thief."

Their first date was on a Sunday, her night off, the restaurant closed. They went down the stairs and out into the nighttime city, and he said to her: "Do you care for Japanese cuisine?" He had rehearsed this line, but it sounded stilted when he said it.

"Sure."

"I know a good place, then. It's down in the Two-Oh. It's

probably the best Japanese restaurant in the city." He had this from two other cops, and he hoped it was true. He had suggested Japanese because it sounded exotic to him, and because it would be fairly cheap. With his own rent and what he gave his mother he didn't have much money, even on sergeant's pay.

"Shall we walk or take a taxi?" he asked her.

"If it's the one I think it is, it's not far."

They strolled down Broadway. It was a warm night, and even this far uptown the lights were bright and there were many people out and cars and trucks moving past them.

He was extremely disturbed by her presence beside him, and this surprised him. She wasn't the first girl he had ever taken out, for crissake.

He tried to keep his conversation bright and amusing by commenting on the shops and businesses they passed. For instance:

"See that store? I had my first homicide in there. Guy got his head blown off. Brains all over the floor. Yeah."

Japanese restaurants were just becoming established in New York at this time. She did know the one he took her to. Had been there several times, in fact. She knew what to order, and that was one reason he let her order for him as well. The second reason was that when he looked at her he was having trouble even talking, much less interpreting the names of the dishes on the menu.

"Stop staring at me," she said once.

"I can't help it."

When the first course came she showed him how to use the chopsticks. She ate like a linebacker, he noticed. She kept asking how he liked the food.

To him everything tasted fishy. "Great," he answered repeatedly. "Really great."

He had thought himself an experienced, sophisticated young man. What was happening to him?

He asked her about acting, about college. She had quit Bennington after two years to come to New York and take acting classes. Her father was furious at her. He would probably be furious to know she was out with a cop, too.

"Bennington," said Bert. "That's in Massachusetts somewhere?"

"Vermont."

"And very expensive. They have boys there?"

"They're thinking of opening it up to boys soon. What about you? Did you go to college?"

"Of course."

He saw the look of surprise that came over her face, and it disappointed him. She was like most people of her social class—thought all cops were morons.

"Where'd you go?" she asked him.

He wished he could have told her Harvard or Yale, but those places cost money, and even before his father died there hadn't been much of that.

"City," he told her.

"Why City College?"

"Because it was free."

"What was your major?"

"Accounting."

"Accounting?"

He realized he wasn't wowing her with these answers. She would have been more impressed if he had studied medieval poetry at some Ivy League school. "I thought I'd try for the FBI," he explained. "They won't take you unless you have a degree in accounting or law."

"But you became a cop instead."

"The FBI wasn't hiring. The police department was."

In a year or two he would go for a master's degree in personnel management, or criminal justice, he told her. Maybe even a law degree, he wasn't sure. "A master's is like a union card," he told her. "Without a master's degree you can't get ahead in the department. Every headquarters boss has one."

She was surprised. "I didn't know that."

"You thought all cops were uneducated louts."

"No I didn't."

"Yes you did. Sorry to disappoint you."

"Please don't be annoyed at me. You're the first cop I ever met. I never even talked to one before you."

He thought of telling her how well he played the piano. It was the one accomplishment he had that might possibly impress her. But he could not think of a way to work it into the conversation without sounding like he was bragging. So he never told her.

The trouble with a Japanese dinner is that it lasts too short a time. In an hour they were out on the street again and he did not know what to do next. He suggested they take a cab down to Greenwich Village and listen to some music, and he was already calculating how much the cab ride plus the cover charge would cost, but she said:

"I'd rather not."

As he mulled over this rejection she said: "I have to go down there in the morning for an audition. Let's stay around here."

So they walked down Columbus and she stopped often to peer into shop windows, sometimes spotting something and enthusiastically pointing it out to him.

He would say: "It's very nice."

Mostly he stood with his back to the various windows, concentrating not on whatever had caught her eye but on the people and cars passing by, for this was what he had been trained to do, and was most comfortable doing. He did not understand shop windows. He did not understand the city. He knew how to look for some detail that was out of place, that was not as it was supposed to be.

"Those are lovely boots, don't you think?"

He turned and peered over her shoulder. "You really like them?"

"Oh yes."

Taking her arm he drew her toward the door. "Come on, I'll buy them for you."

"I can't let you buy me boots."

"Why not?"

"They cost too much."

"My pleasure." But given the state of his finances he was relieved.

"No," she said sharply. "It's out of the question."

Now he felt embarrassed, worried that she had thought his offer crass. They continued walking down the avenue, and after a moment, perhaps to soften her rebuke, she took his hand and said: "I'll let you buy me an ice cream cone, if you like."

So they stepped into a Baskin-Robbins and came out a bit later licking cones and walked along and she said: "You're a funny guy."

Her hand had felt very good in his, but he was convinced he was giving exactly the wrong impression of himself, and he was somewhat frantically trying to think of how to correct this before it was too late.

They strolled downtown as far as Lincoln Center. The three theaters were floodlit, as was the fountain in the center, and there were still a few stragglers hurrying across the plaza. Beyond the fountain was the glass front of the Met with the two massive Chagalls inside, one to either side of the grand staircase. There was nobody on the staircase anymore, but the Chagalls were there, huge and dominating, one mostly red, the other mostly yellow, and Mary Alice began to tell Bert all about Chagall. He kept nodding, and looking up at the paintings, which he had never liked very much, though the colors were nice.

The café tables were out on the plaza, and they sat down and ordered coffee and a man with a guitar came and sat on the edge of the fountain in the center of the vast square and began to play, and a crowd collected around him. They finished their coffees, Bert paid, and they walked over and listened awhile. The musician had his guitar case open on the pavement in front of him, and people tossed coins into it. Bert threw in a dollar.

"We better go," said Mary Alice after a time.

"It's not late."

"I have this audition in the morning."

At her door she permitted him one kiss but did not invite him in. Though she told him she had enjoyed the evening he couldn't be sure. Did she mean it or was she just being polite? Her door closed on him.

He forced himself to let two days go by, then called her. As he waited to hear her voice on the phone his heart was thumping, and he felt not like the hardened detective he imagined himself to be but like a teenage boy.

She seemed glad to hear from him, and asked if he wanted

to see a play in the Village that some of her friends were in. He said sure.

She took him down there, introduced him all around, and there was a smirk on her face as she did it. When they heard the word *cop*, certain of her friends seemed almost to recoil. She was enjoying herself, making a sensation. It was as if he were some dangerous animal that she had on a leash. Bert recognized this syndrome, for he had encountered it before. He didn't like it, but he liked her and thought it would pass.

That was his introduction also to the experimental theater in Greenwich Village, and in the weeks that followed he watched a number of dramatic representations—he didn't want to call them plays because they did not even slightly resemble what he thought plays ought to be.

They took place in lofts, garages, coffeehouses. Often there was no stage, no scenery either, no curtain, and sometimes no audience, or almost no audience, apart from him and relatives of the actors. The scripts, when there were scripts, were sometimes written on the spot. At times there were none. The actors were all supposed to improvise.

It would be midnight before the performance started, which was the earliest most of the actors could get there because the girls were all waitressing; the guys were usually waiters or barmen. Bert would be half asleep before it ended.

In one play a dozen or so actors played the part of boulders. Covered with gray shrouds they lay on the floor in the fetal position. A young woman in a nightdress went leaping about among the boulders yodeling. She would yodel, listen for the echo with her hand cupped at her ear, and then leap a few more boulders and yodel again. Finally her lover came onstage and did the same. This was supposed to have deep psychological meaning—something about finding the eternal shepherd that exists in all of us.

In that one Mary Alice played one of the boulders. When it ended and she asked how he had liked it, he said: "That one was a howler. Yes it was."

As a result she wouldn't speak to him all the way home on the subway.

In another play she got to sing a song. She had a sweet voice, but the words didn't make much sense to Bert, and the song didn't seem to have any tune. None that he could hear, anyway.

Afterward everyone would repair to a coffeehouse or someone's pad, and they would critique each other. But often the focus would turn from the performance to Bert, and they would begin to criticize not themselves but him. They could not believe that anybody would want to be a cop. To them, cops were the enemy.

They would ask him angry, asinine questions.

"Do you believe in capital punishment?"

"Do you believe kids should be busted for smoking pot?"

It helped to be able to zero in on one opponent rather than many. "How old are you?"

"Twenty-four."

"You're not a kid."

"Answer the question, cop."

"You smoke pot in here and I'm out that door."

He was the Philistine among them, and was constantly on the defensive. Mary Alice never attacked him when the others did, but she didn't stand up for him either, just watched him with a slight, fond smile on her face while he fought, figuratively speaking, for his existence.

Occasionally he got angry, and when this happened he found himself making speeches.

"You don't believe in evil, do you, pal?"

"The purpose of cops is to beat up queers, and kids with long hair."

"Well let me tell you something. People are out there killing and robbing and raping other people, whether you believe in evil or not." Evil was a vast concept. It could not even be spoken of in particular terms without being reduced to the level of newspaper headlines. Bert had been trying to define it for himself since he became a cop, but there was no simple explanation he had been able to grasp. He glanced around at these obtuse young people before him. If he couldn't make them see evil, he would at least try to make them feel it, and thereby acknowledge certain of their own duties as citizens. And so he began to describe a teenage salesgirl he had come upon, lying on the floor in an expensive candy shop, shot and killed in a stickup. "The guy had a shotgun. His first shot tears off her left breast." He had decided to make the story as gory as possible, thinking this was the only way to make them believe it. "The girl's looking down stupefied at her missing blouse, her white ribs, and the second blast tears off her head."

He had their attention now. "You needed galoshes to go in there to keep the blood off your pants." Evil was invisible, Bert knew. One could see only its effects. "We caught the guy," he ranted. "Said he thought she was reaching under the counter for a gun. She was sixteen years old. So was he."

They were silent.

"Or the old lady," he said, "strangled in her bed by the burglar who came through her window in the night. Her crime was," said Bert evenly, "she woke up and started to scream. The poor fellow had no choice. He had to strangle her, right? I mean, put yourself in his place. What would you have done?"

One of the young men gave a dismissive wave. "You're making it up."

"Evil is out there," Bert shouted, "whether you believe in it or not, and no one is fighting against it but me and other cops, and you should all grow up and get jobs and learn what life is all about."

This exchange took place in somebody's loft that contained, as it happened, a piano. Bert walked over and began banging on the keys. The piano was out of tune, and at first he was merely angry, but his fingers wanted to do more than make noise, and almost of their own accord they started to coax out an old blues number. Presently the group began to gather around him, and he was aware of it.

"Muddy Waters," one of the young men said. "Where'd you learn that? 'I'm Your Hoochie Coochie Man.'"

"Muddy's good," said one of the girls, "real good."

"Do you know any early rock?" asked another of the girls. Plainly they did not want any more of Bert's speeches that night.

Mary Alice had her elbow on top of the piano and her chin on her hand. There was a special smile in her eyes—pride in him, perhaps, whether for his speech or for his piano playing he did not know. She had never heard him play before, and Bert's fingers moved over the keys.

"'Good Golly Miss Molly,'" said another young man, identifying it. "Little Richard. He's good too."

"Where'd you learn these things, cop?"

"You got anything modern?"

However superior to them he felt, Bert did not enjoy their hostility. By showing he could play the piano he had converted most of it, temporarily at least, into something else, though he wasn't sure what. And he liked the way Mary Alice looked at him—the proprietary glint, as if to say: "I brought him, he's mine."

His fingers picked out another tune.

"'Come on Baby Light My Fire,'" someone said. "The Doors."

"What else do you know, cop?"

Despite himself, he wanted these twerps to acknowledge something else about him—that he was as cultured as they were, perhaps more. This was probably why he had sat down at the piano in the first place, and now he began to play a different piece. As he played he waited for someone to identify it, but when no one said anything, he stopped.

They all looked puzzled. "The Beatles?" someone suggested.

"You think that's what it is?" Bert inquired of the group at large.

"Could be," said someone else.

"It's Chopin, you clucks," said Bert, and he stood up and banged the lid closed on the keys.

They never smoked pot in his presence with the lights on, but sometimes during their performances he could smell the hot sweet odor drifting about the dark loft or garage or whatever it was, and he would deliberate leaving, but he never did. The hold Mary Alice had on him was too strong. He would sit there with every sense alert, literally on the edge of his seat, and imagine cops coming through the door, a raid, and him caught in it, his career over, arrested for failing to take police action in the presence of the commission of a crime.

Most of Bert's own friends were other cops. Most had married soon after coming on the job, already had kids, and lived in far distant suburbs. They liked to meet in bars after work and down pitchers of beer and tell war stories. Before meeting Mary Alice, Bert had drunk his share. He had had more education than most of the others, but was always careful not to let this show.

Most of them liked to hunt. In season they would take a week off and go up into the Adirondacks and shoot whatever they saw. Bert had once killed a deer. It was big, and they were a long way from camp. It took three men, himself and two other cops, to carry it back. But no one had wanted to return to the city just yet. The weather was very warm, and by the time they got the beast to a New York butcher, lifting it off the fender and dragging it into the store, the meat had gone bad.

It was in the company of such men that Bert felt most comfortable. They were profane, they drank too much, and they held prejudices for or against almost everything. But they faced every day the same pressures and dangers he did; they had a love-hate relationship with the department, as he did; and in a crisis, all knew, the only one you could depend on to stand up for you, even at the risk of his life, was another cop.

Although cops belonged to an all-male society, they did occasionally get together with their wives and girlfriends. Bert once took Mary Alice to a dinner party in Massepequa, Long Island, about fifty miles from the city. One of the detectives in his squad had bought a house there, and the others were throwing him a housewarming. The wives had prepared casseroles or salads, and Bert had brought some jugs of wine. The party split up almost immediately into two segments, as these parties always did, the cops on one side of the room erupting constantly into gales of laughter, while the wives and girlfriends on the other side discussed children and recipes. Mary Alice stood on the fringe of the female group for a time but soon drifted over to the men's side, at which point the conversation there faltered. The mordant remarks stopped. The ribald jokes certainly stopped.

These were men who would walk casually into a gunfight but would not talk dirty in front of a woman.

"You don't have to clean up your act for me," Mary Alice said with a smile. "I've heard it all."

But the good humor did not resume. Their observations became bland. Presently Mary Alice walked over to the window and stood staring out at the small lawn and the street beyond.

In the car going back to the city with two other cops who were about to go on duty, Mary Alice sat in silence, and Bert knew she had not had a good time.

He decided that she and his cop friends did not mix very well, and he did not try to inflict them on her anymore—or her on them.

Whenever he came to her house to pick her up to go out, she would buzz him in downstairs and then meet him out in the corridor, or even halfway down the steps.

"You can't come in," she would say. "The other girls are getting dressed."

And when he took her home afterward, their good nights had to be said outside in the corridor also. "The other girls are probably asleep."

He couldn't imagine what was so secret about the inside of her apartment. To him it came to seem that she was keeping him not only outside her apartment but outside her life.

He kept asking to be invited in.

"What for?"

"I want to see how you live."

She shrugged.

"I want to know everything about you."

"You know enough."

That particular night there had been a poetry reading in a coffeehouse on Sheridan Square in the Village. They were on the way home on the subway, standing up because the car was full, swaying with the movement, talking to each other in the stations, silent each time the noise started up again.

"Well," she said, "I want to see how you live too."

This exasperated him. "I've offered to show you my apartment I don't know how many times."

"That's true." She grinned up at him.

The train pulled into the 86th Street station. "Come on," Bert said, taking her arm, "I'll show you my apartment."

As they pushed out through the turnstile, she said to his surprise: "Okay."

He dragged her up Broadway to 89th, and then half a block in toward West End. He had his keys out and he went up the six steps to the vestibule door and unlocked it, pushing it inward so she could enter ahead of him. He opened the inside door the same way, then led the way up the steep narrow stairs. As he climbed up the four flights he was keenly aware of her following. The lights were dim over the hallways at the top of each flight, and the carpeting was frayed, and he kept hoping that his apartment was clean enough, and that she would like it. Though he had brought other girls up here he had never been as nervous as this. In the past he had been almost relaxed, accepting in advance whatever was about to happen. Most times, in fact, nothing happened.

But this was different.

He let them in and turned on the lights.

At first Mary Alice looked all around, and he watched her. Then he decided to go over to the cabinet that served him as a bar. Opening it, pretending to a nonchalance he did not feel, he asked if she wanted a drink of anything.

"Let me think about it."

He watched her peer into the kitchen, into the bathroom, into the bedroom. He hoped the bed was made. He wasn't sure. Often he didn't make it, but on the nights he expected to see her he usually did, just in case.

Mary Alice stood in the center of the room glancing around. "It's nice," she said. "I like it."

"Would you care for something?" said Bert beside his bar.

"A cup of tea, maybe."

In the kitchen he put water on to boil. Waiting for it, they stood kissing. Bert was aware of his gun pressing into the small of his back, and he wished he had removed it as he usually did when he came home. But he didn't want to let her go to do it.

The kiss ended when the kettle began to whistle. Mary Alice broke their embrace and poured the water in on top of the teabags.

They stood in the kitchen sipping their tea, watching each other. Finally Mary Alice gave him a quick kiss on the lips, but she was holding her cup and saucer between them.

"It's very late," she said. "I've got to go home." And she put cup and saucer down on the counter.

Bert felt like an older man in the presence of a much younger girl. If he went too fast he would spoil everything. He took her home.

One night she phoned him at the precinct to cancel a date. She was sick, she said. She sounded sick. When he called the next day she was sicker. He bought flowers and took them around to the apartment she had never invited him into, and saw the wretched place, and got so angry he wanted to arrest somebody, though he said nothing immediately. She had answered the door in a bathrobe. Her eyes were red, her nose was red, she was coughing, and when he felt her forehead she was feverish. He asked who was taking care of her and the answer was no one. One of her roommates happened to be away and the other had temporarily moved out, saying that Mary Alice coughed all night and she couldn't sleep.

"You need a doctor," said Bert.

"How am I going to get a doctor to come here?"

Bert looked around him. Mary Alice had moved into the lower bunk at least, but she needed someone to clean the place, to change the sheets for her, to bring her tea and soup from time to time.

It was night by then. He knew she had a brother who was married. He knew her parents and two younger sisters lived in Scarsdale. "Get dressed," he told her. "I'm taking you home."

He went back to the station house, borrowed a car from another cop, and drove Mary Alice to Scarsdale and turned her over to her mother, who took her upstairs and put her to bed. Her father, meanwhile, poured Bert a drink.

"And what do you do, Mr. Farber?"

It was like a blow to the chest. It meant she hadn't even mentioned him to her parents. He would have hoped by now that she would have at least mentioned him. "I'm a detective sergeant," he said.

"That's very interesting," said her father, meaning that to him it wasn't.

Bert felt like he was fighting for his life again. "And what do you do, sir?"

He was a man of about fifty. He wore tasseled loafers, a turtleneck sweater, and even at this hour a cashmere sports jacket. Even this late in the day every one of his graying hairs was slicked down perfectly in place.

"I'm with a brokerage house."

"Which one?"

"Merrill Lynch."

"What sort of work do you do there?" Bert persisted.

"I'm chairman of the board, as a matter of fact."

The house was a mansion. Bert had driven up a long winding driveway to get to it, and now that he had had a chance to look around inside, it impressed him even more. Those were real paintings on the walls, the carpeting was an inch thick, and the glass he had been given to drink out of was so fine he was afraid he might break it just holding it in his hand.

"I suppose you're asking yourself why my daughter hasn't mentioned you, Sergeant."

This was exactly what Bert had been asking himself.

"I'm sure she will, sooner or later," said Riggs. "She's probably timing it for maximum shock value."

Bert did not have to be told what he meant.

"She probably thinks I wouldn't approve of a policeman as a potential son-in-law."

"Why should you approve or not approve?" said Bert. "And who cares?"

"How well do you know my daughter, Sergeant?"

"Not all that well, as yet."

"She likes to shock me. This little fling she's having in New York is purely and simply a rebellion against her father."

"You know something, Mr. Riggs, she's never mentioned you to me either."

"Sometimes I think shocking me is her principal pleasure in life. Probably you're a very nice young man, Sergeant. You may or may not have some education, I have no way of knowing. And as a policeman I'm sure you're a good deal more realistic than those arty types she hangs around with. But my daughter comes from—" He gave a wave of his hand to indicate his house, its furnishings. "—From all this. So what we're dealing with is a fling. Nothing more."

"I wouldn't be too sure."

"And when the time comes, I'm confident she'll come right back here. Marry the boy next door, or the equivalent. The average actor, the average policeman for that matter, wouldn't be able to give her what she likes, what she needs."

"Why don't you let her decide such questions for herself?"

"Oh, I will. I certainly will. One day she will certainly decide for herself. I have no doubt what her decision will be."

Bert drained his drink.

"I appreciate your bringing her home tonight, Sergeant. Your concern for her. I'm glad she has someone like you to care for her. But I don't think you know her very well yet, and I would advise you not to get too serious about her, in case that's the way you were leaning. That way lies heartache for you, I believe."

Bert had had about as much of this as he could take. He said bluntly: "Your daughter could use a better place to live in."

"Well, all she has to do is come home."

"Her apartment is a pigsty."

"She must like it that way—temporarily. Otherwise she wouldn't have quit college. She'd forget this actress nonsense."

"Have you seen it?"

"She should think about a worthwhile career or getting married."

"It will happen. Don't push it. In the meantime I asked you something."

"What did you ask me?"

"Have you seen her apartment?"

"Well, she does not want her mother and me to help her."

"I have some advice for you. Go see it."

"I don't really need advice from you, actually."

"If you slipped her a couple of hundred now and then," Bert advised him, "it would make all the difference."

They glared at each other. Bert put down his glass and left. As he drove back to the city he was pleased to have given advice to a multimillionaire, and he was amazed at the contrast between Mary Alice and her father. The chairman of Merrill Lynch must get paid millions. His daughter, meanwhile, was living with two other girls in that miserable apartment in the city. She was taking drama classes, auditioning for parts, and living with the constant rejection that was all the auditioning had ever got her so far. Realizing she needed experience, she was willing to accept any opportunity to act, to be onstage—mostly those stupid experimental plays, which humiliated her and for which she wasn't even paid. She was trying to make good on her own and by herself. She was trying to support herself as a waitress. He did not know when he had ever admired a girl more. He wasn't as much in awe of her now as he had been at first, but he really liked her.

Her father's warning had gone completely over his head. He had taken no notice of it whatever, hadn't even heard it.

The next time Mary Alice came to his apartment, ostensibly for tea, there was no kissing at first. She stepped into his tiny kitchen to put the kettle on, while he went to his liquor cabinet, where he drew the .38 out of his belt, getting rid of the weight of it, and also the pressure into his flesh. He broke the gun open to extract the shells, laid it down on top of the cabinet, then stood the five shells upright next to it.

His handcuffs hung off his belt in back. He drew them out and placed them on top of the cabinet as well. Now he felt ready for whatever might happen.

"Handcuff me," Mary Alice said. She had come back into the room carrying the cups, saucers, milk, and sugar on a tray, and had seen him put the cuffs down on the cabinet. She put the tray down on the coffee table and picked the cuffs up, and she held them out to Bert, who took them. "The kettle's on," she said. "Go ahead, do it."

"I don't want to," responded Bert.

She stood with her back to him and her hands behind her.

She was not the first girl he had handcuffed. What was it with females, he had asked himself in the past. Even the most aggressive of them wanted to be submissive. It was a subliminal thing with them, he had decided, playing the amateur psychologist. It's a need some of them don't even know they have.

He stroked one slim, bare arm down to her hand.

"Go ahead," ordered Mary Alice over her shoulder.

"Why?"

"I want to know what it feels like. I might have to act the part some day. I want to know what everything feels like."

"Everything?" said Bert.

She smiled at him over her shoulder. "Almost everything."

"Okay," he said. Being careful not to catch her skin, not to hurt her, he locked the manacles around her wrists.

She marched up and down the room, getting used to them, trying them out.

"Now I don't have to get arrested to know how it feels."

"How does it feel?"

"Odd," she said. She was still walking. "It's a bit hard to keep your balance, isn't it?"

"So they tell me."

"For once I'm totally in your power," she said.

"Yes, that's true." He went to his front door and opened it onto the corridor. "Well, I have to go now, so long."

"You come back here," said the handcuffed girl.

"If you need anything, go to the phone. Dial it with your nose."

"Bert, you can take them off me now."

He went to her waving the handcuff key, but put it in his pocket instead of in the lock. His arms went around the armless woman and when he kissed her, she kissed him back. It was a long, probing, totally satisfying kiss. His hands, meanwhile, slid down her bare arms to the cuffs, to her hands, and then further and he caressed the skirt over her bottom.

"Just making sure the cuffs are secure," he said. "With prisoners you can't be too careful."

"The kettle's whistling," she murmured into his ear.

He went into the kitchen and turned it off, came back, and stood kissing her again, caressing every part of her.

"Hey, don't I get any tea?"

"First I have to search you for any possible concealed weapons. A good cop always checks out the bulges first, like here, and here."

Her eyes were closed and she leaned against him.

He began unbuttoning her blouse, which he pushed back off her shoulders so that it slid down her arms. "Sometimes we have to do strip searches. In this case that is certainly what is called for." Reaching behind her, he unhooked her bra, then bent to nuzzle what he had uncovered. His fingers, becoming more frantic now, went to her skirt.

"Civilian complaint," she murmured into his neck. "The prisoner was defenseless."

"I'm crazy about you."

"The prisoner was taken advantage of." She stood with all her assets disclosed.

"What do you know," he said. "No concealed weapons."

She wasn't a total innocent, but almost. It was all new to her, and she really loved it. She groaned and writhed and embraced him more tightly than anyone ever had. She made him feel like a god that he could fill her so deeply, cause her such pleasure, so many spasms, such long ungodly spasms.

It was about two-thirty in the morning when they started— they had come from a party in Greenwich Village that had begun after her restaurant closed—and the dawn was coming up when he walked her back to her apartment. The night was gone and they had not slept a minute of it. They held hands and walked through the empty streets without saying a word, though from time to time each would turn and smile at the other and give an almost involuntary squeeze to the other's hand. There was no need for any more words. All that needed to be said had been communicated from one to the other long since, but at a level that language alone could never reach— not in language at all but in caresses, glances, sounds, especially the intimate sounds and endearments cried out in the midst of the most intimate of acts. There were times when sex was the purest and most intense communication human beings could reach, Bert felt that night, and this had been such a time for them—in fact not a communication at all but a communion. Communion at the level of ecstasy, of delirium. They had spent hours together in a place so secret it was known only to them.

A state of love now existed between them, and both were still young enough to imagine it permanent—for as long as both should live. Their bodies, their brains, their very beings were sated with the presence of one another, filled up to the top, and always would be. Or so they thought and believed as they reached Mary Alice's door and kissed one last time good night, though obviously, in terms of how things eventually turned out, Bert was much the stronger believer of the two. It seemed to him as he started home again, almost dancing down the sidewalk, that the depth of the emotion between them would only intensify from then on.

And even when he thought about it, clearly, coldly, logically, as he would on certain later occasions when he was alone and pondering his life, still he was convinced that what he remembered of that first night—wanted to remember—had actually been there. That absolute religious communion of bodies and souls, the closest he had ever felt in his life to another human being. Could her lips have lied to him that night, as they did often enough later? He knew about perjured testimony well enough. But he was able to reject this possibility because her body had given out the same message and her body hadn't lied, because bodies can't. A body (alive or dead, as far as that goes) to him was an absolutely reliable witness, compelled to bear witness to the truth because it was incapable of doing anything else.

They returned to his apartment the next night. He met her at the restaurant and they walked over. Without a word said she fell into step beside him. Ignoring the mounting sexual tension, pretending not to feel it, they strolled up Columbus past the museum, past the planetarium, and across 89th Street. They did not talk about love or sex, nor of where they were going or why, though both knew what their intentions were, and he imagined she was contemplating the next hours as much as he, was perhaps even as eager as he. There was a big moon above the buildings. They walked hand in hand with their coats open, for the air was balmy, springlike, and they talked mostly about the restaurant. Most of the tables had been empty tonight, she said. Since the robbery, business had fallen way off. That's always the way, he told her. A place gets robbed at gunpoint and the locals won't go into it anymore, afraid it might get stuck up again. All you get is people from elsewhere who happen to be in the neighborhood and don't know the story. The restaurant might have to close, she said. She might have to find a new job even if it didn't close, unless her tips picked up.

Pretending nonchalance, as if married thirty years, as if walking back from the corner with a newspaper or bottle of milk, they came into his building. They went up the stairs, Bert opened the door, and the nonchalance vanished. Suddenly they could not wait. They were kissing and undressing each other the moment the door closed. There was no time, it seemed, even to turn on the light. They left a trail of clothing from the front door to the bed.

There were no preliminaries. Bert threw himself upon her and she was ready. It was like the night before, only different. This time she writhed and bucked from the beginning, she gasped, she cried out. She clasped him to her, looped her legs around him. From time to time she made a noise that could only be called a scream. Screams of pleasure. The night before she had possibly been surprised by what was done to her, by her own responses, her eagerness for more. She had even been a bit embarrassed, he reasoned. There had been inhibitions. Now there were none. None at all. She held back nothing. She amazed him to such an extent that a part of him simply stood off in the corner and watched her.

At first he was filled with pride as well. The man responsible for the state she was in was himself, Bert P. Farber. He was the one doing this to her. He exulted in himself and in her. She was so wet, so big he could barely feel her. He had transported her to this state, awakened her to herself, to a self she hadn't known was there. Look at her, at the sweat on her upper lip, at her half-closed eyes, her half-open mouth.

But the longer it went on the more disappointed he became. It was not her shamelessness that disappointed him, he liked that part of it, but rather that she seemed to be reveling totally in herself, not in the two of them together. It was as if what they were doing involved only her. She might even have been trying to find out what her sexual limits were, how deep into her being did it run? Perhaps she was so completely uninhibited tonight only because she did not care how she might appear to him. At times she seemed to him so lost in a country of her own, so deeply embedded in herself, that she neither knew nor cared who it was who had taught her this game, had mounted her, was riding her now.

In other words, the intense, religious eroticism of twenty-four hours ago, the communion of souls, seemed to him almost entirely missing tonight. It was not there. Furthermore, its absence was not important to her. She didn't seem to miss it. Had she deliberately set it aside? Worse, had she forgotten last night already?

Despite these speculations, despite his regrets, despite never really having lost himself in it all, still Bert had no difficulty in remaining as hard as required, regularly from time to time spurting forth still another orgasmic dose. This was because her face as she labored was to him so gorgeous, her body so gorgeous. He could look down into those great dark eyes and want to drown in them, want to cease to exist except in her body.

And so he clung to his idealized version of her that he still thought or perhaps only hoped was real. Her body may already have been telling him that although she was part of his dream, he was not necessarily part of hers. But for a time he would continue to believe the contrary. He would continue to believe in love.

Several times they met Harry Chapman in the street, usually as Mary Alice left the restaurant at night. Harry would pull his radio car to the curb and chat with them awhile. It was possible to imagine that on those particular nights Harry had watched the diners through the glass each time he drove by, and had calculated what time Mary Alice was likely to get off work—but this idea occurred to Bert only much later.

Leaving his partner in the car, Harry would stand with them on the sidewalk. The pedestrians would go by, the traffic would go by in the street, and Harry would be careful to direct most of his conversation to Bert. It's me he wants to talk to, Bert told himself, but he doesn't mind looking at her while he does it. Bert saw nothing wrong with this. Harry would talk about his progress through law school, and it pleased Bert that Mary Alice should see the way the younger cop looked up to him.

Mary Alice never flirted with Harry. Mary Alice never flirted with anybody. She showed little interest in him, in fact, although she was polite enough. She would stand a bit apart gazing off into the distance while Harry and Bert talked.

"We should go out to dinner with Harry and his girlfriend," Bert told her one night, as they continued up Columbus Avenue.

"Why?"

"He suggested it. He wants to go out on a double date, so I suggested dinner."

"I only get one night off a week."

"What do you have against Harry?"

"I don't like cops."

"All cops?"

She grinned and stuck her tongue out at him. "All cops without exception."

Bert laughed.

"They're boring," Mary Alice said.

"Harry's almost finished law school." As they walked along Bert told her of Harry's background, his grandiose plans for the future.

"He sounds pretty pompous to me."

"Yeah, a little. Get this: when he becomes police commissioner, who do you think he's promised to appoint chief of detectives?"

"I'm surprised you even like him."

"It's only one dinner," Bert said.

"For a realistic kind of guy you have some strange friends."

"When you get to know him—"

"I can't figure you out."

"I guess I feel like his mentor," said Bert. "Or some goddam thing."

Mary Alice sighed. "Okay," she said.

The double date took place at the Rainbow Room on top of the RCA building. Very elegant. Mary Alice had had to go home to Scarsdale to get a suitable dress out of her closet—red, sleeveless, with sequins across the bodice. It had a tight waist and a swirly skirt. Bert was stunned by her.

Harry's date was named Madge Fellows. She was a bit taller than Mary Alice, and fair where Mary Alice was dark. She was a pretty girl, but Mary Alice, to Bert, was beautiful. Madge was a senior at Hunter College, majoring in psychology, he learned. Of course he did not recognize her as his future wife.

It was a clear night. There was glass all around the restaurant and the view was stupendous, for the lights of the city went on and on in all directions as far as the eye could see. Harry ordered champagne with dinner. He said he had only one more course to pass and he was through law school.

They sipped their champagne, and all around them were people they took to be tourists. All four of them had been born in New York, but up here above the city they felt like tourists themselves. There was an orchestra and a dance floor, and all the dancers were certainly tourists, they told themselves. Many were foreigners, especially Japanese.

After dinner Harry and Madge got up to dance. Bert watched for a while, then felt Mary Alice dragging him to his feet.

"Come on," she said.

"I warn you, I'm not very good at this."

As they moved to the music he said into her neck: "I love holding you tight, but I hate dancing."

"Party-pooper," she said as they went back to the table. It sounded coy coming from Mary Alice, who until that night had always seemed to him a blunt, straightforward girl, and never coy.

Tonight, for some reason, she seemed all girlish and giggly.

"Dance with me, Mary Alice," said Harry.

While Harry danced with Mary Alice, Bert sat with Madge. He received the impression that she wasn't Harry's girlfriend, hardly knew him in fact, though years later he would learn the contrary.

"Harry dances very well," Mary Alice reported to Bert, when he had returned her to the table and gone off with Madge again.

"So it seems."

Her eyes, it seemed to Bert, were especially sparkling, especially bright.

"He took lessons till he was twelve," she said, and she laughed.

"What's so funny?"

"So did I." She was almost giddy.

"Maybe you had the same teacher."

She shook her head, having missed the irony in his tone. "We were living in an apartment on Park Avenue at the time. Harry lived in Washington then."

"The New York public school system," Bert commented, "did not feature dancing on the curriculum."

"His father is the newspaper and TV commentator. I didn't know that."

"I thought I told you," said Bert. And then: "I hate dancing."

He spent much of the rest of the evening talking to Madge, while Harry danced with Mary Alice. Madge was talking about children. She hoped to have three or four, she said, but in fact during her marriage to Bert she was never to have any. Bert tried to listen to her but watched Mary Alice with Harry, and his stomach was twisted up into knots.

In the taxi going home he gave the address of his apartment, but Mary Alice leaned forward and countermanded the order by giving her own. She then leaned back and patted his hand, saying: "It's late. I'm exhausted. Let's both get some sleep."

"Mary Alice—" he began, but soon found that he was pleading with her. Wrong tactics, he thought, and stopped and gazed out the window.

A few blocks farther on she commented airily: "He's very nice, your friend."

Bert said nothing.

And a few blocks after that she said: "We're getting in too deep."

"Too deep?" said Bert. "Mary Alice, I'm in love with you. I want to marry you."

This silenced her, but only for a moment. "You're not in love with me."

"I've told you often enough."

"Yes, in bed. That's just sex talking."

"No, I mean it."

"You don't love me, you just like to fuck me."

In the circles she frequented girls now talked this way. Her circles, not his. Shocked, he said nothing.

"What about my career?" she asked.

"You wouldn't have to give that up."

"That's what marriage would lead to."

"Not marriage to me."

"Yes, especially to you."

"Mary Alice, you may never break through. You may never have a career."

"Well, I'm certainly not ready to quit trying, just because it's been hard to make headway so far."

Ease off, he told himself. She's flaky—a word he had learned from her. It was just coming into use at this time, it's meaning not yet solidified. He was shaken by her attitude, but told himself otherwise. She's a flake, he told himself, and so are all those friends of hers who use words like *fuck* in mixed company. Give her room and she'll come around.

He had been asked to join three other cops who were headed for Canada to hunt bear. But a week of not seeing Mary Alice had seemed to him too long a time, and he had declined. But now in the taxi he changed his mind.

"You won't see me for a while."

"Why not?" she asked sharply.

"I'll be away on a trip." Her initial reaction gave him hope. She would miss him. Absence would make her heart grow fonder.

"How long?"

"About a week. Canada."

"Hunting?"

"For bear."

"Bear?"

"Not teddy bears, for crissake."

"How can you want to kill things that are alive?"

He did go to Canada, where he and the other cops hunted every day for a week without even seeing a bear, or anything else except squirrels; where he drank too much beer, swatted mosquitoes most of the night, and mooned about Mary Alice.

When he returned he found her restaurant had been boarded up again. She had moved out of her apartment too. It took him two days to find her. She was working in a restaurant in Greenwich Village now. He walked in and sat down, and when she came over to wait on him he said: "You're cute. Are you married?"

She wore flat shoes, pants, a sweater. She wore her hair in

a long rope of a pigtail and looked about twelve years old, but he knew she wasn't. His mouth had dried up instantly, and after his opening remark, which he had rehearsed, all he could do was look at her.

She had a new apartment around the corner, she told him, and with only one roommate this time, and this was a better job than the last one, because down here she could come to work wearing whatever she liked. In the old job in the short skirt and net stockings she had felt like a piece of meat. And the high heels, by the end of each night, had given her pains as high up as her knees.

However, it was farther from where he lived, farther still from his station house, and by the time he got down there after work each night she was sometimes already gone, unless he had made a specific date in advance. In the old place he had been able to look in on her in the course of the evening, gauge how early she might get off, even wave to her at times. It had all been almost casual.

Now it was a matter of specific dates, which with this girl, he sensed, was not such a good idea, Especially now it wasn't. But he had to do it to be sure she would wait for him, even though he feared the impression it might give her: that he was hounding her, importuning her at all times.

Wait for me.

Meet me.

And ultimately, at the end of each meeting: come to my apartment.

She did come to his apartment occasionally, though not as often as before. Not as often as he wished.

When summer came she signed up for a job with a summer stock theater company in Lancaster, New Hampshire. She was not hired as an actress but as a general helper—to sell tickets, answer phones, move scenery—whatever needed doing. But it was not so bad, she told him. For three months she would be close to the front lines of the business. She would get to know the actors—

Yeah, thought Bert, the type actors willing to play in Lancaster, New Hampshire.

—She would be able to study their techniques, maybe even

be asked to understudy. Maybe somebody would get sick and she would have to go onstage and save the performance.

Bert listened to her, nodded, and said nothing. He wished she would grow up and stop dreaming and be realistic.

"I'll come up and see you once in a while on my days off," he said.

"I wouldn't expect you to. It's too far."

And so she left for three months.

Lancaster, New Hampshire, is about three hundred miles from the city. But the idea of three months without her was, for him, like the idea of three months in jail.

He waited ten days, during which he was unable to get her on the phone. She was living in some kind of dormitory in the woods behind the theater, and although he left messages, he could not be sure she ever got them. It sounded hectic up there, and she had warned him she would be busy night and day.

He tried to borrow a car, couldn't, and had to rent one. The drive took over seven hours, though he hurried all the way, holding the car at eighty on the interstates, and he got stopped twice by troopers, once in Connecticut, once in Vermont, and although no cop would ever write a fellow cop a summons, still it cost him time. And then once he got into New Hampshire it was all winding back roads.

He got there much later than he had intended. It was past supper time, dark, a warm night, windy. He parked in an empty dirt parking lot in front of the theater and got out of the car into a wind that blew the dust around, blew his hair around. There were posters at the front of the theater, but the doors were closed, for the season didn't open until the following week.

Behind the theater were some outbuildings with lights burning over porches. A man came toward him who pointed out the building in which Mary Alice probably lived. He had just got there himself, he said, and didn't know anyone by that name.

Bert went up three steps onto the wooden porch. The door had glass panes. He tried to peer through the glass, but there were no lights on inside. He opened the door and called Mary Alice's name.

No answer.

He went in. There was a hallway with rooms opening off it. Nothing was locked. This isn't New York, he told himself, no thieves up in these woods. Still, he felt these doors should be locked. Any of the people staying here could be a thief. You couldn't tell by looking. Or someone could come along. No point putting temptation in anyone's way.

"Mary Alice!" he called out.

He called her name several times more, then opened some doors to rooms, switching lights on, then off again. He kept seeing the same things: two beds, a closet, open suitcases.

He went outside and stood on the porch. Where was she? Maybe she didn't want him here. Maybe she knew he was coming and had made herself scarce. He felt more vulnerable than he liked. Suppose she's got someone else among the crew? Probably I shouldn't have come up here at all, he thought.

He thought he could hear music farther into the woods. There seemed to be a path leading in that direction—the bulb over the door threw some light on it. He started into the woods. In a few feet he tripped over a root and nearly went sprawling. He could see nothing. Branches scratched at him. He tried to orient himself according to the dim strains of music, and to feel for the path with his feet, but he was a city boy. Without the sounds, which suddenly seemed to be coming from an entirely different direction, he would be totally lost. Despite his occasional hunting trips, he was not comfortable outside New York City. It was as if he were always listening for sirens. The woods were noiseless, or nearly so, not at all what he was used to. They did not smell the same either.

At last the music seemed to be coming closer.

So was the beam of a flashlight, wobbling toward him, illuminating the path as it approached. When its outer orbit touched his shoes it lifted to his face and Mary Alice's voice said: "My God, what are you doing here?"

When he reached for her she came up against him and stood there somewhat stiffly, it seemed to him at first. But in a moment he felt her relax in his arms, her own arms came around him. The flashlight clicked off, and the metallic weight of it hung against his back, and he felt her soft mouth against his, and he thought he had never been this happy ever. All the doubt, indecision, suffering—the long ride—had been worth it.

Standing on the dark path with the forest pressing in on all sides, he could not even see her, only feel her, hear her breathe, and for a moment, before the sexual urgency kicked in strong, he was totally content. For a further time they engaged in what teenagers called heavy petting, feeling, stroking, rubbing, straining. They were not teenagers, but that seemed the limit of what was possible under the circumstances. It was for Bert the sweetest agony of his life, in its way far sweeter than the total freedom of a room and a bed. It was more innocent, a love more totally pure.

"God," he breathed in her ear. "Oh, God." Why that word, he might wonder later. Perhaps, he would answer himself, because God and love were a perfect match, the one as incomprehensible as the other, man totally awed to find himself in the presence of either.

"I love you," he told her. "Where can we go?"

She had been breathing as hard as he, but she laughed, took his hand, and led him farther into the woods.

Her flashlight had clicked back on again: "Come this way."

Though it wasn't much light, it was enough to dispel the enchantment. Roots to stumble over. More branches that scratched at him. He thought she was leading him to a more private part of the forest. Perhaps they were about to make love under a tree. But the music—a guitar player, he realized now, and someone singing softly—got stronger, and presently they came out into a small clearing illuminated by firelight, and he saw that they were at the edge of a lake.

Six or seven young people sat around the fire. The music seemed to flicker like the flames. Bert and Mary Alice sat down on a log. The firelight did beautiful things to her eyes, made them darker, deeper, and to the planes of her face and to the long dark hair down her back. They sat holding hands, listening, but presently Bert became impatient. He did not want to share her with these others. He did not want any part of her focused on the music rather than on himself.

"That path there," he whispered into her hair. "Does that continue around the lake?"

"I don't know."

"Let's go look."

She gave him an amused, quizzical look, but allowed him to draw her to her feet.

They made off together down the path, which closed around them. It was a deer track probably, although what did Bert know about deer? It was very narrow, and at times curved inland. At other times it was close to the lake, which was visible through branches. There was a small amount of light on the water. Stars. Perhaps the moon was there somewhere, though he could not see it.

Since she had the flashlight, Mary Alice led the way, her hand behind her as if dragging Bert along against his will, which was not the case at all.

They came to a place were there were boulders amid the trees and therefore no underbrush, and Mary Alice's flashlight flicked all about, focusing at length on one that was as flat on top as a stool. He didn't realize it then, but would later: she had known what she was looking for.

"Sit down there," she said.

He sensed rather than saw her step out of her shoes. He heard her working at her belt. Her jeans went down her legs and she stepped out of them.

Her white thighs came toward him. "I thought I told you to sit down on the rock."

She worked a moment at his zipper, then pushed him gently, and he sat down.

"When will you go back?" she asked as she straddled him.

What was it a man felt at such times: that a part of him had penetrated to the core of the world, that it and he were looking all around in wonder?

She moved up and down on him. "Will you go back tonight?"

"Are you crazy?" he growled. "Do you know how long a drive it is?"

He got his hands under her sweater, slid them up her back. How smooth her flesh was, how cool.

"Take your sweater off."

"No."

"Why not?"

"Suppose someone comes."

"You don't have any pants on, for crissake."

She laughed but instead of removing the sweater only continued to move up and down on his lap.

He pushed the sweater up, then the bra underneath it, and bent to nuzzle her.

"Do you have a place to sleep?" she asked conversationally.

"No," he grunted.

She was moving slowly, deliberately. "Stop a minute," he said. "Stop. Please stop."

He attempted to clasp her to him so she could not move, but she laughed and squirmed in his arms, bouncing now, so that he thought: plunging down a ski jump must be like this, the increasing momentum, and then at the end you are soaring. He closed his eyes and moaned softly.

She stood up, still straddling him. "There," she said. "Feel better now?"

She bent to pick up her jeans and for a moment her buttocks, ghostly white in this light, mooned him.

"We have to find a place for you to sleep," she said.

"I know where I'd like to sleep. With you."

"Well, you can't."

"Are you in a room alone?"

"There's another girl."

"Tell her to move out."

They had rearranged their clothing and were walking back.

"The girls' side of the dormitory is completely full."

"I can sleep in the car."

"There may a bed free on the guys' side."

They came to where they had sat around the fire. Although the fire still burned, the guitarist was gone, as were his listeners, and they paused a moment staring into the flames, and Bert put his arms around her and kissed her deeply. She did not resist, but she did not seem to be taking part in the kiss.

She said: "But you have to leave first thing in the morning."

"I may never leave. This is where I intend to retire."

"I'm going to be busy all day. I wouldn't be able even to see you all day."

"There's tomorrow night," said Bert. "Tomorrow night

might be worth waiting for. Now that we know where to find that rock."

He was following behind her, behind the flashlight. She was speaking to him over her shoulder. "We're rehearsing tomorrow night."

"Rehearsals have to end, I find."

"It will go on way past midnight."

"You can wake me up."

"First thing tomorrow morning you'll go. Promise me."

"Sure," he said. At that moment he would have made any promises she asked for. Especially ones he considered in no way binding.

They came out of the woods and could see the outbuildings ahead. Lights burned over the porches, and some of the windows showed light as well.

"This is the guys' dormitory," said Mary Alice. She went up onto the porch, opened the screen door, and led him down the hall. When she came to the room she was looking for she knocked, got no answer, opened it, found the wall switch, and turned on the light.

Inside was a steel cot with the mattress rolled up and tied by string. Two bare pillows and some folded army blankets lay on the springs. Against the wall was a dresser with cigarette burns on top. There was no linen on the bed, and no other light except the one in the ceiling.

"You can sleep here," said Mary Alice. She untied the string and let the mattress roll out. "No sheets or pillowcases, I'm afraid."

Bert swung the door closed and wrestled her down onto the bed.

"No," she said. "Absolutely not. I'm not supposed to be in here at all. You'll make me lose my job."

She pushed him off, rose, straightened her clothes, and opened the door.

"Are you hungry?" Bert asked her. "Want to go into town and get something to eat?"

"There would be nothing open at this hour."

Bert had had no dinner.

Not wanting her to leave, he sat down on the bed. "How's

the job going?" He loved just looking at her. "We didn't even talk about that yet."

"It's going good," said Mary Alice. "Real good."

He quizzed her, and it was as he had suspected. She wasn't getting any theatrical experience, and she certainly wasn't earning much money. So far she and the others had been busy sweeping out the theater, repairing broken seats, answering phones, and stuffing envelopes with tickets ordered by subscribers. But the director was due tomorrow, she said, and everything would change. She gave the director's name, but Bert had never heard of him.

"He's very well known," Mary Alice said.

The actors were due tomorrow too. Bert had never heard of them either, except for one. Mary Alice had been studying the script. "I want to be familiar with it, in case anything happens to anyone."

They're exploiting you, kid, Bert thought. He did not want to be the one to tell her this. He thought she would realize it herself before long.

She stepped away from the door far enough to open it onto the hall. "We can have a cup of coffee together in the morning," she said. "Then you have to go."

"Do I get a good night kiss?"

She grinned at him. "You have to come over here. I'm not going near that bed."

They kissed good night in the doorway.

When she had gone out Bert moved to the window and watched her cross the space between the two buildings, go up onto the porch, open the screen door, and go inside. She did not look back.

He felt pretty good though, and he went out to his car, got his small satchel, came back to the room, stripped down to his underwear, pulled one of the army blankets over him, and fell asleep.

In the morning he stood with her around a coffee urn in the vestibule of the theater. She introduced him to some other young people whose names he immediately forgot. They sipped coffee and munched on doughnuts.

After about twenty minutes an older man came in and started barking orders.

"You have to go," said Mary Alice.

She walked him out to his rented car.

His first stop was in the town, which was about five miles away, where he went into a diner and ordered orange juice, scrambled eggs with sausages, three orders of toast, and three cups of coffee. Except for the doughnut at the theater he had had nothing to eat since noon the day before.

He took his time over breakfast, then got back into his car and drove north toward the Canadian border, just looking over the countryside, enjoying having nothing to do until nightfall. He had lunch in a town called Waterloo, and listened to people speaking Canadian French all around him.

There were some lakes nearby and in the afternoon he went to look at them. It was a warm summer day, bright sunshine and a hot breeze, but the water looked cold. He looked across the water, and to the south there were the mountains he had just come through. He started back.

It was night when he parked in front of the theater. He could tell there was much activity inside, so he took his satchel and walked around the theater toward the two dormitories, thinking that before he went looking for Mary Alice he would reclaim his room from last night.

He crossed the porch under the light, opened the screen door, counted three doors on his left, and pushed open the door to the room. But when he snapped on the light, he saw that another man's open suitcase reposed on the bed.

He heard the screen door bang, and then footsteps on the hall, and then the man came into the room.

It was Harry Chapman.

"Bert," he said with surprise. But he sounded pleased as well. "What are you doing here?"

"Looking for Mary Alice," said Bert.

"This is the men's dormitory."

"The guy I asked said it was the girls'."

"The girls' dormitory is next door."

"I guess the guy made a mistake. Or I did."

"Mary Alice is in the theater."

"Oh, well—"

"Does she know you're here?"

"I happened to be up in Canada," Bert said, "and I thought I'd stop in and say hello on my way home."

"She'll be surprised to see you."

"Yes," said Bert, "I imagine she will."

"She doesn't expect you?" persisted Harry. He seemed to be watching Bert closely. The answer to this question was important to him.

"Not tonight, she doesn't," said Bert, and he saw Harry relax.

"But you," said Bert after a silence. "I guess she knew you were coming, didn't she?"

"Oh yes, we had a firm date. I'll be staying a couple of days."

"I called her several times from New York," said Bert, "but I was never able to get through."

"The same thing happened to me, so I left messages, and she called me back."

"I should probably have left some messages myself."

There was another pause. Then Bert said: "I guess you've been seeing a lot of her lately."

"More and more," answered Harry. "I hope you don't mind."

"Why should I mind?"

"I mean, you're not engaged to her or anything."

"No," said Bert, "nothing like that."

"She's a wonderfully honest, straightforward girl."

"Yes," said Bert, "that describes her." So women lied. So what else was new.

"She'll be glad to see you," said Harry. "And I'm glad to see you too." He beamed as if he actually believed what he was saying. Did he? Could he possibly? Was he that unsuspicious, that naive? It was possible, Bert supposed. If so, he would never make a detective.

"Let's go find her," said Harry.

Bert did not think this was such a good idea. Women did not take kindly to being confronted with their lies.

Maybe she had lied only to protect him. She knew he would be distressed. Maybe she had tried to prevent Harry from coming, but couldn't. Maybe she actually had no interest in Harry at all, but knew that Bert would think otherwise.

This was what Bert wanted to believe. But he could think of other scenarios with no difficulty. Already vague suspicions tugged him this way and that, and they were ugly, and he knew they would get worse.

"Come on," said Harry, "she's in the theater."

"I don't want to cut in on your time with her," responded Bert.

"It's nice of you to say that, but—"

"I was just passing through," said Bert. "I was only going to stay a minute anyway."

"I know she'd like to see you."

"She's busy and I can't hang around. I'm working an eight to four tomorrow, so I better get back on the road. Maybe you better not even tell her I was here. She might get mad at me for not waiting."

Harry walked Bert to his car, and they stood a moment in the lot in front of the theater while Harry talked about the new captain who had taken over command of the Two-Oh. This was Sternhagen, who would play a part in their story later. He had just been promoted up from lieutenant and had replaced Priestly in command, Harry said. Sternhagen was tough. He had put in new controls. Priestly, meanwhile, had been transferred to headquarters.

Bert looked across at the theater. He was not interested in Sternhagen, whom he did not know, or in Priestly either. He thought that at any moment Mary Alice might come out and see him there with Harry. He almost wished she would. She would wave to him. Just to see her would give him pleasure. Maybe she would run up and throw her arms around him and tell Harry Chapman to get lost.

So he watched the theater and hardly heard what Harry was saying. The theater had a porch and three doors. But no door opened and Mary Alice didn't come out, and presently Bert got into his car and drove away.

As he proceeded south the night seemed to get darker, and so did the notions floating through his head. Even now Mary Alice might be leading Harry around the lake to the place where those boulders sprouted out of the ground. In a moment it would be Harry's lap she was straddling. She hadn't found those boulders last night by accident. She had known about them, about the flat one like a stool, meaning she had scouted them out previously. For whom? Not for Bert, for she hadn't known he would arrive. For Harry? For some third party neither of them knew about?

If she was not in love with Bert, then why had she taken him there? If she loved Harry, or someone else, how could she? Was she so sex starved after ten days in the woods that she couldn't help herself? Were girls like that? What did he know about the female gender? What did he know about Mary Alice Riggs? But she hadn't seemed sex starved. She had seemed rather casual in fact. Maybe she was flattered that he had come so far to see her, and had decided to reward him for his long trip. The way you'd tip a waiter. Was sex with him as unimportant to her as that? Did it mean so little to her?

Maybe all she wanted to do was fuck Bert one night, once he had turned up so unexpectedly, and Harry the next night, two different men in under twenty-four hours. See what it was like. Compare them the way men sometimes compared girls. Notches in her gun.

It took Bert six and a half hours to reach New York, and with thoughts like this he tortured himself all the way.

He phoned her two days later, because he was unable not to, leaving a message, and when she called back promptly he was both surprised and elated.

"I thought you might like to know I got home safely."

"I'm glad, Bert. I miss you."

"How are you?"

"Busy."

"Are you lonely?"

"I don't have time to be lonely."

"Does anybody else come up to see you, besides me?"

"Like who?"

"I don't know. Your parents, your brother maybe." He added lamely: "It's a nice drive."

"It's a long drive, you mean. Nobody would drive all this way except a crazy guy like you."

So she didn't know he and Harry had met. Harry hadn't mentioned it. Bert had been reasonably certain he wouldn't.

Even Harry would know better than to take her focus off himself, even for a moment, and put it onto another man.

He wished she wouldn't lie to him all the time.

"Anything new up there I should know?"

"I read for the director."

"And?"

"He said I had talent and should keep at it. He asked me to be his personal assistant."

After a moment Bert decided to say: "I don't like the sound of that."

Mary Alice laughed. "He's old. He must be fifty at least."

"I better come up again, look after my interests."

"I couldn't ask you to."

"I want to."

"I wouldn't want you to. It's too far."

"It's not so far."

"And I'm so busy I wouldn't be able to give you any time."

"Still—"

He could almost see her biting her lip. "If you do come," she said, "call first, okay?"

He phoned her regularly after that, but someone else always answered, promising to give her the message. Invariably it took several days for her to return his calls.

With her grudging permission he did drive up once more. She had been there more than a month by then. She threw her arms around his neck and seemed glad to see him. They went for a long walk around the lake. It was mid-afternoon, a hot day, no wind at all. The lake was smooth, narrowing at the other end, stretching into the trees. The last time he was here he hadn't seen it except under the stars. Walking single file, holding hands when they could, they came to the place of the boulders.

"Well, well," said Bert grinning. "I feel like I've just come across an old friend."

"Don't get ideas," said Mary Alice. But when he kissed her long and deeply, she seemed to kiss him back, and for a moment he thought nothing had changed between them.

Releasing her, he gestured toward the stool-like stones. "Do you suppose one of those might be useful for anything?"

"I'm having my period," said Mary Alice.

At night he attended the play and Mary Alice sat beside him and they watched it holding hands. Afterward they went for another walk, though in a different direction—so he wouldn't get ideas, Mary Alice said. In the dark there was a good deal of kissing and fondling, though no real sex. Confused, distraught, and aching with frustration, Bert slept in the men's dormitory in the same bed as last time. The next morning they had breakfast together, again standing around the coffee urn in the theater, after which he started the long drive home.

So he saw her only those two times all summer.

Meanwhile she was meeting Harry Chapman regularly. Harry was driving up there every week. But he learned this only much later.

She returned to New York discouraged about her career. She had not appeared onstage, and had not even been allowed to rehearse for an understudy role. "None of us were," she told Bert. "All the kids were angry about it. We were promised all sorts of things, but all they did was use us as cheap labor."

They were in a coffeehouse in Greenwich Village. She had a terrible cold and kept blowing her nose as she spoke.

"What about that director who was interested in you?" asked Bert.

The director, she conceded, had switched off to one of the other girls who perhaps seemed more complaisant.

"That's one good thing, anyway," joked Bert.

"To you, maybe," she snapped. "Not to me."

She hadn't gained any ground at all, she said. "I don't know what to do next, careerwise."

"You're just feeling depressed."

"Right now, if somebody offered me an alternative, I'd take it."

Her eyes were red rimmed. The bottom of her nose was red and chapped. She looked beautiful to him nonetheless. "I can think of an alternative," he began, meaning marriage to him.

But she only pushed back her plate, having barely touched her dinner. She said: "Would you mind if I asked you to take me home? I feel really lousy."

"Why don't we go back to my place. I can make you some hot tea, rub your back—"

"I'm sick, Bert. Doesn't that mean anything to you?"

"I was just offering to take care of you."

"I don't need anyone to take care of me."

So he took her home.

She seemed glad enough to see him each time, though a little pensive. She did refuse dates occasionally—always for a good reason, of course: her college roommate was in town, or it was her parents' anniversary and she had to go out to Scarsdale. Other times she broke firm dates they had made, once because she had been hired as a waitress at a private party, and the other time because somebody wanted her to audition. Or so she said.

Bert was beside himself with worry. Her excuses were all reasonable, he kept telling himself. Therefore he should not be unreasonable. Nobody was ever altogether in charge of his or her own life, so why should he expect her to be? She had other obligations besides him. He was perhaps reading more into her refusals than she meant to put there.

But she would no longer come to his apartment at all. "I'm still trying to fight off this bug," she told him. "I don't want to stick you with it."

Or she was having her period again.

Or her doctor had taken her off the pill temporarily.

"There are other methods of birth control besides the pill, Mary Alice."

"I don't like them."

"Which ones don't you like?"

"They're all messy. It wouldn't be as much fun."

It took Bert a moment to come to terms with what he assumed she was telling him. "You're being faithful to someone, Mary Alice. Who are you being faithful to?"

She hesitated for a time, then said: "Well, there is someone else I'm seeing."

"Harry Chapman?"

"I don't have to tell you who I'm seeing."

"Do you want me to stop calling you?"

In a small conciliatory voice she said: "No."

"I think I better."

"Why?"

"I think it would be best."

"I don't think it would be best."

"Mary Alice—"

"Just because I don't happen to want to make love all the time—"

"That's not the reason."

This scene took place in a taxi in Greenwich Village not far from where she now lived. Her voice had risen and the driver, Bert realized, watched them in the mirror.

"You're saying that if I want to keep you interested in me, I have to fuck you."

It seemed to him that she was like all the women he had ever known. When wrong or under pressure, they didn't retreat, they attacked.

"I don't want to be your lover, Mary Alice, I want to marry you."

"I'm not ready to get married. That's all you care about, fucking."

Again the word that, coming from her, Bert hated. "Please keep your voice down."

"Whether I happen to feel like it or not. It's the truth, isn't it?"

"No, it's not the truth. Driver, stop here."

They were still two blocks from her apartment, which was little better than the first one she had had. Her new roommate was messy, and Bert dreaded the idea of her having to live in such squalor. They got out of the taxi and on the sidewalk he said: "Mary Alice—" and attempted to embrace her, but she shrugged him off.

"Fucking," said Mary Alice. "That's what this argument is about. You think you're not transparent? You're transparent."

"Stop talking that way."

"I'll talk anyway I like."

They had reached her building. "You want to fuck?" said Mary Alice. She was fuming. "Come on upstairs and we'll fuck."

"I'll come upstairs if you'll fix me a cup of tea."

"That wasn't what I offered. A fuck is what I offered."

"You sound like those women we round up on Times

Square. When they pile out of the van in front of the station house they sound exactly like you."

"So now I'm a whore. Nice. Really nice."

"Mary Alice—"

They stood on the sidewalk glaring at each other. Her mouth was set in a thin line, her nostrils flared, her eyes were flashing, she looked to him more gorgeous than ever, and he wondered at her ability to cause him such pain. He wondered if he didn't hate her and love her both.

The moment passed. She spun on her heel and went up the steps into the building.

Standing on principle, he didn't see or call her for a week. Instead he stared at his phone that did not ring, listened for a knock on the door that did not come. It was as long and miserable a week as he had spent. Standing on principle was easy when still in the presence of a girl, no matter how in love one might be. He began to realize this. She was still there in front of you, close enough to touch, perhaps to kiss. One could be cool, reasonable. The principle was only a principle so far. It had not yet altered anyone's conduct.

But wait until you began to miss her. Wait until the pain started that was worse than grief, because the cause of it could conceivably be reversed. Try standing on principle three days later, Bert reflected, a week later, when you long for her, when you would pay any price to get her back.

Harry Chapman sought him out in the precinct. Bert was upstairs in the squad room, putting together the paperwork on an arrest made that afternoon. He was of course in civilian clothes, his jacket on the back of a chair, his tie down. Harry was in uniform, the middle of him bulky with all the gear that cops wore. His car waited for him downstairs, his partner at the wheel, the two of them not only out of their assigned sector but out of their precinct as well.

"Can I talk to you?"

"Sure," said Bert.

"I mean in private."

Bert took him into the interrogation room and closed the door. "What's on your mind?"

"I need some advice."

"What kind of advice?"

When Harry wanted something, Bert had noted, he was never embarrassed about blurting it right out.

"I'm considering asking Mary Alice to marry me."

Bert fought with his face, ordering it to show no emotion. "Well, ask her then. What do you want me to do about it?"

"I want to know what you think she'll say."

"How the fuck do I know what she'll say?"

"If I ask her, I don't want to be surprised."

"Women are surprising, I've found."

"You know her pretty well," Harry said.

"What's that supposed to mean?"

"You dated her a few times."

Was Harry probing to find out what had gone on during these dates? Bert looked for the narrowed eyes, the tight lips of the jealous suitor, but did not find them.

"I can't help you, pal. You're going to have to ask her."

"On the one hand I think she'll say yes. I went up to see her every weekend all summer, you know."

"No, I didn't know."

"Yeah."

"Not much privacy up there, from what I could see. Unless you went off into the woods."

Harry grinned. "The woods are for kids. She likes her comfort."

"So where'd you take her?" said Bert.

"I used to rent a motel room."

"And she'd visit you there?"

"Sure."

Bert tried for a disbelieving tone, for he wanted to keep Harry talking, though why? "She didn't strike me as that kind of girl."

"Well, you're wrong there." Harry was nodding vigorously. "We'd go at it for hours."

In the midst of his suffering an image planted itself in Bert's head: the place where the flat stones came up out of the ground. He bit down on his tongue until he drew blood.

"The thing I always hate about motels," Bert said, "is those paper thin walls."

Harry grinned. "It can be a problem. There were times she made so much noise it sounded like I was killing her."

"One of those, eh?"

"Sometimes had to hold my hand over her mouth," said Harry seriously. "I was afraid someone might call the cops. Can you see cops busting in on us?"

"You might have found yourself in another shoot-out."

Harry smiled at this idea.

"I guess she likes to make love," Bert prompted again.

Harry looked a bit uncomfortable that he had revealed so much. "Yes."

"Well," Bert decided to say, "I wouldn't know about that."

"I don't understand why you didn't have a go at her. She's a beautiful girl."

"I was leaving her for you," Bert said.

Harry nodded, but he looked pensive.

After a moment Bert said: "Is that the reason you think you want to marry her? Because she's good in bed?"

Harry shook his head. "Not the only one."

"Her family too," prompted Bert. "Money, influence."

"Her father knows everybody."

"So the marriage makes sense any way you look at it."

"Right."

"What does Mary Alice get out of it?" asked Bert shortly. "Apart from your magnificent body."

"I've explained to her where I expect to be five years from now, ten years, twenty. If she says yes, it will be because she's decided to come along for the ride."

"Interesting," said Bert.

"So what do you think she might say?"

"Ask her and find out." Bert stood up, went out of the interrogation room, and crossed to the window, where he looked down on Harry's blue and white. "Aren't you supposed to be on patrol?" he said. "If I were you I'd get back in that car before someone comes in and asks what you're doing here."

Harry moved toward the door, where he paused. "Thanks. What you said makes a lot of sense."

Bert was unaware that he had said much of anything, sensible or not.

"Well, so long," said Harry, and he left.

Bert remained at the front window, and in a moment watched him come out, get into his radio car, and drive away.

He sat down at his desk and closed his eyes. After a time he began rubbing them, but he could not rub away the searing images that Harry had just put there.

He did not phone Mary Alice that night, or any subsequent night. But finally on a day when he was at home at the stove cooking bacon and eggs for lunch, she phoned him.

"I don't think we should see each other anymore," she said.

Although he had been expecting this call, he nonetheless was devastated. Unable to speak, he took the receiver from his ear and laid it on the counter. "Are you still there?" said her disembodied voice.

"You're getting married," Bert said into the receiver.

"I'm considering it."

"Who's the lucky guy?"

"There's something else I need to talk to you about. Do you have a minute?"

Suddenly Bert felt a steeling of resolve. "Anything else you have to say," he said into the telephone, "you will tell me in person."

There was a tense silence. She said: "Meeting each other will only make it harder."

"On the contrary," said Bert.

"You want to meet me?"

"That's right."

"Where?"

"Here. In my apartment," said Bert.

"Now wait a minute."

"Oh, for crissake," said Bert.

"I don't think I should meet with you alone in anybody's apartment."

"You worried about rape?" said Bert. "You think I'm going to assault you?"

"No, not exactly."

"Tonight," said Bert. "After you get off work. I'll be waiting." He hung up.

It was then noon. Bert put the eggs back on the stove, but could not keep his mind on them. When they began to burn he snatched them off and threw them in the garbage. His stomach was churning and he was no longer hungry.

He was scheduled to work a four to twelve, but went into the station house two hours early, and at ten P.M. he signed out and went home and began to wait for her. There was no telling what time she would come. It depended on when her restaurant emptied out. By eleven o'clock he was pacing and by midnight he had convinced himself she was not coming after all.

At five minutes to one there came a timid knock at his door. He went to open it and let her in.

She walked over to the sofa, and he followed. She did not sit down. He could smell the scent of her and it seemed to him, despite the three feet of air between them, that he could feel her too, the weight of her body, her substance.

"Can I offer you anything? Coffee? Tea? A gin and tonic?"

"No, thank you."

"You're sure?"

"Yes."

"Do you want to sit down?"

"No."

It was clear she was having trouble saying what she had come here to say.

"What have you told Harry?" she said finally.

"About what?"

"About what happened between you and me."

"You and me," said Bert, trying to grin. "What did happen between you and me?"

"You know."

"Oh, that," said Bert.

"He's kind of naive."

Bert had begun to wonder how naive Harry actually was.

"I don't want him hurt."

"What did you tell him yourself? About you and me?"

"That it was fairly platonic."

"You lied to him?"

"I didn't lie. He wanted to think certain things, and I let him."

"Platonic," said Bert. "Is that what it was? I forget."

"Don't mock me, Bert. Please don't mock me."

"I'm sorry."

"It was hard for me to come here. It's hard for me to ask you these things."

Bert looked at her.

"Men always brag about their conquests, don't they?"

Harry certainly did, Bert thought. Suppose he told her how Harry had bragged about the rented motel rooms, about his hand over her mouth because she screamed when she orgasmed. If he told her she would certainly be furious. It might perhaps wreck this marriage right now. But it wouldn't make her love him instead, or get her back, so he forbore doing so.

"I realize I was only one of your conquests. You probably bragged to several people."

"You were not one of my conquests. I was in love with you."

"So what did you tell Harry?"

"Does he think you were a virgin?"

"He doesn't know we had an affair, and I don't want him to know. He looks up to you, Bert. You're practically a god in his eyes."

"Let's not exaggerate."

"I want to know how much he knows."

"I told him nothing. I told no one anything about you and me."

She studied him, trying to decide whether to believe him or not. Finally he saw her relax.

He said: "To me what you and I had was—" He started to say "sacred" but decided this sounded foolish and so said nothing.

"Harry is so naive," she said again.

Bert let this pass. "But he's going places."

"He'll be a lawyer, he's going into politics. Oh yes, he's going places."

"And you're going with him."

She acquiesced by giving an inclination of her head.

"Congratulations," he said, meaning it sarcastically, but she said:

"Thank you. And in addition, I love him."

"I'm going places too, did I ever tell you?"

"I know you are."

"My destination doesn't interest you very much. I can see that now."

She looked at him.

"Thirty years from now I'll still be in this department." He was torturing himself, and was ashamed to be doing it. But he did not seem able to stop. "I may or may not have reached the top of the department by then. Either way, that wasn't for you, I guess."

She said nothing.

He looked at her, at the big dark eyes, the dark hair down her back, at the good cheekbones and the small pointed chin, and for a time she met his gaze, but then her eyes dropped, and she stared at the floor, and in lieu of physically undressing her, he did it mentally, until he could see all of her smooth young body, her fleshy breasts with their big dark nipples, the mattress between her legs. All of which he would not see again, and he felt like weeping. That night on the rock beside the lake was the last time, he told himself, and he hadn't even known it.

Would he have enjoyed it more if he had known? How could he have enjoyed it any more than he did?

"Come on," he said. "I'll take you home."

"No," she said, but when Bert firmly took her arm she did not resist. They descended to the street, where he flagged down a cab. As they settled into the backseat she said: "My father likes Harry, too. You know what he told me one day? That Harry was more like him than I knew."

Bert said nothing.

"Whatever that means," said Mary Alice.

They rode downtown, mostly in silence. As they crossed 23rd Street she took his hand and held it the rest of the way. Once she said: "I'll always be your friend, Bert."

"Yes," he answered, "I'll always be your friend too, and if you ever need me—"

She got out of the cab in front of her building and he watched her go up the steps. At the door she turned and waved to him. He waved back, then told the driver to take him home.

■5■

THE OFFICE OF the chief medical examiner—the morgue—is at 30th Street and First Avenue. Its waiting room walls are decorated with framed blowups of famous New York buildings. The photos are in black and white, which perhaps fits the mournful setting. In here primary colors might jar. One of the blowups shows Grand Central Terminal, and this is perhaps fitting because the morgue is a terminal too, the final one in fact. On the dissecting tables downstairs is where the journey ends.

Chief of Detectives Bert P. Farber, standing in the morgue's reception room, tried to chase such morbid thoughts from his head, but it was hard. He paced in front of sofas, chairs. On the low tables stood boxes of Kleenex to accommodate people come to identify family members.

An attendant came and led him downstairs along a concrete hall past an entire wall of small stainless steel doors. These were the refrigerated lockers that held the naked bodies on sliding trays. There were 126 doors, someone had told Bert once, 126 ex-human beings shoved toes first into the wall. Above flickered an illuminated digital readout showing the temperature inside the lockers. It fluctuated slightly, he noted: 35 degrees, 36, 35 again. The corpses during their term here were kept not quite frozen. Against the opposite wall stood pine coffins in various sizes, seven in a stack. As he passed by Bert could not stop himself from making a count.

The attendant held the door for him, and he stepped into

the long narrow room with its row of stainless steel tables under operating room lights. This was where the morgue's business was conducted. It was a room that saw an unending parade of corpses, traffic that never ceased, so that even this early in the day each of the eight tables bore its nude burden.

The tables were big, eight feet long, almost four feet wide, and had uplifted edges to catch runoff. At some of them, not all, pathologists in white coats labored. At others there was no one except the corpses, certain of them female, lying out waiting. One of the females had gray hair, but two others were young and one, with a stab wound in her chest, was a teenager. Bert, walking by, had an automatic reaction. To leave women uncovered like that seemed immodest. In addition, this was a chilly room and they might catch cold. He almost looked for gooseflesh. He had to shake his head to clear it. These were not women anymore but cadavers. As such they no longer minded the cold, and their modesty, though it might have mattered to their relatives, had become immaterial to them personally.

In any case, this was a room where modesty was unknown, where human beings perpetrated the final indignity on what had been persons like themselves.

In the outer boroughs were a few subsidiary morgues, but this was the main one, headquarters, and into this one room New York City fed most of its violent or suspicious deaths, and all of its important ones. Bert could tell which table was Harry's because there was a crowd around it. The other tables in the long row, those at which men worked, rated only one white coat, or at the most two, but in addition to Dr. Chang, Harry had drawn Dr. Klotz, who was the chief medical examiner, plus three of his principal assistants. These men, all pathologists, nodded at Bert as he approached, and opened a space for him at the table.

Harry lay with his head on a kind of wooden pillow that was dark from scrubbing, or perhaps blood. He looked smaller than Bert remembered, and he seemed to have subsided into the table. His skin had turned a pale, dull ivory. Bert noted an abdominal scar he hadn't known about, a hernia perhaps, and the pubic hair was reddish, or so it appeared under the light. Harry's penis lay flopped over to one side. Whatever blood might have seeped out of his chest wound had been cleaned off and the puncture now looked almost like an extra nipple.

Chang chose this moment to begin speaking into the microphone that hung over the table: he identified himself, gave the date, the time, and the names of the men witnessing the autopsy, including Bert's, and then proceeded to an external description of the corpse. "The body is that of an adult, well-developed, well-nourished white male," he intoned, "scale weight 172 pounds, measured height five feet ten inches."

I thought he was taller than that, Bert murmured to himself.

"There is a bullet wound of entrance approximately one centimeter inferior to the center of the sternum. It consists of a one-centimeter circular perforation and a surrounding abrasion collar that becomes one half inch long inferiorly and medially where the skin is superficially abraded. . . ."

Later a stenographer would type all this up, Chang would sign it, and that would constitute the official report.

". . . No apparent exit wound. Hair brown. Brown mustache present. Teeth in good repair. Rigor complete in the jaws. The irides are brown. Pupils five millimeters, round, equal, dilated. Diffuse hemorrhage in the conjunctivae bilaterally. . . ."

Harry was being rolled, prodded, and parts of him were being spread. Repeatedly his privacy was invaded.

"The foreskin is short. Testes in scrotum. Brown thin feces about anus. . . ."

One of the pathologists was arranging tools. They had some beauties, Bert knew: loppers that looked like bolt cutters, boning knives, skilsaws. And scales—they weighed everything here.

While Chang picked up a scalpel and made his first incision, Bert, who had seen dozens of autopsies, looked off across the room. The view was no better, only different. Other corpses on tables, other knives rising and falling, other skilsaws taking off the tops of skulls. Those were people he had not known. He had known Harry though, and could not help recalling his most vivid recent memory of him, which was a trip they had made together to Washington, where Harry was to testify before the Senate Judiciary Committee. For the ride to La Guardia Harry had laid on a motorcycle escort for himself, something even mayors did not dare do. Bert heard bones crack. Autopsies were noisy. Dr. Chang said into the microphone: "Hemorrhagic track, left fourth intercostal space, anterior pericardial sac, heart, through and through, posterior pericardial sac and inferior vena cava."

In Washington another motorcycle escort sped them to the Capitol. People on the sidewalks must have thought the president was coming. Harry was sworn in, Harry testified—testimony so bold, so forceful, and at times so accusatory that he and it had made headlines and newscasts all over the country.

"Massive hemopericardium," Chang said into the microphone.

Since Washington, because they were both busy men, Bert had seen Harry only in passing. Until this morning.

"Massive left hemothorax," Chang said. "Atelectasis, left lung. . . ." Though the words themselves meant little to Bert, he could see well enough what was being described.

Chang was still cutting. "The left lung weighs 1,020 grams." And then after a moment: "The right lung weighs 1,110 grams. Vessels not remarkable." The heart, when he cut it out, looked shredded. To Bert he said conversationally, "The X ray shows the bullet is lodged in the spine. We'll get to it, don't worry."

"Only one bullet?"

"Only one." Chang leaned toward the microphone: "The heart weighs 405 grams."

On each of the next three tables lay females. Female corpses even more than men seemed to diminish, to subside deep into the slab. With all the air gone out of them, their highest points were not breasts, as one might expect, but the puffs of pubic hair.

"Your friend liked rich food," said Chang. "Probably liked a drink, too. Might have had trouble when he got older." Having excised Harry's liver, Chang passed it around the table. Everyone had a look, and the last man in line, Dr. Klotz, returned it to Chang, saying: "Waiter, take this back, I ordered kidneys, not liver."

"Kidneys coming up," said Chang, cutting and weighing. "Right kidney weighs 190 grams, left kidney 205 grams."

Cops were given to gallows humor too, Bert reflected.

When they fished out floaters, when they confronted tragedies on sidewalks, they made jokes. For people who dealt with the underside of life it was the only way to stay sane.

In fact these pathologists were being remarkably sober this morning, Bert thought. Due to Harry's rank, he supposed. Due to his own presence, too, since they could not be sure how well he had known him.

"Last week I finally worked on a guy named Ernest," Chang said conversationally, and he laughed. The others laughed too. Chang didn't even have to complete the joke, for it was an old one around autopsy tables. Even Bert had heard it before. ". . . The guy on the table was dead earnest."

"Pancreas tan, lobular, and firm," Chang said. "Prostate not enlarged, urinary bladder empty."

"I guess that means he took a piss before he went out to run," said one of the others.

"I hope he enjoyed it," said Dr. Klotz.

Chang was digging deep into Harry. "And there's the baby we're looking for," he said, and he withdrew the bullet at the end of his forceps. Extending the forceps toward Bert, he dropped the bullet into his hand.

It was bloody, with bits of Harry still attached. The head had flattened out. Bert rolled the sticky mushroom through his fingers. The striations still showed on the shaft, meaning it could be matched to the gun it came from, the murder weapon, if it were ever found. With his penknife he scratched his initials into the head of the mushroom, for this would enable him to identify it in court under oath, if the case ever got to court. Chang handed him a plastic evidence envelope, and he dropped the bullet inside, then scrawled the date, Harry's name, and his own name on the label.

Behind him the skilsaw began its tune, and when he turned he saw that Chang was sawing into Harry's skull.

Bert had known this would happen. Nonetheless it gave him a start, for it had pulled a half smile onto Harry's face, as if what Chang was doing tickled. As if Harry were asleep and having a nice dream.

"Be careful there," Bert said. "His wife is maybe going to want an open coffin."

Chang lifted away the power saw. "Is that what she wants?"

"I don't know what she wants."

Chang resumed sawing.

"The mortician can take care of it," said Dr. Klotz over the noise. "They can work miracles these days."

"How long before you get the toxology reports?"

"That might take most of a week," Klotz said.

"I don't think they'll show anything," Chang said. "He looks pretty healthy to me. He wasn't on drugs, was he?"

"How the fuck should I know?" said Bert. This was the first he realized how tense he had become.

"By the way," said Chang as he worked, "there was a key."

"A key?"

"Attached to a rubber thong. He had it around his wrist underneath that designer jacket he had on. We inventoried it. You'll find it upstairs with his effects."

"About the autopsy report," Bert said. "Wait for all the toxology results before you write it up. Take your time. Take a week. Take longer. Anybody asks you, it isn't ready."

"What are you saying, Bert?" said Dr. Klotz.

"This is a sensitive investigation. I don't want copies floating around."

"Relax, Bert," said Dr. Klotz. "This is not the first sensitive autopsy we've conducted here."

"In a week make one copy only." Bert put the bullet envelope in his pocket. "Send it over marked personal and confidential. Anybody calls up wants a copy, tell them to see me."

"Whatever you say, Bert," said Chang.

"Go in peace," said Dr. Klotz with a smile.

Chang was just then lifting out Harry's brain.

Bert jerked his eyes away from there, giving a smile that was closer to a rictus. "Keep up the good work," he said to the assembled pathologists, and walked between the tables and out through the door and up the stairs.

Harry's effects were brought to him in the reception room. They were in a brown paper bag with the inventory stapled to the outside, and he spilled them out onto a coffee table: sneakers, socks, underwear, sweater, muffler, ski hat, and the sweatsuit with the name of a fashion house over the breast.

Bert separated out the key on its rubberized thong. Not a hotel key, from the look of it. An apartment key.

He pushed everything else back into the bag, signed the receipt, and left the building.

Outside, the snow was coming down. The bag was under his arm, and his hand in his pocket was opening and closing on the key that would open the door, obviously, to whatever apartment Harry had been using.

The 20th Precinct station house was new, not the decaying structure he and Harry Chapman had worked out of years ago. On the sidewalk outside a mob of reporters and news crews waited shivering and stamping their feet. Two uniformed cops stood in the doorway to prevent them from entering—orders from Chief Kincaid, they told Bert when he inquired. He swept the newspeople inside with him, found them a room in which to wait, declined to answer questions, and went upstairs.

The squad room was jammed with cops and detectives. The white-haired Kincaid had taken over the office of the precinct squad commander. Bert went in there and closed the door.

"About the newspeople downstairs—" he began.

Kincaid, who was seated behind the desk, did not get up. "I've got men on the door keeping them out."

"Did you take a look outside when you gave that order? Did you see what the weather was doing, by any chance?"

Kincaid looked up at him.

"I countermanded your order. We need those people, for crissake. Let's keep them friendly."

"You need them, maybe. I do not need them."

"Good," said Bert. "That's really good. Brilliant, in fact."

"Give them a place where they're comfortable, they'll start interviewing each other. They'll concoct all kinds of rumors."

This was probably true. Nonetheless, with the mayor about to decide on the next PC, Bert wanted the press on his side, not hostile.

Kincaid said dourly: "They'll interview detectives coming into the building. They'll know things before we do."

"What things did you have in mind?"

"Things we don't want them to know."

"Since we don't know anything ourselves, that's not too likely, is it?"

"Do it your way," said Kincaid.

"That's right, my way."

Kincaid shrugged.

"Be nice to the press, John," Bert advised him. "It will prolong your career."

For ten seconds, perhaps more, they eyed each other, and neither spoke.

"We've finished canvassing the nearby buildings," Kincaid said. He was not happy having to report to the much younger man, and his tone and manner showed it. "Nobody happened to be at the window or saw anything. There's nobody on the street, a morning like this, but I've got men out anyway, stopping anyone strolls by. So far nothing."

Bert nodded.

"The printing section is sending up two hundred photos of Commissioner Chapman," said Kincaid. "When they come I'll send men through the same buildings, the same streets again. See if anybody saw him around this morning. Any morning, for that matter."

Bert nodded again.

Kincaid said: "I've had the telephone company set up two special lines for the public to call in with information. We've released the numbers to the media."

A crime of this nature would generate a lot of calls—every important crime did. Each call would have to be investigated and most would be from busybodies, mental patients, weirdos of one kind or another.

Kincaid knew this too. "One of them might lead to something," he said.

"Yeah," said Bert.

"The PC had no scheduled appointments over the weekend. He left the office at noon on Friday and did not come back. I spoke to his appointments secretary, a lieutenant. He had no idea of his plans for the weekend."

"And his drivers?"

"One of them delivered him to a midtown restaurant on Friday noon and was sent back to headquarters empty. Neither driver was contacted a single time the rest of the weekend. Odd, don't you think?"

"At this point I don't think anything."

"Supposedly Chapman was on his beeper all weekend, but I've found no one who tried to reach him. He didn't once call in for messages either. So we have no record whatever of where he was."

Bert gazed at his fingernails.

"I sent detectives to his office for his desk calendar, his address books," Kincaid said. "Maybe some notes he made. Anything. A starting point. They could not get into the office. It's been sealed by order of the first dep."

"I'll talk to him," said Bert.

"I don't know why he would do that."

"I said I'll talk to him."

"Chapman's movements over the weekend have to be traced," Kincaid said. "What did Mrs. Chapman have to say?"

Bert decided to say "Nothing."

"She must have said something."

"She said she was sorry Harry got killed."

Kincaid looked exasperated. "There are a lot of questions we need answers to."

"That's what you got detectives for."

"I'll send some men down to talk to her later."

"No you won't," said Bert. "You want to know something from her, you call me."

They stared at each other. "I don't want anyone going near her," Bert said. "Is that understood?"

"But—"

"Is that understood?"

Kincaid seemed to be trying to smother his anger. "What kind of shape is she in?"

"Her husband just got shot in the heart." When she was ready he would question her himself. The investigation would have to wait.

Kincaid's lips came together. "We need to know where Chapman was this weekend. We need to know how he got up here from his house."

Bert thought of the key in his pocket. He had intended to

give it to Kincaid, but now he did not. "Maybe he ran all the way."

"It's too far."

The thing to do was send detectives through the streets with duplicates, trying the key in doorways. They should find the apartment quickly. "Did you ever think," Bert said, "that maybe he took a taxi?"

"Why didn't he come up in his official car?" the older man said. He sounded so perplexed that for a moment Bert almost liked him.

"Maybe he took the subway."

"The subway?"

"When they want to get someplace, lots of New Yorkers take the subway. You'd be surprised."

"I'll assign men to check out the cab companies," Kincaid said.

"You do that," Bert said. For the time being Kincaid did not need to know more than he already knew. The work he was doing had to be done whatever happened. It might even lead somewhere.

"The question then becomes," Kincaid said evenly, "why did he come all the way up here to run?"

"He liked to run in Central Park."

"What time did his wife say he left the house?"

"She didn't mention a time."

"Maybe he didn't start out from home at all. Maybe he started out from somewhere up here."

Bert's hand went into his pocket and touched Harry's key. He said: "Then find out where."

The two men eyed each other coldly.

"Can you ask her some of these questions?" Kincaid said.

"Next time I see her I'll ask her."

"Might I inquire when that will be?"

"No you can't."

Nodding curtly, Bert went out through the crowded squad room and down the stairs and out to his car. Hughie was reading the *Daily News* on the steering wheel. He turned the defroster on full, and Bert's face was bathed in cold air.

Ten minutes later he stood again on the corner of 77th and

Columbus, and in the falling snow contemplated the crime scene.

Why would Harry keep a secret midtown apartment? One possible answer: he needed a place to meet politicians or business connections. In the political world people made deals and didn't want to be spotted doing it. Also, police headquarters was far downtown, at least half an hour by taxi from midtown—more when traffic was bad. The men Harry dealt with would not have been willing to make the trip very often.

Bert realized that he did not know who these men might be, that he knew virtually nothing about Harry's life in recent years.

Second question: why didn't Harry sleep at home last night? A fight with Mary Alice? Maybe. The answer could be that simple.

Or he flies in from Washington very late. He has a breakfast meeting scheduled in his apartment. To save time, he goes directly there from the airport.

If he was meeting someone in the apartment, then who? The man who killed him? What was the meeting about? And where was the apartment?

There were two axioms detectives lived by: 1. Crime scenes don't lie, only witnesses lie; and 2. A detective's best piece of evidence is the one on the floor. Meaning in this case Harry Chapman. Bert stood on the corner where Harry had died. The snow was coming down. He glanced all around but did not know what he was looking for exactly—something—anything—he might have failed to observe earlier. Sometimes you could read a great deal at a crime scene. You could make good guesses. Sometimes you could base your case on them.

The cars in the street inched by, wipers beating, drivers leaning forward. The snow on the sidewalk was already two inches thick, and deepening fast. The corner mailbox, the garbage cans, the uncollected Christmas trees wore white overcoats. There had been nothing to see here earlier and it was worse now. It was as if the snow had obliterated any trace of the murderer, of the victim too, had whited everything out. It was as if no murder had ever happened. Harry Chapman was in his office or home or somewhere, still alive. The snow had reversed time.

Bert listened to the smothered noises of the city. He could feel the snow on his hair, and when he looked across at his car, he saw Hughie sitting snug and safe inside. Hughie was not obliged to find a murderer, nor did he hope to be named the next PC. Lucky him. The chauffeur stared straight ahead, seeing nothing while his boss, Bert P. Farber, stood out in the snow and peered all around, trying to see what wasn't there.

When he got back to headquarters and up to his office he took the bag containing Harry's effects, which he ought to have dropped off with John Kincaid, or should send up to him now, and threw it into his safe. The inventory was still stapled to its side, and he swung the safe door shut on it and spun the dial of the lock.

∎ 6 ∎

ONCE A WEEK for four months Detective Sergeant Bert P. Farber attended a police tutorial school—there were several in the city—as he prepared for the lieutenant's exam. The tutors were ex-superior officers who identified themselves in their brochure as being among the most successful test takers in NYPD history.

Texts existed—eight or nine on police administration alone. Certain tomes on criminology had to be studied as well. There were courses in statistics, graphs, rules and procedures, the penal code, the proper supervision of subordinates, Supreme Court decisions.

And there were English courses, for in the exam to come they would be graded on grammar, reading comprehension, and spelling. These students were cops, not college boys, and some had only high school equivalency certificates.

On a Saturday morning in April the exam was held simultaneously at four high schools in four different boroughs. Bert took it at George Washington High in upper Manhattan. He arrived to find hundreds of nervous police sergeants in the street. They were in civilian clothes, and they milled about quizzing each other, or opening and closing textbooks, or their lips moved over something memorized. A few, Bert noted, attached last-minute crib sheets to their arms, their wrists, inside their clothes. A student caught cheating would be arrested; this was one of the few tests in the world of which this was true. But cops didn't roll on other cops.

Inside they filled classrooms, big men, older men, forcing themselves into desks that were too small for them.

Monitors moved down aisles. Each sergeant was obliged to press his thumb onto the monitor's stamp pad and then onto a card, and to sign the card. Thumbprints prevented the use of stand-ins, supposedly. To take care of the inky thumbs, one square of toilet paper was distributed to each sergeant from the roll the monitor carried under his arm.

The exams were passed out: five essay questions, 125 multiple choices: "When is an officer justified in the use of physical force, and when deadly physical force? Discuss, with examples."

The sergeants around Bert were dressed in brogues, jeans or corduroys, sweaters. The majority had gray in their hair. Many had substantial paunches.

"Discuss the theories of criminologist O. W. Wilson relative to recidivism and the warehousing of prisoners."

The face of the sergeant in the next desk, Bert noted, began to glisten with sweat. When he had finished reading the questions the man stood up, tore the pages in half, and walked grimly to the front. He had been clutching a bunch of number two pencils sharpened to a point. He broke them in two, laid them on the monitor's desk, and stalked out of the room.

Bert started through the multiple choices. "To charge a suspect with first-degree burglary, which of the following elements are necessary?"

"How many days after the filing of a UF-61 must a DD-5 be filed?"

A nearby sergeant kept bending to scratch his ankle. He had his gun in an ankle holster, Bert saw, and his crib sheet behind the gun. He kept glancing at it, straightening up to locate the monitor, then bending to glance at it again.

Other men began requesting to go to the bathroom. Though accompanied by monitors, they would lock themselves in toilet stalls, study what they had, flush, and come out again.

It took Bert two hours and forty minutes to complete the test, twenty minutes less than the alloted time.

At four P.M. that afternoon he reported to the Two-Four and worked his regular tour.

* * *

He had not heard from Harry or Mary Alice in weeks, and then one day Harry, off duty and in civilian clothes, walked in on him in the station house.

There had been a series of armed robberies of parking lots and garages in the neighborhood of Lincoln Center. They took place at night about once a week. The stickup men would clean out the till, of course. They would also rob whatever owners came in just then to reclaim their cars.

Most of the victims had attended a performance at one of the Lincoln Center theaters and were starting home. They were patrons of the arts. The gunmen crowded them into the booth or shed and relieved them of cash, jewels, watches, furs.

After the third robbery Chief of Detectives Summers rode up to the Two-Four, took the case away from the lieutenant who commanded fourth district robbery, and gave it to the assistant commander, Sergeant Farber. He told him to put together as big a squad as he needed, and to break the case quickly before somebody got robbed who had access to the mayor, or the media. Before some rich somebody got killed.

Bert glanced from Summers to the lieutenant, whose name was Moore, and whose face showed that he did not like what was happening, and said: "Yes sir."

"This case could be trouble," said Summers.

"I can see that," said Bert.

"So no fucking around. Nail 'em, and let's go on to something else."

Bert's first move, as soon as Summers left, was to try to soothe the humiliated Lieutenant Moore.

"I don't know what he thinks I can do that you weren't already doing," Bert said.

"He's chief of detectives," said Moore bitterly.

"Left alone, you would have locked those guys up within a week."

An officer with ambition was careful to leave no enemies in his wake who might be in a position to hurt him later. Despite his relative youth, Bert knew this. Moore would be a captain before him, and would perhaps rise even higher.

They began to haggle over detectives. Bert mentioned the

names of the five he wanted, but Moore refused him, saying: "I need those particular guys. They're busy on other cases."

"The chief of detectives seemed to think this case takes precedence," said Bert, exerting pressure.

Moore threw up his hands. "Take whoever you want."

"I want them taken off the chart," said Bert. "We're going to have to work every night until we break this thing."

After contacting the detectives he began to construct a pin map of the Lincoln Center area, red pins for garages that had already been hit, green for those that had not, and he worked out which sites he would stake out over the next nights, and which he would have to leave unprotected. Five detectives was not enough men. But one never had enough men. In the NYPD you learned to get by on what you had, no excuses.

Harry Chapman walked in on him.

Bert said: "You're looking well."

"I'm in good shape," said Harry. But as he walked over and peered up at the pin map he looked nervous. "What's this?"

"We're working on those parking lot robberies down in the bottom of your precinct."

Harry still looked nervous, and would not meet Bert's eyes, and he wondered why.

"How's your girlfriend?" Bert asked.

"She's fine."

"Still the same one?"

"Mary Alice, yes. In fact that's what I came in to talk to you about."

"I'm all out of romantic advice this week," said Bert.

"I want you to know," said Harry earnestly, "that Mary Alice has consented to become my wife."

Bert thought: Why does this guy talk so stilted?

"I proposed to her and she consented. It's all arranged."

"Swell," said Bert. But his smile had vanished. For a moment he peered in the direction of the window. "Congratulations," he said. "When's the big day?"

"There are a number of big days, actually. The first is, I graduate from Columbia law May fifteenth. Mary Alice will be there for the ceremony. I'd like you to come too."

"You want me to watch you graduate from law school? Is that what you came in here to talk to me about?"

"No, it's something else."

Bert got up and walked over to the pin map. He had had enough of Harry and wished he would go.

"What are the green pins?" asked Harry from behind him. "You going to stake those places out?"

"Little by little, yes."

"Can I help? I have some time now. I don't mind working for you when I'm off duty."

Bert looked at him.

"I'll stake out one of those places for you."

With Harry's luck, Bert reflected, that would be the place the robbers hit. Harry would be the one to break the case. He'd either be a hero or he'd shoot someone, maybe both.

"Why don't you spend your time looking after your girl-friend. You don't want to leave her alone too much."

"That's true," said Harry, studying the map. "Looks like you could use a few extra guys, though."

"Thanks, but I already got more than I can handle," Bert lied.

"There's a lot of green pins," said Harry doubtfully.

"I don't think I can go to your graduation either. May is the big vacation month around here. We'll be shorthanded."

Still wishing Harry would leave, Bert went back behind his desk and sat down. Harry took the chair opposite and looked at him in silence.

"Well, I really got to get to work on these DD-5s," Bert said.

Looking increasingly nervous, Harry began drumming his fingers on the edge of the desk.

"Was there something else you wanted to see me about?" Bert said.

"Yeah, there was."

Bert waited.

"I resign from the department June first," Harry said.

Bert looked at him.

"I allotted the department two years," said Harry. "I told you my plans the first night we rode in a radio car together."

"So you did."

"Actually, I did a little more than two years."

"But your career is still on schedule," said Bert.

"More or less, yes," said Harry, but he still seemed nervous, was still drumming his fingers on the desk.

"The police department will miss you," said Bert, beginning to thumb through the DD-5s. One of the things the department did not do was miss anyone.

"The wedding is the next day, June second. On June seventh I start as an assistant DA."

Bert nodded.

"In between is the honeymoon."

"Five days," said Bert. "Are you sure that's long enough?"

"It isn't as if we don't know each other already," said Harry seriously.

"Yes, you told me," said Bert. And then, torturing himself: "Does she still like it as much as you said she did?"

Harry's grin became a little more distant. "We have no problems in that respect."

"That's good," said Bert.

"She had only been with two guys before me, but very briefly. Once when she was sixteen, and another time when she was in college."

"That's very interesting."

"The time in college she was drunk."

"What do you know."

"I was surprised at how innocent she was."

"Well, I have to get to work on these DD-5s."

"I guess every man still wants to marry a virgin," continued Harry. "Mary Alice is about as close as you can get these days."

"Congratulations."

"For our honeymoon we're going to Jamaica. Her father's wedding present."

"I met him once," said Bert. "He's got a lot of money."

"Political connections too. I didn't realize how many."

"He'll be useful when your career moves to Washington."

"Yes he will."

Two of the detectives Bert had summoned by telephone had just walked into the squad room and signed in. Seeing that Bert was occupied they moved off toward the coffee machine.

"Mary Alice and I," Harry blurted suddenly, "would like you to be best man at our wedding."

There followed a long silence—nervous on Harry's part, shocked on Bert's.

"I don't think so, no," said Bert.

"Why not?"

"Have you talked to Mary Alice about this?" Bert decided to say. "Did she agree to it?"

"She likes you a lot."

"I hardly know her," said Bert after a moment.

The three other detectives Bert had summoned came into the squad room. He watched them move idly about.

"I think it's fitting that you should be best man," Harry said. "We met her the same night, remember? And also—" He stopped.

"And what?"

"You taught me everything I know about being a cop, and I feel like I owe you."

"You don't owe me a thing. Was this your idea, or Mary Alice's, or what?"

"I talked it over with her. She didn't think you'd agree, but I thought you would. So who's right?"

"Mary Alice is right."

"Don't give me your answer immediately," Harry said. "Think it over first."

"I have thought it over. I wouldn't feel right about it. Talk it over with Mary Alice. See if she doesn't agree."

They studied each other.

"Weddings are family things," said Bert. "You have a brother, don't you? He's the one should be best man, not me."

"I feel closer to you."

"Mary Alice's got a brother too, I believe."

"I don't know him very well."

"You're going to need your father-in-law when you start your political career, right? Having his son as your best man would go over big with him."

"I hadn't thought of that."

"You should think about these things. Now how about leaving me in peace," Bert said. "I have work to do."

"Okay, sure," said Harry, and he got up and went to the door. But there he turned and looked back at Bert. "But I can count on you to attend the wedding and the reception, can't I? I'll have Mary Alice's mother send you an invitation. Do you want to bring someone?"

"No," said Bert after a moment. "I'm not seeing anyone right now."

When the squad room door closed behind Harry, Bert went back to his desk and called together his five detectives.

He had begun to speak to them about the parking lot robberies, and the ideas he had formed, when the phone rang.

"Sergeant Farber," he said into the receiver.

To his surprise it was Mary Alice. "There's something I have to talk to you about."

Bert was in no mood to absorb a second emotional battering so soon after the first. Besides which, he was busy. He said to her: "Now's not a good time."

"When then? It's important."

"Where are you?"

"In Bloomingdale's."

"Don't buy out the store."

"Shopping for my wedding, if you must know."

"I'll be free in about an hour."

"All right, I'll phone you in an hour."

"You say it's important?"

"Very."

"We better meet, then. Walk over to the zoo in Central Park. I'll meet you there."

"The zoo?"

"Five o'clock. Outside the lions' cage." He hung up before she could say anything, and turned back to his detectives.

A yardstick lay on Bert's desk and he picked it up for a pointer and stepped to the pin map, but the map turned into Mary Alice's face, and he had to shake his head to clear it.

The getaway cars, he began, had been stolen off the street in the Two-Eight precinct in Harlem. So that was where the perpetrators were coming from, and where they were trying to get back to.

"We already knew that," one of the detectives said. "Three black fucks, according to the witnesses."

Bert continued his patient explanation. Two of the lots hit so far were on Amsterdam Avenue, an uptown street, with Harlem at the top of it, and the third was on the uptown side of Broadway.

Bert tapped the map with his yardstick. "If they haven't hit Columbus yet, we can assume it's because they don't want to be pointed downtown afterwards. So we're not going to bother with Columbus either. We're shorthanded. We can't stake out everything. So forget Columbus."

"That still leaves a lot of possibilities," a detective said, peering at the map.

"There's only six of us," said another.

Six men did not mean six cars. Bert couldn't put a lone detective against three armed stickup men. There would have to be two men to a car, and even then, if there was shooting, the odds were bad.

"The object is not to scare these guys off but to catch them in the act," said Bert. He had thought of a way to supplement his small force of detectives, and his yardstick drew a circle around the 20th Precinct. "The Two-Oh has eleven cars," he said. "Normally they turn out only eight for the four-to-eight tours. They have a new commanding officer down there, Captain Sternhagen. I have a meeting with him in"—he glanced at his watch—"thirty minutes."

And from the Two-Oh Bert would go into the park to meet Mary Alice; for a moment this thought distracted him. But he forced it aside.

"I'm going to ask Sternhagen to put clerical guys in those three extra cars. Nothing's going to happen to them. I'm going to ask him to have those cars sit on the sites that have already been hit."

There were nods from some of the detectives.

"I'm betting that this will seem normal to the perpetrators, that it won't scare them off. I'm betting they'll drive a few blocks further on and hit someplace else. I'm also betting that once they've seen the parked radio cars they won't hit any place downtown from them. When they make their getaway they won't want to drive up past radio cars they know are there. That leaves these three places here." He tapped them with his yardstick. "Those are the three we'll sit on tonight and every night until we either break this case or headquarters pulls us off. Any questions?"

"Yeah," said one of the detectives. "Suppose the Two-Oh won't cooperate?"

"I know Sternhagen," said another. "He's a prick."

"And he doesn't like detectives," added the first man.

"I'll talk to him," said Bert. Though he had never met Sternhagen, he gave a confident grin. "I'll tell him headquarters is interested in the case."

The first detective grinned too. "Be sure to get out of the room before the stink comes up."

"Yeah," said the second man, "mention headquarters to Sternhagen and he'll shit in his pants."

Bert drove downtown, parked in front of the 20th Precinct, and went into the station house, where he spent thirty minutes being nice to Sternhagen. The older man was about forty that year, still dark haired, tall, and lean, with no hint of the paunch he would develop later. There was no hint either of the confident manner, the sometimes thinly veiled arrogance he would display later. He agreed to all Bert's requests and gave the necessary orders in his presence. Obviously Sternhagen was too new in his job, too unsure of himself, to be willing to stand up even to a sergeant.

By the time Bert was able to leave him he was late for his meeting with Mary Alice.

He drove into the park, put the police plate in the windshield, and left the car in a no parking zone in front of Tavern on the Green. Dodging Frisbees and softballs much of the way, he hurried across the Sheep Meadow. There were many people out, couples lounging on blankets on the grass, teams playing softball on the diamonds at the corners of the immense field. The late-afternoon sun had come partway around and was gilding the sides of the cliff-like buildings along the bottom of the park. The grass over which he trod was very green with spring, and he breathed the air.

Entering the zoo, he found the lion house. Some years later the Central Park zoo would be done over, and in accordance with enlightened new theories of zoology the big cats and certain other large animals would be removed to other more spacious zoos, where they were allowed to roam more or less freely through large outdoor areas. But at this time Central Park boasted a dozen or more lions and leopards that, in fine weather, were allowed to lounge in outdoor cages.

As Bert approached he could see Mary Alice in front of the cages nervously pacing.

"Hello," he said.

He looked at her and didn't know whether to kiss her or not.

She took the decision out of his hands as she glared at him, then said: "You're late."

"Sorry."

"We could have done this over the phone."

"I thought you said it was important."

"Yes, it's important."

"How have you been, Mary Alice?"

This question stopped her for a moment. "Fine. How have you been?"

She was wearing low shoes, jeans, and a blue blazer over a red blouse that might have been silk.

"You look terrific, Mary Alice."

She seemed taken aback by this. "Thank you," she said.

He looked at her and marveled at the hold she exerted on him even now. He wondered why—how—this could be. For him there was not much mystery to her anymore. He knew who she was, and probably marriage to her would be a disaster for them both. So why did his heart turn flip-flops just to look at her? He was reasonably certain that if she said to him "Come away with me tonight" that, yes, he would go with her, would forget the detectives waiting for him, forget tonight's stakeout. He would give it all up for one more night with her.

I'm a sick guy, he told himself.

He said: "So what's so important?"

She stopped pacing and faced him. "For one thing, I'm getting married June second. I guess you should know that."

"Well, that's certainly important news. Congratulations."

"If that's all I wanted to tell you, I could have handled it by sending you an invitation."

"So what else is on your mind?"

She hesitated a moment, then said: "Harry's thinking about asking you to be best man."

"Well, well, well," said Bert. "What do you know about that."

"I want you to say no."

Bert said: "Hmm" and resumed pacing.

She walked beside him and he felt her watching his profile for a sign of what his reaction might be. Although conscious of a sudden ache in the region of his solar plexus, Bert was careful to show nothing. He said: "Why should you care who his best man might be?"

"I don't care. Just so long as it isn't you."

Had she said this angrily, viciously, or only thoughtlessly? It was as if the ache in his gut was attached to something and she was twisting it. He stopped and peered in at the lions. "People are trapped in cages too," he said. "They just don't know it."

"My, aren't we cynical today."

He turned and faced her. "Do you hate me, or what?"

"Of course I don't hate you," she said impatiently. "I just don't think it suitable that you should be at the altar beside the man I'm marrying."

"Why not?" He knew why not, but wanted to hear her say it. He wanted to hear her admit how intimate they had once been—as if this would give some measure of that intimacy back to him.

"Because—" She stopped.

"Because what?"

She seemed to take a deep breath. "Because Harry believes certain things about me."

"Yes, he told me."

"He told you?" she said sharply. "What did he tell you?"

"He seems to believe you to have been a bit more innocent than you actually were."

"When did he tell you this?"

"A while back."

"And what did you say?"

"What do you take me for?"

"I want to know what you said to him."

"You know something? We seem to have had this conversation before."

"What did you say to him?"

"I said nothing at all. Your honor is safe with me."

She looked at him.

"I don't go around bragging about all the girls I've screwed," he said.

Head down, she resumed pacing. "That was not nice. You didn't need to say that."

"No, I guess not. I apologize."

Behind the bars one of the lions yawned.

"Those animals look pretty mangy, don't they?" Bert said.

Mary Alice studied the lions for a moment, but made no comment.

"In winter they're all locked up inside. They don't get any exercise at all."

"I'm not really interested in lions today."

"Suppose I happen to want to be his best man?"

"You don't," she said, "do you?"

"I still don't understand why it should bother you so much."

"Because if he found out certain things later, and if I allowed you to be best man, it might—might wreck my marriage."

"What things?"

"If he found out about—"

He waited, wanting to hear her say it.

"About you and me," she said.

"Well," he said, "who would tell him?"

She said nothing.

He said: "Would you tell him?"

"No."

"Then who else knows about it?" When she did not respond he answered for her. "Well, I do, of course. Are you saying I might tell him?"

When again she said nothing, he said: "You think I would, don't you?"

"It's possible, isn't it?"

"And why would I do that?"

"I don't know."

"Why? Tell me why?"

In a small voice she said: "To hurt me."

Bert looked at her. He didn't want to hurt her, he wanted to grab her and cover her face with kisses.

"I'm tired of lions," he said roughly. "Let's go over and see the apes, or some other goddam animal."

He walked off and she had to hurry to keep up.

"You know something?" he said as they walked. "You shouldn't lie to someone you're marrying. It's a very bad idea."

"I didn't lie to him." She added: "I just let him go on thinking certain things."

"Yes, you told me that already."

"Things he wanted to think."

"And now you're afraid I'll spoil all that good work by revealing to him your innermost secrets."

"Maybe not right now," she admitted grudgingly. "Maybe twenty years from now—when the effect would be even worse. Do you realize how humiliated he would be if you had been best man? He'd remember the two of us standing on the altar during the wedding and imagine that we must have been laughing at him."

"It's a pretty vague possibility, if you ask me."

"Maybe, but it's one I don't want hanging over my head."

The apes were in the outdoor cages too. Bert studied them.

"Can't you understand that? I don't want it hanging over my head."

"I don't know what to say."

"I want you to tell me that when he asks you to be best man you'll say no."

"Look at that big fat ape there," Bert said. "What do you suppose he's thinking?"

"Answer me," cried Mary Alice. "When he asks you, you'll say—what?"

"He already asked me. An hour ago. I told him no."

"What?" Mary Alice said. "What?"

He had thought his announcement would please her, but her reaction was the opposite of what he had expected.

"Then why did you let me make a fool of myself just now?

Why did you put me through this—" She was sputtering. "—this charade. This stupid conversation. This excruciating—"

"Calm down," said Bert. Suddenly he was trying to keep from laughing.

"Were you just trying to embarrass me, or what?"

"Not at all, Mary Alice. Calm down."

"Don't you have any respect for me? Do you think it was easy to call you up, and then to come here to meet you, to plead with you? Do you ever consider my feelings at all?"

"I'm afraid I wasn't thinking of anything except how much I wanted to see you, talk to you."

There were tears in her eyes, she was so angry, which he hadn't expected either.

He said: "It was obvious to me you wouldn't want me on the altar with you, so I turned him down. I told him the best man should be his brother, or your brother."

She said: "There are times when I really hate you, you know that?"

"Is this one of those times?"

Instead of answering she spun on her heel and strode off. He didn't know what to do, so he did nothing. He stood watching her back as the crowds on the pathway parted to let her through, then coagulated behind her, until finally he could not see her anymore. He turned then and for a time studied the gorilla in its cage.

After a few minutes he started back across the park to his car.

At nine that night he and his five detectives went out in the unmarked cars and staked out the lots he had selected, and the time began to pass and he sat wondering if he should not have borrowed a few more cars and men from somewhere. There were too many uncovered lots, and it bothered him.

Bert's own stakeout was at Amsterdam Avenue and 70th Street, which was almost outside the Lincoln Center orbit, except on a night like this when all the theaters were operating. It was on a corner where a number of small buildings had been demolished and the rubble paved over. It was surrounded by a chain link fence and there was a small house trailer in the center of it, where two black guys kept the time clock, the ticket stubs, and the keys to all the cars. A skyscraper would go up on this spot beginning probably later in the year—the chain link fence was hung with signs announcing this. In the meantime whoever owned it was making money parking cars.

Bert's second team was at Broadway and 60th Street, across from a lot like this one. If the robbers hit there he was in position to get across to Broadway fast enough to intercept them as they raced uptown getting away. His third team was three blocks south of him, just off Amsterdam, outside a garage under a building. If the robbers chose to hit that one his men would not see it happen. They would have to react to the loitering getaway car, and to two men running up the ramp and piling in. Was this too much to expect of them? Maybe he should have stationed himself there instead of here.

He began to torment himself with worry about the operation. Suppose a detective got killed, a prominent citizen got killed. Or the robbers got past him and his men and escaped. Or they hit an unguarded lot. Or somewhere else entirely. It seemed to him his whole career rode on this one case.

Bert keyed his hand radio and spoke to the other two teams: "See anything?"

In each case the answer was no.

Every fifteen minutes the radio was as close to his lips as if he were kissing it. Every transmission ended the same way: "Stay alert out there."

He was slouched low in the backseat so as not to be seen. But he could barely see out the window himself. Time dragged. His mind went off. It went in one direction only, to Mary Alice, and stuck there, the way their bodies had sometimes stuck together with sweat. What had gone wrong? That was what was important. This tonight was only a game, cops and robbers, of no importance whatever. In a month she would be married. What could he have done to change that? What, if anything, could he still do? Who was Harry Chapman that he could take her away from him?

The detective beside Bert was named McClain. Suddenly he sat up straighter and said: "Oh, oh."

And there the perpetrators were, or at least so Bert imagined, in a red Cadillac that had just pulled in toward the curb. It stood double-parked, its engine still running, half blocking the entrance to the lot. In it sat three black men, and all three were facing into the lot.

Bert too studied the lot. Near the house trailer, waiting patiently for their cars, stood two well-dressed couples. One of the attendants was jockeying cars to get theirs out. The other was standing talking to them, grinning at something, his hand full of ticket stubs.

As Bert watched, more car owners entered the lot on foot and approached the office, and Bert counted them, three men, two women: a total of eleven innocent persons inside the chain link fence. All were potential hostages, and his problems began to compound exponentially.

Two men in raincoats had got out of the Cadillac and entered the lot. The guns appeared, and the terrified people— Bert could see by their movements how terrified they were— were herded into the house trailer.

Still clutching the radio, Bert tumbled over the backrest into the front seat, slid behind the wheel, and started the engine. Keying the radio, he said in a tense voice: "It's going down. Get up here as fast as you can. A red Cadillac." He read off the plate number. "There are too many people present to take them here." He had many decisions to make, and he began to make them. He would not call for backup. He and his five men were enough for this, if they did it right. A bunch of uniforms bailing out of radio cars only made for clutter, and if the shooting started it made for too many bullets. At 77th and Amsterdam there was a school yard that would be empty at this hour. They would pinch them off and take them in front of the empty yard.

He steered out into traffic and went forward to the traffic light, where he pulled into the curb, doused his lights, and waited.

"We'll come up alongside them and at the school yard turn them in toward the curb," he told McClain in the backseat.

These are experienced detectives, he told himself, you don't need to tell them anything. "The other two teams should be here by then," he said. He willed himself to stop talking. All you're doing is revealing your own nervousness, he told himself.

The second unmarked car went past them and pulled into the bus stop half a block ahead.

"Mockler," said McClain.

"Where's Carbone?"

"Is that him?" said McClain. A car had come out of 72nd Street. It turned up Amsterdam a few feet and stopped. "It's him," said McClain.

"I got you in sight, Sarge," said Carbone's voice.

"Here they come," said McClain, turning from the back window.

"Here they come," said Bert into the radio. Dropping the radio, he yanked his gun out of his belt and laid it on the seat beside him.

In the mirror he saw the two men in raincoats running out of the lot. One was carrying a bag that looked heavy. Pulling open the Cadillac's back door he slung the bag in on the seat, then dove in after it. The second man jumped into the front seat. The car took off with a peal of rubber, the two doors not even closed yet, but Bert pulled slowly away from the curb directly into its path, forcing it to slow down. He had to hold it to a reasonable speed to have any hope of stopping it where and how he wished. There was a taxi to Bert's left moving slowly uptown with its roof light lit, the driver cruising for fares, so for two blocks the getaway car was behind them both, unable to get past. In his mirror Bert noted that one of his other cars was directly behind the Cadillac, and the second was half a block ahead. So far this was working out better than he had hoped. Textbook stuff. The school yard was four blocks ahead, then three.

The driver of the Cadillac blinked his lights, leaned on his horn trying to pass, but Bert slowed even further, waiting for the cab to pull ahead—he didn't need a cab driver in the middle of this.

It was by then close to midnight. There was other traffic on the avenue, but not much, and a few people on the sidewalks, but not many. The taxi's turn indicator came on, and at the next corner it turned off. Bert accelerated until he had come up alongside his lead car, the two of them slowing, the two of them far enough apart to block the entire avenue, and in his mirror Bert watched his trailing car advance on the Cadillac until it was beside it.

"I got the driver," cried Bert to McClain, as they drew level with the school yard. "You get the other two guys."

He jammed on the brakes and was out of the car, running back toward the Cadillac. His other cars had stopped also, for he could hear the doors flung open, could hear or sense men running.

All the windows of the Cadillac were closed and there was rock music on the radio, the volume up so loud Bert could hear it outside, and he swung the heel of his gun into the glass beside the driver's ear and it shattered into a million crumbs that rained down onto the driver's lap. By then Bert's arm was inside the car, driving his gun barrel into the side of the driver's face, lacerating the cheek, feeling teeth go underneath the flesh.

"Police, freeze," he shouted, but doubted anyone heard him because of the music. The music was booming. It was so loud he thought it might knock him down. How could they have stood so much noise? The smell of bodies washed out at him too. To Bert an arrest of this kind was an extraordinarily sensual experience, it was as vivid as sex, a rush like no other.

The guns of six detectives were pointed inside the car, and there was no resistance whatever. The three black men were yanked out of their seats and thrown spread-eagled up against the fence. When one of them turned to say something, Bert clubbed him in the head with the side of his gun and he went down. Two detectives lifted him to his feet and flung him once more at the fence. He clung to it like a spider, the blood running down his cheek and neck.

"Somebody turn off that goddam music," ordered Bert.

One of the detectives reached into the Cadillac and the music stopped.

The three clinging spiders were searched for weapons. They were carrying two guns each.

"Fucken cowboys," snorted Bert, tossing the guns in on the floor of his car.

The prisoners were handcuffed and driven to the 20th Precinct station house. Upstairs in the squad room they were read their rights, then thrown into the cage. They sat sullenly on the floor in full view of the detectives who kept moving back and forth outside, always grinning, and frequently slapping one another on the back.

For Bert the rush was over—it never lasted very long—and the slave work began. He put one detective on the phone to make the necessary notifications, and sent two others back to the parking lot to bring in tonight's victims, take their statements, and hold them until the assistant DA arrived and decided whether or not to have a lineup. In the meantime the prisoners had to be fingerprinted and their belongings inventoried. Their guns had to be traced, if possible. The bag that contained the loot sat atop the desk Bert was using, and its contents had to be inventoried also. The precinct-wide alert had to be called off, and the extra radio cars called in. The red Cadillac had to be traced, its owner found and brought in.

"And I want DD-5s on everything," said Bert, and he left them for a moment, went to the phone, and dialed the chief of detectives' office, but at this hour it was empty except for the duty sergeant, who refused to give him Chief Summers' home number.

"All right," said Bert, "then you call him at home."

"It's after midnight."

"Wake him up."

"I can't wake up the chief of detectives."

"Wake him up," said Bert. "Tell him to phone me here forthwith."

"Forthwith" was the strongest command in the police lexicon.

"Forthwith?" said the sergeant. "The chief of detectives? Are you crazy?"

Bert giggled. The rush was over, but he was still a bit giddy. "Forthwith," he said again and hung up.

Ten minutes later the phone rang on the corner of Bert's desk and it was Summers, who sounded groggy.

"This better be good, Bert."

"Those guys you wanted, Chief. We got them."

Silence on the end of the line.

"There won't be any more parking lot stickups for a while, Chief."

"I only gave you the assignment yesterday."

"We locked them up twenty minutes ago."

"Well," said Summers. "Well, well, well."

"We were lucky," said Bert modestly.

"Shots fired?"

"No shots fired."

"Even better," purred Summers. "So tell me about it."

Bert described his plan, the stakeouts, the arrests.

"Perpetrators Negro?"

"Negro, Chief."

"What kind of shape are they in?"

"We hardly touched them."

"Good. Can't be too careful these days."

Bert waited.

Summers said: "You'll get another meritorious out of this, Bert, if I'm not mistaken."

"Thanks, Chief."

"I'll call a press conference at headquarters tomorrow. Three o'clock. Be there. And in the meantime don't speak to the press."

After hanging up Bert stared at the phone. The idea of a press conference had not occurred to him, but would from now on.

He worked all night—they all did. At dawn the prisoners were brought downtown and arraigned, and by noon, on three hours' sleep, Bert was back in the office and the work continued.

At the press conference later he and his men were allowed to stand behind Summers and were introduced and praised, but Summers did all the talking. However, in the next day's papers Bert's name and picture appeared in print for the first time. At lunchtime he went out and bought a scrapbook, and when he got home that night he pasted the clippings into it. Mandatory retirement age in the New York Police Department was sixty-three. Bert, who was still not quite twenty-seven, expected to be a cop for the next thirty-six years, and in that time to fill many more scrapbooks like this one.

More than two dozen previous victims were contacted, and Bert lost track of the number of additional lineups he set up. The case, and the sheaf of papers that went with it, got fatter and fatter. He worked on the case eight straight days and scarcely thought of Mary Alice at all. Good, he told himself, I'm over her.

Then the wedding invitation came to his flat in the mail. It had been sent by Harry Chapman personally, and he had scribbled on it: "Best man to be my brother, but I won't be happy unless you're there standing up for me at least symbolically."

The wedding, Bert saw, was to take place at St. Patrick's Cathedral. Well, where else was good enough for the daughter of a man as rich and powerful as Mary Alice's father? Bert had known only vaguely that Mary Alice's family was Catholic. He and she had never talked about religion. They had always had too many more important matters on their minds. Like bed. Well, that was over.

There was a second envelope out of which Bert pulled a heavily embossed invitation to the reception afterward. RSVP—a Scarsdale phone number. Mary Alice's mother would answer, Bert supposed. Or perhaps a butler, who the hell knew.

He propped the invitation up on his dresser and looked at it every day as he knotted his tie, but could not make himself answer it one way or the other.

Finally Harry phoned him. "My in-laws want to know if you're coming to the reception."

"They're not your in-laws yet."

"You know what I mean."

"Tell them I'll try to be there."

"You gotta come. It means a lot to me. Promise me."

"Sure," said Bert, "I promise."

Two days before the wedding he dialed the number on the invitation. A woman answered, and Bert said he would not be able to make it to the reception.

"Oh, I'm so sorry," she said.

"Is this Mrs. Riggs?"

"No, this is Annette. I work here."

"Well, please express my regrets to Mrs. Riggs. And—"

"Yes, sir?"

"Can you get a message to Harry Chapman for me? I don't have a number for him anymore."

"Mr. Chapman is living in an apartment they bought in New York on the East Side," Annette said. "It's where they'll live together after the honeymoon. Do you have a pencil?"

Bert duly copied down what she told him. "In case I should miss him," he told Annette, "please express my regrets to Mr. Chapman as well. Tell him I have to be in court on a case and can't get a continuance."

"A what?"

"A postponement," Bert said. There was no such case.

He was at his desk in the squad room at the Two-Four, and when he had hung up he stared at Harry's new address and phone number for a moment. That part of the East Side was known as the Silk Stocking District, and he wondered how much the apartment had cost, and who had paid for it, and he crumpled up the phone number and threw it into the basket in his kneehole.

When he woke up on the morning of the wedding, he told himself this was just another day, but in the station house there was a clock on the wall above Bert's desk and he kept watching it, as if watching for the hour when someone was to be executed. About now Mary Alice in her long white dress—he supposed she would be in a long white dress— would be entering the cathedral. The marriage ceremony would take only a few minutes, she would be officially, legally married and would have only the nuptial mass to wait through before leaving with her new husband.

As a sergeant Bert was entitled to a car and driver. Abruptly he went downstairs and got into it and ordered his driver to take him downtown to St. Patrick's.

They parked on the opposite side of the street.

That part of Fifth Avenue was a no standing zone. Bert got out and stood leaning over the car, his elbows on the roof, and watched the great bronze doors of the cathedral, waiting for them to be thrown open, and for the bride and groom to come out. His driver, a detective, said: "Can I ask what we're doing here, Sarge?"

Bert turned to him. "We're on an important surveillance."

"What are we surveilling?"

"In a few minutes a woman is going to come out those doors over there. She'll be wearing white like a bride. She's a very bad piece of work, and bride is only one of the many roles she plays. I want you to go across and arrest her. Be sure to search her for concealed weapons."

"Only a policewoman can search a female perpetrator," said the detective. He studied Bert a moment. "You're putting me on," he said doubtfully, "right?"

"Go look into the shop windows or something," said Bert. "There's nothing on Fifth Avenue for a cop."

"Go look anyway."

The crowds moved by behind him, and more crowds passed in front of the cathedral across the street, and four lanes of traffic cruised by his parked department car, and he stood there with his elbows on the roof, his face showing nothing of the emotion he felt, and he waited.

There were limos with drivers in them parked in front of the cathedral, which was permitted, but Bert's car was the only one parked on his side of Fifth Avenue, and a uniformed cop approached it, walked around it once, eyed Bert briefly, then got out a pen and his summons book.

Bert was so concentrated on the cathedral that some seconds passed before he was aware that the cop was ostentatiously writing out a parking ticket on him.

"What the fuck do you think you're doing?" Bert shouted, and ran over to him.

"You're illegally parked," the cop said stolidly. "This is a no standing zone."

"So what?"

"So you're going to get a summons for illegal parking," the cop said.

"This is a department car," Bert shouted.

"What department?"

"Your department, you fucking moron. Are you blind?"

"A department car?" the cop said, as if trying to work out what the words meant.

Bert slapped the fender. "Every criminal in the city would make this for a police car on sight, but not you. You see all the aerials? You see that it's a plain black Plymouth? Look a little more carefully and you observe the police radio under the dash. And if you're really sharp you might even notice the police plate in the windshield."

The cop was beginning to look stubborn. "Who are you?" he demanded.

"I'm on the job, same as you."

Bert's driver had come back to the car and was watching carefully.

The cop gestured toward the driver. "Who's he?"

"He's on the job also."

A small crowd had gathered around them. Bert was afraid that the cathedral doors would open right now, that before he got this settled Mary Alice would come out onto the steps in her white dress and would notice the altercation. She would notice him, would realize how miserably, ineluctably he had been drawn to her wedding.

"Can I see some ID?" the cop asked.

Bert thrust his shield under the cop's nose. "You see that, you jerk-off? You see what it says?"

"Oh," said the cop, "a sergeant."

"That's right, a sergeant," Bert snarled. "And you're a patrolman. So beat it, okay?"

"Can I ask what you're doing here, Sarge?"

"I'm on surveillance."

Looking perplexed, the cop peered down at his summons book. "I already started the ticket," he said.

Bert snatched the summons book out of his hand.

"Hey, give me that," the cop hollered.

Bert tore off the half-written summons, ripped it in two, then allowed the cop to grab back the book.

"Now look what you've done!" the cop cried. He held up the torn summons. "How am I gonna explain this?"

"I don't know," said Bert, "and I don't fucking care. Now get the fuck away from me before I give you a complaint and you wind up in the trial room."

Just then the cathedral doors opened and people and photographers spilled out onto the steps. The cop must have wandered off. In any case Bert's gaze was fixed absolutely on the dark maw just inside the doors, and in a moment it was filled by Mary Alice on the arm of Harry Chapman. They came out blinking onto the stoop, where pictures were taken and people began throwing rice.

Her dress looked like satin to Bert. It was white, of course, which used to attest to the virginity of the bride but didn't anymore. It had a long white train that was presently engaged in sweeping up filth. Harry and Mary Alice were both grinning.

To Bert, Mary Alice looked absolutely gorgeous. Although across the street and watching through traffic, he was still a very young man, his eyesight was perfect, and he could see her eyes, her smile, even her teeth.

People kept coming out of the cathedral. They were kissing Mary Alice and wringing Harry's hand.

Well, Bert thought, that's the end of that. And he got into his car and had himself driven back to the station house.

■ 7 ■

OUTSIDE THE first dep's windows snow fell heavily. The day was so dark that the lights were on. Bert came in. In a semicircle in front of the desk sat Sternhagen and two FBI agents: Ed Croke, who ran the New York office, and his immediate subordinate, whose name was Butler.

Bert shook hands with the two agents, whom he knew. "I wasn't aware that murder is now a federal crime," he said. "Even the murder of a police commissioner."

"It's not," said Croke.

"The Justice Department asked us to look into it because of the funeral," said Butler.

Bert had the New York street cop's natural animosity toward FBI men. They were too well educated, too well dressed, and they did not like to get their hands dirty. Also, they had untold amounts of money with which to buy informants and information.

"There are some important people," explained Croke, "who might want to come up for the funeral."

"Like who?" said Bert.

"The president maybe."

"To demonstrate his concern about violence in the cities," said Butler, "and the need for strong gun control legislation."

"Did he and Harry Chapman know each other?"

"I don't know."

"The police commissioner is, like, a symbol," said Butler.

"Symbolic, right," said Croke.

One minute Harry was on a slab having his organs handed around, and the next he was a presidential symbol. The juxtaposition was so extreme, and to Bert so obscene, that he felt an impulse to laugh, or perhaps scream.

"If it could be made to seem that Chapman died in the line of duty," said Butler, "that would be perfect. I think the president would come."

"Defending someone," said Croke, "intervening in a crime—something of that nature."

"Unfortunately," said Bert carefully, "there's no evidence to that effect as yet."

"Maybe something will turn up," said Croke.

"Maybe," said Bert. He was trying to control himself by taking slow deep breaths.

"If that was what it was," said Croke, "the president would be almost guaranteed. The vice president at least."

"Assassinated by a terrorist group," said Butler, "would be almost as good."

"Not really," contradicted Croke. "Assassinations are sometimes tricky."

"A devoted public servant knocked off by some group," insisted Butler.

"I don't think it was an assassination," said Bert carefully. "He was shot only once. Assassins usually like to make sure."

"Maybe they fired off a whole magazine but the other shots missed," offered the first dep.

"Possible," said Bert.

"Went sailing off down the street," said Croke, "and your guys aren't good enough to find them."

Bert decided to ignore this remark.

"If it wasn't an assassination, what was it then?"

"We don't know yet."

"Can we rule out hanky-panky?"

"Hanky-panky," said Bert.

"There are a lot of people in Washington want to come to the funeral," said Croke. "Under certain circumstances. Even if the president decides not to come himself. People who need to make plans. We need to rule out hanky-panky right away, so they can decide."

"That's really why we're here now," said Butler. "To rule out hanky-panky."

"Call it something else," said Bert. "Call it what you mean, for crissake."

"Was he into something?"

"He means corruption," said the first dep from behind his desk.

"Not to my knowledge," said Bert.

"You admit the investigation has just started," said Croke.

"I said not to my knowledge."

"How long before you can be certain?"

"How the fuck do I know?"

A profound silence fell upon the room.

Bert addressed Croke directly: "What else do you want to know? So I can answer you and then get the hell back to work."

Croke had the rank of assistant director. In the federal bureaucracy no one spoke to him this way, and his lips tightened. "Who's in charge of the investigation?"

"Chief Kincaid."

"What's his phone number?"

"You want to know anything, you call me."

"I'd rather call him directly."

"Or if it's a tip on how we should conduct our investigation, you call in on the public phones. We got two special numbers installed just for people like you. You should get right through."

"Give him the number, Bert," said Sternhagen mildly.

Bert withdrew his notebook and read out the number.

Sternhagen said mildly: "What did the autopsy show?"

"That he was shot dead."

"What else?"

"We'll have the report tomorrow or the next day."

From behind his desk the first dep said: "Was the bullet recovered?"

"No." Bert could not have said why he lied, perhaps because he so detested the two agents. He was not going to give them any information at all.

"Meaning we won't be able to match it to the eventual

murder weapon," the first dep said, "assuming we ever find it."

"No," said Bert. Having lied, he could not immediately reverse himself. "Anything else?" he said, still glaring at Croke and Butler. "No?" He nodded all around and left the room.

In his office he locked the door, retrieved the evidence envelope from his attaché case, and spilled its contents onto his blotter: the lead mushroom that had killed Harry Chapman.

The police academy, on East 20th Street, was the site of the ballistics unit—of all the department laboratories. The bullet should be logged in there. It was what regulations called for, but Bert hadn't done it yet and he realized now he wasn't going to. He would lock the bullet in his safe instead. The fewer people who knew about it, the better. The department was too big. Log it in and the news would leak out. The guy who killed Harry, who might otherwise keep the gun and get caught with it, would throw it away. Without a ballistics match to the murder weapon a successful prosecution might prove impossible.

Of course the murderer might throw the gun away anyway.

Bert had begun to flounder, to do things he did not normally do, and in the end he did not even lock the bullet in his safe but threw it back into his attaché case and from then on carried it everywhere he went.

Sitting far forward on the sofa, tense, his knees high, Assistant Chief Earl Coxen watched the noon newscast. Beside him sat his wife. Coxen was in uniform, about to go to work. There were two stars on each shoulder, and gold braid on the cap on the sofa beside him.

When the credits came on the screen, superimposed over footage of Harry Chapman being sworn in, Coxen got up and turned off the set.

"Poor Harry," he said.

"There goes my dinner party," said his wife, whose name was Marlene.

"How can you even think of such a thing now?"

"I've put a lot of time and energy into it." She had invited the Chapmans, the Priestlys, and the Sternhagens to dinner later in the week. She had made the calls herself, and although her husband had feared she would be refused everyone had agreed to come.

"I have to get to work," said Coxen. He came over and picked his cap up off the sofa.

"How do you feel?" asked his wife, watching him closely.

"I liked Harry. I liked him a lot."

"I never liked him."

"I rode in a radio car with him almost two years."

"So who's going to be the next police commissioner?"

"He was a nice man," said Coxen.

"You even campaigned for him when he ran for Congress. You made him look good."

"It was a favor I knew he'd repay, and he did."

"He was one of these people," mused Marlene, "who never knew there was anyone else in the room but himself."

"You didn't know him."

"We went to his wedding," Coxen's wife said. "We went out with them in Washington that time."

"I've got to go to work," Coxen said.

"The next PC. Who'll it be?"

Coxen fingered the gold braid on his cap. "He gave me this," he said. "Jumped me over a lot of men."

"You didn't answer my question," said Marlene.

"Priestly or Sternhagen. Those are the two likeliest ones."

"What about you?"

It gave Coxen pause, but only for a moment.

"I don't think so, no."

"Why not?"

"Let's mourn the guy for a day or two before we toss that one around."

"There isn't time for mourning, if you want it."

Coxen's driver was waiting outside with the car. "I'm late for work," he said.

"You're the boss. You can come in anytime you like."

But Coxen, who commanded the Brooklyn North patrol forces, had put himself down on the chart as working a noon-to-eight tour, and today his lateness would be remarked upon. There would be calls from headquarters, from other commanders. Calls from reporters looking for anecdotes about Harry.

He said: "The mayor would never appoint a black man."

"Have you seen the statistics?" his wife said. "The city is now less than fifty percent white."

"Not the police department, though."

"The mayor is a politician. All he cares about is votes."

"I doubt my name would even occur to him."

"We could see that it does."

"How?"

"Enlist support."

Coxen was silent.

"There's a congressman from this district," said his wife. "He seemed to be black, last time I saw him."

"Branford? I doubt he'd do anything. He's like me. He knows when he's already well off."

"There are other possibilities as well." And she named some of them.

"Why should those men stick their necks out for me?"

"Because if you got the job they would feel part owners of the New York Police Department. Don't you know anything?"

Coxen was again silent. Finally he said: "Some things you probably don't understand. For instance, there are men in the department who already hate me, because I got jumped over them."

"What do you care? You give the orders and they obey them."

"Men I don't even know," said Coxen, "who would wreck my career, given the chance. Probably working on it even now." He smiled and embraced his wife. "Inside the department there are intrigues within intrigues. You don't realize that. You're a tough lady and I love you, but making a run for the PC's office is not a good idea."

"Why not, if you get it?"

"Supposing, what is far more likely, that I don't get it?"

"You don't have to make the calls, I'll make them."

"There are two ways to get ahead in the department. One is to acquire a powerful rabbi—"

"Like Harry Chapman." She affected a deep Harlem accent: "Some o' mah best fren's is niggahs."

"That wasn't Harry."

"Oh no?"

For a time both were silent.

"What's the second way?" said Marlene Coxen.

"You go along doing your job, never making an enemy of anyone, and finally seniority puts you over the top."

"You don't have a rabbi anymore," said Marlene. "Harry's dead. And since you now have enemies that you don't even know about, as you say, the second way is out too. So I don't see where you're risking anything."

"Marlene, Marlene. I'm forty-six years old. I like my job, and I don't want to lose it. If I were known to be lobbying for PC, and if I lost out, then whoever did get it would run me out of the department. Don't you see?"

"Not really."

"I think it's an idea we should just forget about." He put his cap on and started toward the front door. "I have to go to work."

A tall, broad-shouldered man with short hair, he went out the door and down the steps to the sidewalk. His car was there, but instead of getting into it he looked up at his house. He lived on 139th Street, the so-called Strivers' Row, in an elegant brownstone designed by the famed architect Stanford White before the turn of the century, at which time Harlem was the richest of the city's all-white suburbs. Stanford White had designed the entire block, identical buildings, and the entire block had long since been designated a historic landmark. In the houses today lived the elite of Harlem: black judges, politicians, businessmen. And Assistant Chief Earl Coxen as well, he reminded himself. Coxen was in overall command of ten precincts, about three thousand men. His immediate staff was composed of one deputy inspector and eight captains. By the standards he had set himself starting out, he had made good in a very big way, and he got into his car grieving slightly for Harry Chapman but in all other ways a happy man.

His wife had stood at the front window watching him go. As soon as his car had turned the corner she went to the phone and dialed the office of Congressman Branford. She said she was calling on behalf of Assistant Chief Earl Coxen, New York Police Department.

Branford was not in, but the secretary promised he would

call back, so Marlene stayed close to the phone. There were other calls she might have made, but she wanted to get a feel for Branford's reaction first. About three o'clock the congressman did call back, and she spoke to him for twenty minutes or more. He said he liked Earl, having met him somewhere. He seemed to like the idea of a black police commissioner very much, and before hanging up he promised to speak to the mayor. The mayor owed him some favors, he said.

Feeling more confident now, Marlene phoned the publisher of Harlem's newspaper, the *Amsterdam News*, and after him the pastor of the Abyssinian Baptist Church, Harlem's most prosperous and influential church. Both men said they would speak to the mayor on Earl's behalf.

Another conference. Also chaired by First Deputy Commissioner Priestly. He sat behind his desk and spoke with a tremor in his voice that came and went, Bert noted. He did not look well either, he thought; this murder had marked him.

The other men present were Sternhagen and Monsignor Casey, who was the department chaplain. According to Casey, Harry Chapman would lie in state downstairs in the rotunda. An honor guard would stand watch over the bier, he said. The public would be admitted, he said. He seemed determined to let no detail go unmentioned. The inspector's funeral was scheduled for St. Patrick's, the same grandiose funeral rated by every slain cop. The regular units had been notified. The cardinal would give the homily—Casey had spoken to him— and would also concelebrate along with a number of bishops.

Casey had seen the widow, it seemed. She had agreed to everything.

This interminable, lugubrious conference was followed by another in another part of the building, called by the Secret Service to discuss security arrangements in case the president or the vice president chose to attend the funeral. Present were the commanders of every police unit even peripherally involved. Air Force One would put down at JFK; the presidential helicopter would land at the 30th Street heliport eight minutes later. The motorcade would come up the East Side Drive, etcetera.

In his office Bert sent a detective out to buy him a ham and Swiss on rye and several Cokes. His phone kept ringing. He drank the Cokes all afternoon. He had been drinking too much coffee lately, especially when under pressure. The literature said too much made you a candidate for a heart attack, even someone his age.

The mayor scheduled a press conference for late in the afternoon. Chief Farber, who was not formally invited, or even officially notified, decided to attend anyway. In his car driving to City Hall, he was both furious and worried. The mayor had not phoned to ask for a progress report, either, which meant he was getting his information from someone else—John Kincaid, obviously. Which meant the mayor was operating behind his back. Kincaid too, but with the mayor's connivance, meaning there was nothing Bert could do about it.

He went into City Hall past the salute of the cop on security duty, and then he was marching down the corridor past portraits of former mayors hanging on both walls, men a hundred to two hundred years dead, and they eyed him gloomily as he strode by. Ahead was the mayor's office, and he could hear the buzz of noise from the Blue Room, which was where mayoral press conferences took place, and then he saw the mayor come out of his office into the corridor accompanied by several men, one of them John Kincaid.

The mayor looked surprised to see him. "What do you know that I don't?"

Bert glanced coldly at Kincaid, who to his pleasure seemed to cringe slightly. "Did John brief you?"

The mayor only nodded. He was a politician used to pressing flesh, though not this time, a bad sign.

"Nothing new since then."

"I called down about the autopsy," interrupted Kincaid.

The mayor eyed Bert. "Are you going to solve this case?"

"Don't worry, we'll solve it." Well, what else was he supposed to answer?

"They told me to be patient," said Kincaid.

Bert only glanced at him.

"Gave me some crap about toxology tests."

"You and I will have to have a long conversation," said the mayor to Bert.

"Sure," said Bert.

"Maybe you can talk to Dr. Klotz for me," Kincaid suggested nervously, "get them to hurry with that report."

"They only just finished cutting him up, for crissake," said Bert.

"Have one of your men contact my appointments secretary," said the mayor. "Better wait till after the funeral, though. We don't want to seem ghoulish, do we. We have ten days, they tell me."

This did not mean Bert was to be the next PC, but it seemed to him a step forward. He was being actively considered. It was certainly encouraging. But he found himself eyeing John Kincaid, who, however discomfited at this minute, was perhaps being considered also. It was possible.

All the more reason to tell him nothing.

They moved into the Blue Room and its buzz of noise, the mayor jumped up onto the platform, and the noise stopped. As the bright lights came on, Bert, Kincaid, and the mayor's other aides stepped back against the wall, and the mayor began to speak about his murdered police commissioner.

When he had finished there came a babel of questions.

"Who will be appointed to succeed Harry Chapman?" Everyone was shouting. "Who's in line?"

The mayor said he was considering a number of names.

"Which names?" the voices demanded. Did he have a short list? Was Chief Farber on the list?

"There are a lot of names on the list," said the mayor.

"If Chief Farber solves the case, will he be the next police commissioner?" someone shouted.

The question surprised the mayor. Turning quickly toward Bert, giving him what in the political world is often considered a fond smile, he said: "If Chief Farber solves the case, I would certainly have to consider him very strongly."

The press conference ended there. The mayor stepped down, the newspeople hurried out of the room to get their stories in by deadline, and John Kincaid was gone before Bert could even glance in his direction. Bert himself remained standing against the wall, digesting what the mayor had just said. Tonight's newscasts and tomorrow's papers would describe Bert as a possible next PC—for his had been the only police name mentioned. How would Priestly react? How would Sternhagen react? Their noses would be out of joint certainly. In what ways were they likely to try to hurt him?

He was driven back to headquarters through the dark slushy streets. In his office his in-basket was full and the sheaf of phone messages that awaited him was as thick as a deck of cards. But he had barely sat down before the red phone rang still again.

He went up the stairs two at a time and strode impatiently into the first dep's office. Priestly and Sternhagen were both there. The drapes were drawn and they looked ready to go home.

However, the television was on, and Bert glanced at it on its small table: Channel 2 News, what else. The two men had been watching the mayor's press conference, they said.

Bert looked from Sternhagen to Priestly and back again.

"We wondered what you were doing there," Sternhagen said.

"Briefing the mayor."

"From now on," said the first dep, "you brief us. We'll brief the mayor."

Again Bert looked from one to the other. "Sure," he said, "we can try it that way." But he added carefully: "However the mayor wants it."

A heavy silence followed. Bert broke it: "By the way, Commissioner, Kincaid wants to search the late PC's office. You've ordered it sealed, I believe."

"I'll go in there myself," said Priestly. "See what's what."

It was not in the interest of either of these men, Bert reminded himself, that he break this case quickly. "Fine," he said to the first dep, "just as long as the detectives go in with you."

Giving a brief nod to both men, he walked out.

One of Mary Alice's sons opened the door. A tall kid, seventeen years old, Bert believed. He had seen him at a campaign rally eight or ten years ago. Of course he looked much different now.

"I'm a friend of your mother's," Bert said, and walked past him.

The house was full of Harry's relatives and friends. He had hoped to talk to Mary Alice alone, but saw at once that this would be difficult. People stood talking, laughing, eating, many of them in the dining room, where the table was heavily laden with food and opened bottles of wine.

Mary Alice came toward him. She wore a black skirt, a gray sweater, and around her throat was knotted a red silk scarf. Her hair was in disarray and she looked distracted.

"Oh Bert," she said. Her face was flushed. "So nice of you to come." She squeezed his hands for a moment, but her attention was caught by someone else and she went away.

Though the corpse was not present, this was a wake nonetheless.

As he helped himself to some roast beef and potato salad Bert wondered if he were the only person in the room actively thinking of Harry. Mary Alice didn't seem to be grieving, but of course she was very busy. She kept replenishing the food, carrying dirty plates, glasses, and utensils out to the kitchen, and greeting guests as they arrived.

For a time Bert talked to people he did not know. Some of them recounted anecdotes about Harry that he had not heard before. Most had to do with his time in Washington in the Justice Department, or in Congress. Some were funny and everybody laughed. Bert could have contributed anecdotes about him as a young cop, but chose not to. These were personal memories, they were all mixed up with memories of Mary Alice, and he had no desire to share them.

Finally the crowd began to thin. He thought he might soon get a chance to talk to Mary Alice alone, but those who were left showed no sign of leaving and at length he realized they were not going to leave at all, that they must be relatives who would spend the night in bedrooms upstairs.

Bert's coat was lying on one of those beds. He came back downstairs carrying it, and as he reached the hall Mary Alice was there, en route to the kitchen or somewhere.

"Are you leaving, Bert?" she said, and she accompanied him to the door, where she turned and said: "Thanks for stopping by." Even when he took both her hands she did not make eye contact, glancing instead over her shoulder at others who had just come out into the hall. She did not seem able to keep her head still, and the effect was to accord Bert no sense of intimacy whatever.

When she opened the front door he saw that it was snowing again outside, but he lingered a moment.

"What did Harry go to Washington for, I wonder," he said.

"He was mysterious sometimes," she said vaguely.

"Did he have an office up there on the West Side? An apartment? Something he used?"

She brushed back a strand of hair. "With Harry you could never be sure."

Because he did not want her to think he had come tonight merely to interrogate her, he stopped there. Perhaps he would be able to talk to her tomorrow. After kissing her on the cheek he stepped out into the night.

When he got home he found that Madge had waited up for him.

"You've been to see the widow," she said. Her tone was not quite accusatory.

"Yes," he admitted. "There were a lot of people there."

"How was she?"

"I don't know. How do you tell?"

He went into the kitchen and put water on for tea. When he turned he saw that Madge was standing in the doorway. He said: "You were with her this morning. How did she seem to you?"

His wife thought about it a moment. "Stunned, I would say."

"Not grieving?"

"Stunned."

He stood waiting for the water to boil. "How long did you stay with her?"

"Until one of her sisters came. About two hours. Two hours I could have done without, by the way. Why me?"

"What did you do all that time?"

"She took a shower and got dressed, while I read a magazine. She made a few phone calls, while I read a second magazine. I was afraid I would run out of magazines. Finally she hung up, and we went out and bought food for the party.

The streets were all slushy. I ruined a perfectly good pair of shoes, and I was two hours late for work."

Madge, who had a master's degree in child psychology, was the assistant director of a home for delinquent girls.

"Did she talk about her husband?"

"Not much."

"She must have said something."

"I don't think it was such a hot marriage. But then few are, are they?"

"She said something specific. What did she say?"

"Nothing that I remember."

"Try hard. It could be important."

"It was just an impression I got. She said she had thought he was still in Washington. He was a fairly ruthless man from the sound of it. Didn't confide in her much, apparently."

Bert took the kettle off the stove. "You want tea?"

"Sure." She studied him a moment. "As you don't confide in me."

Bert poured boiling water over the tea bags. "Are you saying I'm ruthless?"

"No. I'm saying that in good marriages people confide."

"Look," said Bert, "I'm not in the mood."

"The way is clear for you now, isn't it? You can make your move on her. You couldn't before because if Harry found out you would have lost your job."

"What are you talking about?"

"Now she's a widow."

Bert picked up his cup and saucer and moved past her into the living room, but she followed.

"You've been obsessed with her for years," Madge said.

Bert was at the window staring across at other windows, at ledges with fresh snow on them, at snow falling down into the chasm in between. He was sipping his tea and trying to ignore his wife.

"Every time you would see her, you would talk about her for days."

"Our paths crossed maybe five times in seventeen, eighteen years, and that's all they did, they crossed."

"You were obsessed with her when you married me, and you're still obsessed with her."

"What bullshit," said Bert. "I'm going to bed."

"You may not even realize it. I'll grant you that much. Men are so blind."

But in bed in the dark he reached for her. One of the purposes of sex was to reaffirm life. A man could get to believe too much in death. Particularly a detective could, since he saw so much of it. Sex was not so much the act of making love as the act of making life. It was doubly reaffirming if the woman took part, and finally, without a word being spoken on either side, despite herself probably, he felt Madge begin to succumb to his manipulations. Her breath began to come quicker, and a low moan escaped her. Good, Bert thought, and he continued what he was doing until at last her whole body stiffened and the spasms began, whereupon he rolled on top of her and took his turn, two separate actions, not one, but the best he was capable of this night. The best she was capable of too, probably, and perhaps both felt more alive afterward than before. He hoped so.

Lying in the dark he wanted not to think at all—not of Mary Alice, not of his own marriage, not of Harry Chapman dead on a slab in the morgue, not of the investigation that so far had made no progress at all. He wanted only for what seemed like the longest day of his life to be over, and at last it was and he fell asleep.

■ 8 ■

WHEN CHIEF of Detectives Bert P. Farber came awake the other side of the bed was empty and he could smell coffee brewing. He shaved, dressed, and went out to the kitchen, where his wife poured coffee into two cups. She drank hers standing up, watching him, her rump against the sink. She was wearing the same purple dressing gown she had worn the night before, and matching purple mules. The gown was of some slick material, and her hair was combed and she looked very nice to him.

He always noticed her appearance, though she often accused him of ignoring her, of hardly knowing she was there, much less how she looked or what she was wearing. He tried to go through life noticing everything, he had retorted more than once in annoyance, including the way she looked.

As he sipped his coffee he brooded about Harry, and about the case.

He drank two cups of coffee, ate two slices of toast with marmalade, and his wife did not interrupt his brooding until he had finished and stood up from the table.

"If I were you," she said, "I'd look for a woman."

Bert studied her a moment. "Well, there's no evidence in that direction."

"That's where I'd look."

"Why do you say that?"

She shrugged. "An impression I got from Mary Alice."

"Something she said?"

"Not in so many words, no."

Bert continued to gaze at his wife, but she said nothing more.

When he got to his office he made several brief telephone calls, after which he called in Potter, his chief of staff.

"Close the door," he said. "Sit down."

Potter, as he took the chair beside the desk, looked mystified.

"The PC was in Washington over the weekend," Bert said. Since he had brought Potter's career this far, he thought he could trust him. "We don't know when he came back. Probably on one of the last shuttles Sunday night. I want you to go to the airlines and go over the passenger manifests of every flight until you find his name."

Potter was a man of rank. In uniform he would have worn eagles on his shoulders. In the army he would have been a colonel, and he started at once to protest. "Me, Chief? Personally?"

"Personally."

Poring over manifests was a job for an ordinary detective, not an inspector, and Potter said so.

Bert cut him short. "There's a man named Bronfman at Delta, vice president for security. I've already called him and he expects you." He tore a page off his memo pad and handed it across. "If you don't find what you're looking for at Delta, you go to the other shuttle airline. Here's the guy to see. I already called him too."

Inspector Potter protested that he would send someone on his staff, a lieutenant, even a captain.

"No," said Bert, shaking his head. "You go yourself." Bert saw him begin to digest the order. For a man of his rank it was a hard swallow.

"The PC is supposed to be in contact with his office around the clock," Potter said finally. "His appointments secretary should have the information you're looking for."

"He doesn't."

Potter was gazing at the names on the paper in his hand.

"Once you find out what plane he came back on," Bert said, "start looking for the one he went down on. His appointments secretary has no record of that either."

"Jesus," said Potter. "If something heavy had happened

in his absence—a bomb, an assassination, a hostage situation, a riot—and he couldn't be reached, the mayor would have fired him."

"Maybe," said Bert.

Potter was shaking his head. "He took a helluva chance, didn't he?"

"He could have gone down there Friday night," persisted Bert, "or anytime Saturday or Sunday."

"To do what?"

Potter had begun reacting like the street detective he once had been.

"Why did he go down there, Chief?"

"I don't know."

"Does anyone know?"

"His wife maybe. And whoever he went there to see."

"Something's fishy," said Potter. "What's fishy? What am I really looking for?"

"I don't know," said Bert.

"You think he had a secret life?"

"He intended to run for president. So his political life may have been secret. Somewhat secret, anyway."

"And the other parts?"

"I don't know."

The two men sat there, eyes locked on each other, both heads nodding.

"Are you thinking," Potter asked, "that he was killed by someone he met on the plane?"

"It's possible," Bert said. "At this stage anything is possible."

After a moment Bert added: "The detectives working the case, including Chief Kincaid, don't know he was in Washington, and they don't need to know as yet. For the time being, this part of the investigation is between you and me. We need to trace the PC's movements, but we don't need to start any rumors or speculation that might reflect badly on the department, or cause his wife additional pain." For a moment his thoughts became glued to Mary Alice, her face, her form, her future. But he forced them away from her. "Let me repeat how sensitive this case is."

* * *

As soon as he was notified that Harry Chapman was in place in the rotunda, Bert went down there. He found that the coffin was closed, a flag draped over it. Cops wearing white gloves stood at attention at the four corners. In a few minutes the public would begin to be admitted. Through the glass doors Bert could see long lines of people waiting outside. To keep them from wandering through the building, police academy trainees in gray uniforms were in place at the stairwell and to either side of the elevator bank.

Mary Alice, in a black dress, stood at the head of the coffin. Her eyes were downcast, her hands clasped at her lips as if in prayer, and he watched her. Her sons, motionless and solemn, were back two paces, and a few feet farther back than that were Monsignor Casey and two uniformed lieutenants who were no doubt responsible for arranging all this.

Bert waited, for he thought Mary Alice would soon turn from the bier, at which point he could speak to her. But the minutes passed and she did not move from her position. Finally he stepped into an elevator and rode back up to a conference the first dep's office had called to discuss details of the funeral.

There were eight officers in the room. Both New York senators and most of the state's congressional delegation would attend, Bert learned, as would nearly all high-ranking New York City officials, of course. There would be five thousand cops in the street representing departments as far away as Ohio. A plane had been chartered to carry the coffin and the official party to Washington after the service, for permission had been received for interment at Arlington National Cemetery. Neither the president nor the vice president would come to New York for the funeral. Later in the afternoon one or both would drive across the Potomac for the burial service, however.

When this meeting ended First Deputy Commissioner Priestly drew Bert aside. The chartered plane was for family, close friends, and officials, Priestly said. He and the mayor would be on it. There would be no other official NYPD delegation at the graveside. Bert's presence at Arlington would not be required.

This was a harsh dose, and as he absorbed it Bert stared at the rug. It was a decision he would somehow have to reverse. No one who aspired to be appointed PC could afford to leave Priestly alone with the mayor all afternoon. Not to be seen at graveside by the mayor, by the other officials, and especially by the press, could be equally disastrous.

"Chief Sternhagen going?" inquired Bert. Since Sternhagen was in the running for the PC's job as well, he would feel exactly as Bert did.

"I told Chief Sternhagen exactly what I've just told you."

"And his reaction, Commissioner?"

"I gave him his orders as I've given you yours."

"I'm sure Chief Sternhagen feels he should be at graveside."

"What he feels is immaterial."

"Just as I do."

"You have duties here. I suggest you see to them."

"I'm afraid the family expects me to be with them at the graveside."

"Your name was not listed on the charter."

"So they made an oversight, what do you expect. They're half blind with grief over there."

"The family does not expect you," said Priestly, but he looked less sure of himself than before.

"I'm afraid I have to be there, Commissioner," Bert said. "Not as chief of detectives but as a friend of the family." Bert realized he didn't even know the names of Mary Alice's two sons.

"The department won't pay for it," said the first dep lamely.

Bert shrugged and left him.

In a sour mood he stepped into the elevator and descended to the rotunda again. Mary Alice's position had not changed. She stood in her black dress at the head of the bier and the public filed past, in one door and out the other. To people who spoke to her she gave a half smile. "Thank you for coming," she said. She kept saying it, the half smile firmly in place. Otherwise she did not seem to move a muscle.

Bert watched this for a time. He did not understand why people who had not even known Harry should want to walk past his coffin. They used to stage this scene in communist

Russia every time a party dignitary died, the coffin open, the corpse rosy cheeked. Bert had seen it on news broadcasts. But this coffin was closed, nothing had been staged, and the lines outside in the cold were as long now as they had been earlier.

Nor did he know why Mary Alice felt obliged to stand there acknowledging this lugubrious tribute to her late husband. She did not seem grief stricken to him, although he was not sure what her grief ought to look like. In the past he had several times gone from murder scenes to the victim's home to notify next of kin. He had seen widows who screamed and would not stop. He had seen women literally pull out their hair. Scenes that a young cop never forgot. But Mary Alice had been composed from the start and was still composed. There had never been any wailing or even weeping, and there were no tears or sighs today, just the sad little smile and the fixed position at the coffin that she would not quit.

What kept her there? Loyalty to Harry? Some obscure guilt she was trying to work off? Was she perhaps only playing a role? The supreme role of her life so far: bereaved widow. But he dismissed this idea.

Finally he stepped to her side and when she failed to acknowledge him he touched her shoulder. "You need a break, Mary Alice."

She gave him the same sad half smile she gave everyone. "I'm all right, Bert."

"It's lunchtime." He looked at his watch. "Actually it's past lunchtime. Let me take you to lunch."

"I can't leave Harry."

Even her sons had departed by now. "He won't mind if you leave him long enough to grab a bite to eat."

This time her smile was broader, a real smile, not the sad one. "You don't know Harry," she said. Her smile turned into what was almost a grin.

Bert was obliged to go off to lunch by himself, where he sat alone in a restaurant and wondered what that smile—that grin or rictus or whatever it was—might have signified.

He had left his alternate driver, a detective named Vince Powell, in the car to monitor the radio, and now as he sipped an espresso Vince came in to say there had been a double homicide, and he gave the address, which was nearby. "It just came over the radio, Chief."

Bert liked to stay close to cases that might attract attention, as double homicides sometimes did, so he finished his coffee, paid his check, and had himself driven there.

He saw at once that it was nothing. The bodies lay in an alley, a man and a woman. He had to squeeze past a car to get to them. A number of uniforms and detectives were standing around, and a small crowd had collected at the entrance to the alley and was trying to peer around the car. The medical examiner had not yet arrived. The dead man lay facedown with a gun in his hand. His back pocket had been pulled out and one of the detectives handed Bert his wallet.

He read the driver's license: Hector Rodriguez. Hector had been thirty-eight years old.

"Who's the woman?"

"His wife," said another detective, and he handed over the woman's handbag. "It was on the seat of the car, Chief."

"Who owns the car?"

"The dead guy, Chief. We checked it out."

"Murder-suicide?" Bert gazed down on the driver's license of Juana Rodriguez and tried to match the photo to the face on the corpse.

"Looks like it, Chief."

Another ghetto tragedy. What had gone so wrong in the lives of these two people? Would the detectives ever learn the answer? Probably not. They were too busy to ask why Rodriguez had shot his wife and then himself—they didn't have the time, and ultimately they didn't care what the answer might be. Having seen too many similar cases, they were no longer that curious. The Rodriguez case was solved. The perpetrator was dead on the ground there, they didn't need to know anything more about him, and they would close the case as quickly as possible. The file would go into a drawer and that would be the end of it.

Bert's attention was drawn to the dead couple's car, which was old and half rusted out. There were bags of groceries on the backseat, so he opened the door and peered into them. At the bottom of both bags he noted gallon containers of milk.

"There are kids involved here," he said to the detectives. "They've left them alone somewhere. Find the kids."

"How do you know, Chief?"

"Nobody buys milk by the gallon except for kids," muttered Bert. "When you find the kids call me up and tell me, so I don't have to worry about them anymore." He turned and left the alley, pushing out through the crowd to his car. Vince Powell was still seated behind the wheel. He hadn't been curious enough even to get out and look at the results of a fellow human being's ultimate act of despair.

"Where to, Chief?" said Detective Powell.

But another call came over the radio: a teacher shot in a high school in the Ninth Precinct.

Bert was in no hurry to return to headquarters, which for him was heavy with the presence of Harry Chapman's corpse and Mary Alice's lonely vigil. He was in no mood for more unpleasant meetings with the first dep either. "Turn around," he ordered Detective Powell. "Let's see what that is."

Another crowd to push through, this one composed mostly of silent, staring teenagers. More cops and detectives standing around. The body was lying half covered by newspapers on the gymnasium floor. Protruding were one outflung arm and two worn sneakers. Also the top of a head of graying hair.

The dead man was the gym teacher, the detectives told Bert, shot by a fifteen-year-old boy. The gym teacher was white, and the kid who killed him was black. At present the killer was in the principal's office being grilled by other detectives.

Bert went in there. He watched the detectives question the kid. Surly little bastard, and either a mental defective or close to it. Claimed the gym teacher had insulted him. "When I put some holes in him, he found out who was who."

There had been about fifty witnesses, most of whom were other kids. The detectives in the gym had their names, and now they had a confession that the lawyers might or might not get thrown out of court later. Nonetheless, as far as the police were concerned, the case was closed. Bert left the school.

This was not the first teacher killed this year by a gun-toting juvenile for a real or imagined insult, and most probably it would not be the last. Bert got into his car, and Powell steered it into the downtown traffic.

"Three violent deaths already today in this one little corner of Manhattan," muttered Bert.

"It happens, Chief," commented Detective Powell.

Bert looked out the window. "My poor city. My poor country." And then a little later: "What has happened to us all, to the world?"

"Excuse me, Chief?"

"Never mind."

Without any other detours, they drove back to headquarters.

Bert rode up in the elevator, and as he walked through his anteroom, Inspector Potter got up and followed him into his office.

Seeing him, Bert carefully closed the door, hung his coat and muffler in the closet, sat down, and Potter handed across what looked like a long printout.

"The PC came back from Washington on Delta's nine-thirty shuttle Sunday night," Potter said. "You got the passenger list there. I didn't recognize any of the other names, but you may. His driver was not asked to meet him at the airport and did not do so, meaning either that somebody else meet him or he took a cab."

Bert was scanning the passenger list.

"It seems strange, doesn't it?" said Potter, who was reading over his shoulder. "I mean, Commissioner Chapman was a guy liked to ride to airports with motorcycle escorts."

Bert looked up from the lists. Everyone had heard about Harry and his motorcycle escorts.

"He phoned operations as soon as he landed," Potter said. "They have a record of it. He asked if anything was happening and said he would be on his beeper if needed."

Bert said nothing.

"If he took a cab," said Potter, "it doesn't make sense. Even forgetting the motorcycle escorts. I mean, it's a thirty-dollar cab ride from the airport to midtown, sometimes there aren't even any cabs there, and the city provides him a car, for crissake. Besides which, when he's been out of touch that long, you'd think he'd want to get back on the radio as soon as possible."

Bert looked at him.

"Unless—" Potter said, and waited for the response from Bert that should have been automatic.

But a good detective made it a point of avoiding automatic responses.

"—Unless," Potter continued, "he didn't want anyone to know where he was going."

Bert remained silent.

"Someone he didn't want to be seen with?" suggested Potter.

Bert still did not speak.

"A woman, maybe?" said Potter.

"I could think of a lot of people he would not want to be seen with. There are two lists here."

"Right, Chief. The other one is from the four-thirty shuttle to Washington Friday afternoon. That's when he went down there, you'll notice. He was out of touch with the department more than forty-eight hours."

"Yeah, well, he got away with that part of it, didn't he?"

"We ought to check the cab companies, see if a driver remembers him, can tell us where he took him."

Of course this was what should be done, but there were dozens of cab companies, and hundreds more independent drivers. Bert did not have enough detectives on hand to do it. John Kincaid had all the detectives, and if Bert told him to check the cab companies, he would have to tell him why, at which point Bert himself would no longer control this part of the case.

"It'll take ten, fifteen detectives," Potter said. "I can get them from Chief Kincaid. Unless you want me to use men out of this office. But I'd have to strip all the desks."

"No," Bert said.

"No?"

"Forget the cab companies."

"I don't understand, Chief."

"You don't have to understand."

Potter's eyes dropped and his face got red. As a man rose in rank in the NYPD fewer and fewer men could say such things to him.

But Potter was stubborn. "Are we running an independent investigation here, or what?"

"No," Bert replied. "We're just trying to straighten this thing out quietly, at least until the PC is in the ground. Is that clear?"

"Perfectly."

When Potter had gone out, Bert telephoned Delta and asked for the security chief, Bronfman. He and Bronfman, who had once been chief of police in Atlanta, sometimes shared information, sometimes did each other favors. Now Bert asked him to assemble the cabin crews from the two shuttle flights, and he gave the flight numbers. He wanted the two crews kept separate, and he wanted to talk to the individuals one at a time in private.

"At your shop, Chief?" Bronfman asked.

"I'll come out to La Guardia," Bert decided.

"May I ask where your investigation is going, Chief? I mean, if it involves us—"

This time Bert was more polite. "I'll have to keep that confidential, I'm afraid, at least for the time being."

After a momentary silence, Bronfman said: "I won't be able to assemble them all today. Tomorrow is possible, though."

"I've got a funeral tomorrow. It will have to be the day after."

A time was decided upon, and Bert rang off.

A pile of DD-5s, faxed down from John Kincaid, waited on his desk. He went through them carefully. Kincaid had sent detectives into about thirty hotels by now, and also into the building department archives looking for Harry's name on a deed. Obviously Kincaid believed Harry had started his run close to the site of his death—which of course he had.

No one could say Kincaid didn't know his job.

A number of the DD-5s, Bert saw, related to tips from the public. Dozens must have been logged in by now, and he read the reports of those that had been investigated so far. One had led to two drug arrests, another to the arrest of a Harlem man on a gun charge, crimes that had nothing to do with Harry Chapman. Well, that always happened. Announce a special phone number and people would call up to report all sorts of suspicious activity. Detectives followed up on every call. Criminals were falling into the police web almost by accident.

Near the bottom of the pile Bert came to a report that made him reach suddenly for the telephone and dial Kincaid's number. A ten-year-old boy on a bicycle had delivered a note to the 41st Precinct in the Bronx. The note took credit for the assassination of Police Commissioner Harry Chapman in the name of a group calling itself Freedom Fighters for Puerto Rico. The boy had been interrogated at length, and the note had been hand-carried to the fingerprint lab.

When Kincaid came on the line Bert demanded details.

They had grilled the kid two hours, had him in tears most of the time, Bert gathered. A man had given him a dollar to deliver the note.

"Other than that," said Kincaid, "the kid knew nothing."

At present Kincaid had men all over the Four-One precinct trying to learn more, he said. In the meantime the lab had called to say the note bore the left thumbprint of a man named Jesus Villa Lopez. According to the intelligence division, a so-called Freedom Fighters for Puerto Rico group did exist, and Villa Lopez was supposedly its leader. He was a violent radical who had been arrested as part of a plot to bomb Madison Square Garden but was currently out on bail.

So the note was perhaps genuine.

Kincaid had sent out more men to arrest as many members of the group as could be found, he said.

"All right," said Bert. "Just keep it away from the press."

"How long?"

"Until we have something hard. I shouldn't have to tell you that."

Bert might have spoken longer but a man named Jim Flynn was standing in his doorway waving to him, so he hung up.

Flynn was from management and budget. He sat down beside Bert's desk, and for most of the next two hours they argued about money. Bert wanted more detectives. There's no money, said Flynn. Especially Bert wanted more first-grade detectives. No additional first grades, said Flynn.

"We've got to find a way to reward the best guys," insisted Bert. "There has to be some incentive for detectives who really put out."

"Then give up something else," said Flynn.

For paying informants Bert wanted more money as well. The FBI and the DEA were outspending the department, he told Flynn, who was surprised to hear this.

"By informants you mean criminals?"

"Most informants are criminals," Bert conceded. "Federal agencies are able to offer their best informants two or three times as much as we can. As a result the best informants will work only for the Feds."

"You'll have to take that one to the PC," Flynn said.

"Hard to do at the moment," said Bert dryly.

"Take it to the mayor then," said Flynn. "If he says give you the money, I'll give it to you."

"I don't think I can go to the mayor right now."

"Why not?"

"It's a sensitive time."

Flynn shrugged. "I can't give it to you unless he says so." Flynn left.

With a sigh Bert turned to his phone messages.

Then came the regularly scheduled monthly meeting of his detective borough commanders—he had forgotten to cancel it. Six men were ushered into his office, for the department had broken the city down into seven boroughs, not five. Missing was Kincaid, who was busy elsewhere, as they all knew. The meeting was supposed to work on manpower allocation, the spreading of too few detectives ever more thinly, but all anyone wanted to talk about was the PC's murder. Hypotheses were offered, suggestions as to which directions the investigation ought to take, and little other work got done.

Outside the windows darkness fell. Lights came on across the way. By the time Bert left his office the corridors were silent. There were duty sergeants in some of the offices, no one in most of them. Descending to the rotunda, he found that the big doors had been locked. The lines were gone. Even Mary Alice was gone. The bier under its flag waited in silence for whatever tomorrow would bring.

As he stood a moment at the coffin Bert too was waiting. Waiting for the funeral of course, same as everyone, waiting to talk to Mary Alice too, and most of all waiting for the mayor to decide—would he take the whole ten days, or decide quickly?

He went home to dinner with his wife. She served lamb chops, frozen peas, and rice, and he poured himself a bottle of beer. They sat at the same table but ate mostly in silence while Bert mulled over what she had said at breakfast—it had raised a question in his mind that had bothered him off and on all day.

This question he wished to put to her now, but how was he to phrase it? If he phrased it wrong she would not answer. Ask her outright and she would say angrily: "Just what are you insinuating?"

She wore a white blouse pulled taut across her rather big bosom. She had big blue eyes set wide apart in what he had always thought of as an honest face, and he studied her. He could not see her legs under the table, but they were nice legs. Her tummy was still flat. Of course she had never had children, which she regretted; he did too. She was thirty-nine years old, the same age as Mary Alice Chapman. He remembered the first night he ever met her, Harry's date, sitting across the table from her at the Rainbow Room. He could not remember what they had said to each other—he had been too concerned about the way Harry was monopolizing Mary Alice. Anyway, he did not see Madge again until a year or so later, when he had met her at someone's house. After three months they had got married. They had been married seventeen years, and some of them had been good ones.

He had decided to lead up to what he wanted to know by asking: "What makes you think a woman killed Harry?"

"Did I say a woman killed Harry? I don't think I did."

"You said to me: look for a woman." He was hoping that when he came to the question on his mind she would be in a mood to answer.

"It seemed like a good idea."

"Why?"

"I used to know him, you know."

"Yes, I remember." But how well had she known him? This was what he wanted to know. He wanted the details.

Admit it, he told himself, you've been nagged by jealousy all day.

She laughed. "I could well imagine a woman wanting to kill him. For a few days back then I could have killed him myself."

"I had the impression you only went out with him one or two times."

"No. It was more serious than that."

"How long then?"

"About four months."

"So why did you want to kill him?"

They sat in their dining room having dinner together as they did almost every night. Nonetheless, for the moment she seemed to have receded from him and from this room. She was somewhere else with someone else in another time, and talking almost to herself. "Harry had a way of making you think you were the most fabulous girl in the world."

She stopped, and Bert prodded her. "Go on."

"It wasn't that he just piled on the flattery. The flattery was only occasional, and only for something you thought you deserved. He had very keen instincts in that respect."

"He made you feel fabulous," Bert prodded.

"Fabulous? No, not exactly. But when we were together he focused on me and only on me. What I thought, what I felt, what I liked. Everything he did or said was to please me, as if he enjoyed me more than any girl he had ever met, and it lasted right up to that double date we had with you and Mary Alice."

"He danced with her a lot that night," said Bert.

"He told me on the way home that he danced with her only to find out about you. He said they talked about you the whole time."

"Interesting," said Bert.

"But they didn't. I knew that right away."

"He lied to you," said Bert, to keep her talking.

"I was very young, but he was too. He lied whenever it suited him, but I didn't realize that at the time. He gave the impression of being naive, and so up until that night I believed everything he told me. I believed him absolutely."

After a pause she said: "Harry wasn't naive at all. I was

the one who was naive. Harry always knew exactly what he wanted, and at the end of four months he wanted another girl, and he dropped me. He just dropped me."

This was the aspect most painful to her, but the one most painful to Bert was something else.

"And the sex," Bert probed.

"He made me feel like the sexiest girl anybody ever saw."

They nodded at each other. Bert thought he saw moisture in his wife's eyes, and he deliberated asking the key question. Finally he asked it.

"Did you fuck him?" There, it was out.

"Yes."

"A lot?"

"A lot," she conceded.

For a moment, despite himself, Bert could not speak. "You never told me."

She looked at him sharply. "All you ever asked me was how many men, not who. And I didn't answer that question either, as I recall."

Bert studied the food he was no longer eating, and said nothing.

Madge's gaze dropped to her lap, and a half smile came onto her face. "In bed he couldn't get enough of me. That was part of what made me feel so special."

Bert said nothing.

"He made me feel terrifically attractive. That I could provoke him to that extent."

"Was that your first love affair?"

"Yes."

Bert realized he was torturing himself, but he could not stop. "Those were the days before easy sex," he heard himself say. "So where did you used to go?"

Madge shook her head. He noted that the half smile had left her mouth. Nonetheless, her eyes did not come up.

"Where?"

"I don't remember."

"I'm curious."

"Anywhere we could," she said.

He could feel his emotions moving across his face. "Like where?"

"The back of cars."

"Where else?"

"A field one time." She had begun watching him closely. Bert supposed she could see the jealousy that he felt so strongly, and seemed unable to smother, though he was trying hard, the questions that he did not seem able to stop asking. She had answered with some reluctance, but she had answered, and it was she who had brought the subject up in the first place. So perhaps the reluctance was a sham. She had stuck the knife in and was twisting it. Lately they had not been getting along, and whether she did this to hurt him or to make him appreciate her more, he could not decide.

She said: "And then he met Mary Alice and dropped me."

After a moment Bert was able to say: "He had met her already. There was this robbery."

"From one day to the next he dropped me. I didn't know it was over between us. He never told me so. He had me calling him up, beseeching him to meet me. He kept putting me off. He was always nice about it, always charming. I couldn't believe he didn't want to see me again. But finally I got the idea. That was when I wanted to kill him."

"This thing is getting very incestuous, isn't it?" Bert said. Working hard at controlling what he felt, what he might say next, he took a deep breath. "Mary Alice and me, Mary Alice and Harry," said Bert. "You and Harry, you and me."

"You're jealous," said Madge, watching him.

"Of course I'm not jealous," said Bert. "It was long ago. I mean, what do you take me for?"

"I met another girl about that time," Madge said. "Harry had done the same thing to her. It was the way he dealt with women, apparently. It turned out that her time and my time overlapped slightly, as my time overlapped with Mary Alice's."

Bert moved food around his plate.

"Was he faithful to Mary Alice?" Madge asked.

"How do I know if he was faithful to Mary Alice?"

"Probably not," said Madge. "Men like that don't change, and later on he got to be so high and mighty he could get any woman he wanted, I imagine. If he was still dealing with them the way he dealt with me, then I wouldn't be surprised if one of them up and killed him."

"Well," said Bert, "it's possible, I guess."

Presently he asked her: "Are you going to the funeral?"

"I don't think so, no."

"If you were that intimate with him, I should think you would want to go."

"I don't feel I owe him attendance at his funeral," she said. "No thank you."

In their bedroom she put her nightdress on, turned back the bed, then walked over and took his hand. "I shouldn't have told you any of that," she said.

"No, it's perfectly all right."

"I'm sorry."

"Nothing to be sorry about."

"I've caused you pain."

"You didn't cause me pain."

He went into the bathroom and Madge, barefoot, came and stood in her nightdress in the doorway, watching him brush his teeth.

"It's just that—" she said.

"Just what?" He had finished and put the toothbrush away.

"You've been so cold to me lately, so distant." Her arms came around him and she buried her face in his neck. "I guess that's why I told you. I was feeling a bit desperate. I wanted to see if I could still make you jealous. If you cared enough to be jealous." And then she added almost humbly, "If you got jealous, I thought it might prove you still loved me."

"I love you," said Bert. "It's late. Let's get to bed."

He got in on his side and turned out the light, but two hours later was still awake. His wife, who lay six inches away in the dark, presumably slept easily. His mind was churning, his stomach too, while Madge perhaps dreamed pleasant dreams. What she had told him about herself with Harry was entirely too vivid. He could not comprehend it, or else comprehended it too well. Harry had put him through this once already with Mary Alice, and the jealousy that had nagged at him only sporadically during the day consumed him now, and he did not see what he could do about it.

* * *

The funeral. Fifth Avenue was closed off for the event, and it was an event, the police department's proudest production, the so-called Inspector's Funeral.

Nearly all cops killed in the line of duty were patrolmen or detectives. Even sergeants were killed rarely, and men of higher rank worked in offices, and were not killed at all. Patrolmen and detectives were usually very young men with young families, who lived in tract houses in suburbs fifty or more miles out of the city. When they became slain heroes their funerals took place in those distant suburbs, the cortege sometimes wending with infinite slowness through their entire town. It was led by the department's bagpipe band in kilts, marching slowly and blowing dirges to match the mournful occasion, and by motorcycle cops moving so slowly in front of the hearse that the men could barely hold their machines upright. In front of the small church waited thousands of cops representing departments from miles around, and as the coffin was lifted onto shoulders and carried up the steps the thousands of white gloves at once snapped into a salute.

Harry Chapman's funeral differed from these others only in its location—crowded midtown, the cathedral—and in the impressive number of civic, state, and national dignitaries who crowded into the pews, so many that Bert found himself fifteen rows back from the altar, with much of the rest of the police hierarchy extending even farther back than that. More than half the pews were taken up by cops in blue uniforms who sat primly upright, white gloves on their knees, the other thousands of their fellows having remained in place in ranks outside on Fifth Avenue. The mass began. Bishops milled around the altar. The cardinal in his homily pretended to have known Harry far more intimately than he had. The mayor, who climbed up into the pulpit as the cardinal was climbing down, read a speech: he said Harry had been a devoted servant of his fellow man, the highest type of human being, his death a tragedy for all. The police department bugler blew taps.

Bert's car was among the scores that clogged all the nearby streets. It took him a while to find it. Because the burial at Arlington would not start until four P.M. he went back to his office, where he worked for a time, before being driven out to La Guardia and boarding the shuttle to Washington. At that very hour at the other end of the airport Harry's coffin was being loaded onto the charter, and his family, the mayor and his entourage (which included the first dep), plus those dignitaries returning to Washington had begun to board. But Bert was on this plane, not that one, and he was worried about it.

Just before the door closed Chief Sternhagen in civilian clothes ducked into the aircraft. Bert watched him come down the aisle.

There happened to be an empty seat beside Bert, and he patted it. "The department picking up the price of your ticket, Chief?" he said, and he grinned.

Sternhagen, as he sat down, was mouthing imprecations under his breath. They were directed against First Deputy Commissioner Priestly, and Bert heard them well enough. "What's that, Chief?" he inquired. "I didn't quite catch what you said."

Sternhagen muttered that it was outrageous.

"What's outrageous, Chief?"

It made Sternhagen begin to sputter. As the highest-ranking uniformed officer, he said, his place was in the other plane with the coffin: "Besides which, I was once his commanding officer, for God's sake."

"Priestly may have made one helluva mistake cutting you out like that," agreed Bert. "I mean, if you're the next PC, he's out on his ass, wouldn't you say?"

"I know who my enemies are," said Sternhagen grimly.

The chief of the department was fifty-seven years old, a big man, gone heavy. He had pale blue eyes and a full head of gray hair that he wore parted in the middle. As a sergeant he had worked with juveniles in the community affairs division, then had gone to the 19th Precinct as desk lieutenant. He had had a desk lieutenant's mentality then, and still did, Bert believed. After serving as commander of the 20th Precinct as a captain, he had gone to the personnel bureau in headquarters, and had never left headquarters after that. To Sternhagen the traditional way was the best way. To get ahead you did perfect paperwork and protected your ass. You put in your time in grade, you studied hard for the exams, did well in them, and got promoted regularly.

In temperament Sternhagen was a volatile man. He sometimes told off subordinates, and used strong language to do it. When he laughed it was usually at the expense of someone. Otherwise he smiled only rarely.

He was rather too easy now to twit.

"So why would he do that, Chief, do you think? Take a chance on insulting you to that extent?"

Instead of responding, Sternhagen only scowled.

"Unless," said Bert, "the job is already his. You think that's it, Chief?"

"Ridiculous," said Sternhagen. But the question had hit home, and for a moment he looked shaken.

"Ridiculous?" said Bert, still twitting him. "I don't know. Maybe not."

"I have friends who are close to the mayor," insisted Sternhagen. "They assure me that no decision has been made. These same friends tell me I have the inside track."

"Say, that's terrific," said Bert. "Who are these friends?"

"I am not at liberty to say."

"But they're close to the mayor?"

"Very close."

Bert was barely repressing his amusement. "I wish I had friends like that."

"Yes."

"What do they say about the first dep?"

"No chance."

"Are there any other candidates?"

"No."

Bert continued with his questions, and by the time the seat belt sign came on, he was satisfied that Sternhagen knew no more about the mayor's intentions than he did himself.

With the plane descending, the chief of detectives leaned toward the porthole. Washington began to spread out below, and he thought of how easy it had been to agitate Sternhagen, and about how nerved up all of them were, himself included, over the possibility of being named the next commissioner.

As the plane came in low over the river, the cemetery at Arlington passed by under the wings, and Bert's thoughts went suddenly from his own future to the deep open hole that waited down there to receive the body of the late Harry

Chapman. One minute you're on top of the world, he reflected, and the next you're under six feet of dirt—not an original thought by any means, but possibly the most profound one any man ever tried to comprehend. To Sternhagen beside him, Bert said soberly: "The last time I took this flight Harry Chapman was sitting where you're sitting now."

"This time," Sternhagen commented, "he's making the trip in a box."

■9■

AT THE TERMINAL at La Guardia the police commissioner's motorcycle escort peeled off. With airline security people pointing the way, Commissioner Chapman's official car was driven through a gate, under part of the terminal building, through another gate, and out onto the tarmac directly to the airliner. There were two hundred people waiting to board this flight, the noon shuttle to Washington, but they were still milling around inside the terminal, and would be kept waiting for some time longer.

When the car came to a stop at the foot of the boarding stairs Chapman remained inside until his driver, a detective sergeant, had jumped out and come around to hold open the door.

Chief of Detectives Bert P. Farber, who had got out the car's other door without help from the sergeant or anyone else, had watched this scene—this succession of scenes—and the expression on his face was either inscrutable or bemused, depending on how well you knew him.

Commissioner Chapman stood beside the car glancing around, though there were no spectators to admire the magnificence of his arrival. He was almost preening, Bert thought.

During Bert's twenty-three years as a New York cop, nine different men had served as police commissioner, not one of whom had resembled what Harry Chapman was turning out to be.

"Thanks, Jack, 'preciate it," said the PC to the sergeant, and he bounded up the steps and ducked into the plane.

Except for the crew, it would still be empty inside.

Like an old-world footman, like a native gun bearer perhaps, Jack ran up the steps behind his master carrying the royal luggage, which was an attaché case. One of the stewardesses came out onto the landing to relieve him of it.

Small things. The chief of detectives was trying to notice all of them, trying to fathom the new PC. This was Harry Chapman, after all, with whom he had once shared a radio car. He had thought he knew him well, but was discovering that he didn't. He had imagined him to be a friend, but Harry had given no recognition that any friendship had ever existed between them, which left Bert, at the moment, thoroughly confused.

He had watched Harry take control of the department quickly and forcefully, which was good, but mostly Harry had done it in two specific ways that were not so good. First of all he had fired almost the entire police hierarchy, and he had done it brutally, called men in, told them he needed the vacancy, and demanded their resignations by nightfall. He was a man in a hurry. Career commanders in their fifties were given no time to get used to the idea, no time possibly to find some other job, were simply told to clear out. Some of them tried to bring political pressure to bear on Harry. He ignored it. When one assistant chief defied him, he reduced the man on the spot to his civil service rank of captain, and that captain, assigned by Harry to a backwater job under men ten years his junior, was still serving.

To the vacancies thus produced Harry appointed men closer to his own age, and some of these younger men were not in the normal line of succession. One such was Bert, only a deputy chief and executive officer of Brooklyn South detectives, who was jumped to three-star rank over the heads of others and made chief of detectives. Another was Earl Coxen, Harry's other ex-partner, jumped from inspector to two-star rank and given command of Brooklyn North patrol forces. Harry had called in six officers that day. They had stood in front of Teddy Roosevelt's desk, Harry's desk now, and he had promoted them simultaneously, and although he had a smile and warm handshake for all six, there had been nothing special for Bert. Nor for Coxen either, in fact. An outsider would have imagined that he knew them no better than any of the others.

All these firings and hirings made headlines, which presumably was what Harry wanted.

His second method of taking control was to lay on imperial trappings for himself such as no previous PC had dared. For instance, whenever he moved through the streets on official business, motorcycle outriders escorted his car. This too made headlines.

In a matter of weeks, unlike his predeccessors, Harry had become a personage known citywide, known by all. The mayor himself did not travel with motorcycle escorts, and if he had to fly he mingled with the passengers in the boarding lounge, shaking hands. Mayors, it seemed to Bert, did not like to be outshone by people they had appointed. They did not take kindly to subordinates who reared up like rivals. Previous PCs had always played God within the department, but outside it they had tended to make themselves inconspicuous. They were in direct command of thirty thousand armed men, after all, and the city did not like to be reminded of this fact. PCs served at the pleasure of the mayor—call it the whim of the mayor—and according to law could be dismissed at any time without explanation. This included Harry. So his conduct was risky, to say the least, and Bert wondered if he might have grown into one of those men who loved risk, who went looking for risk. If so, what did this mean and where would it lead?

Jack, the detective sergeant, had come back down the boarding stairs to the car, and Bert handed him his gun in its clip-on holster, saying: "Take care of this for me," for that was the deal with the airline security people: no guns on board. When the PC had decided that he wanted special boarding privileges from the airline it was his chief of detectives who had had to arrange it for him. It hadn't been that easy for Bert to do, and one of the conditions was no guns.

He didn't know if Harry, already on board, was armed or not, and he felt so estranged from him that he didn't see how he could ask him.

The detective sergeant in turn handed over the heavy briefing books, and it became Bert's job to carry them onto the plane. They were the PC's books, not his own, and as he carried them up the steps and ducked in through the door he felt a bit like an old-world servant himself.

As he had expected, the flight attendants were clustered more or less closely around the PC. The handshaking had already been concluded apparently. One of the pilots was there too, though he soon broke off and went forward. Bert dropped into a front-row seat and peered out the porthole.

Almost as soon as Harry had sat down beside him, one of the women came from the galley with a tray.

"Coffee, Commissioner?" she offered. "Tea?"

She was about twenty-five, and not dumpy like the professional stewardesses the airlines seemed to favor these days. She resembled instead the girls who had had the job when Bert was a young man. She had moist lips that made her look sensuous, which perhaps she was, but lovely eyes that made her look chaste, in the old sense of the term, which these days surely she was not. She poured coffee for the PC, and was all smiles doing it. "And you, sir?" she said to Bert.

He and the PC were still sipping as the passengers filed on board, glancing at them curiously as they passed.

In the air Bert supposed Harry would either study the briefing books or ask questions about the detective division—probably both. After that he could be expected to relax. Inevitably they would talk of old times. The old intimacy would return.

But something quite different happened. For a while, closed in on his own thoughts, Harry Chapman stared at his hands. After that he lay back with his eyes shut, either brooding or dozing. No way to tell which. Bert had counted on this trip, for it had seemed the best chance he would get to find out if they were still friends or, from now on, business associates only. They would spend the whole day together, possibly eat dinner together.

At the very least he would get to observe his new boss close up—what exactly did Harry want from his top subordinates? From his chief of detectives? What did Harry mean to

do with the department, and with Bert himself, now that the
bloodbath was presumably over?

The Washington PD met the plane with a car and two
motorcycles. Bert had been obliged to arrange this too, though
surely the PC or his secretary could have done it. It had
annoyed Bert to have to phone the chief of the Washington
PD. A lot of people owed Bert favors, and he liked having
these favors out there. He hated to have to call one in for
something frivolous, and a motorcycle escort, to Bert, was
certainly frivolous.

With Bert sitting beside him and Harry saying nothing, this
particular escort sped them to the Senate office building in
under twenty minutes. There were no sirens, but they arrived
with about as much ceremony as most visiting heads of state,
if anyone was watching. Quite a few were, as it happened.
Tourists just standing there. Maybe a senator entering or leaving—Bert wouldn't have recognized many of them. Harry
got out of the car and Bert noted that he stood on the sidewalk
in the warm November afternoon pulling down on the hem
of his suit coat, probably waiting until someone recognized
him, and his name started around. Probably he wanted a
description of his arrival to make its way inside the building,
thereby impressing the senators before whom he was about
to testify. The reporters, when they heard, might not use it
in their pieces, but they would be impressed also. Despite
themselves, probably. Reporters, Bert had found, were not
nearly as blasé as they pretended.

If you wished to move onward and upward in the world,
obviously you had to impress people. It was clear that Police
Commissioner Chapman believed this, and Bert did too, up
to a point. Until they remembered your name not much else
was possible. But Bert liked to believe that at this high level
what counted was performance, whereas Harry, to judge by
the way he had behaved since becoming PC, seemed to believe
that self-promotion, which was only froth, counted for just
as much, very often more, possibly because people could
never understand what was keeping the froth up there. They
were waiting for it to collapse. Harry seemed to be trying to
reach deep into people's psyches to touch emotions—call
it areas of respect—they scarcely understood. Respect for

motorcycle escorts, for instance. Bert thought this was over-kill, and that if Harry didn't give it up fairly soon it would destroy him.

In the hearing room they took their places at the big table, Harry in front of the microphones, Bert beside him holding in his lap the briefing books that four men had worked on all week, and that Harry had not yet so much as glanced at. The television lights came on. When Bert glanced around he saw that crews from all the networks were represented, alerted no doubt by Harry's office. If Harry said anything noteworthy, and Bert had no idea what he intended to say, he would be on the national newcasts tonight. CNN had cameras in place as well, Bert noted, and they usually televised live, he believed.

This was the Senate Judiciary Committee, and the subject of the hearings was organized crime in America's major cities. Commissioner Chapman, as head of the country's largest law enforcement agency, was to be the first witness.

Senator Davidson, Democrat from Illinois, rapped his gavel for order, and in the ensuing silence asked if Harry wished to make a brief opening statement. Harry said he did, and he removed some folded pages from his inside coat pocket.

"Ready, Bert?" he whispered teasingly into Bert's ear. "Then here we go." And he leaned forward into the micro-phones and began by touching all the right nerve endings. He thanked Davidson; he thanked the committee. It seemed to amuse him then to introduce Chief of Detectives Bert P. Farber. He knew, and Bert also knew, how many noses this would put out of joint back in headquarters: Priestly, Sternha-gen, all of them. Why was Harry doing this? Why had he chosen to place Bert in the limelight in Washington, and not one of them?

To the senators Harry described Bert as "enormously com-petent," which was nice, but then he leaned over and whis-pered: "Wave to the camera, Bert."

The microphones picked this up and the roomful of people laughed. Greatly annoyed, Bert scowled at the tabletop, to which Harry responded with a broad grin.

Bert was astonished by what came next.

"You senators," said Harry into the microphones, "are

here to investigate organized crime, which to you means the Mafia, which to the whole country in fact means the Mafia, and supposedly your object is to write new and stronger legislation against this Mafia, and I am here to tell you that the Mafia is in disarray in all our cities, it is fragmented and falling apart. Those laws that already exist are strong enough. The focus of this committee is dead wrong. You are ten years out of date."

It was an astounding beginning, a police commissioner criticizing and disparaging a Senate committee in public at the very moment its highly publicized hearings got under way. The room was buzzing, the cameras were turning, the reporters were scribbling. The senators' faces had darkened, and their bodies had begun to squirm.

"I came here with briefing books prepared on the Mafia in New York. We are blessed with five Mafia families, as you know, four more than other cities. They are still out there, we have much work still to do, but we can handle them now by ourselves. Chief Farber, hand me those briefing books."

As surprised as everyone else in the room, but not showing it, he hoped, Bert passed them across, and Harry Chapman waved them in the air. "I'm not going to read to you from these books. I myself have not bothered to look into them. I'll leave them with you. You can study them if you like. But I would not consider that a worthwhile use of your time."

He paused and peered dramatically about, looking for an attendant of some kind. Finally one came forward. "Deliver these briefing books to Senator Davidson," he ordered.

While this was being done, he touched a few more nerve endings, but this time with praise. "The Mafia is in disarray because Chief Farber's detectives, and the FBI, and the DEA, working with the laws you men and women gave us, have all performed brilliantly. So have certain prosecutors." And here he named several, probably because, unlike most law enforcement officers, prosecutors were likely to have sponsors, and connections—in other words, constituencies. They were, after all, lawyers. For all of his bravura performance Harry Chapman was being careful about who he offended, and how much.

He continued: "Organized crime as it threatens New York

and other cities today has become something else completely, and if you wish me to talk about it, I will. But if your focus is to remain on the Mafia, then I cannot offer you anything of value and had best return to New York on the next shuttle and get back to work." And he stood up as if to leave the hearing room.

After swallowing hard, Senator Davidson leaned forward into his own microphone: "Please continue, Commissioner."

All those cameras were turning, and Bert glanced wildly around.

Having gauged the situation perfectly, or so he obviously imagined, Harry sat back down, and resumed speaking. "Organized crime today is becoming more and more fragmented, and the new groups are more unruly and therefore far more dangerous to the general population than the Mafia ever was. In New York we have black groups controlling the drug market in Harlem and Bedford-Stuyvesant, Dominican groups taking over parts of Washington Heights. We have Chinese organized crime operating in Chinatown and parts of Queens, Jamaican groups in Harlem, Russian groups in the Brighton Beach section of Brooklyn. All these groups are heavily armed. When riled they tend to spray whole neighborhoods with bullets, as I'm sure you have all read in your newspapers. We have had babies getting shot in carriages, old ladies getting shot as they peer out upstairs windows, teachers getting shot in school yards. This is organized crime today, and I do not see what broad legislation you could write that would help us against it."

Again Chapman paused dramatically. "—Except in one small corner of the law." And he stopped speaking altogether.

Davidson prompted him. "And that is, sir?"

"You can help us get these guns off the street," Harry said harshly. "You can enact meaningful gun control legislation. Why haven't you done it? You talk and talk and talk, and year after year you do nothing. Why? I demand to know why?"

Bert sat there in a state of amazement. Most of the police organizations were on Harry Chapman's side. New York City and State, which had the strongest gun control laws in the country, were certainly on his side, but the guns kept coming in by the truckload from unregulated states.

Most of the country was on Chapman's side, the polls said, but those same people might turn against him if he seemed to be attacking the United States Senate—which was what he was doing.

The risk to Harry's career, as Bert saw it, was beyond all imagining.

But in a low, intense voice Harry went even further. "I'll tell you why you do nothing. Because many of you are in the pay of the gun lobby, especially the National Rifle Association, that's why. Americans think the power of the NRA comes from its membership, several million members sending deluges of letters to Washington. But it isn't the letters from the gun fanatics that cause you to vote against sensible gun control laws, and a good many of you are not voting your consciences either, are you, gentlemen? You vote against gun control because the NRA gives you money. It buys your votes. Often it isn't even very much money, is it? Some members sell their votes for five thousand dollars a year. Others are expensive. One senator took two hundred thirty-five thousand from the gun lobby last year. The gun lobby calls this, and you call it, campaign contributions. Campaign contributions. Sure. If any of my cops got caught doing anything even remotely similar to this that you men do as a matter of course, they'd go to jail."

The hearing by now was in an uproar. Senator Davidson was banging his gavel for order. Shouting into his microphone so as to be heard over the noise, Harry Chapman said: "You, Senator Davidson, have never taken a nickel of this gun money. I wish the same could be said for all of your colleagues. As for what to do about organized crime as it exists in my city today, I suggest you pass some meaningful laws against the proliferation of the traffic in guns. Apart from that, I have nothing further to say to you, and ask now to be excused."

He stood up, gathered his papers, and turned from the table. Bert stood too, not knowing what else to do. Senator Davidson was rapping for order and calling into his microphone:

"Please sit down, sir. Please sit down."

Harry sat down. So did Bert.

"You have given us a dressing down, sir," said Davidson when he could at last be heard. "One that perhaps we needed. Please bear with us, if you would, as we have some questions to put to you."

That was when Bert knew that Harry was not going to be cited for contempt of Congress but would come away with a victory. It had been an immense gamble nonetheless.

An hour later the committee thanked Harry Chapman, he was excused, and the hearing recessed. A horde of people crowded around him, reporters mostly, but including Senator Davidson and one other senator as well, and Bert, who saw that the PC would be held there for at least another thirty minutes, went out of the building to see that the car was still out front.

The car and the two motorcycles were there and he spoke to the men.

When he went back inside he saw that Harry had made it only as far as the back of the hearing room, where he stood under hot lights giving a television interview. Others still waited to talk to him, but when the interview concluded he broke away momentarily and drew Bert aside.

"Something's come up, Bert, and I'm going to have to stay overnight. You go on home."

Bert waited, hoping for an explanation, but Harry said nothing more, merely returned to his fan club, or whatever it was. Bert nodded to his back, moving away from him.

The chief of detectives went out of the building. In the street he hailed a taxi, and ordered himself driven to the airport.

That was then. This was now. At Arlington National Cemetery Bert waited near the open grave. It was a nice afternoon, sunny, and for January almost warm. People were in topcoats. It had not snowed here, but the dirt beside the hole looked moist. The president of the United States stood about five paces off, holding the arm of Mary Alice Chapman, who appeared solemn but dry-eyed. Newsmen and photographers were scampering about among the nearby graves, trying for a better shot, a better view; the Secret Service men were trying to keep them back.

A Marine Corps guard fired a volley into the air. A Marine bugler played taps. The flag was removed from the coffin, folded, and handed to Mary Alice Chapman. The coffin was lowered into the ground.

■ 10 ■

KINCAID CALLED. "I still haven't received the autopsy report. Do you know anything about why?"

"Talk to the medical examiner, not me."

"Have you seen a copy?"

"No."

"I call up those people and can't get through."

"Who'd you ask for?"

"The Chinese guy, Wang, Fang, whatever his name is."

"Chang," said Bert. "He's Korean."

"He's either cutting some guy up downstairs, or he's out in the field bending over some gunshot victim who's still warm."

"Lot of murders in this city," said Bert.

"When I finally get him, he says it's not ready."

"Those serum reports take weeks sometimes."

"I don't care about serum reports in this particular case."

"But the ME's office does," said Bert.

"When I ask when will it be ready, guy acts like he doesn't speak English."

"I never had any trouble with him."

"I tried Dr. Klotz, but he's on vacation. Tomorrow I'll go by in person."

"You do that," said Bert. "What else? I'm busy."

"Chapman's office is still sealed by order of the first dep."

Bert was not thinking about this but about Chang. When Kincaid went by tomorrow, maybe he would be out again.

"My detectives have still not been permitted in there."

"I'll talk to the first dep."

Kincaid's frustration showed. "It's absolutely essential that we get in there," he said. His tone was accusatory. A confrontation with the first dep was required. Clearly, he didn't think Bert would be willing to risk one.

"I said I'll talk to him."

When he had hung up, Bert went up to the fourteenth floor. The men and women who worked in the PC's office were already at their desks in the various anterooms, he noted. That was their assignment, and so they continued to report for work each day, even though there was, by now, little to do. Mail addressed to the PC still poured in, and would continue to, most of it complaints, or tips on crimes, or else threats. It had to be rerouted, and Harry's phones answered, but that was all. As Bert entered most of the officers were sitting sideways at their desks sipping coffee, or reading the morning papers.

In a bureaucracy like the NYPD this was only to be expected; no one had taken command; no one had told them what else to do.

Inspector Martel, Harry Chapman's chief of staff, looked up from his desk outside Harry's door. "What can I do for you, Chief?"

Bert pointed. "I need to get in there," he said, and strode past him.

But Harry's handle did not turn and the door did not open.

"It's locked, Chief, sorry to say," said Martel.

"Open it, please."

"The first dep—"

"Open it."

"I can't, Chief. First dep's orders."

"I'm countermanding them."

"Chief—" pleaded Martel.

Bert studied him. "Reach out for the first dep," he said. "I'll speak to him."

He waited while Martel dialed the number.

"He's not there, Chief, sorry to say."

Jaws working, eyes narrowed, Bert went back downstairs to his office.

* * *

At that moment First Deputy Commissioner Priestly sat beside
the mayor in the backseat of the mayoral limousine en route
to Harlem, where the mayor would dedicate a new school.
The car was stuck in traffic, and the mayor was on the car
phone, but then he hung up and turned to the first dep. "Did
you bring that thing I asked you for?"

"My resume, yes," said the first dep, and he handed it
across. "I don't know why you wanted it, though. You know
me well enough, I thought."

The mayor eyed him speculatively, then turned to the
resume, which was three pages long. As he read he sometimes
thumbed back to reread one of the previous pages. It was the
typical resume of a high-ranking New York cop, the mayor
thought, and most of what was important was not on it. It
gave all the dates: graduation from the police academy, promotion to sergeant, lieutenant, captain, and the command grades
above. It gave all the postings. Priestly had started his police
career in the Coney Island precinct. Nothing but sand and
sunburns out there. As a sergeant in midtown he had arrested
an armed bank robber outside the bank, no shots fired, no
one hurt. He had got a commendation for it, had been promoted
to lieutenant, and moved to headquarters. He had commanded
the 20th Precinct as a captain, and then gone back to headquarters again. In forty-one years as a cop he had served less than
five years on what cops called "the street."

Promotions had been steady, the mayor saw. Apparently
Priestly had gone to school nights for years. Well, they all
did that. He had got his college degree from N.Y.U. at the
age of thirty-six, and his master's in criminal justice from
John Jay five years later. By the time he was forty-five he
had a law degree as well, and had been admitted to the New
York bar. These high-ranking cops were all supereducated,
but the degrees, the mayor reflected, all came late. It was part
of the mores of the department—if you wanted to get ahead
you went out and sat in classrooms with kids, and you piled
up these meaningless degrees. The mayor had always imagined that the men running the department were trying to prove
to the city, and especially to themselves, that they were not

the dumb flatfoots people supposed. But in the mayor's view degrees did not make the man.

Priestly had three grown children and a second wife. His first wife had died of cancer after about two years of agony. The mayor, who had been only a city councilman at the time, had attended the first wife's funeral. A very sad affair.

After her death Priestly had remained a bachelor for a number of years. His second wife, formerly a policewoman, had worked in his office as a secretary. Well, these things happened. The trouble was that you paid such women police salaries and police benefits to serve as secretaries. Civilians ought to be hired to do those jobs. Save the city a lot of money. The resume gave her name, but not her age, which the mayor thought was about forty; she was younger than Priestly, anyway.

The first dep was supposed to be a genius at interpreting statistics. He was the one who had handled the department's long-range planning. Probably still did. As first deputy commissioner he had served three different PCs. It was the mayor's guess that all three had considered him a bookish type, and nonthreatening. Otherwise they would have forced him out and brought in their own man.

Each time the incumbent PC had moved on—or had got shot, in the case of the present one—the then mayor had considered appointing Priestly to succeed him. He himself had considered Priestly not three months ago, had met with him in this very car in fact, before listening to the recommendations of his search committee, which had found him Harry Chapman. Chapman was a congressman at the time, but was willing to resign to come back to New York and serve as PC. The search committee had argued that Chapman was already a big man on the national scene, a star, and that to appoint him PC made the mayor a bigger star.

A man like that, I'll have to compete with the sonuva bitch for headlines, the mayor had thought, and he had been about to appoint Priestly, who was not likely to attract much attention at all. Priestly had known of his impending appointment, had probably even told his friends and his wife that he had the job.

But finally the mayor had listened to his search committee and had appointed Harry Chapman.

A mistake, he told himself now, and he took a long look at Priestly beside him. The man was tall and thin. And sixty-two years old. You could not get away from that little detail. He was bald, but the hair over his ears was black. He did not nearly look his age, but in eight months time he would be obliged by law to retire. The mayor was sixty-two also, no such law governed politicians, and he figured that his political career still had ten years to go. Perhaps more. Who could say? The mayor considered mandatory retirement laws useful if you were trying to get rid of old farts who worked for you. Otherwise they were a pain in the ass. Nonetheless, the law was the law.

Of course, if he appointed Priestly and the guy turned out to be a strong commissioner, it was always possible to push through a waiver, or a new law.

"So who should I appoint?" said the mayor. "In your opinion?"

"You don't have much time," said the first dep carefully. "A few more days, you have to decide."

The mayor tended to conduct his meetings, no matter how important they might be, in his car. That is, on the fly. As soon as he got where he was going, the meeting was over. The bulk of his time and energy was reserved for what was really important: votes. Appearances at dinners, at funerals. Handshaking. Shoring up his political base. Getting reelected.

"You don't have time for a search committee to find you another Harry Chapman," said Priestly.

"You put your finger on it."

"Assuming there is another Harry Chapman out there."

"I hope there's not." said the mayor, watching him. "So what do you think I should do?"

"Terrence Sternhagen is the chief of the department," said the first dep carefully.

The mayor nodded. "Chapman appointed him. Fired the guy had the job, and appointed him."

"Sternhagen was commander of the Twentieth Precinct when Chapman was a rookie cop there, did you know that?"

"No."

"That's why he appointed him. Wanted to lord it over a guy who had been above him when he started out. Other than that Sternhagen had no qualifications for the job."

"You were Chapman's precinct commander back then, too," the mayor reminded him. "Maybe that's why he let you stay." It never hurt to stick in a dig, the mayor thought. See how the guy reacted, see what he was made of.

"He let me stay because somebody had to run the department and he certainly didn't know how to do it."

A good answer. The mayor felt renewed respect for the man sitting next to him.

"As chief of detectives he appoints Bert Farber, who has no qualifications either, except that he was his first radio car partner."

"I knew they had been partners years ago."

"Farber was his mentor. Now the situation is reversed. The teacher has been reduced to pupil. The pupil is now in charge."

The car was inching forward again. The mayor looked out the window.

"Very satisfying—for the pupil," said Priestly. "Not necessarily for the city."

The mayor was nodding thoughtfully.

"Chapman takes the oath of office," continued Priestly, "and fires the guys who are there, and appoints his cronies, Sternhagen and Farber, to the two big jobs. Then he begins firing other guys. The department hasn't worked right since."

"He fired a lot of people," conceded the mayor.

"And each time appointed cronies in their place. Coxen, the black guy, he was another one. He's a former radio car partner too."

"You were there and could have stopped him. Why didn't you?"

"If I had tried, I would have been the next man out. And there would have been nobody at all to run the department."

"I know Coxen," said the mayor.

Priestly waited, but the mayor was looking out the window again.

"Chapman's mistakes ought to be corrected," said Priestly. "But if you appoint Sternhagen or Farber they won't be."

"So who should I appoint? You?"

"Do you know anyone more qualified?"

"You're sixty-two years of age."

Priestly permitted himself a small smile. "So are you. Prime of life, wouldn't you say?"

The limousine moved slowly through traffic. The driver, who was also the mayor's bodyguard, was a detective named DeGaetani, and from time to time he watched them in the mirror. The mayor was so used to conducting meetings in his car that he did not notice, though Priestly did, and would have wished for a more private meeting. But after a while Priestly too forgot DeGaetani's presence. How much could he hear up there? Probably nothing.

The mayor said cruelly: "In eight months you have to retire. Why should I want to have to go through this selection process again in eight months' time?"

"There's another way to look at it," said Priestly. "You would have eight months to pick my successor. No time pressure. All the time in the world."

Obviously Priestly was under great stress, and from time to time there was a tremor in his voice, and the mayor heard it. "And it would crown your police career," the mayor said.

Priestly stared at his hands, and to the mayor they too seemed to be trembling slightly. The man gave an almost imperceptible nod, plus a second small smile. "It would give you time to send out another search committee. Find yourself another Harry Chapman."

The mayor said: "Yeah."

"Time to get the retirement law changed, maybe."

"If I made you police commissioner," said the mayor, "how would you handle the job?"

"I'd go back to tradition. I think that's what you want. If not, we could talk about it. I am well aware that I would be working for you first, the department second."

"If Farber breaks this case in the next couple of days," the mayor said, "the city will make him PC by acclamation."

"He's not going to break it," said Priestly, and the tremor was back in his voice.

"He might."

"He's got about a thousand detectives working on the investigation. So far they got nothing."

"Nothing?"

"They don't even know where Harry started out from on his last run."

"Why should that be so hard to find?"

"Because he didn't want it found. I'm not sure Farber wants it found either."

The car drew up in front of the school, where a hundred or more black children milled about on the sidewalk. As soon as they saw it was the mayor's car they began cheering.

"How will you get back to headquarters?" the mayor asked suddenly.

"I'll wait and ride back with you," said Priestly. "How long will you be?"

The mayor seemed already to be thinking about something else. "That won't be possible, I'm afraid."

Just then, looming above the children, Priestly spied Terrence Sternhagen in uniform. Sternhagen, who had gold braid on his hat and four stars on each shoulder. Obviously it was Sternhagen who would ride back to City Hall with the mayor.

"The media might consider Terrence Sternhagen a fine choice," Priestly said. "I would not, however."

"Oh?"

"He's a man who has avoided all controversy, all responsibility his whole career. A perfect desk lieutenant is what he is. If you base your police department on him, you are going to have problems."

"And Farber?"

"He's secretive, trusts nobody, can't delegate. Wants to do even the routine jobs himself."

"What's wrong with that?"

"He's got three thousand detectives," responded Priestly. "If you named him PC he'd have ten times that many men. A major organization can't be run without putting together a staff and delegating responsibility. All of which he has proven is beyond him."

"Could you explain that a bit?"

"We've seen it in every command responsibility he has had."

The mayor was silent.

"All of his commanding officers have commented on it," said Priestly.

"Hmm," the mayor said.

"He's brusque, he's blunt, sometimes to the point of insubordination. He doesn't get on with others." The tremor was gone from Priestly's voice now, as if he were giving a speech he had given before. Or had considered giving before. Also he was speaking fast, as if trying, in the short time left to him, to get it all in.

Both men were out of the car by now. "Did your car follow?" the mayor inquired abstractedly. "To take you back to your office? No? There's a subway on the corner. I suggest you try public transportation. Find out how the other half lives."

Bert at his desk studied the manifests from Harry's two shuttle flights, looking for a name that appeared on both. Someone Harry might have been traveling with. But on each manifest were over 150 names, and after a while he got bored. He was chief of detectives, did not have to do work like this, and so carried the printouts out to Inspector Potter, who rose immediately to meet him.

"Put a couple of detectives on this," Bert told him. "See if they can find any names common to both lists."

But as he took the lists, Potter said in a low voice: "There's a detective asking to see you, Chief. I told him you were too busy, but he won't go."

The man sat in a straight chair near the outer door, and when he saw Bert glance in his direction, he stood up and gave a slight nod.

"What's his name?" said Bert, though he knew.

"Detective DeGaetani."

Bert pretended to give the matter some thought. "I guess I can afford five minutes," he said.

Leaving his door open, he went back behind his desk, and in a moment Detective DeGaetani stood before him.

Before DeGaetani could speak, Bert said to him: "Close the door."

DeGaetani closed it.

"Aren't you supposed to be driving the mayor?" said Bert.

"I'm on meal period."

"So what did you want to see me about?"

DeGaetani began to recount what he had heard from the back of the mayor's car. The mayor was considering appointing either Priestly or Sternhagen to be PC, and had just interviewed them, first one, then the other. Bert himself was perhaps under consideration too. At least the other two men seemed to think so, for both had spent a good part of the time running him down.

"They don't like you much, Chief," DeGaetani concluded.

Bert studied DeGaetani. "What makes you think this was something I needed to know?"

DeGaetani was silent.

"Those conversations were private, were they not?"

"Well, I suppose they were private, Chief."

"Does the city pay you to eavesdrop, or to drive the car?"

"To drive the car." DeGaetani had begun to look extremely uncomfortable.

"A detective with ears like you got shouldn't have such a cushy detail. You should be out in the street catching criminals."

This was not what DeGaetani wanted to hear. Street detectives worked irregular hours and sometimes got shot.

"I don't have many detectives with ears like you."

DeGaetani looked sorry he had overheard anything, much less brought it to this man.

"You're maybe too good to be driving the mayor," Bert said. "Your talents are being wasted, you might say."

"I like the work," DeGaetani pleaded. "It's a good detail."

"On the other hand," Bert said, walking him to the door, "you look like a bright young guy, how old are you?"

"Forty-two."

"How long you been a detective?"

"Eighteen years."

"I guess you hear all sorts of things."

"Sometimes I do, Chief."

"I'll keep you in mind if anything better comes up." There, that was enough. He didn't have to draw pictures, and it certainly wouldn't do to thank him. If DeGaetani heard anything more, he would be back.

As the detective went out, Inspector Potter came in carrying the airline manifests. "What did he want, Chief?"

"You know who he is?"

"I didn't have a chance to look it up."

"He's one of the mayor's drivers. Wants a transfer out. Feels unappreciated."

"Ho-ho," chortled Potter. "I'll transfer him out. I'll put him in Harlem or Bed-Sty. See if he feels appreciated there."

"Leave him where he is," Bert said negligently. "A guy like that, I don't want to do him any favors."

"Whatever you say, Chief." Potter put the two printouts down on Bert's desk. "Six doubles, Chief. Four men, two women. I had the fellas circle the names for you."

Still smarting from what DeGaetani had told him, Bert strode uninvited into the first dep's office and planted himself in front of the desk.

"We still need to get into the PC's office," he said. Though on a diplomatic mission, his manner was less than diplomatic. "You told me you'd take care of it, but you didn't."

Priestly looked up from some papers he was studying, and said mildly: "It must have slipped my mind."

"Sure."

"I don't understand what you think you might find in there."

"I think you do, Commissioner."

"Tell me again," said Priestly mildly.

"His memos, his address books, his desk calendar. Anything that will tell us a little better what we're looking for." Bert was thoroughly exasperated, and it showed.

"I ordered the office sealed."

"You got the place guarded around the clock. What for, for crissake?"

"Whatever is in there belongs to his wife."

"This is a criminal investigation, Commissioner."

"There's nothing in there."

"Do you mind if we look for ourselves?"

"Let me think about that," said the first dep.

"So when will I have an answer?" demanded Bert.

The first dep said: "Something else has been bothering me. How many detectives you got working on this case?"

"I don't know. A lot. Every detective in the city wants to break this case."

"Suppose it was Mr. John Q. Public got shot. How many detectives would be working on it?"

"What are you talking about?"

"Two maybe. Ten at the most, but only if the victim was very important. Mr. John Q. Public gets killed, normally we assign two detectives for a week and if nothing falls into our lap we close the file."

"What's that got to do with anything?"

"A cop gets killed, we go all out. A hundred detectives is not too many. The file never gets closed till we collar the guy. Well, the public is tired of us behaving that way. I'm tired of it too."

He got up and began to pace behind his chair. "I want this case treated like any ordinary case. No more favoritism. There aren't enough leads to keep so many detectives busy anyway. Assign ten detectives. Send all the others back where they came from. Put a sergeant in charge, and send Chief Kincaid back where he came from too. You understand me?"

"Perfectly," said Bert. "And you want me to tell this to Kincaid?"

"That's your job."

"I think maybe you should call up Kincaid and tell him yourself."

"You're the chief of detectives."

"I think he should know where the order comes from, Commissioner."

There was a long stony silence.

"And send out a T.O.P. into every precinct," Bert said. "Everybody ought to get the message simultaneously, don't you think? Sign your name to it. Every cop in the city should know where the order comes from, don't you think?"

"Of course if the case opens up again," said Priestly hurriedly, "and you need more detectives—of course at that time you could bring additional men in."

"When you talk to Kincaid," said Bert carefully, "you should make that clear to him."

"You heard my instructions. Now do what you're told."

At any other time Priestly's behavior would be counted bizarre; under the present circumstances it made perfect sense. It's not in his interest for me to break this case quickly, Bert told himself. He wouldn't care if I never broke it at all. He'll block me any way he can.

"I'm ordering you to pass on my orders to Chief Kincaid."

In the New York Police Department, men who resisted the will of superiors did not survive.

Bert said carefully: "I'm not sure I would be able to do that, Commissioner."

"I'm acting police commissioner," said Priestly in a soft, menacing voice. "You will obey or I'll have your shield."

The two men stood glaring at each other. Then Bert spun on his heel and strode out the door.

Back in his own office he paced from his desk to his window and back again. In his agitation he dragged his fingers through his hair.

Finally he went to his telephone and punched in Kincaid's number—then hung up before Kincaid came on the line. After that, he continued pacing. He stared at the phone from time to time, but did not take it up again.

Abruptly, he rolled up the airline printouts, shoved them into the pocket of his suit coat, took the elevator down to the garage to his car, and had himself driven to La Guardia. If he was going to disobey, it was best he got out of the building.

En route to the airport he studied the printouts, and he saw that two of the passengers Potter had circled, a man and a woman, had the same last name—most likely a married couple traveling together, who most likely had had nothing to do with Harry Chapman. That left three other men and one other woman, but their names meant nothing to him.

Delta's security chief, Bronfman, worked out of an office in the Marine Terminal. Since Bert was early, the two men shared a pot of coffee, and Bronfman gave him a list of the crew members he was about to meet: four women from one flight, five from the other.

"Someone missing?" inquired Bert.

"One of the women went home sick."

Bert studied the list a moment. "The one who's missing, what's her name?"

"Caroline Connolly."

"You say she was here but when she heard I was coming she went home?"

"I don't know," said Bronfman. "I never saw her."

He led Bert to a small office down the hall. It was bare, unadorned, its window looking out on the flight line.

"This okay?" asked Bronfman.

"Can you get me the address and telephone number of this Caroline Connolly?"

"We don't normally give out that information."

"Come on," said Bert.

"I can have her call you."

Bert gave him a look.

"All right, I'll get it for you."

There was a coat tree in the corner on which Bert was hanging his coat. He tugged the passenger printouts from his pocket and read off the names his detectives had circled. "Two of these people appear to have been a married couple, and the other four appear to have been traveling alone. If they paid for their tickets with credit cards, which they most likely did, the airline should have their credit card numbers. I want you to find me those numbers."

"Hold on a minute, Chief, that's a helluva job."

"Put somebody on it. And if they have time, have them call up the credit card companies and get me billing addresses for each of the names. You do those things for me and I'll owe you one."

He was in no mood to treat Bronfman or anyone else gently. "Now I wish you'd start sending in those women one at a time. Thank you."

With a yellow pad in front of him he sat at the desk in the bare empty office and interviewed the crew members. He asked each woman her name, address, age, place of birth, marital status, airline experience. To make them as nervous and therefore as cooperative as possible, his questions and manner were deliberately blunt. They came in nervous, and got more so. When they wondered aloud what this was all about he did not reply. They knew they had somehow got involved in a criminal investigation.

Finally he would sit back and with pretended casualness question them about crewing on shuttle flights. How many flights did a crew make in a day? How many in a month? Was it interesting work?

Pretended casualness was the opposite of casual, and all recognized it. He watched the women get more and more on edge.

"Harry Chapman."

As he threw the name out his voice became suddenly crisp, challenging, unfriendly. Had they recognized him when he came aboard last weekend? Where did he sit? Did he talk to anyone? Did they notice anyone who appeared to be with him? Who sat next to him? Had they noticed him on any other flights?

A woman named Hanna Klein admitted having noticed Harry last weekend.

"Was he with anyone?"

"I don't know." Then she added: "We had him on at least one previous flight as well."

Hanna Klein was older than the others, about fifty. She had gray hair.

"Was he with anybody that time?"

"He was with you." She gave him a brilliant, nervous smile.

Bert studied her in silence. He did not remember her at all. He said: "Is Caroline Connolly on your crew?"

"She was on that earlier flight too. Surely you remember her."

"Remind me."

"A tall girl, mid-twenties. Dark hair. Bangs."

"A beauty, or what?"

"Very attractive, I would say."

"Do you know if the police commissioner noticed her?"

"How do you mean?" said Hanna Klein. But to get the words out, it seemed to Bert, she had had to take a deep swallow first.

"Did they talk to each other, or what?" said Bert impatiently. There was something there, and he wanted to know what it was.

"I remember he gave her his autograph."

"That was some weeks ago. Did he talk to her this weekend?"

"I was in the back of the plane. Caroline was up front."

He paused and pretended to study his notes. "How sick is Caroline?"

"I don't know. When they took us off the flight and told us you were coming, she said she was sick and went home."

He interviewed all nine women. He put two hours into it, and learned more than he had ever hoped to know about serving businessmen on shuttle flights, but nothing at all to advance the investigation into the murder of Harry Chapman. As he was finishing up Bronfman came in and handed him Caroline Connolly's address, together with the other information he had asked for.

Caroline Connolly lived in a brownstone in Chelsea. A nice building but no doorman. A vestibule, an intercom. Bert looked out through the glass doors at his car and driver in the street, and waited for a returning tenant. When one came, he shouldered in behind him. The tenant shrugged, but said nothing.

No elevator. Bert walked up four flights, thinking: I hope she's home. He rang Caroline's bell. If she was actually sick she might come to the door in a bathrobe, with a stuffed up head and knots in her hair.

He didn't know what he expected. What he got was an extremely beautiful young woman wearing a black cocktail dress and about to go out.

"Yes?"

He showed his shield, said: "May I come in?" and marched past her without waiting for an answer.

"Wait a minute," she said, "just wait a minute."

There was a guy there too. About her age. Wearing a dark, well-cut suit, and moving up until he stood only half a step behind her.

Bert had recognized her at once from the flight he and Harry had made to Washington, and thought she recognized him too. Had she been warned by Hanna Klein? In any case she had seemed to go rigid the moment she saw him.

"I have to ask you some questions."

"I've got nothing to say to you. I called my union delegate before and—"

So it was going to be a confrontation. "Perhaps," Bert said, "you'd prefer to come down to the station house and answer questions there."

"No, but—"

"What's this all about?" asked the young man.

An interrogation was a performance. To get information out of someone, a detective had first to decide what attitude to project. In some cases compassion kept people talking. Boredom had its uses. Anger could be extremely effective. Attitude was a disguise. Masks. Roles. Select one. Unfortunately the detective never had much time to decide.

Bert turned brusquely on the young man. "Who the hell are you?"

The girl clutched his arm defensively. "My fiancé," she said.

"Name?" Bert said. "Show me some ID."

The young man began to fumble for his wallet.

"Hurry up, I haven't got all day."

He carried the wallet over to the light and on a yellow pad out of his attaché case took down the particulars. When finished, instead of giving the wallet back, he dropped it into his pocket. "Wait outside while I talk to your girlfriend."

The young man was obviously rattled.

"Unless you want a trip down to the station house too."

"You don't have to do what he says, Larry."

"Out."

"Can I have my wallet back?"

"No."

"You can't come busting in here," the girl said.

Opening his attaché case, Bert rattled his handcuffs. "Out," he said to Larry.

After eyeing the handcuffs Larry said to the girl: "I'll wait downstairs."

When the door had closed, Bert and Caroline stared at each other. Bert's gaze was truculent. Caroline's showed fear.

"Sit down there," ordered Bert.

She sat. With Larry gone she looked suddenly cowed.

"How well did you know the police commissioner?"

"Not well at all."

"How long had you been fucking him?"

She gasped.

"I'm waiting for an answer."

"How dare you say such a thing?"

"More importantly, where did you go to fuck him? Here and where else?"

Her eyes moved past him and fixed on the door. "Will you keep your voice down? Will you please keep your voice down?"

If she thought lover boy was out in the corridor listening hard, this was all to the good.

"We——" she said, "Larry and I—we're supposed to get married next month, and——"

"That didn't stop you from fucking the police commissioner, though, did it? Did you kill him too?"

"Oh God," Caroline said, and began to cry.

Intimidating a twenty-five-year-old girl was rather too easy. "Let's start from the beginning," said Bert.

The beginning, as by then he expected, was the flight to Washington he and Harry had made some weeks before.

Just prior to landing, Bert remembered, Harry's eyes had come open, and he had excused himself and gone aft to the toilet. Turning, Bert had seen him talking to the women back there, including the one he now knew as Caroline Connolly. A girl as beautiful as that, Bert remembered thinking, probably had to fight off male passengers every day of the week.

If she had caught Bert's eye, then she had probably caught Harry's eye too. And Harry was a celebrity. Suppose she did something to invite Harry's interest, Bert remembered thinking. Blinked her eyes at him, or whatever? How would Harry react? The question was only half formed in Bert's head, nothing specific had put it there, he had thought it only because he realized he didn't really know Harry anymore, and he dismissed it almost at once. Harry's conversation with Caroline had not lasted long enough. And there were all those other women listening in.

Besides which, Harry had Mary Alice at home, so why should he bother?

But Bert had been wrong, he now learned.

When Harry had come up and asked for a glass of water, Caroline now confessed, and when she had poured it out and handed it to him, Harry had said to her: "Do you stay over in Washington?"

Ignoring the presence of the other two women, Police Commissioner Chapman had focused on her completely. The other two women had seemed to take half a step backward, as if getting out of the way of an accident.

"No," she had told Harry, "I fly right back to New York."

Giving in to the impulse to lead him on, she added: "And then I fly back to Washington again. And *then* I stay over." And she swallowed hard.

"We'll have dinner together tonight," said Harry decisively, and he mentioned a restaurant. She recognized the name, one of the best known in Washington. Expensive. Hard to get into.

"Sure," she said.

It had taken altogether about fifteen seconds.

Walking back down the aisle to his seat, Harry had worn a slight smile. Bert had attached no importance to the smile at the time, though he did now. More and more he was coming to see Harry as a man who took risks. Who enjoyed taking risks of whatever kind, even to trying to make a date with an experienced airline stewardess who might have brushed him off in front of two other women.

"So he took you to dinner," said Bert. "Then what?"

"There were some important people in the restaurant," Caroline said, and began to name them. "They came over to the table and Harry introduced me." Her voice dropped, and she again wiped her eyes. "After dinner he asked me if I wanted to come back to see this town house he keeps in Washington."

Mary Alice's town house, thought Bert. Mary Alice is the one with the money.

"By that time," continued Caroline, "I thought he was really nice, so I said—I said sure."

"You stayed all night."

"What if I did?"

"Suppose his wife had come in?"

"His wife was in New York."

"She could have turned up."

"I doubt it. They weren't getting along at all."

"Is that what he told you? And you believed him?"

Caroline's head was down and it took Bert a moment to realize that tears were streaming down her face.

"And in New York you went on seeing him. Where?"

"We used to meet in this apartment he had."

"The one near the Museum of Natural History."

"Yes."

Bert said casually: "It's on Seventy-seventh Street, isn't it? What's the number?"

"I don't know. It's the brownstone next to the Ethiopian restaurant."

Gotcha, thought Bert. "How often did you see him?"

"Often enough."

"I'm sure you were both deeply in love," said Bert. "Where was your fiancé throughout all this, if I may ask?"

"Larry didn't know—doesn't know about it."

"He simply continued to be your fiancé. Very good. You still planned to marry him."

"I know it doesn't sound too—too—"

"Jesus," said Bert. "This torrid love affair between you and the police commissioner, how long did it last? Two weeks? Three weeks?"

"I kept trying to call him at police headquarters but I could never get through."

As a teenager, and even into adulthood, Bert had been in awe of girls, and then young women. They had seemed to him so cool, so smart—smarter by far than the males who sniffed after them. Now he thought the opposite. Women were not cool, and they were dumb. Men were led around by their perpetually swollen cocks, they couldn't help it. Women did not have this problem, but got in trouble anyway, and to Bert there was no explanation for it except stupidity.

"So you didn't see him again until he got on your flight Sunday night."

"Yes."

"And," said Bert, guessing, "he had a woman with him."

"They were practically sitting in each other's laps," Caroline blubbered. "It was disgusting."

Bert got the Sunday night passenger manifest out of his attaché case. "Mrs. Russo. Is that her name? Mrs. Anna Russo?"

"I don't know. She had on this nice Chanel suit. Dark green. Very expensive. I used to be a model. I knew it was Chanel." Caroline nodded truculently. "I spilled a tomato juice on her lap. You should have seen Harry's face. But he couldn't do anything, could he?"

Bert laughed, and for a moment almost liked her.

"You should have seen her face, too."

Caroline was grinning and wiping away tears at the same time. "I got lots of paper towels. I pretended to blot up the tomato juice, but what I really did was rub it in."

Her grin did not last, and when it vanished she was sobbing again. Bert walked to the window and peered down on his car. The light inside shone on part of Hughie's newspaper spread out over the steering wheel. Since there was no sign of Caroline's Larry pacing the sidewalk down there, this probably placed lover boy in the corridor outside this apartment, ear pressed to the door.

Bert returned to Caroline. "Let me tell you what happened next," he said. "The plane lands, you come home to your apartment, but you can't sleep. You pace up and down all night. You are tormented by jealousy. It is a torture to you. It becomes hatred. And when the dawn comes up you are waiting out on Seventy-seventh Street with your gun. The snow is coming down. Harry Chapman comes out to jog and you shoot him to death."

Somebody had probably paced up and down all night unable to sleep, either this girl or someone else, and it was this someone who had shot Harry Chapman. This had been Bert's theory from the beginning. He had never believed in street muggers or political assassins or any of the other possibilities. He had believed instinctively that when the case broke he would find that the killing of Harry Chapman was purely personal. Which should come as no surprise to anyone, he reflected. Most murders were personal: murderer and victim were known to each other.

But was Harry's killer this girl, or someone else? Some other woman—the woman on the plane, perhaps? Or even someone's husband or boyfriend—someone like Larry Lover Boy listening so hard out in the corridor.

But Caroline Connolly was the suspect at hand, and Bert wanted to hear how the accusation sounded. "You killed him," he told her. "What did you do with the gun?"

Unfortunately the accusation did not sound good at all. A girl who would spill a drink on a rival had already had her revenge. Caroline did not sound like a killer to Bert.

The accusation hung there in the air, and Caroline stared at him.

"Hand it over and we can go down to the station house and you can talk and get it all off your chest."

Caroline wiped her eyes. She said: "You're weird. You're really weird."

Bert decided to press her further to be sure. Glancing around, he saw that there was a side table under the window, and end tables to either side of the sofa. All had drawers, and Bert went to each of them in turn. "Where do you keep the gun, in this drawer here, or where?"

"Get out of my drawers."

"You can claim temporary insanity. The jury will be understanding, I assure you."

"And get out of my house. Do you have a search warrant? Do you have an arrest warrant? Then get out. Get out, get out, get out."

She was shrieking. Bert watched her through narrowed eyes. Her mood was outrage, not guilt, and it sounded genuine. He was willing to consider it genuine for the time being. He had no probable cause to arrest her anyway. Besides which she had already given up more information than he had ever dared hope for: the probable name of still another woman in Harry Chapman's life, and the location of the apartment that a hundred detectives had failed to find. Bert visualized Harry's key on its rubber thong, which was presently in his attaché case. He was already visualizing what the apartment would look like. He was anxious to get inside it. He wanted to be there, not here.

"Maybe I believe you," he told Caroline. "If I come back you're going to need a lawyer."

He went out of her apartment into the dim stairwell outside, and Larry Lover Boy came toward him with face dark and fists clenched.

"She wants to see you," Bert told him. "See if you can comfort her. Here's your wallet back."

How much had Larry overheard? She would have to give him some story or other. She would have to think fast. It was a problem. Maybe now there would be no marriage. Bert had no sympathy for her on that account. He was a man with a strong moralistic streak—not religious tenets but a personal code. Caroline had had a fiancé, for God's sake. She should not have been fooling around with a married man fifteen years her senior. Nor Harry Chapman with her, for that matter. Bert did not like what he was finding out about Harry. He was beginning to see him distinctly, and what he saw was not heroic.

In the streets it was the last of rush hour. Hughie got the car out onto West Street, where once the West Side Drive, three express lanes in each direction, had run overhead. The drive had rotted out some years ago and been torn down and the environmentalists and other groups had thrown up lawsuits every time the city tried to replace it. The result was the pouring of all these cars onto a single north-south city street. Bert sat there fuming while progress was measured in yards.

"Put the siren on, Hughie."

The chauffeur did so. They gained some ground, not much. Once Hughie went up onto the sidewalk. They gained about six car lengths, and lost half of it trying to edge down into the street again. Plumes of exhaust rose into the streetlights from the tailpipes of hundreds of becalmed cars.

"Try Sixth Avenue, Hughie."

Sixth was a little better, not much. There was gridlock at many of the cross streets. Only when the street entered the park were they finally able to roll more or less freely, but it had taken nearly an hour to travel fifty blocks.

They came across 77th Street, and ahead Bert spied the Ethiopian restaurant Caroline had mentioned.

"Park in front of the restaurant, Hughie."

Bert got out and went up the stoop of the brownstone next to it. The key slid easily into the lock, a simple act that he had expected but which, in his excitement, caused him to miss a breath. He turned the key, opened the vestibule door, and found himself facing a flight of steps. Steep, narrow. They seemed to climb straight up. There was an apartment door to his left, and the name on the bell was Brooks. Bert rang but got no response. When he banged on the door and listened he heard nothing, so he tried to insert the same key. It would not go in. He went up the stairs to the second floor. There was only one apartment up here, and the name on this bell was Brooks also. Again he rang, then banged on the door. Again there was no answer. Again the key in his hand did not fit the lock.

Up another flight. He peered at the third-floor bell: still Brooks. No answer, no fit. Bert kept climbing. On the fourth and top floor the bell bore no name at all, no one answered when he rang, or when he banged either. The key went into the lock, no problem. A great sigh escaped Bert. He turned the key, entered the apartment, and began switching on lights.

He went through every room, every closet, starting in the back of the building and working forward. The bedroom had two windows overlooking a small courtyard, in the middle of which stood a bare scraggly tree. The bed was made, the walls were bare, and the closet was empty. If Harry had started his run from here, this room ought to contain his street clothes, his nightclothes too, but it didn't.

He peered into the closet a second time. Still nothing.

Taking the flashlight from his attaché case, he knelt and moved the beam of light under the bed, illuminating a few balls of dust, nothing else. He peeled the counterpane back and saw that the sheets were tucked in tight. They didn't look entirely fresh, but they didn't look well slept on either.

This apartment had the feel of a place where no one lived. Perhaps it belonged to this man Brooks, who used it for houseguests. Brooks would have to be checked out. Presumably his most recent guest had been Harry.

The next room was a tiny kitchen. The sink was clean and dry, the counter spotless, no dishes on it. Bert opened the dish cabinet. The dishes, there weren't many, stood in racks. The dishwasher, he saw when he peered into it, was empty. There were other cabinets. In one he found a little food, not much: coffee, tea, cereal. Staples that might have been there a long time. When he opened the fridge he found two bottles of soda water, a six-pack of soft drinks in cans, and an opened container of milk. He sniffed the milk, then tasted it to be sure. It was not sour, and the final sale date stamped on the carton was tomorrow's. Which proved that someone had been here recently, though not necessarily Harry. But it had to have been Harry. Bert was trying to reassure himself, because nothing in this apartment reassured him at all.

The front room was long, narrow, and sparsely furnished. Occupying one half of it were a dining room table with four chairs; a sofa, a coffee table, a cabinet, and two armchairs occupied the other half. The cabinet contained a half-empty bottle of scotch and nothing else. Bert did not touch the bottle. There was a mirror on one wall, but the others were bare. There were no books. On the coffee table stood a number of decorating magazines, not new.

The chief of detectives stood in the center of the room biting on his thumbnail. There was not a thing in this apartment that pertained to Harry Chapman. Either there had never been or the place had been cleaned out after his death. If so, by whom? How? And why? The thoughts tumbled like clouds through Bert's head. They were amorphous, they collided without sound. He could not get a grip on any of them.

Having stepped to the phone, he dialed the 24th Precinct, and when John Kincaid came on said to him: "Take down this address. I want a full forensic team here forthwith."

Forthwith again. At once. Faster than that—the strongest command there was.

"What's it in reference to?" said Kincaid.

Bert had had to call on Kincaid. The closest forensic team was the one Kincaid was using, and if he phoned the police academy and ordered up another, Kincaid would hear about it anyway.

"I want to know if there are any prints, any pubic hairs in this place."

"I take it you found the apartment I've been looking for."

"Maybe."

"May I ask how?"

"A little birdie told me."

"An informant?"

"A confidential informant." This too was police department jargon. The word *confidential* enclosed sacred terrain. A good detective never divulged the name of a confidential informant. Since it was clear Bert would ignore any further probing, Kincaid fell silent.

Bert said: "This building may be owned by a man named Brooks. Check him out. Put as many detectives on it as you need to. Who is he? Find out how he knew Harry Chapman. You got that, so far?"

"Yes," said Kincaid.

"Here's a phone number for you." Bert read the number off the phone in his hand. "I want a printout of all calls in or out of this place for the past month. Put detectives on it right away."

"Anything else?" said Kincaid coldly.

Bert thought about it a moment. "Nothing else." He hung up.

As soon as the line was clear, he rang up his own office. "A woman named Anna Russo," he told Inspector Potter. "Here's her American Express number. I want to know her billing address and her phone number. No one is to go near her, but have detectives ask around and try to find out who she is."

As he stood waiting for Kincaid and the technicians, the apartment seemed to echo with silence, and with questions.

He started through it again, for maybe he had missed something. The bathroom when he looked into it was as small as before. He was on his knees with his flashlight, hanging over the bathtub, the toilet, the sink, all of which looked recently scrubbed out. He was becoming more and more perplexed. In the medicine cabinet stood the same bottle of aspirin as before, and nothing else, not even a toothbrush. But as he turned and was about to leave, something made him glance up.

Half concealed in the folds of the shower curtain, where presumably they had been left to dry, hung a pair of ladies' panties.

Bert made a grab for them. Whoever cleaned this place out had missed them, and Bert himself had almost missed them.

He examined them under the light over the mirror. They were perfectly clean, without clinging pubic hairs, without stains. He brought them to his nose and sniffed. They smelled of soap, maybe.

Despite the length of time he had been married, and the liaisons before that, Bert believed he knew little of women. He knew that some of them had a fetish about their underwear. When they slept over in hotels or other people's apartments or houses they washed out their underwear before going to bed. They hung it to dry on towel racks or shower rods, and the next morning packed up and left, sometimes with their underwear still hanging in some stranger's bathroom.

Which must have been what had happened here.

In any case the panties in his hand had been overlooked, and he sniffed them again and wondered about the identity of the woman to whom they belonged.

He was so concentrated that he did not hear the footsteps on the stairs outside; the ringing bell startled him. Only at the last moment, as he went to open the door, did he wonder what to do with the panties. Deciding that no one should know he had them—he could not have said why—he rammed them into his trench coat pocket.

The forensic team, four men headed by a sergeant, trooped into the apartment. Someone else was coming up the stairs so Bert waited in the open door: John Kincaid.

"This man Brooks," Kincaid said as he reached the landing, "he owns the apartment. That's why we couldn't find anything in the PC's name."

Kincaid moved past Bert and started through the rooms. He moved slowly, peering around. "We would have found this place ourselves, probably today. I knew about Brooks. I sent men to Washington two days ago to find out who the PC's friends were. They came back with a list. Brooks was on it. We were in the process of checking the list against the building department's names."

"So who is he?"

"Not much here, is there?" said Kincaid. He stood in the

front room glancing around. "Newspaper reporter. Friend of the deceased from when he was in Washington. Evidently they were great buddies. Are you so sure Chapman was using this place?"

"If we find his fingerprints on something, that will confirm it for us, won't it."

"If we find them. It's been too many days. Most prints don't last that long."

They went into the bedroom, where they watched the technicians work. Floodlights hung over the bed. The blankets had been folded and were on the floor. A technician with tweezers was going over the sheets. He had a loupe in his eye like a jeweler.

"Getting anything?" said Bert.

"A few hairs, Chief. Couple of fibers look like they came from somewhere else."

"If this Brooks was such a close friend," said Bert to Kincaid, "why didn't he come forward?"

"He's in the Balkans covering the war. Probably doesn't even know his houseguest is dead."

In the kitchen the two fingerprint men worked meticulously. Bert and Kincaid stood in the doorway watching.

"Some of this stuff looks like it's been wiped," one man said. "Nothing on the door handles. Who wiped it, Chief?"

"You tell me."

The air was so heavy with fingerprint powder that Bert sneezed.

"You could wait outside if it bothers you, Chief," said the technician apologetically.

"Whoever wiped the place," said Bert, "might have missed something."

"Probably. There are always surfaces people overlook." The technician was working on a soup tureen, and he pointed with his brush. "There for instance." Peering over his shoulder, Bert noted a smudge that had just appeared on the side of the tureen. In it he could discern faint whorls and arches.

Just then the phone rang on the kitchen wall, and Bert reached for it. "Farber," he said.

"That female's name you wanted me to look up, Chief,"

said Inspector Potter. "I have some information for you. Can you talk?"

Which female—he must mean Anna Russo. "No, I can't," said Bert, after glancing around quickly. Kincaid was gone—he was out in the front room probably, where there was a second phone. He had perhaps picked up on the same ring, and was listening.

"I'll call you back," said Bert, and he hung up.

He went out into the front room. "What was that?" said Kincaid.

"My office."

The two men looked at each other a moment.

One of the technicians had found the half-empty bottle of scotch and was dusting it. "Here's something," he said. "I got a couple off the glass coffee table too."

Bert went down to the street and called Potter from a phone booth.

"That name Anna Russo," said Potter, "It rang a bell. As soon as we got her address from American Express, I looked her up, and she's Dominic Russo's wife."

Bert was not surprised. He had almost expected it.

"The head of the Gambino family," said Potter.

"Alleged," Bert said, and gave a broken laugh. "Alleged." He looked up Columbus Avenue at the headlights coming toward him. It was a raw, blustery night and the booth he stood in was open at the back and from the waist down. The wind tugged at him. With his free hand he was trying to button his trench coat at the throat.

Potter said: "What's she got to do with this, if I might ask?"

"I don't know yet," said Bert, but he did. The police commissioner in bed with a Mafia guy's wife. Wait till the newspapers get hold of this, he thought. Jesus.

"Anna Russo is Mafia through and through," said Potter. "Her father ran the Lucchese family until his untimely death last year." And he chuckled, as if to say: these people keep killing each other, one can't take them seriously. "She's about forty, I'm told. Three children."

Bert remembered the very young Harry Chapman with whom he had once patrolled these same streets every night.

The boy who brought his books along in the radio car. The boy who studied every chance he got. The boy who killed two men in a post office shoot-out, and then wept about it afterward. The young Harry Chapman was the one Bert wanted to believe in. Could that eager boy have grown into a police commissioner as careless, or stupid, or self-indulgent as now seemed to be the case?

"I have several phone numbers for her address, Chief, all unlisted by the way."

Bert's fist was opening and closing on the panties in his pocket. Anna Russo's, maybe? Caroline Connolly's? Whose?

Finally he said: "Leave those phone numbers on my desk, and then do one more thing for me. Try to find a photo of this Mrs. Russo."

"Unless she's been arrested we wouldn't have one, Chief."

"Call over to Intelligence. They may have something. A surveillance photo from one of those Mafia funerals. Her father's, maybe. Ask them to send it over." Bert, who had begun to shiver and stamp his feet, looked at his watch and saw how late it was.

"And after that, Chief?"

"After that go home to your wife and kids."

"By the way," said Inspector Potter in his ear, "your wife called to remind you you're going to a concert tonight."

Bert glanced at his watch again and realized that the concert would start in thirty minutes. Madge was no doubt pacing the living room cursing him and smoking. He said to Potter: "Call her up for me, please. Tell her to take a taxi. I'll wait for her in front of the box office."

It was so late that the taxi might not get her there in time. She would climb out angry, and would be hissing in his ear as they found their seats. At least he wouldn't have to listen to her during the performance. He would try to make it up to her afterward, take her to dinner or something.

Since he was closer to Lincoln Center than she was he had time for a stiff drink first. He took it standing up at a bar across the street, then went and stood outside Avery Fisher Hall waiting for Madge. He was cold and stamping his feet again. Hordes of people were moving across the plaza and entering the various halls. Although it was winter the fountain was on, brilliantly lit and blowing in the breeze.

The drink had relaxed Bert a little. He hoped the music would relax him more. The program was to be Beethoven's Sixth, the Dvořák piano concerto, and Haydn's Surprise symphony. The scheduled soloist was a new young pianist named Klemf, whom Bert was anxious to hear. He had once dreamed of becoming a concert pianist himself, and as a boy had put in seven years of lessons paid for out of his father's wages as a tailor. When the tailor died, the lessons stopped and Bert went to work after school in a supermarket. Later he learned how to make money playing the piano at parties, but it wasn't the same thing.

He turned and spied Madge coming toward him through the stragglers who now hurried across the almost empty plaza.

"You—" she said.

But he cut her off: "If we hurry we can just make it." He had the tickets in one hand and he took her arm with the other, pulling her forward.

In the dark he sat back and waited for the music to sweep over him, transport him perhaps into another world, somewhere, anywhere, but this did not happen. Because the investigation would not stop its urgent movement through his brain, the music failed to captivate him or please him. He thought the Beethoven came out too loud, and that Klemf played without subtlety, his tone too sharp, his fingers too mechanical. The music did not come from inside him, it was merely something he had learned.

Sometime during the next several days the mayor would decide on a new PC. Was there a way for Bert to influence this decision? Should he attempt to move his own candidacy forward, or would this be counterproductive? Could he hurry the investigation to a conclusion before the mayor decided? And would it influence the mayor, if he did?

A few more days. He began to worry about the information he was withholding from John Kincaid. If it became known that the chief of detectives, himself, was conducting his own investigation in secret, and not sharing what he found with the main body of the investigation, he would be severely criticized, and perhaps voices would be raised demanding his resignation. But if in the meantime he broke the case wide open, this wouldn't matter. Or would it?

He was worried about the direction the investigation seemed to be taking—that Harry's reputation would not survive it. If Harry came out of this thing totally discredited, then the men he had appointed—himself, for instance—might appear discredited too.

Bert had launched himself into the investigation with a certain innocence, but was not innocent now. He had started with some vague notion of trying to protect Mary Alice Chapman. Now it was himself he was trying to protect, nothing vague about it.

The concert ended. As they moved up the aisle in the crowd Bert could feel that Madge was still angry at him, but she was not one to make scenes in public. They crossed the plaza to where Hughie waited with the car.

"Anything come over?" Bert asked him.

"Nothing, Chief."

"You want to go get something to eat?" Bert said to his wife as they settled into the backseat.

"I had my dinner at dinnertime."

"Okay," said Bert. And he leaned forward over the backrest: "Take us home please, Hughie."

In the car in the presence of the driver Madge was silent. She sat half turned from Bert, peering out the window.

"What did you think of Klemf?" Bert asked her.

"Who?"

"The pianist."

"Was that his name?"

The chief of detectives was concerned that Hughie would read the weight of the silences between them. "He hit all the notes, but—"

She did not answer.

"Would you like a drink?" inquired Bert when they had come into their apartment. He had dropped his coat on the chair beside the door.

"I won't be treated the way you treat me."

He marched into the kitchen, where he got out two glasses and put ice into one of them. "Yes or no?" he asked her.

"You never tell me where you are, what you're doing, when to expect you. Tonight—"

"I'm sorry about tonight, but—"

"You're always sorry."

"There's a very heavy investigation going on. I don't know if you heard."

"You—" She spun on her heel and walked away.

Bert took his drink into the living room and sat down at the piano, where he played what he could remember of tonight's concerto. He had studied it once. He had once imagined it as the piece with which he would make his concert debut.

It was late and he held the pedal down to muffle the sound as much as possible.

Madge must have gone to hang up the coats, for in a moment she stood in the doorway holding up the panties that had been in his pocket.

"And what's this, if I may ask?"

"That's evidence." Bert got up and grabbed them away from her.

"Evidence is supposed to be vouchered and turned in to the property clerk, last I heard."

"Well this hasn't been."

"I'm waiting for an explanation."

Bert sometimes wondered if he was secretive by nature or only by profession. Perhaps it was in his genes and could not be helped. With age he had become more and more secretive, he believed. He hated to tell anyone anything until absolutely necessary. If you wanted a secret to stay secret, then you shared it with no one.

He put the panties on top of the piano and sat down again. To Madge he said: "I think they belong to the last woman Harry Chapman went to bed with."

"Who, his wife?"

"I don't know who yet."

"They're Mary Alice Chapman's, aren't they? Was it difficult to get them off her?"

"Oh for God's sake, Madge."

"A little trophy. Bring the little trophy home to your little wife."

He began banging on the piano, drowning her out, and finally, weeping, she left the room.

He got up from the piano and phoned John Kincaid at home. The apartment on 77th Street had been resealed, Kincaid told him. Prints had been lifted belonging to a number of individuals.

"Harry Chapman's?" said Bert.

"Congratulations," said Kincaid. "Chapman's prints were all over the place."

"Good."

"You found the apartment we were looking for," said Kincaid. "You found it an hour or two sooner than we would have. How, I don't know."

He waited for the chief of detectives to provide an explanation, but Bert said only: "What else?"

They would try to identify the other prints tomorrow, Kincaid said, but it might be difficult. "Especially if the person or persons we're trying to identify should happen to be female."

Bert said nothing.

"A man who's been arrested," Kincaid said, "or he's been in the armed forces, his prints are on file. Most women, on the other hand, have never been fingerprinted. That's what we're hoping to identify, am I right? A woman?"

"Maybe," said Bert, and rang off.

Next he called Inspector Potter at home, waking him up apparently. He gave a perfunctory apology and asked for a report. There was no picture of Anna Russo, Potter told him. Intelligence had nothing on her at all. She had never been arrested or even questioned in connection with any mob business.

Bert had hoped for a photo he could show Caroline Connolly. *Is this the woman you spilled the tomato juice on*? He needed a positive identification. Without one it was difficult to proceed.

When he went into his bedroom later it was dark. It was cold too, for the window was open. Sitting down on the edge of the bed he stroked Madge's hair. "Believe me or not, I don't care, but those panties are evidence. I found them late this afternoon in an apartment Harry was using. They could be Mary Alice's. I don't know who's they are."

His wife did not move under his hand. Presently he stood up and began to get undressed. When he came out of the bathroom he got into the bed on his side and after a time he fell asleep.

■11■

THE MORNING WAS crisp and cold, the low sun streaming onto the roofs and sidewalks of the city, the air so exceptionally clear that Chief of the Department Terrence Sternhagen decided to walk part of the way to work. At the corner of Broadway and Canal he got out of his car, sent his driver on alone, tugged his cap down firmly on his head, and started toward headquarters on foot. All around him people were moving toward the subways, the bus stops, funneling into buildings. Sternhagen wore his greatcoat and muffler and gloves, and he could see his breath as he strode along.

Most New Yorkers had never seen a cop of his rank before—so much braid, so many stars—certainly not marching alone down the street. He drew stares. This pleased the chief of the department. He saw himself as an important personage in the most important city in the world. The stares proved it. The braid on his cap and the stars on his shoulder proved it. He had reached the top, or nearly so, and in the next few days—perhaps in the next few hours—the mayor's decision would be announced, and he would go higher. His chances of succeeding Harry Chapman were excellent, he believed. He had the stature, and who else was there? Priestly was too old, Farber too young. This fine cold morning it was easy for Terrence Sternhagen to believe in himself. He would be seen as the perfect choice.

It was a long, invigorating walk, but he came into headquarters well past his normal time and found his outer office buzzing with the news that Assistant Chief Earl Coxen had been spotted entering City Hall not an hour ago. He had remained closeted with the mayor twenty minutes or more with the door shut, and when he came out he was seen to be smiling.

There was only one possible explanation: the mayor was considering the appointment of a black police commissioner. You could make a good political argument for it. Most of the criminals and all of the high-crime precincts were black. The city's black ghettos were dangerous and they were in turmoil. Other cities had gone to black police chiefs and commissioners. In New York in these times a black PC made sense. The mayor might well decide to do it.

As he passed through into his own office Sternhagen overheard some of this gossip, and his chief of staff followed him to his desk and filled him in on the rest. "What do you think, Chief?"

Momentarily Sternhagen's confidence had been shaken. However, he did not believe the mayor would risk naming a black man, much less Coxen, who was two stars below him in rank. He himself was still the most likely candidate. "Whoever the new PC happens to be, we will give him our best efforts, won't we?" he said. "Close the door on your way out."

Nonetheless he kept brooding about Coxen, and later in the morning his phone rang, and it was Marlene Coxen on the line. This disconcerted him much more than the earlier gossip. Perhaps she knew something he had not yet been told.

But ostensibly all she wanted to talk about was her dinner party tomorrow night.

"Oh yes," said Sternhagen, searching through his desk calendar until he found the entry.

"Sorry to call you at the office, Chief," said Marlene, "but since the time's so close I felt I had to."

Sternhagen was listening for other messages in her voice, but so far had not heard them.

She had tried his wife at home, she added apologetically, but had got no answer. The dinner party, despite the death of the PC, was still on, she hoped. She had phoned Florence

Priestly. The Priestlys were still coming, and she hoped the Sternhagens were too.

Sternhagen thought it would be wise now to stay as close as possible to Earl Coxen. "I'm looking forward to it," he told Marlene. "Mrs. Sternhagen is looking forward to it too."

They murmured a few platitudes to each other. Life, they agreed, did not come to an end just because someone died.

When he had hung up, Sternhagen scratched out the question mark beside the entry in his desk calendar, but not the new one in his head. Coxen. Was he a threat or not?

The phone numbers Potter had left him, the ones that went into the Russo residence, lay on Bert's desk, and he dialed the first of them.

The man who answered had gravel in his throat. He growled: "Who's this?"

Bert hung up, drew a line through that number, and dialed the next one.

This time he got a woman with a thick accent that he judged to be Italian—a maid perhaps. "La Signora, she maybe here, I see if."

After a long wait a second voice came on, and when Bert asked for Anna Russo the voice replied: "This is she. Who may I inquire is calling?"

A well-modulated voice, cool. Educated. Pseudo-educated, more likely. All right, she spoke the way you would expect a mobster's wife to talk. Bert gave his name and rank, and said he wanted to ask her a few questions.

Her response was a sharp intake of breath. "What would it be in reference to, if I might inquire?"

To jolt her, Bert said gruffly: "The murder of the police commissioner."

"I wouldn't know anything about that," she said, "I'm sure." But there had been a pause.

Smoothly, casually, as disarmingly as possible, he said: "Let me explain."

The police commissioner, he told her, had ridden the shuttle back from Washington last Sunday night, and the police were merely trying to interview every passenger on the flight. The airline had identified her as one of the other passengers and—

"My mother happened to be ill," Anna interrupted. "That is why I happened to be in Washington."

"Yes of course," said Bert. "And probably, you won't be able to help us. But—"

But she was one of the last people to see Harry Chapman alive, he told her. Perhaps Harry spoke to her, perhaps she observed some little detail, heard something that could help the investigation. Or could point them toward some other passenger who might provide some detail.

"Unfortunately I was very fatigued that night, and so noticed nothing. So I shan't be able to help you."

"Shall we say three o'clock in my office?"

"When one is as fatigued as I was, one can't be expected to notice anything, can one?"

"Three o'clock it is, then."

"Also, I may have forgotten to mention it, but I have a previous engagement for that hour. I have previous engagements all the rest of the week, in fact."

"We're a little pressed for time, so it will have to be three o'clock."

"I would like to meet with you very much, but what can one do? My previous engagements won't permit it."

"If transportation is a problem," said Bert, "I can send some detectives with a car to pick you up and drive you in."

He heard the threat register. She lived in Westbury, twenty miles out, behind a ten-foot-high wrought iron fence. She could not afford to have detectives drive up in front and take her away in an unmarked car.

"Or you may prefer," Bert said smoothly, "to come into town and maybe do some shopping. You can stop in at police headquarters on the way home." He waited the proper amount of time, then added: "No one need know we ever met."

When he had hung up he made additional calls, alerting the men he thought he would need, then went to his closet, where he pulled the panties out of his trench coat pocket. They were white with lace around the thighs. Silk, he thought, not synthetic. Probably there was a matching bra to go with them. Were they Anna Russo's? He tried to picture this unknown woman standing in them looking at him across, say, a bedroom. She was a mobster's wife, and with such a woman in the old days the police could be as heavy-handed as they liked. They could have brought her in and stripped her. See if the panties fit. See if they matched whatever else she had on.

Unfortunately, those days were over now.

Bert had spread the panties out on his desk. What would be the shock value when he showed them to Anna Russo? She comes in the door and he throws them in her face. What might she blurt out?

Unfortunately he could not be sure the panties belonged to her. He could not be sure she was the woman who had sat beside Harry Chapman on the plane, much less the one who had accompanied him back to the apartment on 77th Street. If her fingerprints had been on file he could have matched them against the prints and partial prints found in the apartment. But he did not have her prints. He had no photo of her to show to Caroline Connolly or anyone else.

Gazing at the panties on his desk he felt like a teenager studying a pornographic picture. Once he even put his hand inside them, the better to note how sheer they were. A woman wearing these things would not be hiding much. Through them, if he wanted, he could count the hairs on the backs of his hands.

Anna Russo turned out to be a platinum blond who swept into Bert's office wearing a white mink coat over a gold lamé pantsuit. A big woman, tall and big boned with big hips and big tits. She was heavily made up. It looked as if she couldn't smile without cracks appearing. Like cracks in glass, cracks in ice. She wore dark glasses under which, he was to learn when she finally took them off, rode false eyelashes.

Although not involved in mob activity herself, according to the Intelligence Division, she was not in any sense a virgin. Her husband was head of a vicious crime family. He ordered hijackings, murders, extortions every day. She was certainly aware of this, and either ignored it or condoned it. Obviously she had no difficulty flaunting the profits.

The mink coat, for instance, was worth a fortune. Bert offered to hang it up for her but she said: "I prefer to keep it on, actually. We're not going to be long, are we?"

She did open the coat though, as if to impress him with the weight of her breasts. Earrings dangled, and she wore diamonds the size of hangman's knots on three of her fingers. The word *moll* came to Bert's mind. How could Harry have got involved with a Kewpie doll like this?

Assuming he had been involved with her. As yet Bert could not be sure.

"Will you share a pot of tea with me?" he asked her.

"I don't care for any, thank you."

Nonetheless he went to his intercom and asked the detective who answered to bring in a pot of tea and two cups, and while waiting he asked after the health of the woman's husband, the health of her children, the health of her mother in Washington.

"Here we are," said Bert, when the tea arrived. A policewoman set down the tray, and he began pouring from the pot into the cups.

"I really don't care for any," said Anna Russo, but Bert went on pouring.

"Sugar?" he asked her.

"I never take sugar."

"Milk?"

She shrugged.

She was sitting on his sofa, pretending to be at ease. He had taken the chair across from her. When he held out the tea on its saucer she did not reach for it, and he was obliged to set it down on the table close to her knees.

"So how well did you know Harry Chapman?"

"Who?"

"The police commissioner who was killed."

"Oh yes."

"You did know him?"

"I'm afraid I didn't have the pleasure of his acquaintance."

"Someone told me you knew him."

"I may have made his acquaintance socially," she said, cautiously.

He looked into her dark glasses and could see almost nothing.

"I meet many people socially," she said, "as a matter of fact."

"Where might you have met him?" Bert persisted.

"That would have been a social occasion of some kind. If in fact I met him."

"I find afternoon tea so civilized," said Bert. "Don't you?"

She shrugged.

She watched Bert carefully. Or at least so he thought. The glasses were so dark he couldn't be sure. And she still hadn't touched the tea he had set before her.

"Mr. Chapman went down to Washington Friday night," Bert said. "You were on that flight also, according to the airline."

"How coincidental. I find life full of coincidental occurrences, don't you? Coincidences are amazing, aren't they?"

"He came back Sunday night and you did too." Bert got up and went to his desk drawer, where he removed a cardboard chart. It related to detective manpower allocation, but she didn't know that. "According to the airline's seating plan, which I have in my hand," Bert said, "you were seated next to him Sunday night." He replaced the chart in his drawer and returned to his chair.

"I was seated next to a gentleman," she conceded. She took off the dark glasses and blinked her false eyelashes at him. "That's true."

"Harry Chapman."

"Was that his name? He was quite charming."

Was she deliberately and specifically lying? Or was it merely a reflex action—she was conditioned by the world she lived in to lie whenever anyone questioned her about anything at all.

Perhaps she was merely stupid. Bert said: "Your tea is getting cold."

It seemed to him that the hand she reached for the tea was trembling slightly. He could not be sure; these things were almost imperceptible. If so, it perhaps signaled the equivalent of a stress fracture in her moll's carapace—the equivalent of a crack appearing down the middle of her caked-on makeup.

"Coming back from Washington you were wearing a Chanel suit, I believe. Green, wasn't it?"

"I seldom wear green. It doesn't happen to suit my complexion."

"Were you able to get the stains out of it?"

Now she was holding the saucer in both hands as if to prevent it from rattling. "I don't comprehend to what you might be referring to."

"On the plane the stewardess spilled something on you."

"I don't recall."

"I was worried it might have ruined your suit."

"Hardly."

"It spilled all the way down your front, I'm told."

"Oh yes, now I recall a slight accident of that nature. A minor thing. I scarcely recall it."

Although encouraged, Bert let nothing show. Instead he again went to his desk, this time bringing forth an eight-by-ten photo of Harry Chapman, which he handed to her.

"Is this the man who sat beside you on the plane?"

"I have a poor memory for faces," she said, "unfortunately." She handed the photo back, but instead of taking it, Bert gestured to her to put it down on the table.

"But it could have been him?"

"I'd like to help you, but—"

"But what?"

"There must have been a hundred men on that plane."

"More tea?" He lifted the pot and began pouring.

He kept her another twenty minutes, kept asking questions, but somehow he lost control of the interrogation. She went on denying everything, and because he had no hard evidence with which to confront her, she seemed to get stronger as he got weaker. The nervousness he had detected earlier was perhaps only that: nervousness. Any woman summoned to police headquarters by a chief of detectives relative to she knew not what would be nervous. Particularly one of this type with so much to hide.

Her replies had become increasingly confident. If it was all lies, then she lied beautifully. All women lied well, Bert had noted, this one perhaps better than most. She had been on the plane with Harry. Since she admitted to having a drink spilled on her, probably she had been sitting next to him, though even this was not sure. There could have been another drink spilled elsewhere in the plane.

All the rest was still guesswork.

So he never confronted her with the underpants that might

have shocked her into an admission of some kind. More likely she would only have denied they were hers. They stayed in Bert's drawer, waiting, he hoped, for a more viable opportunity. Next time, he promised himself.

At the door he told her he might have to see her again.

"Anytime," she said.

He thanked her for coming in.

"My pleasure, I'm sure," she said.

Every detective in the outer office, Bert noted, watched her flounce out the door and down the hall toward the elevator.

Standing in his doorway, Bert nodded to one of his detectives, who got up from his chair and went out behind her. This was Lieutenant Mosconi from the organized crime control bureau, whose entire professional life was focused on the Russo crime family. Mosconi got on the elevator with Anna, and they rode downstairs together, but he did not speak to her. Nor did he even look in her direction as the two of them came out of the building almost side by side and crossed Police Plaza. But the appearance of Mosconi was the signal that a detective named Crosse had been waiting for. Crosse, who was from the photo section, had a camera equipped with a motor drive and a 200mm lens, and he snapped a dozen pictures of Anna Russo before she was ten yards out of the building.

Meanwhile, in Bert's outer office two other detectives, one with a black satchel on his lap, looked up from the straight chairs on which they had been sitting.

Bert said to them: "Will you gentlemen come in please."

Having closed his office door, Bert gestured toward the coffee table. "The cup, the saucer, the photo," he said.

He watched for a moment while the two men broke open the satchel, got out their powders and brushes, and arranged everything on the table. They were slow, meticulous men, which was what their job called for, he supposed. But the technicalities, as they began to employ them, were not new to Bert, nor did they concern him overmuch. In the meantime he had the detective division to run, his in-basket was again stuffed with papers, and he began to go through them, signing or initialing some, rerouting others.

"Nice and clear," he heard one of the detectives say.

There was a shaft of sunlight that came down onto the coffee table, and when Bert glanced over there he saw that it had become a shaft of fingerprint dust.

"Yes sir," said the other, "nice and clear."

A bit later he heard their camera clicking as they photographed whatever prints they had found before lifting them onto their cards, and a bit after that the two men were standing beside his chair showing him two cards, one from today, one from the 77th Street apartment, and pointing out comparisons with a pencil.

From the underside of the saucer they had lifted this print here, probably her left pinky. It matched this print here, found on the soup tureen in the kitchen of the apartment. You needed eight points of similarity for a print to stand up in court, and you had them here, for both prints were clear.

Prints tended to aviate. *Aviate* was a fingerprint word: it meant evaporate, vanish. The print in the kitchen was at least five days old when found, Bert reflected, and Anna had been in Washington for the three days before that. How long would it have taken the print on the soup tureen to aviate? Would it have lasted those eight days?

Unlikely. Even five days was pushing it.

Therefore, to make the print on the soup tureen, Anna must have been present in the apartment about the time Harry Chapman was shot. Either that or she entered the apartment and handled the soup tureen afterward. But this was unlikely, as by then there were detectives all over the neighborhood. She would have had to run a veritable gauntlet to get in there, and to Bert she hadn't seemed anywhere near brave enough to try a thing like that.

Which made her probably the last person to see Harry alive, apart from the killer. Almost certainly it did. Maybe it made her the killer as well.

So what did he do with this information?

"What's her name, Chief?" said one of the technicians. He had his pen poised over the card with today's latent prints taped to it.

Bert looked out the window.

"Since it's the same person," said his partner, "we can put her name down on both cards."

"Put down Miss X," said Bert curtly. He wanted these men out of his office before they had time to do too much thinking. "What else you got?" he said with pretended impatience. "I don't have time for conversation." He started toward the door, the signal that they had been dismissed.

But they did not go, for they had him at a disadvantage, and seemed to sense it.

"Who is this Miss X, Chief?" asked the younger technician. "What's her connection to the PC?"

"Yeah," said the first man with a grin. "Was she a relative, or what?"

Bert looked at them, and did not smile. These two men were detectives. Lab detectives, rather stodgy types, but still detectives. They were not stupid, and their profession had made them cynical. They had stumbled onto an important piece of the case, and knew it. By now a lot of other detectives were in possession of other pieces, and when these two got outside this room they would ask questions. They would give up what they knew in return for what someone else knew.

Before long, talking among themselves, the detectives would have put together most of the story, which would then race through the department. It was juicy enough, was it not? How do you keep something like this quiet? In a few hours, news of the PC and the Mafia floozie who may have killed him would be all any cop could talk about. It would then be only a matter of time before some reporter overheard them talking and the story got out.

"I don't think she was a relative, no," said Bert. It was no use lying to these men. "Listen—" he said urgently.

He began trying to impress on them the sensitivity of the case. They should keep their mouths shut, tell nobody. Give him two days of silence and he would deliver the killer—

But they interrupted with more questions, which they would not normally have dared.

"If she's the one who shot him, Chief, I just don't see how you could let her walk out that door."

"She's not the one. Of that I'm certain." He was certain of no such thing. "But she may lead us to the killer—unless you guys blow the case by shooting your mouths off." His lips came together and he gave each of them a hard stare.

"Let me give you a warning. If word of what's on those fingerprint cards gets out, I'll know exactly where it came from, and you two'll be back in uniform so fast you won't have time to shine your shoes first. You got that?"

They began apologizing. They made promises all the way to the door. Bert had no illusions—promises, under circumstances like these, were meaningless. They might last an hour or two. The time it took the men who made them to belly up to a bar. He had very little time.

As he showed them out, he saw that Lieutenant Mosconi had returned and was waiting for him.

"Well?" said Bert, inviting him into his office.

"She had a car waiting for her, Chief—a white Cadillac in fact. The driver was a young guy named Willie Boy Benvenuto. He's what they call a zip—straight from Sicily. Doesn't even speak proper English yet. He's just a gofer. Mostly he's assigned to drive her wherever she wants to go."

Bert wasn't interested in Willie Boy Benvenuto.

"And Chief, listen to this. I got an informant tells me Willie Boy adores her, even though she's close to twenty years older than he is."

Bert looked up sharply.

"I know what you're thinking, Chief, but you're wrong. As far as we know she doesn't reciprocate, and I doubt Willie Boy would dare try anything. Her husband would have him whacked so fast—"

"Did Crosse get photos of her?"

"He said he'd have them on your desk in an hour."

"I want you to go out to Westbury," Bert said then. He was thinking it out as he spoke. "Go yourself or send guys you trust. She brought her green Chanel suit to be dry-cleaned the other day. Monday, maybe Tuesday. Tomato juice stains all down the front. Find whatever dry cleaner she patronizes. Give them a story and get me the suit, preferably with the stains still on it. Then bring it back here."

This order made Mosconi uncomfortable. "You really should have a warrant for that kind of work, shouldn't you, Chief?"

Bert would have preferred a warrant too but judged there wasn't time to get one.

"Maybe," said Mosconi, "we should consult the DA first before taking such a step."

These were reasonable objections and they forced Bert to pause. An assistant DA had been assigned to the case from the first day. His name was Petrie. He was there to go into court to procure warrants or wiretap orders as needed. He was the one who would sift through whatever evidence the police brought in, and would decide when—whether— enough had been accumulated to make an arrest.

Bert had met him on a previous case, and had talked to him twice by phone about this one. Like most assistant DAs Petrie was a young guy not long out of law school. Bert knew without being told that there was not enough evidence to arrest Anna Russo, or anyone else, and also that getting a judge to sign a warrant to seize Anna's suit was unlikely.

And just to explain to Petrie what he was thinking, what he was trying to do, would cost him two hours, maybe more. These were two hours Bert didn't have. Besides which, Petrie would probably order him to step back from Anna Russo and her Chanel suit or risk tainting the case legally.

Anna, meanwhile, would be on her way home to Westbury, where she might go straight to her cleaner, reclaim her suit, and then destroy it. Better, Bert decided, to possess evidence that couldn't be presented in court rather than no evidence at all.

"Let's say I manage to get hold of the garment," Mosconi said. "Without a warrant the court might rule it inadmissible as evidence and—"

"Just do it," said Bert.

"—And an illegal seizure of property."

"Fast," said Bert.

Mosconi shrugged and went out.

In an hour the pictures came up, and Bert brought two detectives into his office, briefed them, and sent them out to find Caroline Connolly—at her apartment, at the airport, wherever—and show them to her: "Get her to identify this woman as the one who was sitting next to the PC on the shuttle. Have her sign a statement to that effect."

Late in the day Lieutenant Mosconi returned. Outside it was already dark by then. Mosconi had the Chanel suit in a paper bag, and he spilled it out onto Bert's desk, where it lay as inert as a dead animal.

Mosconi had had to sign a receipt to get the cleaner to hand it over, he said. "The guy would have been within his rights to refuse me, Chief."

"He gave it to you, didn't he?"

"Well, yes."

"Most people," Bert said, "the police want something, don't stand up for their rights. It's called fear." Bert fingered the suit. "I wonder if you ever noticed?"

"Yes I have, Chief."

"I'm glad to hear it." Bert examined the stain down the front of the suit. Tomato juice.

Mosconi gestured toward the suit. "If you're hoping to use it as evidence in court, Chief, I think the judge would have to throw it out."

Bert tossed the Chanel suit at Mosconi. "Take it to the lab. Ask them to verify that the stain is tomato juice, and to check it against whatever fibers they found in the apartment."

Mosconi nodded.

"After that throw all your men into the street. Go to the social clubs, the restaurants—wherever mob guys hang out. See what they're saying out there."

Because mobsters could not keep their mouths shut, you could count on it. They were even worse gossips than detectives. They lived in such a grotesque world that this was understandable. Hit contracts and rip-offs were difficult not to talk about. Detectives who paddled around in the Mafia's muddy waters almost always heard who had done what to whom. This was not the same as being able to prove it in court, but it made for a solid body of information.

That Bert had questioned the wife of a Mafia don would cause talk, if it got out. The streets would boil with it. "You hear something," Bert said, "you come back and tell me."

When Mosconi had left him, Bert went to his window and stared out.

The possibility of tainting the case was a worry. Holding back information and evidence, including now Anna and her Chanel suit, was a bigger one. Men would be furious when they found out: the DA, John Kincaid, Priestly, Sternhagen.

Not to mention the mayor. Bert would explain that the case had been unraveling fast, that he had had to move equally fast to keep up with it. How would this argument be received?

Not well.

About the case itself: was he making assumptions before he had facts to support them? Relying on guesswork? Risking his career on guesswork?

The mayor did not have to wait ten days to appoint a new PC. He could announce his choice anytime. He could do it five minutes from now. How much longer could Bert risk holding back what he knew?

He returned to his desk and phoned Anna Russo at home.

He got the same maid as the last time, and was put on hold.

When Anna came on she sounded out of breath. "I just this minute got home," she said. "Who is this?"

He apologized for bothering her again so soon, but—

There was a scared sound to her silence.

Some additional facts had just come to light, he said. He wanted to check them out with her. Would she please come in to see him tomorrow morning: "How does ten o'clock sound?"

"Unfortunately, I won't be able to—"

"It's settled, then. Ten o'clock."

She said: "Now wait, just wait—"

He could, he told her, send detectives to bring her in, if she preferred. Or come to her house himself. Or else, she could come to his office at ten A.M. tomorrow.

Silence.

"It will only take a few minutes," he assured her.

She became angry and abusive. She wasn't coming, he couldn't make her—

"Maybe," interrupted Bert, "you'd rather I spoke to your husband."

Silence again.

"I don't know if he knows yet," insinuated Bert.

"All right," she said in a small voice, "Ten A.M. But this is the last time." She slammed the receiver down, which only made him smile.

It was decision-making time, and he returned to his window and brooded. It had got very dark out there. The day was over, and it was night. The lights of the city seemed to go on to the horizon.

Bert too knew about Earl Coxen's visit to City Hall. Abruptly he dialed the mayor's office.

When the mayor came on, Bert offered to come over at once and brief him in person.

"Now?" said the mayor.

"Now," said Bert.

"I'm pretty busy," the mayor said. "Can't we do this over the phone?"

"I don't think so, no."

The mayor sighed.

When Bert reached City Hall most of the offices were empty and dark, but the mayor was waiting for him. So were two deputy mayors, who occupied chairs in front of the mayor's desk. Bert shook hands with them.

"You can speak freely," the mayor said. "These fellows know everything I know."

Seeing that Bert looked hesitant, the mayor added: "Let's hear it. What's so important you couldn't tell me on the phone?"

Bert glanced at the two deputies, and a heavy silence fell upon the room.

"Well?" said the mayor.

Bert held his ground. "Maybe you and I could talk first," he said stubbornly, "and then if you want I could brief these men after."

The mayor sighed again. "Marv, Julius," he said, "give us a few moments in private."

The two deputies took it with bad grace. Shaking their heads in annoyance, they rose from their chairs and left the office.

"All right," said the mayor to Bert, "what's so goddam secret?"

"Whatever you choose to do with my information is your own business," answered Bert, "but you deserve to hear it first in private." Now he began to describe in guarded terms some, not all, of what he had been holding back. Harry Chapman, he began, had started his last run from a secret apartment he kept near where he was killed.

"Doesn't surprise me," said the mayor.

"Yes," said Bert cautiously, "well, he seems to have used it to meet women."

"And one of them killed him," chortled the mayor. "I told you it was a woman."

Bert said guardedly, "We don't know that for a fact as yet. But it certainly seems possible."

"How many women was he boffing at one time?"

"I've found two. Maybe there were more."

"Jesus," said the mayor, "two plus his wife, I suppose."

"I don't know about that part of it. I guess so."

Bert could feel the mayor shaking his head in amazement.

"Here's the thing," said Bert. "One of the women is a Mafia guy's wife."

This caused a long, stiff silence.

"I felt you should know about it," said Bert, "before anyone else did."

Another silence.

"Which Mafia guy?" the mayor said.

Bert told him.

"The biggest mafioso we've got," said the mayor. "Three cheers for Harry Chapman."

"I don't know yet whether it was a one-night stand, or what. I may find out tomorrow when I interview her again."

"Harry Chapman," said the mayor. "My search committee's gift to the city of New York."

"I wanted to warn you. I wanted to give you as much time as possible to figure out what to do. This case could get messy."

"Messy, the man says."

"I'll sweep as much under the rug as I can," said Bert piously.

"Thank you."

"But I don't know how much that will be."

"The press vultures will be on this the minute they get a whiff of it."

"I guess they will."

"On me, that's who they'll be on. They'll make me responsible for the scandal of the century. The Mafia. That's all I needed."

` The mayor was shaking his head.

"Of course," Bert said, "I'll confer with you every step of the way."

"Any chance," said the mayor, "of the case going in some other direction?" Although the tone of his voice hadn't changed, Bert understood him to be almost pleading.

"I don't know. We have nothing conclusive as yet."

"At some point you have to tell the press something. How much are you going to tell them?"

"My instinct is to stonewall them until we're sure of what we have."

"My instinct too," said the mayor.

"John Kincaid has been sending someone out to brief them every night. The investigation is following up on some new leads, blah blah blah. The guy he sends is very good at it."

"Congratulate him for me."

After another pause the mayor said: "So what do we do next?"

"With luck I may be able to put a solid case together before too long. When we make an arrest, you can call a press conference and announce it."

"You call the press conference," said the mayor. "I think I'd prefer to be left out of this one."

"However you want to play it."

"Harry Chapman," the mayor said. "Christ."

Bert left shortly afterward. The mayor did not ask him to brief the deputy mayors first.

As he strode down the long corridor past all the gloomy former mayors and out to his car it gratified him to imagine that he was now at the top of the mayor's consciousness, and would remain there until the case was concluded. Being the custodian of incendiary information had its advantages. Sometime soon the mayor would decide on a new PC, but he would not do so now without considering Bert's reaction first.

An hour later Bert sat in the office of Acting Police Commissioner Priestly and went over the same information a second time. Also present were Chief Kincaid, who had come down from the 24th Precinct for the occasion, and Chief Sternhagen. The others had known of the secret apartment since the night before; now they heard about the stewardess, and about the

Mafia don's wife whose fingerprint matched one of the ones from the apartment. They heard certain other particulars too. To career policemen, it was doleful news.

"This is going to smear the department like nothing else that has ever happened to us," said Sternhagen. Late as the hour had become, his uniform shoes still gleamed, the pleats in his trousers were still razor sharp. He was tall, white haired and, despite his somewhat protruding paunch, a man of ramrod posture—in appearance every inch the commander. "It will take the department twenty years to get over it." He was stiff in demeanor at the best of times, but at the moment he looked ready to cry. "We'll all be gone by then," he said.

Kincaid's mood was the opposite, not tears but outrage, and he turned to Bert. "How long have you known all this? Why wasn't I told?"

"I told you now," said Bert.

"What else do you know that you haven't told me?"

"You have it all," lied Bert. He had said nothing about the white panties with the lace around the thighs, or that he possessed the bullet that had killed Harry Chapman. Nor had he outlined certain other ideas that had been floating through his head all day.

"I'm up in the Two-Four spinning my wheels," Kincaid said, outraged, addressing the other two men, "and he's conducting his own private investigation, and not telling anybody."

"This is information that fell into my lap," said Bert, and he too turned to the first dep and Sternhagen. "I did what any detective would do. I checked it out before I went forward with it."

He looked into the unreceptive faces of his two superiors.

"I mean, it's somewhat sensitive stuff, wouldn't you say?"

"True," admitted Sternhagen.

"Should I have shared it with however many detectives are working on this case out of the Two-Four?"

"I don't know," said Priestly.

"Maybe not," conceded Sternhagen.

"I resign from the case," said Kincaid. "Either I'm running this investigation or I'm not. If I'm not, I'm out of here. Get somebody else." And he sprang to his feet and started for the door.

Because the authority of Priestly and Sternhagen was being more directly flaunted than his own, Bert gave them a moment to react. But they did nothing.

"Come back here," Bert shouted at Kincaid's back.

Kincaid had reached the door but there he hesitated.

"Sit down in that chair," ordered Bert in a hard cold voice. "Sit down right now."

Kincaid, fifteen years his senior but one step below him in rank, did not move.

"You will resign from the investigation when I say you can resign, and not before," said Bert. "Go out that door now and I want your shield. You'll be resigning all right. Not from the case, from the department."

Kincaid returned sullenly to his chair. He met no one's eyes and did not speak.

There was a long heavy silence, broken finally by Sternhagen. "I knew Harry Chapman had a zipper problem back when he was a young cop in my precinct," he said.

Bert doubted this. He himself had ridden in the same car with Harry every night and never suspected it. It must have come on later, perhaps because of the adulation politicians receive, or because his marriage went bad.

"Do you tell Mary Alice Chapman?" said Sternhagen.

"What for?" said Bert.

"Maybe she knows," said Sternhagen.

"Maybe," said Bert.

"Women usually do," said Sternhagen.

A platitude. In Bert's experience women usually didn't know. They didn't want to know. Usually you had to rub their faces in it. "Whether she knew or didn't know has nothing to do with the investigation."

"Of course not," said Sternhagen.

Sternhagen and the first dep began to discuss other commanders they had known. This one and that one had also had "zipper problems." To lighten the mood, Bert mentioned a cop he had known who used to hit on women who had just been burglarized. "They were all distraught and easy pickings, apparently."

Since this idle chatter was designed only to gloss over the disturbing confrontation that had just taken place, it began and ended spontaneously. Staring alternately at the floor or the wall, Kincaid took no part in it.

"Do you think it was a Mafia hit, Bert?" said Sternhagen finally, and they got down to business again.

"There are other possibilities."

"If it's a Mafia hit," said the first dep, "you'll never solve it."

"Mafia hits are very difficult," agreed Sternhagen.

"Or you solve it five years from now," said the first dep.

"Five is about right," said Sternhagen.

"You catch some guy facing twenty-five to life on something else, and he turns, and agrees to testify on this," said the first dep.

Neither man seemed too disturbed at this possible outcome.

"That's the only way you solve Mafia hits," said the first dep.

"If you don't solve it," Sternhagen said, "nobody needs to know Chapman was screwing a Mafia don's wife."

"Or that he was screwing anyone," said the first dep.

"The department won't be smeared," said Sternhagen.

"We have to go forward with the investigation," said Bert impatiently. "We have to investigate the possibility that a Mafia hit is what it was. If we investigate it, word is going to get out."

"But you can soften it, Bert," said Sternhagen. "You can, can't you? So as to protect the department as much as possible."

"I don't know."

"Russo finds out the PC is banging his wife and has him whacked," said the first dep. "Why didn't he whack his wife as well?"

"It may happen," said Bert.

"Should we protect her, or what?" asked Sternhagen.

"How are you going to protect her from her own husband?" said Bert.

"The witness protection program," suggested Sternhagen.

"Her and her children," said Bert. "That's not something you arrange overnight—even if she agreed to it. It would leave her husband plenty of time to whack her if that's what he wanted to do."

"You could pick her up and hold her as a material witness," suggested the first dep.

"For the moment, Commissioner, we have nothing to hold her on, and as for the witness protection program, I doubt she would go."

"What rubbish," snorted Kincaid suddenly. He had not spoken in ten minutes or more. "The Mafia had nothing to do with this."

All eyes turned to Kincaid.

"When was the last time the Mafia killed a cop? Never, that's when. It's almost a religion with them."

Sternhagen said: "Normally, you'd be right. But this is not a normal situation. I can see it happening."

"Kill a police commissioner? They'd have to be out of their minds. They know they'd bring on an investigation they'd never survive."

"They're in such an investigation now," Bert said, "like it or not."

"Maybe they didn't know who he was," suggested Sternhagen.

"Before they kill anybody, they know very well who he is."

"Maybe this one time—"

"Anything leads the investigation toward the Mafia," stated Kincaid, "is a total waste of time."

"The woman is Russo's wife," mused the first dep. "This was personal, you might say. He was beside himself at her infidelity. So he had the PC whacked. It makes sense."

"The Mafia never hits cops," said Kincaid bluntly.

Bert had been troubled by the same thoughts himself. The men who ran the five families were hardheaded businessmen, not hotheads. They ordered murders all the time, but for business reasons only. If Dominic Russo ordered the murder of Harry Chapman without clearing it first with the other dons, and if they found out about it, they would do away with him. He was probably the most powerful Mafia guy in New York, but he was not the only one. All those guys had triggermen working for them, and Russo knew it. All of them, in a pinch, could pull triggers themselves. At bottom the Mafia was a disciplined organization, which was why it had stayed in business so long.

As a solution to the murder of Harry Chapman, Anna Russo was almost too good to be true.

And yet—

The first dep said: "What are your thoughts, Bert?"

Bert looked at them. "Bizarre behavior is not the exception, it's the norm. For all human beings, but especially for those guys."

"What does that mean?" said Kincaid.

"It means there is more here that we don't know. It means that maybe Anna Russo had something to do with the PC's death, and maybe she didn't. Maybe Dominic Russo did, and maybe he didn't. It means we will follow the investigation wherever it may lead."

Kincaid said: "The Mafia is a dead end, I tell you. It's a blind alley."

"You don't have to do the Mafia part of the investigation," Bert snapped. "I'll do that part of it myself."

"But do you have the time, Bert?" asked the first dep.

"I'll make time."

"And what am I supposed to be doing meanwhile?" demanded Kincaid.

"Whatever you've been doing all along," said Bert in a low dangerous voice.

The first dep looked from one man to the other and felt the need to inject a calming presence. "And what is that, John?"

"Commissioner," said Kincaid earnestly, "we've had over five hundred phone calls from the public, and another couple of hundred letters. Everybody's got a tip for us. We've checked out almost all of them, but there are still some to go. We're still canvassing and recanvassing the neighborhood, trying to find somebody who saw something. We're going through Chapman's phone records, his canceled checks. Do you realized how many death threats he received since he became PC?"

"All PCs get death threats," said Bert. "Chiefs of detectives too, as a matter of fact."

"We had to go back and check all those death threats out again," said Kincaid plaintively. "I've got detectives working on the Puerto Rican angle—they're staked out all over Spanish Harlem waiting for any of those guys to come home. I've got detectives in Washington trying to find out who Chapman saw there, what he did there—maybe that's got something to do with who killed him. I've got other detectives interviewing his political connections here. I'm still looking for some secret life Chapman had, other than women. I don't believe he was shot because of unrequited love, whatever the rest of you believe."

"The department has confidence in you, John," said the first dep.

To Bert this sounded patronizing, but Kincaid seemed to accept it. "Thank you, Commissioner," he said.

Priestly stood up, which signified that the meeting was over. But as the others filed out of his office, Bert stayed back.

"I still need to get into Chapman's office," he said to Priestly.

Priestly said; "Hmm."

"Not me personally, Commissioner," Bert said, "the investigation."

"There's nothing in there that will help you, I'm afraid."

"Well," said Bert, "you never know."

"It's personal stuff. Belongs to the widow. We'll have to make arrangements soon to move it out. As soon as she's able to tell us where to move it to. I didn't want to bother her about it during the worst part of her grief. We should give her another week or so, don't you think?"

He's trying to stall the investigation, thought Bert. And he'll go on stalling it until the mayor names a new PC. Then whatever happens to the investigation will be too late to help me personally.

"I'm beginning to understand Harry's life," said Bert. He was not pleading but explaining. "At the very least, there should be a little black book somewhere with the names of bimbos in it. It's an angle, Commissioner, that we need to investigate."

"No," said Priestly, "there's nothing like that, I assure you."

"What about his safe?"

"I'm afraid Harry took the combination with him to the grave."

"In other words we don't know what is in the safe?" Bert had always assumed this.

"If anything. No."

"We can get people in here to open it. We can burn it open if necessary."

"Oh, I hardly think this calls for extraordinary measures like that, do you?"

"Yes I do," said Bert bluntly.

"Blowtorches in the PC's office? I'm afraid that would make a very bad impression. The news would go all over the building. The press would hear about it. It would look like we were accusing him of something, and trying to find evidence against him."

"I don't think that's how it would read at all."

"It would to me."

"Commissioner, the investigation has to get into that office and into that safe. Failure to do so, if the press heard about it, would look, I'm afraid, like a cover-up."

Priestly again said: "Hmm." He had gone behind his desk and sat down, and he looked at Bert over steepled fingers.

"If we wait," he said finally, "the combination might turn up. There would be no need for blowtorches, and all the commotion that would go with them."

"Commissioner, we can't afford to wait."

"Let me think about it overnight," Priestly said.

He got up and patted Bert's shoulder all the way to the door. "You're young yet," he said in a fatherly tone. "Young men are always in a hurry. They tend to exaggerate, too."

In the corridor headed for the stairs down to his own office on the thirteenth floor, Bert told himself that tomorrow the first dep would only find new arguments, and would stall him again.

The investigation couldn't wait. Bert himself couldn't wait. And he began to formulate a plan.

■ 12 ■

CHIEF OF DETECTIVES Bert P. Farber did not phone first; it seemed better simply to drive up and ring the bell.

Wearing a gray sweat suit and mules Mary Alice opened the door and immediately looked surprised. Finally she gave a smile that was so brief he almost missed it, and let him in.

He followed her back into the living room, where he saw that she had been sitting on the sofa playing solitaire on the coffee table. Over in the corner burned a single lamp. All the rest of the vast empty house seemed to be dark.

"If you're busy," he said, "I can go."

"Busy?" she said. Her voice to him was as musical as ever though a bit flat, like champagne when all the bubbles have gone out.

She scooped up the cards on the coffee table and walked over and put them in a brass bowl on a sideboard. He watched her carefully as she moved about turning on lamps. Even with all the lamps lit, it seemed to Bert that the room remained gloomy.

"How are you, Mary Alice?" he asked, and hoped she would hear the concern in his voice.

"All right," she said, and tried another half smile. "Getting used to being a widow, is all."

"The boys gone?"

She nodded. "They went back this morning."

"Do you have anyone to stay with you?"

"No."

"You should have, perhaps."

"There's no one. I prefer being alone, anyway."

"Do you?"

"I think so."

He had work to do here, but couldn't just barge in and do it.

She said: "Would you like a drink?"

He could use a stiff drink. "If you're having something."

She went to a sideboard and began to prepare his drink. "Still scotch over ice?" she asked.

He followed her into the kitchen, where she put ice in the glass and handed it to him.

"Have you had dinner yet, Mary Alice?"

"I'm not very hungry lately."

"Well, you should force yourself," he said, for she looked as if she had lost ten pounds in a few days.

There was a kitchen table and several chairs, but she did not sit down, nor did he.

He said: "Why don't I take you out and buy you something to eat?"

She looked down at the sweat suit in which she stood. "I'm not dressed for it."

"You could change into something."

She shook her head. "I'd rather not."

They stood looking at each other. It was awkward.

"I could fix something here, perhaps." She bent and peered into the fridge.

"I don't like to put you out."

"Potato salad," she said, "cole slaw, cold roast beef."

"That would be fine."

"Left over from our party the other night. The wake, or whatever it was."

She served out tiny portions for herself, large ones for him, and they sat opposite each other at the kitchen table.

She did not eat, and presently put her fork down. "This is like trying to bring the wake back to life," she said. But then, seeing that he was eating with good appetite, she added: "I'm sorry. I didn't mean to spoil it for you."

He had not had time for lunch and had been drinking coffee all afternoon. He could have eaten almost anything. In addition

to which, he could not leave until he had asked his questions
and acquired some answers. As he ate he kept watching for
a spot to begin interjecting them, but none occurred.

"Do you still play the piano?" she asked him, looking
wistful. "Do you still go to Japanese restaurants?"

She had resumed picking at her food, he noted, and from
then on the questioning was all done by her. He felt like a
former classmate, one she barely remembered, cornered at a
high school reunion. She kept looking for topics to keep the
conversation going.

"Mary Alice," he interrupted finally, "I need to get into
Harry's office, and into his office safe."

Immediately her listlessness dropped away. "What for?"

Bert put his fork down and wiped his mouth on the paper
napkin. "Because we might find a lead as to who killed him
and why."

"Why come to me?" she asked somewhat frantically.
"What do I know?"

"His office is locked. His safe is locked. Does he have a
place in this house, a room or somewhere, where he might
keep an extra set of keys, where he might have written down
the combination of the safe?"

"You just want to dig up dirt on Harry," she said.

"I want to catch whoever did this."

"You want to drag Harry's name down into the dirt, and
mine with it."

"Mary Alice," he said, and attempted to take her hand, but
she snatched it away.

"I have so little. Can't you just leave me with what I
have?"

Her chest was heaving. He watched her for a while.

"You've hated me ever since Harry and I got married,"
she said.

"How can a man hate someone he loved as much as I
loved you?"

She shrugged this off.

He waited until she seemed a bit calmer. "Did you know
about the apartment on Seventy-seventh Street?" he asked
then.

"No." He had the impression she was lying.

"Brooks' apartment."

"Chet Brooks," she said.

"Is that his name? I never met him."

"You're lucky."

"Harry must have kept the apartment for when he had business meetings in midtown."

She was dabbing at her eyes with a paper napkin. "That's not why he kept it."

Bert registered this remark but decided for the time being to ignore it. "Mary Alice, I'll do everything in my power to protect Harry's reputation, and especially your reputation."

He got up and made tea for them both, all the while talking to her as soothingly as he could. Probably, he told her, he would find nothing in Harry's headquarters office, or in his safe there, but it had to be checked out. He would be severely criticized if he didn't check it out. He could break into the office, and they could blow the safe open if they had to, but why make such a mess if it wasn't necessary?

Presently she led him into a small room off the second-floor hall that, she said, Harry had called his den. He had made and received phone calls in this room, paid household bills here.

There was a desk, and she stood in the doorway as Bert began to open its drawers and to shuffle through their contents. He found a ring of keys at once, one of which was the same make and general shape as the key to his own office, for he took his own out and compared it. He looked up at Mary Alice in the doorway, and when she nodded to show she acquiesced, he dropped the keys on their ring into his pocket.

"I'll bring them back," he promised, and she nodded again.

In another drawer, lying loose amid pencils, paper clips, rubber bands, and other such junk, was a scrap of paper with a series of numbers scribbled on it. Numbers to a combination lock of some kind—what else could it be? But not just an ordinary lock, for there were five numbers. A safe then. This had to be the combination Bert was looking for. How many safes—or other locks involving a combination—could Harry have owned?

He glanced up at Mary Alice, who returned his gaze without blinking.

She asked: "Did you find what you were looking for?"

"Maybe," he said, and stuffed this paper too into his pocket. He stood up. "What would he be likely to keep in his office safe—if anything?"

"Some jewelry of mine, I think. You might bring it back to me."

"I'll do that," he said.

They gazed at each other a long time, but finally he broke it off. One couldn't actually look into someone else's soul. One couldn't actually look into the past either. This moment in time was not going to lead anywhere, and to stand this close to her and do nothing was painful to him.

"I have to go," he said.

"Eat and run, eh?" She tried a smile but managed only to look forlorn and lost.

"No, of course not," he said. But now that he had decided what he intended to do, he did want to run.

"You can't stay?" she asked, but he could not tell if she cared about him personally, or wished only not to be left alone.

"I really can't."

He went down the stairs and then along the hall to the front door, and she trailed him. His trench coat was on a chair near the door, and as he put it on his hand went automatically into its pocket, encountering there the lacy underpants he had been carrying around since last night, and his fingers clenched around them.

It made him stand stock-still and think for a moment. Should he show them to her or not? Maybe they were hers. Maybe she was not the grieving widow at all but the suspect he was looking for. But he chased this thought at once. Not Mary Alice. He would never believe it. But what was the correct thing to do here? Correct as a detective. Correct as a man. Correct as someone who cared about this defeated, grieving woman.

His hand kept opening and closing. The lace was rough, the other surfaces slick and cool. But if he did show them to her, how would she react? Perhaps with such shock that she would do or say something to give herself away. Herself or another. He didn't think so, but having conjured up the possibility, he considered that he now had no choice but to bring the panties forth. "Do you recognize these?"

She handled them, turned them this way and that. "No. Should I?"

"Not yours, by any chance?"

"That's not the type of panties I wear. As you know very well."

It was her first acknowledgment of the intimacy that had once existed between them.

She touched his arm. "Or don't you remember?"

Good, he thought, these panties have nothing to do with her.

So he gave a mischievous grin. "It's been a while since I checked out your underwear personally."

But then her face darkened. "What do those things have to do with Harry's death?"

"Maybe nothing," said Bert.

"Where did you find them?"

The habits of a lifetime reasserted themselves. "I'm not sure," Bert said. He shoved them back in his pocket.

"A trophy from Chet Brooks' apartment," said Mary Alice bitterly.

"No, I don't think so."

"A little souvenir of Harry's."

"You're mistaken."

"Anything you found there, it wouldn't surprise me."

"Mary Alice—"

"Why'd you show them to me?"

Bert could not think how to answer.

"To humiliate me, that's why."

"That's not true, Mary Alice."

"Why don't you go?" she said, her voice rising. "Why don't you just go?"

"I'll bring the keys back tomorrow. And your jewelry too, if it's there."

"Don't bother."

Putting his hands on her shoulders, he bent to kiss her cheek, but she shrugged him off. "Go, just go."

He went out into the cold dark night and stood on the

sidewalk and shook his head back and forth and tried to breathe deeply, but couldn't.

Twenty minutes later he got out of the elevator on the fourteenth floor of police headquarters, and hesitated, and glanced toward the offices of the late police commissioner at the end of the hall. He could see a light on down there, and thought he could hear someone moving around.

The fourteenth floor was the province of the PC and of various deputy commissioners: the first dep of course, but also the deputy commissioners in charge of legal matters, management and budget, and departmental trials. These were big offices employing many people, and at this hour all were locked and dark. Normally the PC's offices would be locked and dark too, and any calls would be routinely directed to the operations division, the department's nerve center. But it was not dark tonight because Priestly's guard was in there, a uniformed cop guarding Harry's office as if it were a crime scene, which it was not. The office staff guarded the door by day, and a relay of cops at night. To Bert the night guards seemed a prodigious waste of police manpower. He wondered how Priestly would be able to justify it, if called upon to do so.

What did Priestly imagine was in there that was worth guarding? What had been his purpose in sealing the office off?

But Bert had already asked himself these questions several times.

Walking as softly as possible he moved along the corridor, but in the absence of any other noise his footsteps sounded incredibly loud to him.

When he came to the door to the first dep's offices he stopped. After listening carefully, he withdrew a tire iron from his attaché case. He could not hear the cop on guard down the hall, but was afraid that in a moment the cop would hear him, that the noise he was about to make would sound like an explosion.

Inserting the tire iron into the first dep's doorjamb, he pushed, heard a crack, then another crack, pushed again, and saw the door swing open.

But it left splinters and other mess on the floor that he worked at scuffing inside with the side of his shoe. Studying the broken jamb, he tried to convince himself that little or no damage showed from the outside, and that nobody would be looking for sign of forced entry anyway, not at this hour, and not up here on the fourteenth floor. But his handiwork did show. It was plainly visible to anyone who, happening by, happened to glance at it.

Like who for instance?

Answer: high-ranking men worked up here, any of whom might come back after dinner to work late, or to fetch something left behind earlier.

Well, it was too late to worry about that now, and Bert stepped into the office, closed the door, and leaned his back against it, while he waited for his heartbeat to slow down, and to catch his breath. It was not every day that the chief of detectives of the New York Police Department burglarized the offices of the first deputy commissioner, and he was having more trouble getting used to the idea than he had anticipated.

Reaching, he pulled a chair over and braced it to hold the door closed. In addition to the splinters, part of the jamb had been ripped out and lay on the floor, along with part of the lock. There is going to be hell to pay here in the morning, Bert thought, and he looked around.

He had no difficulty orienting himself, for the night glow of New York came in through the various windows, and he went through into Priestly's office to his desk, where he pulled out some drawers and dumped them to the floor. He pulled file jackets out of cabinets and dropped them with a splash, and books off shelves that fell with thumps, and at a certain moment he had to drop down into Priestly's chair to let his breath catch up with the hilarious reckless exhilaration he now felt, the vast mirth that was bubbling up inside him.

Out in the anteroom he upended a few more drawers. Having accomplished this much, he went through to the door to the conference room, which he found unlocked. He opened it, stepped inside, and closed it behind him.

He was in a long, narrow windowless room—the flashlight out of his attaché case showed an immense table and the twenty or more chairs that fit around it, and nothing else. How many conferences had Bert attended in this room? The answer was countless, almost all of them presided over by whoever was PC at the time, and almost all of them absolutely boring. A few commanders talked to hear themselves talk, while the others watched to see what answers the PC was looking for before daring to open their mouths—which the various PCs had never seemed to recognize, Harry Chapman included. In this regard Harry had been no better than his predecessors. High-level conferences were not the answer to running an organization as enormous and as rank structured as the NYPD, in Bert's opinion. That these thoughts should come to him now in the midst of what could only be described as criminal activity should not seem surprising because he was by training and temperament not a burglar but a three-star chief of the New York Police Department.

The conference room had three doors. One connected to the outer corridor, and this was the one entered by ordinary members of the hierarchy, such as himself, each time a conference was called; the other two connected with the offices of the PC on one side and the first dep on the other, and once the mass of commanders had assembled and were in their places these two exalted personages could enter privately from opposite ends of the room, the first dep first, of course. It was always rather galling to sit there and wait for the two of them to get around to making their appearance.

Bert listened at the middle door and could hear nothing moving out in the corridor, so he crossed to the far door and turned the handle, but found it locked. He tried various of Harry Chapman's keys, and one of them opened it.

Now he was inside the PC's private office, and there too he stepped to the outer door and listened for movement. What he heard was a TV playing. He remembered that it hung halfway up one of the walls. Whoever was on duty was presumably glued to it, feet up on the desk. Good, Bert thought, for the TV noise would help cover any noise he might make himself.

He withdrew from his pocket the scrap of paper containing the combination to Harry Chapman's safe—he hoped it was the combination—and moving up close to the safe he placed it on the rug, the beam of his flashlight beginning now to dart repeatedly from the paper to the face of the safe, as he worked the dial with his other hand.

The safe door opened almost soundlessly. It made not even as much noise as Bert's vast intake of breath, and he shone his flashlight inside.

The first thing to catch his eye was a stack of money: hundred-dollar bills in packets of twenty. He did not count it, but he took it out, hefted it, and judged he was holding about $100,000. This seemed an exhorbitant amount to leave in an office safe drawing no interest, and as he put it back he wondered where it had come from and why it was there. The phrase "campaign contributions" crossed Bert's mind, and he shook his head in a mixture of annoyance and disgust. To him campaign contributions and bribery were the same. He did not see how any man could keep a straight face while pretending otherwise. Harry, in his speech to the judiciary committee, had been right. Cops went to jail for accepting bribes. Politicians called it campaign contributions.

As a practicing politician Harry had certainly taken money.

Next the flashlight illuminated three Russian ikons, which Bert withdrew. He supposed they were Russian ikons. They were magazine sized, though much thicker of course, and he laid them on the floor and played the flashlight over them. A Cyrillic Christ, Cyrillic saints. He supposed they were worth plenty, and he remembered news reports involving Harry some years ago, an incipient scandal that got smothered before it really broke. Harry had been part of a congressional junket to Moscow, and afterward the ikons were found to be missing. The congressional party, with Harry's name at the top of the list, was accused of smuggling the rare ikons—part of the Russian national heritage—out of the country. Harry was supposed to have bought them on the black market for very little money. When he denied it on television, he had seemed so open and frank, so young and almost naive, that people believed him, and the whole thing had blown over.

Bert put the ikons too back in the safe. Mary Alice's jewelry was there in a pouch. He looked into the pouch, but after a moment's thought decided to leave it where it was.

On one shelf was a pile of papers, which he spread out on the floor. Birth certificates, car titles, insurance policies, titles to the two town houses, the one here and the other one in Washington. There were also two small notebooks. The first listed people's names, and next to each of them sums of money. Campaign contributions again, Bert thought. Some of the sums seemed to him enormous, and he put the notebook in his attaché case. Eventually he might want detectives to check out every name, and he gave a grimace at the thought of the work involved, which would be truly stupendous.

The second notebook was for phone numbers, but not just ordinary ones—Bert scanned page after page of prominent names: politicians, film stars, business leaders. The numbers beside them, he presumed, would be unlisted.

And there were people identified only by initials, sometimes with asterisks beside them, and this to Bert was more interesting still. If he had indeed found Harry's little black book, then the initials should correspond to women who had occupied parts of his life, some of whom Bert already knew about, and others of whom he was still ignorant. Anna Russo's initials should be there, Caroline Connolly's as well, and he checked quickly for initials that might be theirs, and found them, and a smile came onto his face.

There were initials and asterisks on a number of pages, he saw as he flipped through.

This notebook too went into his attaché case.

His flashlight probed the depths and corners of the safe, but nothing else of interest was revealed, so he swung the door shut, levered the handle into position, and spun the dial.

But he had been so concentrated on the safe and its contents that he had lost any sense of the rest of the room, and as he stood up he backed into and knocked over a chair.

The noise this made rang out like a detonation. Since entering the office he had been vaguely conscious of the TV noise just outside. This noise now stopped, and he heard footsteps approach the door.

He went stock-still, shut off his flashlight, and for some minutes not only did not move but scarcely dared breathe. If the cop came in here, what would Bert do? He glanced wildly in the direction of the conference room door, but it seemed to him he could not make it that far in time, and in any case the guard would see or hear the door close and would come after him.

There goes my career, he thought. Would he go to jail?

All these thoughts, this panic, lasted more than a minute. A very long time.

Finally outside the door the TV noise came on again.

Another minute passed before Bert could breathe normally again.

He moved to Harry's desk, where his flashlight beam bounced off objects. There ought to be a desk calendar on top of the desk, but there wasn't. And a phone directory or Rolodex for numbers Harry dialed every day. Again there wasn't. Bert had been in this room several times during Harry's tenure and had seen both, but they were gone. Who took them? The first dep? If so, why?

Quickly, silently he went through the various drawers, but found nothing of significance, not even any quick notes Harry might have made to himself, and this too seemed strange.

Listening again for the TV noise, he reassured himself that it was still there.

All he had to do now was get out without being seen, and he tiptoed back through the conference room, turning his flashlight off as he crossed it lest someone out in the corridor glimpse a line of light under the door.

Standing once again in Priestly's office he paused to survey the damage he had made, decided it was not sufficient, and so took a vase full of flowers off the sideboard and upended it on the floor. Water ran all over the place. Headquarters personnel often remarked on the flowers in Priestly's office, for they were fresh every week, a gift from his wife. Usually she brought them in herself and arranged them.

Bert was careful not to break her vase.

Ready to leave now, he put his ear to the door he had jimmied. He would have to cross the hall to reach the staircase that would take him down to his own floor. He would have to cross directly in front of the men's room, and so he waited listening for some minutes—time enough for anyone in there, the guard or anyone else, to finish his business, come out, and go back down the hall into an office.

Finally he lifted away the chair tilted against the door, listened hard, then stepped out into the corridor and pulled the door shut behind him.

But it swung back open again. It was important that the

broken door, and the mess inside it, not be discovered until morning, so he stepped back into the office, found a sheet of paper that he folded into a wad, and this time from the corridor side wedged the wad under the door to hold it shut.

Even as he did this he heard footsteps approaching, and he sprinted across the hall and into the stairwell, grabbing the stairwell door as it closed so it would not bang, letting it ease gently into place even as the footsteps moved on past. When he heard the men's room door open and then close, he went slowly and carefully down to the thirteenth floor, his own floor, where his presence would seem normal, and there he boarded the elevator and descended to the garage level. His car and driver were waiting, and he ordered himself driven home.

It was a cold night and the sidewalks were empty. The streets began to pass. He was in the front seat, which was where all commanders sat so as to be within reach of the radio, and scenes from the past half hour—the burglary he had just committed—moved back and forth behind his eyes, begging to be reexamined. There was going to be a helluva stink in the morning, detectives running around, Priestly screaming. He had just risked his entire career. He had risked being prosecuted, going to jail. For what?

I'm trying to break the case, he told himself. But this explanation seemed to him insufficient.

Why had he done what he had done?

Was it because he owed something to Harry Chapman? He owed nothing to Harry Chapman. Was it in the interest of seeing justice done? But he was past the Boy Scout stage; justice rarely got done. Why then? Was it because he had personal capital invested in this case? But he did not think he did. Like surgeons, lawyers, and other such practitioners, he had learned never to do that, no matter how gruesome or tragic the case might be.

Did he truly believe that if he broke the case he'd be appointed the next PC? Is that what had motivated him? But at the moment it seemed certain to him that someone else would get the job, whether he broke the case or not. He was too young, too junior, and he had no heavyweight rabbi who might lean on City Hall in his behalf. He might or might not be the best possible candidate, but politicians did not risk appointments that might be criticized. The mayor was not going to name him.

He could easily have blustered his way past the guard outside Harry Chapman's door. It made no sense at all to have broken in via Priestly's office. The guy on guard duty was a patrolman probably, at most a sergeant. Was he going to dare stand up against a determined chief of detectives? Or Bert might simply have gone to the DA and got a subpoena. Or harried the first dep for another day or two and eventually got his permission.

What was his motive? Why do it the way he had?

Having no answer he shut these thoughts out, or tried to, fighting off one after another the various notions that continued, of their own accord apparently, to crowd his head. He had done what he had done because he felt like it. He had lived the disciplined policeman's life for too long. He had needed to commit an act of rebellion, and for thirty minutes he had committed one. And got away with it too. Or so he thought. And he was tired of thinking. The hell with it all.

In the morning the red phone on his desk rang and it was Priestly.

"Will you come up here, please, Bert."

Here we go, thought Bert. He went up the stairs and as he entered Priestly's outer office he noted the broken doorjamb, the papers still scattered on the floor, and he made a show of surprise: "What the hell happened here?" he said.

Wearing a dark gray suit, his bald pate shining, Priestly stood amid the desks. People hovered around him, some in uniform, some not. No one was sitting down. No one was smiling.

"Someone broke in last night," said Priestly, and his voice sounded under tight control.

Bert allowed his eyebrows to rise, and he moved from desk to desk, surveying the damage. "What's missing, Commissioner?"

"Nothing, as far as we can tell," said one of the men.

"Something scared him off," muttered Priestly. "He didn't have time. Whoever he was."

Bert said: "Do you think he could have been a cop, Commissioner?"

"Who else could get into the building and up here at night?" Though extremely agitated, Priestly seemed to be trying to hide it.

"When I was a sergeant in the Two-Four," said Bert, "somebody carried a bolt cutter into the station house and up to the locker room on the fourth floor, cut the lock off a locker, and stole all a cop's guns."

"We're not talking about stealing guns," said Priestly. "This is not guns."

"That particular thief, it turned out, had come in off the street."

"When you were a sergeant is of no interest, none whatever."

Bert ignored the rebuke. Gesturing all around him he said: "The guy who did this, Commissioner, what was he looking for?"

"I don't know," said Priestly. "How am I supposed to know?"

As first deputy commissioner, Priestly was in direct command of the department's most sensitive functions: intelligence, internal affairs, and inspections.

"Something sensitive probably," suggested Bert. "Has anyone done an inventory?"

"Only a cursory one so far," one of the men said.

Bert had moved to where he could see into Priestly's own office. The door was partly ajar, and he expected to see the effects of his handiwork by daylight, but what he did see surprised him. The office was in pristine condition, no upended drawers, no papers scattered around, nothing.

Bert pointed down at the litter at his feet. "Is this the extent of the damage?"

"Yes," stated Priestly.

"He didn't get into your office?"

"No."

"Curious," said Bert.

The vase, empty for once, was back on the sideboard, he observed through the door. The stain on the rug had dried.

"It's obvious he didn't," said Priestly. "What do you mean, 'curious'?"

"If I were looking for something sensitive," said Bert, "I'd look in your office, Commissioner, not out here."

"Well, that wasn't the way it happened, was it?"

Disconcerted, Bert glanced around at all the faces. "Who was the first one into work this morning?"

It was Priestly who answered. "I was the one discovered the break-in." His voice sounded to Bert very tight.

And cleaned up your own office before anyone else arrived, thought Bert. Why did you do that? Why are you lying about it now? "What time did you come in?" he said.

"About seven-thirty. I'm always in by seven-thirty."

Let it go, Bert told himself, but he couldn't. "You didn't touch anything, Commissioner?"

"No."

"Nothing at all?"

"You see exactly what I saw when I got here."

"That's good. You know what they say about crime scenes." Bert was confused and as a result was talking too much. "At a crime scene the best place for a cop's hands is in his pockets."

"This is no time for jokes, Bert."

"You're right, Commissioner. I'll send some detectives up right away." In the doorway he turned. "I don't know if you would want a fingerprint team up here or not."

"Why wouldn't we?" Priestly demanded.

"They'd make a mess of your office, for one thing. And I doubt they'd find anything conclusive. You got a big staff here, and many other cops going and coming on legitimate business. That's a lot of prints to have to eliminate. Besides which, if it was a cop broke in, you have to assume he had the sense to wear gloves."

"Skip the fingerprint team," decided the first dep after a moment. Nervously he smoothed both hands back over his pate.

"Okay," said Bert, "no fingerprint team." He glanced around one last time. "Some corrupt cop trying to find out what you had on him, that's my guess." But as he went out he could not resist adding over his shoulder: "By the way,

Commissioner, I still need to get into the PC's office. When you have a chance." At the wrecked door he stopped again. "Better call building maintenance, have them come up and repair this," he said, and went out.

He was sure he had got away with it now, which seemed hilarious. His relief was such that it was all he could do to keep from semi-hysterical laughter. This internal laughter died in the stairwell, and then he was in his own office standing behind his desk, thinking: Priestly lied to me. People who lied were usually hiding something. What was Priestly hiding? Why did he lie?

Was he merely trying to downplay the break-in? It was possible. He didn't want his name in headlines in connection with a cheap break-in. He was waiting to be named police commissioner. A statesman-like image was the one he was trying to project.

Or did he believe somebody had broken in to steal something specific? Something he was hiding in there? Of course the burglar, Bert P. Farber, had stolen nothing. Once Priestly had satisfied himself of this fact, he had had to decide what to do next—and he had decided to downplay the break-in. The alternative was detectives nosing around his private office, so he had cleaned up and started lying.

So what could he be hiding? Harry Chapman's desk calendar for one thing. Harry Chapman's Rolodex for another.

Bert cursed himself that he had not thought to look for them last night. If they were in there it wouldn't have taken five minutes to find them.

But why would Priestly have taken and hidden them? What did they reveal that he wanted no one to know?

What else from Harry's office had he made disappear?

Or was he hiding something unrelated to Harry altogether? This too was a possibility.

For thirty minutes or more Bert chewed on all this as if it were a wad of gum in his cheek. If he was right in his brooding, then Priestly must imagine that the burglar had broken in for a specific purpose. He must wonder who the burglar was, how he knew what he knew, and how soon he would strike again.

After locking his office door Bert opened his attaché case

and got out Harry's notebooks. One he put aside almost at once—the one that apparently related to campaign contributions. Obviously it was meant to be cryptic, and to him it was impenetrable. He did not know who these people were, and the investigation did not lean in their direction anyway. Detective work meant making choices, most of which were based on instinct. If there should be no break in the case soon he would perhaps assign detectives to interview every name listed in this first notebook, but he would not do so now.

The second notebook, with the phone numbers, seemed more promising. Obviously these were extremely private numbers.

Studying, he turned pages slowly. Particularly he studied the numbers that were linked only to initials. There were many such, and they could not all relate to women. Even the satyr he was beginning to imagine Harry to have been could not have handled that many women. In addition about half the numbers were not local.

Now Bert copied out all numbers with New York City or local suburban area codes, sealed them into an envelope, and phoned the telephone company's vice president for security. He was sending a detective over with some phone numbers, he told him. He would appreciate it if the company could attach a name and address to each number, together with itemized bills for each number for the last two months.

The vice president said this was highly irregular.

If the company was unwilling, Bert said into the phone, obviously he could subpoena the information, but this would take time, and he hoped it wouldn't be necessary. He would prefer to do this on a personal basis, a favor from you to me, which favor Chief of Detectives Farber might someday be in a position to repay.

"Well—" said the vice president.

"Call me as soon as the information is ready," said Bert gruffly. "I'll send the detective back to get it." And he hung up.

A little after this Inspector Potter announced that Anna Russo had arrived in the outer office. "But we got a problem, Chief. She's not alone." He spoke in a low voice that would not carry outside the room.

Bert looked up from the papers he had been signing. "She's brought a lawyer, I suppose." He had been afraid of this.

"Worse," responded Potter. "There's three of them. Her husband's here too."

Bert went to the door. Anna and the two men sat on straight chairs along the wall and pretended to ignore the roomful of detectives at their desks who were staring at them.

Street detectives assigned to the Mafia had seen Dominic Russo, who was known also as The Fist, many times, and had even arrested him, or brought him in for questioning, on occasion. But the detectives who worked in Bert's outer office were not street detectives, and Russo to them was the enemy in person, suddenly in their midst in a place where they had counted themselves safe. His was a face and name as well known as most film stars. He was the most powerful gangster in the city, and a hardened killer on whom arrests did not stick. He was also a celebrity. The detectives were looking at him, and it made them extremely uncomfortable. Work out there had completely stopped.

Though their reaction was almost comical to observe, Bert was not amused. To Potter he murmured: "About ten minutes after I start interviewing those people you are going to hear voices raised. When you do, call me up on the phone at once."

"To say what, Chief?"

"Anything you want. And have a policewoman in uniform standing by. Got that?"

"Of course, Chief," said Potter, looking mystified.

"All right. Send them in."

In a moment the three visitors came through into his office. Smiling, he shook hands with Anna Russo. "Mrs. Russo," he said warmly, "thank you for coming in." To Dominic Russo he said curtly: "You I know." He recognized the third individual also, but pretended not to: Aaron Rosenthal, a former assistant district attorney who now used his immense legal skills—honed at public expense—to keep Mafia hoodlums out of jail. Of course Rosenthal had other clients too, but his Mafia work was what he was known for.

"And you are?" Bert said to the lawyer.

"Attorney Rosenthal. I represent Mrs. Russo."

Bert nodded as if digesting this information, but otherwise kept his face expressionless.

He closed his door, then placed chairs in a semi-circle in front of his desk, and everyone sat down.

"I must inform you," Rosenthal began, "that upon advice of counsel my client will answer no questions of any kind on the grounds that her answers might tend to incriminate her."

"I see," said Bert.

"She has that right."

"Did you hear him, dickhead?" said Dominic Russo. "I think you heard him. The interview is over." And he stood up to go.

Rosenthal was in his mid-forties, a little guy, somewhat plump, with a big black mustache. Russo was no taller but much more physically imposing. He had a barrel chest, thick arms and thighs, and enormous hands, which was probably why he was called The Fist. He weighed over two hundred pounds, none of it fat. He was fifty years old but his hair was still jet black.

"Sit down a moment, please," said Bert courteously. And although The Fist remained standing, Bert turned to Rosenthal, to whom he said: "Your client is not under arrest, counselor. She is not being detained. She is not at this time a target of any investigation. However, she may have information critical to solving the murder of Police Commissioner Harry Chapman, and a court might rule that the withholding of such information comes very close to the crime of obstruction of justice."

This speech caused Anna to glance wildly around, first at Rosenthal, then at her husband.

"We don't have to listen to this shit," said Russo, whose face had got very dark.

Bert ignored him. "Conviction on the crime of obstruction of justice carries a jail term, I believe," he said to the lawyer.

"Wait a minute," said Rosenthal, "just wait a minute."

"I also could throw her into the grand jury, where she would be obliged to answer questions or be faced with a citation for contempt of court."

Anna was becoming more and more agitated.

"You motherfucker," her husband said.

"One more outburst from you and I'll have you escorted out of here," said Bert.

They stared at each other. The Fist's fists clenched and unclenched.

"Your client," Bert said to the lawyer, "rode back from Washington last Sunday night on the same plane as the victim. In fact she happened to sit down in the seat next to the victim. This makes her one of the last persons to see the victim alive. That is what I want to question her about."

Rosenthal glanced at Russo, who was momentarily silent. "All right," said Rosenthal to Bert. "You may address your questions to Mrs. Russo, and I'll advise her whether or not to answer."

"Thank you."

Well, it was a start. Anna, who was about to be interrogated in the presence of her husband, would not know what the next question might be, or what the question itself might reveal, and this was going to terrify her, terror being the state Bert wanted her in.

And so he took her back over the same ground as previously, posing mostly innocuous questions about the flight, about what she was wearing, about the stewardess spilling the drink on her. She did not protest, or even remark that she had answered these same questions already. Rosenthal nodded his permission at each one, and she answered, even as her eyes pleaded with the lawyer, or so it seemed to Bert, to end the interview and get her out of there. Apparently Rosenthal did not see this appeal, or perhaps he was so used to defending Mafia husbands rather than their wives that he was not on his guard.

"All right," said Bert to Anna, "the plane lands at La Guardia, and what does Commissioner Chapman say to you?"

Again the mute appeal to Rosenthal, who chose, however, not to intervene.

"He said, 'Pleased to have made your acquaintance, I'm sure,'" responded Anna.

"That's all?"

"Or something of that nature." Her voice had got very small.

"And you said?"

" 'The pleasure is all mine.' "

"And from the airport, where did you go?"

Under the thick makeup Anna's face was already gray. Now she began to shake.

For the first time Rosenthal seemed to realize the state his client was in. "She has said good-bye to the police commissioner," he interrupted. "He goes one way, she goes another. She knows nothing more. This interview is terminated."

"Answer the question," Bert shouted, and Anna jumped in her chair.

"You cocksucker," snarled Russo. "You gotta pick on a woman? Where's your manhood? You don't have the balls to face another man? You big brave cop. You fairy fuck."

"Shut up," said Bert.

"You want to know anything else, you ask me, not her." Russo was not shouting. His voice was low. He was almost hissing. In the world he inhabited, this was perhaps an effective ploy. When the men who worked for him had to strain to hear him, they knew they were in trouble, and their blood turned to ice.

Russo went on hissing. "You hear me? She don't know nothing. You want to know something, you ask me direct."

"One more word," shouted Bert, "and you're out of here." If Russo was not going to shout, Bert had to.

At last his phone rang. He picked it up, listened, then said: "I'll be right there," and hung up.

He shuffled through dossiers and envelopes on his desk, selecting what he needed. "Wait here," he muttered. "I'll be right back," and he went out the door, closing it behind him.

For a moment he hovered beside Potter's desk, waiting for the voices to start up behind the door.

Russo, angrily: "What the fuck is he driving at?"

Anna, barely audible: "I don't know."

Russo, angrier still: "So where in fact did you go when you got off that plane?"

Anna: "You were away."

Russo: "I said, where?"

Anna: "To see my mother."

The policewoman whose presence Bert had requested was seated beside Potter's desk, and Bert drew her out into the corridor, where he gave her certain instructions, then watched as she turned and went back into his office.

By this time Russo was berating his wife. The policewoman could hear this through the door, and she knocked and went in. The lawyer, Rosenthal, stood at the window gazing out. Russo stood over his wife and looked about to hit her.

Chief Farber had been called in by the acting police commissioner relative to another matter, the policewoman explained to the visitors. He would be delayed a few minutes and asked them all to wait for him. She smiled, but no one smiled back.

In the meantime, she said, if anyone would like to use the facilities—

"No," snapped The Fist.

"I'm all right," said Rosenthal.

"Perhaps if you'd like to freshen up," suggested the policewoman to Anna.

Anna seemed ready to grasp at any excuse to get away from her husband. "Yes I would," she said quickly, and the policewoman led the way out through the desks and into the corridor. But when she glanced over her shoulder she saw that Russo was only half a step behind. He was taking no chances that this was a ploy to separate him from his wife.

The policewoman led Anna to the door to the ladies' room. Russo was right behind them both. Did he intend to follow his wife all the way into a toilet stall?

Anna's gaze flickered from one face to the other. She looked frightened, even as she pushed open the door and went in.

Russo attempted to push past the policewoman, but she stopped him. "Sir," she said, "you can't go in there."

"Why not?"

"Sir!"

"You think I never saw her take a piss before?"

The policewoman stood with her back to the door blocking him. "I'm sorry, sir. I can't permit it."

"I've seen her do worse than that."

To get past the policewoman he would have to push her aside or knock her down, and if he did either he would probably get arrested for assault—this was not the first time the cocksuckers had tried to provoke him. His mouth hardened, but after a moment he nodded slightly and backed off. The policewoman remained with her back to the door, while he retreated some distance down the corridor, still watching her.

Anna, meanwhile, had pushed through the second door and into the washroom proper. There was a row of sinks and mirrors along one wall, a row of toilet stalls along the other, the place looked empty to her, and then one of the stall doors opened and a man stepped out, and it was the chief of detectives.

He was carrying a file folder and a manila envelope, and he reached into the envelope and pulled out a pair of white woman's underpants.

"These yours?" he said.

Anna stared at them.

Bert said: "I should show them to your husband. He might recognize them too."

Anna said: "Oh God."

After that he hardly had to mention that her prints had been found in Harry's apartment, or that he had also found and seized the Chanel suit stained with tomato juice. He hardly had to threaten her at all. She sagged and he caught her. Dragging her to a sink, holding her upright, he one-handedly wiped cold water on her face, then propped her against a wall. "Let's hear it," he said. "Everything."

Her affair with Harry had been going on for some months, she confessed. Since before he became police commissioner. She was half blubbering, half gagging. They had first met on the shuttle flight to Washington. After that they met usually in Washington, but sometimes at the apartment on 77th Street too. She would go to Washington ostensibly to see her mother. Harry had a nice house there in Georgetown, did Bert know that?

Yes, Bert knew that.

Last weekend they had gone to Washington on the same plane. They hadn't been together in a while. Unfortunately her mother chose that weekend to have an attack, and she wasn't able to spend any time with Harry. But she had made it up to him Sunday night on 77th Street. This was possible because her husband was in Atlantic City, where he had "business interests." He was probably in a hotel room with his gumatta, she said bitterly.

When she woke up the next morning Harry was dressing to go out to jog. As she watched him she was feeling very, you know, mellow, and after he went out the door she had walked, wearing nothing, out to the front room to watch him come out of the building. In the street below she saw someone come up and accost him.

"Man or woman?" said Bert.

She couldn't tell, didn't know. It was dark and it was snowing. Harry and the other person went down the street to the corner and then she heard something, or afterward thought she had heard something, she wasn't sure. A shot maybe. She didn't know. She didn't really worry about it. After spending some time in the bathroom, bathing, fixing her makeup and all, she put on Harry's bathrobe and slippers and went into the kitchen and made the coffee and cooked some bacon and put it to dry on a piece of paper towel, and got ready to fix the rest of breakfast the minute Harry came back.

He did not come back. She kept going to the front window to look for him. At first there was nothing down there. The snow had turned to rain and the streets and all the sidewalks and streets that she could see remained empty—and then suddenly they began to fill up with police cars and detectives. She got dressed. She picked at the bacon until it was gone. She poured herself coffee, but spent so much time at the front window that she forgot to drink it.

A little after that there were detectives outside on the landing banging on her door. She could hear them talking. She stood close to the door listening and learned that Harry had been shot dead. She became terrified that the detectives would find her there—terrified that she would become involved.

"Terrified that your husband had done it."

"He didn't know anything about Harry and I. But if he found out—"

She waited hours inside the apartment. She knew there were detectives all around outside. But she had to get out of there before they found her, and she had to get home to her house in Westbury before her husband returned from his weekend in Atlantic City. Finally she got up her courage and left the apartment. She carried nothing with her, not even her overnight case, because she feared this might attract the attention of any detective who saw her. She simply walked out through the ring of them and took the subway away from there. One detective did try to talk to her. She told him she was late for work, didn't have time to talk, and he let her go.

But the police still might find the apartment, and if they did they would find her things, they would connect her to Harry, and it would be in the papers and her husband would find out. By the time she got home she was beside herself with anxiety, and she phoned Willie Boy Benvenuto. He didn't speak much English, she said, but she knew he was in love with her—"do you think a woman can't tell?"—and would do anything she asked. Willie Boy came over to her house and calmed her down. She got him to do what she wanted. It was Benvenuto who returned to the apartment later that day and cleaned everything out of it, Harry's belongings as well as her own—

"His wallet?" interrupted Bert.

She nodded.

"His gun?"

"I didn't see any gun—and wiped away all the prints."

"Most of the prints," commented Bert. "What happened to Harry's gun?"

Bert's one weakness as a detective, he sometimes admitted to himself, was that under certain circumstances he tended to believe the avowals of women. Women were good liars only up to a point. Beyond that point they were transparent. Fear made them especially transparent, and Anna Russo was terrified, and he tended to believe her now.

"Go back to my office," he said in a gentler tone. "I'll rejoin you in about five minutes. Five minutes after that you'll be on your way down in the elevator." As he watched her dry her eyes he added: "Maybe you better not tell your husband or your lawyer that we had this conversation. I mean, I don't think it would be to your advantage."

"No," she said.

Though her eyes were now dry there was a further delay while she renewed her thick makeup. Bert waited by the sinks while she did it. She was fairly well composed by then and he noted how meticulously she wielded the mascara brush.

"I wasn't Harry's only girlfriend," she remarked suddenly into the mirror.

"How could you know that?" said Bert.

"Because he liked to talk about them in bed. What he did, what they did. He might be doing the same thing to me. He liked to get himself all excited in that way."

"Did this bother you?"

"Why should it bother me?"

"I guess you were enjoying it too much yourself for it to bother you."

"You might say so."

"He actually," said Bert, "liked to describe what these other women did for him? Is that what you're telling me?"

"So men have dirty little minds." She shrugged, watching him in the mirror. "So what else is new?"

"I'm a little surprised it didn't bother you?"

"That men have strange tastes?"

"No, that he spoke of other women while with you."

"I wasn't trying to marry him."

"But you were very much in love with him, I bet."

"If you want to know why I was in bed with him, it was because he was good looking, and a congressman who then became the police commissioner, and I was flattered to be asked."

"Any other reason?"

"Yeah. My husband gives me a pain in the ass."

"I see," said Bert, and he did, sort of. Despite all the years he had been a cop he was still puzzled by the thought processes of some people, still amazed by the acts of which they were sometimes capable.

"If you're looking for Harry's women," she said into the mirror, "there are lots of them to find. I'll give you a hint. One of them's a policewoman."

This did not surprise Bert very much. There would have to have been at least one policewoman. "Do you know her name?"

"No, but I can tell you what she liked Harry to do for her in bed, and what he liked her to do for him."

After surveying her makeup and herself from several angles, she put her tools back into her handbag, gave Bert a half smile into the mirror, and pranced out the door and was gone.

Bert went to the sink, slapped water on his face, and washed his hands.

Carrying the same file jackets as before, he stepped back into his own office, met no one's eyes, and pretended to be distracted, preoccupied. "Sorry to have been so long," he said. "Something unexpected has come up. We'll have to continue this interview some other time."

"Next time you'll need a subpoena," threatened Rosenthal.

"We'll see," said Bert vaguely, and he showed them out.

As soon as they were gone he sat down and pondered his next move. Presently he telephoned Lieutenant Mosconi, instructing him to move his men up as close to Anna Russo as they could get.

"Do you fear for her life, Chief?"

"No," said Bert, but perhaps he did. He had no sympathy for organized crime people, male or female. However, a detective's role often required him to play God—often it was he who decided who would be arrested or placed in protective custody and who would be left out on the street, which crimes would be punished and which ones overlooked. That is, at times it was left to him to decide what was right and what was wrong. Certainly he manipulated lives, and there were times when he could not escape responsibility for what ultimately happened to someone.

"Just move up close to her, and tell me what you see," Bert said. He did not think Russo would murder his wife, or order her murdered, but he might, so Bert would keep an eye on her. Apart from this, there wasn't much he could do.

As an afterthought, he added: "And keep an eye on Willie Boy Benvenuto, too." Willie Boy was in far more danger, Bert believed, but there was no way he could be protected by anyone.

That same evening there was a demonstration scheduled in the Bedford-Stuyvesant section of Brooklyn, a black ghetto and part of Assistant Chief Earl Coxen's command. It was to be led by the Reverend Hoke Highsmith, pastor of the

Missionary Baptist Church, who was one of the most influential black churchmen in the city and not a firebrand. Coxen
had met with him twice in the past week, and now just before
noon there was a third meeting, which the commanders of
the 14th Division and the 77th Precinct also attended. What
Highsmith had planned, and still planned, was a kind of can-
dlelight parade through the Seven-Seven ending in front of
the station house. Its purpose, he said, was to dramatize the
community's concern with drug addiction and violence. He
thought about three hundred parishioners would take part,
most of them middle-aged women and kids, and he had long
since obtained the obligatory permit from City Hall.

After Highsmith left, Coxen and his two field commanders
made the necessary manpower decisions, and all prudent measures were put in place. At four P.M. Coxen signed out and
went home to help his wife get ready for the night's dinner
party.

"Did the mayor call?" Marlene asked him as he came in
the door.

He kissed her on the nose. "Relax, Babe," he said. "He'll
either call or he won't call. There's nothing we can do about
it now."

Still in uniform, he unfurled the tablecloth and sailed it out
over the dining room table, then laid out the place settings.
He was interrupted twice by the front doorbell. First came
the caterer Marlene was using. He brought the smoked salmon
and the other hors d'oeuvres. The man from the city's number
one wine purveyor was right behind him with appropriate
wines.

About this same time a memo reached Sternhagen's desk
in headquarters. It was from Assistant Chief Rider, commander of the Intelligence Division. Ripping open the envelope, which was marked personal and confidential, Sternhagen
read that an undercover cop had penetrated a group calling
itself the NBR. The letters stood for The New Black Resistance—militant groups were as in love with acronyms as was
the police department itself. This NBR—heavily armed young
blacks—planned to infiltrate tonight's scheduled demonstration out in Brooklyn. Reverend Highsmith's peaceful march
through the 77th Precinct was to be turned into a violent

disturbance if possible. This would tend to discredit the moderate Highsmith and, if enough woolly skulls got broken, the police department as well.

According to Chief Rider, a riotous confrontation could well occur outside the 77th Precinct station house.

Sternhagen put the memo down and thought for a minute. Rider did not presume to advise what action to take; this was of course up to the chief of the department and to the commanders in the field.

Chief Coxen ought to be alerted, Sternhagen knew, and he actually picked up his telephone to do it. Coxen would then alert his subordinates, the news traveling downward through channels as was proper. But after only a moment, not having dialed, Sternhagen put the phone down, for Coxen would not be in his office in Brooklyn. Coxen was no doubt at home preparing for tonight's dinner party. The peaceful demonstration was scheduled to start out from the Missionary Baptist Church at eight P.M., about the time the first course would be served at Coxen's house, and it would finish up in front of the station house about an hour later, in time with the dessert.

Sternhagen decided there was no need to disturb Coxen with such alarming news when he was so busy at home.

Instead he put the memo into an envelope and directed his secretary, a deputy inspector in uniform, to send it to Coxen at Brooklyn North headquarters in the next department mail. The secretary was to mark the envelope personal and confidential.

Sternhagen was satisfied that even if it got there quickly, which was unlikely, no one would open it in Coxen's absence.

Later he himself signed out and went home but kept his car waiting outside. Night had fallen. Upstairs he changed to a brown suit with a red striped tie and Italian loafers with tassels. On the other side of the room his wife was getting dressed also.

His car and Priestly's car pulled up in front of Coxen's house almost simultaneously, and the two couples got out and stood together on the sidewalk.

"I don't know what this is going to be like," said Florence Priestly.

"Grits? Chitlins?" said Mrs. Sternhagen, and everyone chuckled.

"Well," said Priestly, eyeing the building's handsome facade but unimipressed by it, "let's get this over with."

"Right," said Sternhagen, and they went inside.

The first phone call to Coxen came at nineteen minutes after eight.

Sternhagen was pushing smoked salmon around his plate at the time; he hated smoked salmon. Coxen took the call in the kitchen but the chief of the department, who was seated beside Florence Priestly, could make out part of the conversation.

When Coxen returned to the table he looked worried.

"What was that?" Sternhagen asked, feigning ignorance.

"There seems to be some trouble building up in the Seven-Seven," said Coxen. "I'm wondering if I shouldn't get out there."

Marlene Coxen looked extremely alarmed at this possibility.

"Nonsense," said Sternhagen jovially. "That's what you have a staff for."

Until this minute there had been no suspicion by Coxen or any of his subordinates that the Reverend Hoke Highsmith's march would be other than peaceful. And so Coxen hesitated.

"Maybe you're right," he said, and as he sat down again his wife relaxed so visibly in her chair that it was almost comical.

Presently the two hosts got up and cleared the table. Sternhagen could hear them murmuring to each other in the kitchen, Marlene's voice muffled and angry, Coxen's muffled and conciliatory. Then Coxen came back carrying the main course on a silver salver, quails that must have been sitting in the oven keeping warm for some time.

Marlene behind him bore a dish of mixed vegetables and a second dish containing wild rice, and she sat down and began to ladle food onto plates. When all were served Sternhagen, wishing it were something simple like steak, attempted to cut into his quail without sending it skittering onto the floor.

"This is certainly delicious, Mrs. Coxen," he said.

She gave a small smile and asked him to call her Marlene. He told her to call him Terry, which she proceded to do. Her husband meanwhile would continue to address him as sir, or chief, Sternhagen well knew.

The phone rang again.

This time when Coxen came back from the kitchen he looked tense. An hour had passed since the first call. "It may be building up to a major disturbance," he said. "I really should get out there, sorry to say."

His wife's eyes flashed daggers at him.

"Let your staff handle it," ordered Sternhagen. "Finish your dinner first."

The others seemed to agree, and so Coxen was confused.

"It's all right to be conscientious," suggested Florence Priestly, "but you mustn't take any of these disturbances personally."

And Amanda Sternhagen said: "If Terry went out every time they called him, we'd have no home life at all."

These were police wives and so for Coxen their testimony had weight.

"With traffic the way it is you're almost an hour away," said Commissioner Priestly. "Nothing you can do now."

"No hurry," said Sternhagen.

Looking doubtful, Coxen sat back down. He had graduated from St. John's with a bachelor of science degree at the normal age, twenty-two, had passed all the police promotion tests with high marks, and as a captain had been accorded a two-year leave of absence to attend Harvard Law School on a foundation grant. After graduating cum laude, he had passed the New York bar exam on the first try. But he was a black man meeting socially in his own house for the first time with white men who outranked him, and he did not know what they would have done in his place. He was unsure what good manners called for, could not decide what was the correct thing to do. He sat fidgeting another thirty minutes at the head of the table, then got up, apologized to everyone, and hurried from the house.

Even the news crews got to the riot before he did. By the time Coxen was filmed getting out of his car in front of the station house much of the 77th Precinct had been wrecked, cars were burning in the street, four cops were in the hospital, one rioter was dead, and about twenty were under arrest.

And by then an anonymous tipster had phoned Channel 7 news. Borough Commander Coxen had arrived late, the tipster revealed, because he had been hosting a dinner party and had been reluctant to leave his guests, and this news went out live from the riot scene on the eleven P.M. newscast. Sternhagen watched this newscast at home on the small screen in his den, and was satisfied that the mayor could not now name Earl Coxen to succeed Harry Chapman. Had Coxen ever been a real threat? Sternhagen did not know. In any case the threat was gone now, and he went to bed vastly relieved.

■13■

AT SOME POINT, Bert told himself, and sometimes on very little evidence, the detective in charge—in this instance himself—had to narrow his focus, zero in on somebody, point his men at a particular target. Decide who was guilty, and close off the rest of the investigation.

However, Bert assured himself, such a solution to the present case was a long way off. It was not close at all.

Though perhaps it was.

Because the phone numbers from Harry's little black book had come back from the telephone company with names attached, and one of these names had shocked Bert. He had unfolded the list and the name had leaped off the page at him. From one moment to the next he found himself faced with a problem he had not anticipated, and did not know how to deal with.

It was noon. He had been about to go out to lunch. He sat at his desk on the thirteenth floor of police headquarters and tried to study all the other names, none of which he recognized. All of them, not just the one, would now have to be checked out, he told himself, no matter how many detectives it occupied, or how many days it took, or whether or not it led in a believable direction.

He was already in a panic, stalling, trying to calm himself. He folded the telephone company envelope list, then spread it out again. In the metropolitan area alone the investigation would now have seven new names to work with. Six of the seven meant nothing to him. The seventh lay there blinking at him like a neon sign.

Bert was trying to think it out, but he couldn't think. He could hardly take his eyes off that seventh name.

The first admission he made to himself was that he could not hand that name to a detective and ask him to check it out. He would have to do it himself. He was so thoroughly shaken that, having made this one decision, he had reached the limit of his powers. He seemed unable to move in any direction at all. He had no idea what came next.

The seventh name that the telephone company had found for him, the one that corresponded to the initials F.P., was at the bottom of the list.

It was Frederick Priestly.

The phone number that went with it was Priestly's home number.

Which meant that the first dep paid the bill on this particular line. Unfortunately that's all it meant, for this was not the number Bert, or any other police official, would dial if trying to reach the first dep at home. The city had put second lines into all their houses, and those were the ones they used when telephoning each other on official business.

This one was not Priestly's line; it was his wife's line.

Bert's mind had begun bouncing about. As the first shock wore off there came dismay, then a dozen other emotions one after another. The initials F.P. must refer not to Frederick Priestly, first deputy commissioner, but to Florence Priestly, his wife. Otherwise why would Harry have used initials? He would have written the name out. Why get cryptic for no reason?

And if Florence Priestly was in Harry Chapman's little black book, it meant she had been still another of his girl-friends. There was no other explanation. And this opened up the deadliest possibility of all, for Florence Priestly, ex-policewoman, owned a gun or at least had access to a gun, and furthermore knew how to use it.

If Bert was still a romantic, this was because his profession demanded it. A detective had to be a romantic to believe that what he did for a living, the locking up of wrongdoers, did any good at all, purified society in any way. Most wrongdoers, after all, were never caught, and those who did get caught were immediately replaced from an inexhaustible pool of others. Did a detective really accomplish anything worthwhile? So at the same time that he was a romantic, Bert was also a cynic. He looked down at Harry Chapman's address book in his hand and saw Florence Priestly compromised, and the first dep, and Bert P. Farber as well. The Priestlys would have to be investigated, he would have to do the investigating, and news would get out. The Priestlys' marriage would be destroyed certainly, and the police department pulled apart, and the investigator, himself, would be destroyed too.

Florence was not an immediate suspect, he tried to tell himself. Not yet. She was a potential suspect.

Boffing the wife of his top subordinate was just the sort of thing Harry would have done, wasn't it? It fit the Harry Chapman that Bert had come to know these last few days.

It fit also his deepest fears. He realized now that he had been afraid of this case from the beginning, and he had been right. This one meant trouble for everyone, for himself most of all.

He went back to see Mary Alice Chapman. The interview took place in the living room, the bedroom, the kitchen, and then the bedroom a second time.

Once again she had been playing solitaire in her darkened living room, turning up soundless card upon soundless card, and he had interrupted her. Although she hadn't expected him she smiled as she opened the door to him. He dropped his coat on the chair in the entrance hall and followed her back into the living room, where again she began turning on lamps.

She looked a little better, meaning that today she had at least bothered to get dressed. She was wearing a plaid skirt, and a green sweater with the sleeves pushed up, and her hair was combed.

"I should think it would make you gloomy, sitting in the dark like that," said Bert.

She smiled. "I'm not gloomy. Or at least not as gloomy as I was. I was not really paying attention to the cards. I'm going to have to remake my life, and I was trying to decide what I wanted to do with it."

Bert handed over Harry's keys, pretending this was the purpose of his visit. He had been unable to get into Harry's office, he told her, because the first deputy commissioner had ordered it sealed. "So I couldn't get your jewelry out of the safe for you."

"It doesn't matter." She gave a faint smile. "I won't have occasion to wear any of it for a while, will I?"

"If you want it, I suggest you ask the first dep directly."

She did not respond.

This seemed to Bert the best opportunity he was likely to get to ask the questions most on his mind. He said: "How well do you know the Priestlys, by the way?"

She shrugged. "Slightly. We had dinner at their house once, and they came here once. Why do you ask?"

"No reason," he said. "Were these dinner parties with the wife who died, or with his present wife?"

"The present one."

"What's her name?" said Bert. "Florence, isn't it? What did you think of her?"

She looked at him with that level gaze she had that seemed to see into him. He had always been flattered that she seemed to know him so well, though it could be a little discomforting too.

She said: "You're investigating the women in his life, aren't you?"

This comment shocked him. He said: "What makes you think that?"

"Bert," she said. "Come on, Bert."

He decided to drop the subject of Florence Priestly for the moment. "By the way, how many guns did Harry have?"

She seemed surprised at the question. "Only one, as far as I know."

"We haven't been able to find it."

She shrugged. "So? Is that significant?"

Bert was watching her closely. "Of course he was going away for the weekend. It's possible he didn't have it with him."

"I wouldn't know."

"He may have figured it wasn't worth the hassle of getting it on and off the planes."

"What are you asking me, Bert?"

"If he left it in his office or his official car, it hasn't turned up. Maybe it's here in the house somewhere. Where did he usually keep it?"

"Follow me," she said, and led him up the stairs to the master bedroom on the second floor. Bert had shared bedrooms with this woman—she was a girl then—but never this one, and his gaze was caught and held by the big bed in which she now slept alone, and certain thoughts came to him, he could not help himself. The bed was made. The counterpane was a bit lacy, something a woman like Mary Alice would choose. There were bedside tables with lamps on them, a clock on one, a telephone on the other. He wondered which side Mary Alice slept on.

She was rummaging in a bureau drawer. Because she might turn at any moment and catch him staring at the bed, he forced his gaze to move on. She was bent over the drawer and because her skirt was momentarily stretched tight he allowed his eyes to mold her waist, her hips. He noted what he could see of her legs, her thin ankles.

"He's been keeping it in his sock drawer lately," she said. And then: "Ah, here it is." She held the gun out to him by the barrel.

Bert took it from her. "I'm glad to have this."

"Why is that?" she asked.

"I was afraid," said Bert, watching her closely, "that maybe he had been shot with his own gun. But inasmuch as you had it here all the time, that can't be the case, can it?"

She grinned at him. "Sorry to disappoint you. I'm not the killer type, I'm afraid." And then: "You are the most suspicious guy. Should I resent you for thinking what you were thinking?"

Bert only studied the revolver. "I'll hold this for the time being, if I may?"

"Sure. I don't want it. Take it. Do all the tests on it you usually do. Would you like a drink?"

Again he looked down on her bed, and then at the closed closet door that would hold her clothes. What's so intimate about bedrooms? he asked himself. Everybody's got one.

Mostly what people do there is sleep. "A drink?" he said. "Yes I would, as a matter of fact."

They went back to the living room, where she stood at the liquor cabinet and poured scotch into a glass, after which there was another trip toward the kitchen for ice.

"So what did you think of Florence Priestly?" asked Bert as they walked down the hall.

"Was she one of his girls?"

"I wouldn't know anything about that."

"If she was, I wouldn't be surprised."

"Why not?"

"The way she looked at him one time."

"One time?" said Bert. "I don't understand." But he understood perfectly well.

"One time can be enough. She was passing him the salad, as I recall. And the way he so studiously ignored her all night. That wasn't normal either."

"You said: 'One of his girls.'" They came into the kitchen. "Were there such a great many?"

"There were a few," said Mary Alice Chapman, "quite a few."

"If you knew about them, why did you stay with him?"

"I ceased to care."

"That's not an answer."

"I stayed because of the boys, and because it was my own fault I got into this mess, and also because—" She stopped, but after a moment continued. "—Because I really thought he would be president someday. And if he made it to the White House, so would I."

Bert did not know what to say to this.

"That sounds pretty silly, I guess," said Mary Alice Chapman.

When Bert still did not respond she added: "Everything else he said he would accomplish he did accomplish: the Justice Department, Congress, and now police commissioner. So why shouldn't the rest of it come true too? Why shouldn't he be one of the next presidents? He was only forty-two years old."

She had not met his eyes as she spoke.

"Did you ever imagine yourself in the White House, Bert?

Everybody wants to be a star, and that's the ultimate stardom, isn't it? After that I would have been able to do anything I wanted."

She reached into the freezer, and withdrew an ice tray. "The White House is not a place I could get to on my own," she said. "I mean, who am I?"

This was the first Bert realized that a beautiful girl, and now a beautiful woman, though seemingly so cool and assured where men were concerned, could also possess a hidden inferiority complex—hidden, but of substantial dimensions. And he looked at her for what seemed like the first time.

"To me," he said bluntly, "that doesn't seem such a good reason to stay with a man who runs around on you."

She was at the sink, where she broke the ice out of the tray. "You're not me, are you?"

"No," he conceded, "I'm not."

She dropped ice into his drink. "By last year I had pretty much gotten over that White House notion. I was ready to leave him." She frowned. "No, not leave him, kick him out. It has always been my money we were living on."

"But you didn't kick him out."

They had sat down at opposite ends of the kitchen table.

"Because he got appointed police commissioner. It was a serious job and would take all his time, I thought. He was still on the schedule he had set himself for reaching the White House. And away from Washington I thought he might change. Maybe we could start to have a marriage again."

Watching her, Bert sipped his drink.

"At which point," she said somewhat bitterly, "somebody shot him."

"Do you think it was a woman?" asked Bert.

"Who else?"

"Well, there are other possibilities."

"I suppose so."

"When he rode with me in the Twentieth Precinct," Bert said, "he seemed like such a solid guy. Rather naive."

"Harry was never naive."

"People thought he was."

"Cops," said Mary Alice.

"Other people too. I did myself for a time."

"Did it ever occur to you that from the outside, naive and ruthless look exactly alike?"

Bert was silent.

"Harry played at being naive because people thought it was charming. He always went straight where he wanted to go, but at some point he learned that if he acted naive and blundering people wouldn't mind so much."

"Naive or not," said Bert, "he had all his priorities straight, or so it seemed. He was brave, dedicated, ambitious. Obviously he changed." Bert studied her. "So when did he change?"

"When he got elected to Congress, I think. He had this big staff, and nothing much to do, and there were all those women around. At first he used to complain that politics was boring. That soon stopped. He began to claim to be busy nights, busy on weekends, and I didn't hear about him being bored anymore."

"How'd you find out about the other women?"

She studied him again with that level gaze. "I was in a restaurant and I overheard somebody talking. Washington is a very gossipy town. Nothing stays secret long. If you have ears you can't miss hearing what you're not supposed to hear."

"Did you confront him?"

"That first time I did. He swore to me how faithful he was. A faithful but very busy congressman. After that I didn't confront him anymore. My pride wouldn't let me."

Bert felt terrifically sorry for her.

"And then pretty soon," she said, "I no longer cared what he did."

"Were you faithful to him?"

"Oddly enough I was. That was pride too, I suppose. Proved I was a better person than he was. In fact I was more than faithful. I became almost a nun. He knew what that meant well enough, but we never talked about it."

She said this with downcast eyes, then glanced up and caught him staring. "You still like to look at me, don't you, Bert?"

He nodded.

"You're the one I should have married, not him." She put

her hand over his on the table. This sent a shock through him. Of course it did. Why was he so surprised? "Oh, Bert, I was such an empty-headed girl."

They stood up and she came into him, pressing her body against his, her face in his neck. One hand went to her back on top of the bra strap, the other to the back of her head. Today she wore her hair pulled straight back, a ponytail held in place by a rubber band that he was aware of because his hand was on it. He was trying to decide what he wanted to do. He was not immune to her, never had been and was not now. If you kiss her, he told himself, you are lost. But no sooner had this thought come into his head than his fingers, which seemed to be working of their own accord, had grasped the ponytail and yanked her head back and she was looking up at him wide-eyed, the way she used to do, her lips slightly parted, and then his mouth came down on hers and he kissed her hard and could feel her teeth.

He was not really surprised that she kissed him back, but was very surprised that her side of the kiss seemed to contain so much hunger. When their lips finally parted she took his hand and led him up the stairs again. Two steps inside the bedroom there was another long kiss. When it ended she pulled her sweater over her head saying: "Would you like to see my scar?"

He had not seen her body in eighteen years, and so it was familiar to him and unfamiliar at the same time. Her belly was less flat than before, there was a slight droop to her breasts, but what the hell, he was no longer a boy himself. The scar was new to him. It was about an inch long and situated about an inch above and slightly to the side of her left nipple, and it was still red. His finger traced the line of it. In themselves scars weren't important, he thought. Everybody had scars. Why had she wanted him to know about this one before he had even seen it, before she was even fully undressed? Was she apologizing to him in advance because the body she offered him now was less perfect than before? Did she think such a scar made her less attractive to him? To men in general? She had lost her husband—not this week but years ago—and had nearly lost her breast, obviously, which might be enough to give any woman a complex, he supposed.

What kind of life had she led? Was it as out of scale as all that?

He did not want to talk about her scar, not then, and he finished removing her clothes and moved her toward the bed. He had brooded about this woman and this moment off and on for eighteen years, at times obsessively. To Bert now, Mary Alice Chapman was unfinished business. She represented a life he might have lived. She was what might have been, rather than what was. She represented what he had once seen as his future. However, eighteen years of that future had been used up without her, and was gone, could not be called back, and now here she was again, a woman who was the same but different, a potential new future, a woman with her legs apart and her head on the pillow, and literally and figuratively he wanted only to plunge into whatever that future would be, and he came down on top of her and during that moment and the few moments following he was consumed not so much by passion as by many other emotions he could not sort out. One of them was memory of the eagerness he had known as a very young man on the rare occasions when a girl, this girl for instance, presented herself to him in this manner, his unbelievable luck; he could not believe it even as it was happening—that the girl—this woman now—was going to let him do this thing, meant to go through with it, he had best hurry before she changed her mind, get it done so it could not be taken away from him, plunge into her quick. Which he did.

"Oh Bert, it's been such a long time," she said.

"Bert, Bert, Bert," she said.

"Oh Bert," she said, and he saw that she had bitten down on her lip so hard she had made it bleed.

Afterward, when they were lying close together, half on top of each other, no longer being driven forward into the future, one of the few times in life when one was totally content with the present, his finger traced the line of the scar on her breast, and he said: "What happened?"

One day she had discovered a lump there, she told him. Alone and in a panic she had rushed from doctor to doctor. There was nothing to do but operate, see what it was. She had gone into the operating room having signed all the papers.

If it was malignant, then when she woke up, she would have no breast.

He said: "You must have been so scared."

The biopsy had been performed while she was unconscious. She woke up in the recovery room and felt herself and started to cry. "I've been fine since," she said brightly.

Life not only separated two people, it pushed them around to such an extent that when they came together again after many years they didn't know each other anymore even if they thought they did. This was principally because each was unacquainted with the traumas the other had lived through. Bert had observed this before, but did so again now. Mary Alice Chapman did not much resemble the person she used to be, and neither, most probably, did he.

"Tell me about Madge," said Mary Alice, "is your marriage in trouble?"

Bert found that he did not want to share Madge or their marriage with Mary Alice Chapman. "Well," he said, "we have our disagreements from time to time."

"Don't want to talk about it, eh?" she said, and grinned at him and placed her hand over his crotch. You could not start up again from where you had laid off, Bert realized now. If you wanted to start up again it had to be from somewhere else.

It was Mary Alice who changed the subject totally. "About your investigation," she said, "when you find out, well, whatever you're going to find out, don't drag Harry's reputation down into the dirt."

"I'll try."

"Leave me that much at least. His reputation. My reputation. Promise me."

"I don't know what's going to happen, Mary Alice."

"Promise me."

"I promise I'll do my best to protect you."

Had she gone to bed with him solely for the purpose of extracting such a promise? With Mary Alice it was possible, he supposed.

Her hand still lay on his crotch, which he thought was about as familiar as a woman could get with a man, but he removed it. To lessen the rejection this implied, and also to ease himself out of bed, he kissed her on the nose.

She watched from the bed as he began to get dressed. "Want another go first?" she offered.

"I don't have time, Mary Alice."

She put on a bathrobe and accompanied him down the stairs to the front door.

"When will I see you?" she said.

"Soon," he said, and again kissed her on the nose. He went out the door.

The shock of the cold air against his face was just that— a shock. He stood on the stoop a moment and Hughie, who was parked beside a hydrant some distance up the street, saw him, and the headlights came on.

He went straight to the police academy, where he watched Harry Chapman's revolver fired into a box stuffed with cotton. The bullet was then dug out of the cotton and placed into one side of a double microscope. From its envelope in his brief-case, Bert produced the murder bullet, and he watched the technician lock it into the microscope's other side.

The technician, a detective, studied the two bullets through the microscope, trying to line up lands and grooves.

"Does it match?" said Bert impatiently.

"Not even close, Chief."

Bert nodded. This meant Harry Chapman had not been murdered with his own gun, and therefore not by his wife. Bert ought to have been somewhat relieved, but wasn't. Mary Alice as murderess was a possibility he had never much believed in.

Unless of course there was another gun somewhere to which she had access. She might have used that one. Had Harry kept other guns around the house? Cops often had extra guns. Saw something they liked and bought it, and kept it around. A cop's gun became so normal to him, so much part of his wardrobe, that he came to see nothing sinister in it. It was heavy lethal steel, but not to him. Most cops became interested in guns in general—not to fire but to look at, to heft from time to time. To wear from time to time. A cop might get up in the morning and select this one because it had a different grip, or that one because it was silver and matched his watch. His gun was an accessory, and he changed it the way another man might change his necktie, or his cuff links.

So Harry could well have owned another gun.

It occurred to Bert that he kept coming up with suspects, and in his head exonorating them, at least for the time being: Caroline Connolly, Anna Russo, and now Mary Alice. He had still not exonorated Dominic Russo, or Willie Boy Benvenuto, or, now Frederick or Florence Priestly.

In addition to which John Kincaid was working his way down all the other dark and unexplored streets, and it was entirely possible he would come up with a direction and a killer whom Bert had not yet considered.

Having removed the murder bullet from his microscope, the technician was studying its blunted damaged nose, and there was a perplexed expression on his face. "Where'd this come from, Chief, if I might ask?"

"There's some question about that," said Bert vaguely.

"I mean—"

"It's a mystery," said Bert.

It meant he wasn't going to answer the question, and the technician shrugged.

"However," Bert said, "that gun you have there was the PC's gun. We know that much. So log it in. Log in the bullet you fired from it, too. Give me back the other one."

But the technician held it a moment longer, for he could see bits of flesh still attached to it. He knew well enough it had come out of somebody.

He said: "This ought to have a case number, Chief."

"Not just yet," said Bert, replacing it in the evidence envelope it had come in.

"Is it the bullet that killed the PC?"

"I wouldn't say that," said Bert. "I wouldn't say that at all."

He started away, then turned back as if to deliver an afterthought. "By the way, you're a detective, right. You work for me. So if I were you I wouldn't say anything about this bullet"—he waved the transparent envelope—"until I tell you you can. Understood?"

The technician looked startled. "Right, Chief," he said.

* * *

The mayor was at home at Gracie Mansion. "All right," he said, after leading Bert into an office off the foyer. "Where are we as of this minute?"

It was late. The summons to Gracie Mansion had come as Bert was about to go home.

Earlier, he told the mayor now, he had interviewed the Mafia don's wife for the second time, and he gave the gist of what Anna had said, but without details. If in his narrative the Harry-Anna liaison came out sounding more sordid than he intended, if he himself sounded overly judgmental, this could not be helped. Sordid was the way he saw it.

He did not mention that he had separated Anna from her lawyer, thereby tainting any possible case against her. Even if it turned out that she was involved in the killing of Harry Chapman, most probably she could never be prosecuted now. Nor did Bert describe lurking in the toilet stall in the ladies' room to waylay her, nor the toilet odors that had overlaid their conversation. These were less than heroic images of himself, and he did not want the mayor pondering them after he had left.

He did report finding and testing Harry's gun. "Which proves that the PC was not shot with his own gun," said Bert. "That's a good thing, don't you think?"

"Unless he had another gun," commented the mayor. "It could still be his wife who shot him."

The mayor's cynicism and astuteness continued to surprise Bert. "I don't think so. I just interviewed her, in fact. She was entirely forthcoming." Forthcoming? The word made such a pleasant tingle in his groin that he was forced to wonder about himself.

"What else you got?" said the mayor.

A desire to be appointed PC himself was what he had.

Bert hesitated. Tomorrow he would interview Florence Priestly, but the evidence against her—and by extension against her husband—was flimsy. It was worse than flimsy. There wasn't any. It didn't exist.

"I don't know how close you are to appointing a new PC," said Bert carefully. "But I think you should hold off a few more days while I check certain things out."

Watching him suddenly closely, sharply, the mayor waited for him to go on.

"I wouldn't want you to make an appointment now that would embarrass you later," said Bert.

"I bet you wouldn't."

"Or embarrass the police department."

"What have you got?" demanded the mayor bluntly.

He had the Priestlys' home phone number in Harry's little black book, but if he mentioned this the mayor would laugh derisively, and say: That's all?

So Bert shook his head. "Nothing I can talk about at this time."

"You got something on Priestly, or Sternhagen," guessed the mayor. "On one of them or both?"

"I've got nothing hard on anyone."

"Chapman was boffing their wives," guessed the mayor.

How close had the mayor been to appointing one of them or the other? "I don't want to say anything at all," said Bert. "I don't want to spread rumors."

"Not much you don't."

"I need time to check something out."

"I'm the mayor, for crissake."

To mention either of the Priestlys by name seemed to Bert, at this stage, too big a risk to himself. "I'm not asking for anything more than that. Time."

The two men looked at each other. "I better go," said Bert.

"Not Sternhagen's wife," said the mayor. "She's too old. Priestly's wife then. Chapman was boffing Priestly's wife."

Bert said nothing.

"You afraid to tell me, or what?"

Bert edged toward the door.

"He doesn't want you to get the job either," the mayor said.

Bert tried to bring forth a grin and some charm. "You mean I'm under consideration? Little ol' me? Imagine that!" But he was too tense, had been buffeted by too many emotions already today, and it didn't come off.

"You should hear the things he says about you."

"I can imagine," said Bert.

Finally the mayor released him.

By the time he came into his apartment Madge was in bed asleep. He made himself a drink and sat at the piano brooding. Tomorrow he would interview Florence Priestly. She would say what? He would say what? Where would the investigation be by tomorrow night? From time to time he touched a piano key, making a soft isolated tone.

Finally he closed the piano, rinsed out his glass in the kitchen, and went into the bedroom and slipped into his pajamas. When he got into bed he could feel the warmth coming off Madge, and he stroked her flank once, and chased away thoughts of Mary Alice Chapman, and lay there feeling guilty until he too fell asleep.

To investigate Florence Priestly he would have to move carefully.

The first job was in some ways the most delicate one. From his doorway he looked over the detectives who worked in his outer office. He would have to pick one of these men to do what he wanted done. Which one?

The detectives at their terminals, as his gaze traveled over them, realized he was there, but none looked up. Often he would stand there silent, expressionless, a looming presence over the room, and over their lives, so that by now they were used to him. They had given up trying to figure out what he was thinking, much less what he was up to.

Most of these detectives had sat at the same desks since Bert was a captain, if not before. The chief of detective's office was good duty, eight to four, five days a week. No one requested reassignment; vacancies occurred by retirement only.

For the job he had in mind Bert could not risk using one of these old-timers. They knew too much, and they tended to talk too much. Although the gossip they purveyed made them resemble old ladies in a sewing factory, they had nonetheless been street detectives once and they were rather too good at unraveling thin clues, at ferreting out secrets, at explaining to each other the intricacies of cases they weren't supposed to know about at all.

There was one new man, however. His name was Baumgartner, and because he was on the sergeant's list he had been brought in from the field while he waited to get made. This had long been customary. Baumgartner would soon be a superior officer, and headquarters experience, however brief, would be useful both to him and to the department.

Calling Baumgartner into his office, Bert questioned him. He learned that he had been a cop eight years, all of it spent in south Brooklyn. Good. This meant that names familiar to men who worked in headquarters might be unknown to him. One could hope so. In any case, Bert needed someone, and Detective Baumgartner seemed the best choice.

He asked him to go down to the fingerprint section and pull the fingerprint card of a woman named Eberstat.

"Florence Eberstat," said Bert. "Bring it up to me."

Eberstat was Florence Priestly's maiden name, which the old-timers would know. But Baumgartner's face showed no reaction, so he apparently didn't.

"Has she got a B number, Chief? What's she wanted for?"

"Never mind all that. Just bring me the card."

"Suppose it's not there?"

"It's there." Of course it was there. She had been a police-woman, and every cop on the day he or she came into the department was routinely fingerprinted.

The young man was too new to dare ask the chief of detectives what this was all about, though obviously he was dying to know. "Right, Chief," he said, and went out the door.

About twenty minutes later he reappeared, handing the card across Bert's desk. "I see she was a policewoman," Baumgartner said. "What happened to her?"

"She died."

"That's too bad."

"Yes it is." Bert continued to study the card, which of course told him nothing.

"I have to bring that card right back, Chief."

"When I'm finished with it."

"But—"

"Keep this confidential."

Bert forced himself to wait an hour before sending a different detective, Inspector Potter this time, back down to the fingerprint section, which was on the fifth floor. He was hoping he had waited long enough, and that no one down there would associate Baumgartner's visit with Potter's.

In a few minutes Potter was back, bringing with him as instructed all latent prints from the apartment on 77th Street that were still unidentified.

After ushering Potter out, and ordering his phone calls held, Bert locked his door. There were eighteen latent prints, all but one of them partials, and on Florence's card there were ten inked, perfect prints.

The partials were indeed partials, in some cases a third of a finger or less. Others were little better than smudges. He had to try to match each indistinct pap to each of Florence Eberstat Priestly's ten inked fingers, and he began studying the cards under his desk lamp under a magnifying glass, sometimes turning one or the other card every which way looking for a fit. There were a hundred and eighty different possibilities.

Down on the fifth floor they had projectors for this kind of work. They could project blowups onto screens, the latent print side by side with the inked print you were trying to compare it to. Huge images. Matches could be made more or less quickly. His puny magnifying glass was a poor substitute. But he couldn't afford to go near the fifth floor on something as delicate as this. With the point of a pencil he counted ridges from one bifurcation to another. He counted ridge after ridge. Whorls and arches began to blend into each other. He blinked a great deal. By the end of the first hour he began to think he was going blind.

He expected to find at least one match, and at last he did. Then he found another. He had five points of similarity on one partial, four on the other—not enough points to stand up in court, but they satisfied Bert. One partial, he saw, had been lifted off a candlestick holder, and the other off an opened coffee can.

It proved Florence Priestly had been in that apartment—and it caused a lurch in the pit of Bert's stomach.

It meant that the case would go forward to wherever it might lead.

He got up and paced from his chair to the window and thought of Baumgartner and Potter and the fingerprint men who had served them just now, and the other fingerprint men who had lifted Anna Russo's prints off the teacup, and the pathologists at the morgue who had dug the bullet out of Harry, and the technician at ballistics who had seen the bullet, and the mayor, and the detectives working for John Kincaid—pieces of Bert's investigation were now in the hands of too many people. How long before certain of them found each other, and began talking, and the news leaked out? How long did he have? Did he even have another whole day before all this exploded into the public consciousness?

He sat down and stared at Florence Priestly's fingerprint card once more, perhaps hoping for additional answers that he knew were not there, but finally he picked up his telephone and dialed the first dep's number.

"Is he in his office?" inquired Bert when the secretary came on. "I may need to see him later."

"He'll be in the rest of the day, Chief."

"Good," said Bert, and he hung up.

Having localized the first dep, he dialed Florence Priestly's home number, intending to localize her too.

She picked up and he heard her voice say "Hello?" And then a second time: "Hello?"

He hung up again, went down to his car, and was driven uptown to the apartment building on West End Avenue in which the Priestlys lived. He went up in the elevator and rang the bell, and a moment later felt Florence peering at him through the spyhole. There was a long silent moment during which he wondered if, instead of opening the door, she might choose to let him think there was no one home.

But she did open. "Hello, Bert," she said.

She was wearing jeans and a rumpled blouse, and her hair was tied up in a kerchief. The vacuum was out on the floor behind her, though he hadn't heard it a moment ago. In any case he had interrupted her chores.

Seeing him, her color appeared to have gone off. Her breathing seemed to come a bit too fast. Was he imagining this? She must know what he was there for, perhaps had been expecting the knock on the door for days.

"You surprised me," she said. "Let me change into something more presentable."

"Not necessary," said Bert, but too late. He was addressing her departing back.

She went down the hall into the bedroom and closed the door.

As he waited for her to return, Bert reviewed what he knew of her. He had first met her in the 20th Precinct when both of them were young cops. Priestly was precinct commander then. Florence came into the precinct about the same time as Harry Chapman—they may even have been in the same police academy class.

Fresh out of the academy, Florence Eberstat was assigned to desk duty. It was what you did with female police officers in those days. But she had kept clamoring for a seat in a radio car, he remembered, claimed she wanted to be a real cop out on patrol, and finally Captain Priestly, who much later would take her as his second bride, got fed up and ordered some cop to ride with her. The cop screamed about it but Priestly was adamant. Male-female radio car teams were to become common enough later, but back then no cop wanted to ride with a female. It wasn't considered manly. A woman couldn't help you wrestle some guy to the ground, and if you got in a shoot-out she would probably run.

But Florence proved a reliable partner. She even made a few good arrests, Bert remembered. She had a big bosom and usually wore tight uniforms. He also remembered she had the foulest mouth of any woman he had ever known. She liked to stand in bars with cops, and she talked as rough as they did. Rougher. She talked rough to prisoners too, but never to superior officers. There were rumors she was screwing some cop up in the Three-Four. Bert's own tastes ran toward sensitive, artistic, very feminine girls like Mary Alice Riggs. Being around Florence Eberstat always made him extremely uncomfortable.

She had long blond hair—bleached of course—that she wore in a bun under her cap, for the regulations were pretty strict then. Without the bun it was long. After work she would come out of the station house with her hair half hiding her face and hanging down below her shoulders, and this always surprised Bert.

During those years he never noticed any familiarity between her and Captain Priestly. Priestly was a married man and bucking hard for promotion, not at all the type to risk his career by carrying on with a policewoman in his own station house. Of course Bert hadn't exactly been looking for anything. Still, he did not think so.

As for Harry Chapman, if he ever looked twice at Florence Eberstat, Bert did not notice this either. But Harry certainly knew her back then, and probably talked to her a few times.

After Bert left the 20th he lost sight of her. Once he heard that she and her partner got involved in a shoot-out with two men in a liquor store. One of the stickup men was killed. That Florence Eberstat had stood her ground was the talk of the department. Later she was married for several years—to a lawyer, Bert believed. She had a child who died. Of what, Bert no longer remembered, if in fact he ever knew. But it must have been highly traumatic for her. Afterward her marriage broke up.

She remained in the 20th on patrol until she was promoted to sergeant. Priestly, meantime, went to headquarters. He kept moving up in the department, and eventually he was promoted to chief of personnel. Florence must have been tired of the street by then, for she moved to headquarters and went to work as his secretary. When he became first dep he took her with him. She was still a sergeant, and in fact never rose any higher. Bert encountered her several times during those years. She had cleaned up her mouth a little, not much. He still did not like to be around her.

Priestly's wife got sick and after many months died. The next thing Bert heard was that the first dep, who was by then fifty-nine or sixty, was making a fool out of himself over a woman twenty or more years younger, a sergeant, one of his secretaries, Florence Eberstat.

When they got married, she took her pension, resigned from the department, and the gossip stopped. She was still seen around headquarters from time to time, fixing her flowers in his office, or at official functions, and she was always nicely turned out. She seemed to be spending most of her pension on clothes.

* * *

By the time the bedroom door opened and she came back out ten minutes had passed. Under the circumstances, a long time—much longer than necessary. Now she wore a black skirt and a pink sweater, and those big boobs stuck out at him. Her hair was combed, and she had applied light makeup to her face. Her demeanor had changed too. She was no longer obviously nervous but had herself together. Maybe she had herself under tight control, how was he to know? She was on her guard. She was ready for him.

"Sorry to keep you waiting," she said. "It's good to see you again, Bert." She gave him a smile that looked almost genuine. "What can I help you with?"

They stood in the center of the living room rug. She did not take his coat, which by now hung over his arm, or ask him to sit down. She did not offer him coffee or tea or anything else. This was either simple bad manners, which Bert did not believe for a second, or it was a statement of fact—she recognized that this was not a social occasion and she was not going to pretend otherwise. She saw it as exactly the confrontation Bert had meant it to be, and she would stand and wait for him to make his move.

This caused Bert's morale to plummet. She had been a cop, knew the rules, and would refuse to answer questions that did not suit her. Or else she would lie. He could interrogate her all he wanted but was not going to get any admissions out of her. Probably he would not get anything out of her at all.

Having come this far, however, he was obliged to try.

"How well did you know Harry Chapman?"

"I met him on a few occasions."

"No better than that?"

"No."

Her attitude—any cop's attitude—toward accusations or threats would be: prove it in a court of law. Which he couldn't do. She would realize this quickly enough. She had probably realized it already, because if he had had anything solid on her he would simply have sent somebody to arrest her.

"What did you think of Harry, anyway?"

"He seemed like a nice man."

"You knew him back in the Twentieth Precinct?"

"Barely."

Bert was already on the defensive.

"He was always studying, as I recall," said Florence: her only gratuitous remark so far.

"I thought you might have known him better than that?"

"Then or now?"

"Now."

"No."

Her manner seemed to him a virtual confession of the guilt he was looking for. If she were not guilty she would be reacting some other way. Guilty of what? He had not decided.

"Harry had a little black book. Private phone numbers. Your private number was in it." The chief of detectives recited the number from memory.

"He sometimes called my husband on that number."

"I see."

"My name or my initials?"

Bert said nothing.

"My husband and I have the same initials, as you know."

Bert studied her, hoping that under his direct gaze she would flinch, do something else to give herself away. But her composure remained solid.

"When you were in the department, how many guns did you own?"

"Only one, as a matter of fact."

"You carried the big gun off duty?" He was surprised. Most cops had a second, off-duty gun. It had a short barrel and was much lighter.

"I never carried any gun off duty."

"The regulations said you were supposed to."

"Well, I didn't."

They looked at each other. "My handbags were heavy enough already," Florence said.

"You had only the big service revolver, then. When you left the department, what did you do with it?"

"Got rid of it the next day."

Had she? If she had applied for a permit to keep her gun or guns, the license division would know it, and he should have checked this out in advance. It was important. They were perhaps talking about the murder weapon.

"Most of the men keep their guns afterwards."

"I'm not a man."

He looked at her and thought that her control over herself was less than absolute. She seemed to be getting increasingly uncomfortable.

"I was happy to get rid of it," she said.

"And you sold it?"

"That's right."

"Harry Chapman kept an apartment quite near here."

"Did he?"

"On Seventy-seventh Street. Ever go there?"

"Am I supposed to have gone there?"

Wherever possible she was answering questions with questions, and his own questions were lousy anyway. They were designed to try to prove to her and to himself how smart he was, but appeared to be doing the opposite, and the result was that he felt frustrated and inept.

"What would you say if I told you your fingerprints had been found in that apartment?"

"That would be odd. I heard someone went through the place and wiped it clean."

"Your husband tell you that?"

"Somebody."

"The guy missed a few. Including yours."

"If you had found my prints there," she said, "you'd have been here long before this." But for the first time she looked rattled.

"In two places," said Bert, watching her carefully.

"Really," said Florence. "Is that so."

Bert watched her.

Finally she said: "Which two places?"

"A candlestick holder and a coffee can."

"You don't say."

"Do you remember making a pot of coffee the last time you were there?"

"And when was this," she said, "that I was supposed to have been there?"

"It could have been the night before he was killed," said Bert, watching her carefully.

Silence.

"Harry comes back from Washington," said Bert, "and you're there waiting for him with the candles lit." He was inventing as he went along. "But unfortunately he is not alone. He comes in with another woman. She's got a small suitcase with her, obviously planning to spend the night. You have to leave. He asks you to leave."

"If Commissioner Chapman was as debonair as people seemed to think, that wouldn't be his style."

She was perhaps remembering a different scene, and Bert tried to imagine it. "You're right," he said. "Harry would have done it differently, wouldn't he? As I see it, he sits down with both of you." Bert paused, working it out. "It becomes a question of which of you will get in a huff and leave first. He finds this highly amusing. The stilted small talk between you two women makes him nearly laugh out loud."

"You have some imagination, you know that?"

Bert nodded knowingly. "So you were Harry Chapman's girlfriend," he said, nodding to himself as if he had just realized it. "One of them, anyway."

Florence went over and peered out the window.

When she turned back he thought he saw sweat on her upper lip.

He said: "A stewardess, a Mafia guy's wife, and you, all at one time. You all overlapped, you might say."

"I wouldn't have thought," she said, "that he was that type of man."

"Well he was. The Mafia wife was the one you met."

Now he thought he saw moisture in her eyes as well. The tongue lies, Bert thought. The body tries to lie but sometimes can't.

"Three women?"

"Plus his own wife. That makes four. That's all I've been able to find so far."

She had turned and was again peering out the window.

"I was thinking about going to your husband," Bert said, talking to her back.

"To tell him what?"

"About Harry Chapman's love life." He wanted her to turn around. He wanted to see her eyes, so he added cruelly: "And about his wife's love life."

"He doesn't like fairy stories."

"He would be interested in this one."

Her face when she turned had gotten very dark. "Tell him whatever you please. What do I care?"

"All right, I will."

"He's not a jealous man."

"All men are jealous men."

She shrugged.

Changing to a conversational tone, Bert said: "By the way, I made this as a woman's crime the minute I saw it. Didn't you?"

She looked at him.

"I mean," he said, "you were on the job. You've looked down on a lot of people who got shot. What did you think?"

When she did not answer, he said musingly: "One shot straight into the heart. That reads crime of passion, right? Any experienced cop would read it as a woman's crime immediately, don't you think?"

Which of course wasn't true. Kincaid hadn't, Sternhagen hadn't. Priestly maybe had, but suspected his wife and was protecting her. "What else could it have been," Bert continued rhetorically, "besides a woman's crime? An assassination? Nah. A stickup? Nah. A random shot? Impossible."

Her eyes were getting narrower, her mouth tighter.

"A woman," said Bert decisively. "One of Harry's girlfriends. I was pretty sure that's what it was. The only question was which girlfriend."

"You worked all that out by your own little self?"

"From the start."

"You must be pretty goddam brilliant." He had had her cowed for a time, but she was coming out of that now.

"Which girlfriend do you think it was?" he asked rhetorically.

"Do you think it could have been me? Assuming I was his girlfriend, of course."

"I've pretty much eliminated the others," said Bert, watching her.

"Do you mind if I laugh?" She didn't laugh, but she had her reactions under tight control again, and in addition she was getting angry.

"If you were the shooter," Bert said, "which gun did you use? That's the second question."

"You tell me."

"You say you turned in your own gun when you left the department, which I can check, by the way."

"I know goddam well you can check it," said Florence, "and I suggest you do so."

"Your husband's gun, then."

"I also suggest you leave. I've had enough of this horse-shit."

"You borrowed your husband's gun and afterwards put it back where it belonged."

He was accusing the first dep's wife of murder on no proof, and if he was wrong the risk to his career had just passed all understanding.

Though knowing this, Bert kept doggedly on. "So you were one of Harry's girlfriends. Your fingerprints prove that much. So I ask myself, how could you let yourself get involved in such a love affair? You were susceptible, that's how—happens all the time. Your husband is sixty-two years old and going nowhere except into retirement. Whereas Harry Chapman is young, virile, famous. He could be the next mayor, governor, president—whatever he wants. He makes a play for you and he seems so sincere that you fall for it. You don't know what the future holds for the two of you, but you can hardly wait for it, you are thrilled, you believe everything he tells you, you are in love. You and Harry will go forward together."

Had her mouth tightened further during this recital? He could not be sure. He had the impression she was about to turn on him, perhaps strike out with her nails or her fists.

"Then it turns bad," Bert continued. "You find out about the other women. The night before his death he's up in his flat with one of them. Maybe you only guessed this. Maybe you were up there too with the candles already lit, and he rubbed your face in it until you left. At home you can't sleep. You're up all night pacing. You are consumed by jealousy, or maybe only anger. Maybe both. The love of your life has turned away from you. You despair of getting him back. You are sick with jealousy."

He paused, then said thoughtfully: "Jealousy like that goes into hatred, I believe. I don't really know. I know the result, because I've seen it so often, but not the thought process that goes into it, because it's never happened to me personally."

He saw the emotion building in her, she would soon react. He could not predict what this reaction would be, and so began to hurry, wanting to shake her up as much as possible before it happened. He did not expect to force her into a damaging admission, but she might make some other egregious mistake, it was certainly possible.

"The night hours pass," he continued quickly. "You are half out of your mind with emotions you have never encountered before. You are tormented. You know Harry goes jogging at six A.M. no matter what. You want to see him, talk to him, plead with him, make him see how much he has made you suffer. You dress, grab your husband's gun—he is sleeping peacefully in the other room—and by now you are half crazed. You go out into the night. It's snowing and very cold. You go around to Harry's flat. You huddle in a doorway out of the snow. You are shivering, and perhaps crying as well. Your head is filled with images of another woman and Harry up there, rolling all over each other."

She started to speak, but at the last minute clamped her lips shut.

"Finally Harry comes out in his jogging suit. He pulls his hat down over his ears. You run across the street and accost him. He doesn't want to listen. He keeps going toward the corner. You are half running to keep up. You curse him for betraying you. You tell him you love him. He brushes you off, he wants to start his run. You are losing him forever. You pull out the gun. Mostly this is to make him stop and listen to your avowals of love, but the gun goes off."

"That's enough of this horseshit," said Florence. "I want you out of this house."

"Did you pull the trigger on purpose, or was it an accident? No one will ever know. You don't even know yourself. You saw right away that he was dead though. So you ran. What else could you do? There was no one on the street, you thought. No one saw you, you thought."

"At that hour in that kind of weather," Florence snarled, "I doubt anyone saw anyone, whatever you may be trying to imply. Now get the fuck out of here."

"No one," Bert continued, "would ever link you with the crime, you thought. By the time you let yourself back into your apartment you would even have convinced yourself that Harry had had it coming to him. And in a way maybe he did."

"Every time you open your mouth," said Florence, "more shit pours out. I suggest you take whatever evidence you have and go to the grand jury with it. You get an indictment, you come back and see me." She paused, breathing hard. "But you don't have any evidence, do you? You got any witnesses? Any forensic stuff? You got shit, that's what you got. The grand jury'll laugh you out of the fucken courtroom."

She strode to the front door and held it open. "Now get the fuck out of my house."

Slowly Bert threaded his arms into his coat. Slowly he walked past her and out the door.

The door closed behind him with a violent slam.

■14■

BERT STOOD AT his window staring down at New York at night. One way or the other, this case was almost over, he believed, and there was now a distinct possibility that his police career would end with it.

It was quite late by then. The night city was coldly, brilliantly lit. The white sparkle went on for as far as he could see. At this hour the corridors of police power were largely empty, so there was no noise outside his door, and he looked out over the city that had been his home all his life, and that excited him still. New York was cold, glittering, uncaring, and he loved it as much for its coldness as for its occasional warmth, as much for its lack of compassion as for its austere strength. The police department could be equally cold and austere, but warm too, if you fitted in. He was a lucky man to have fitted in as well as he had. He loved the department and the city equally, as a man might love two women similar in beauty and identical in temperament. Especially he loved being chief of detectives. He loved the authority, of course. More than that, he loved being close to events that, one way or another, were of an extraordinary brilliance. Everything about the city was outsized, its mischief, its mystery, its glamour, its mindless violence. There was a brilliance to it that only a detective could penetrate, and of all the detectives, his was the only jurisdiction that was citywide.

He wondered if he was trying to commit career suicide, or what.

He had accused Priestly's wife of a crime, which he could not prove. Not now and possibly not ever, which she had certainly perceived, and which left her free to demand all manner of sanctions against her accuser. She could go to her husband, to the mayor, to the district attorney.

She might do one or all of these things before he had even decided what his next move was to be.

Then what would happen?

He had exposed himself and his career to ruin. Why?

Had he taken the murder of Harry Chapman as some sort of personal affront? But Harry Chapman, he now saw, had not even been a very nice man. Human kind would not weep for him long, and some of those closest to him, his wife for instance, were apparently not weeping at all.

So what did Bert P. Farber care who killed him?

And yet something was driving him forward, which was scary, because he did not know what it was. Was it some sort of moral righteousness? If so, no one would applaud. Not being God, he had no right to be more right than anyone else. Was it mere professionalism? Was it perhaps only curiosity? Curiosity was always a strong factor in the affairs of men, often the strongest of all, and a detective's curiosity had a longer and stronger reach than most people's, extending further out over the void. Because finding out who had done the deed was, for a detective, not the end of it. His curiosity could not be satisfied until he had enough evidence to get an indictment. Only an indictment satisfied it totally. Only an indictment was the end. He was not responsible for convicting the wrongdoer; what happened in court later was out of his hands.

Whatever might be motivating Bert, he had found few tools to work with and so had decided to attack Florence Priestly head on hoping she would crack. She hadn't cracked. What next?

He knew he would go forward, but he did not at the moment know how.

Just then his door burst open. He turned from the window and found himself confronting First Deputy Commissioner Priestly, whose face was livid, whose fists were clenched, and who was shouting at him.

"How dare you? How—how—" Already the first dep was sputtering. "How dare you?"

It was as if he was so overwrought that no other words would come into his head.

Though his own heart had taken a lurch to see him there, Bert attempted to project calmness, to speak calmly. "How dare I what, Commissioner?"

Priestly's rage was so great his whole body shook. "How dare you go to my wife? How dare you accuse her? What proof have you? What right have you? It's, it's—you, you—" And his clenched fists waved in the air.

What exactly had Florence told her husband? What did it mean that she had told him anything at all? There were drawers in Bert's mind and he was ransacking them, but he did not find what he was looking for. Whatever she had told him, did this indicate guilt, or collusion between them, or guilt and collusion both? Did it possibly indicate innocence?

"Pack your things and get out," shouted Priestly.

"Please keep your voice down, Commissioner. There are people out there." There could be men going by in the corridor. At the least there was Bert's night duty sergeant at his desk out front, all ears no doubt. Word of this would be all over the building by tomorrow.

"I'll keep my voice down," shouted the first dep. "I'll do whatever I goddam please. I'm the acting police commissioner, and you're fired. You're finished. Out."

"I don't think so, Commissioner." Bert was still trying to project a calmness he in no way felt. "I think we both have to let the investigation run its course first."

"I'm in charge of this department and you're fired. Fired, fired, fired."

"Your wife is a suspect in a murder case, Commissioner. I don't think you can fire anybody just yet. I think you have to step aside—"

"Step aside?" shouted the first dep. "Step aside? While you harass my wife. While you ruin her life, ruin my life, I'm just supposed to step aside?"

"The evidence led in a certain way, Commissioner. I followed where it led."

"You're trying to destroy my name and reputation in order

to get yourself appointed PC. I'll show you who steps aside—I'll—" He began sputtering again, gasped for breath, and for a moment could not speak.

"And you," he cried. "You were the one who broke into my office, weren't you? I can see that now. You did, didn't you? You broke into my office—"

"The investigation into that break-in is continuing, Commissioner."

"—Looking for evidence against my wife that you didn't find. Because it doesn't exist. You hear me, it doesn't exist."

There was froth around the first dep's mouth. His face was red as a boil that might at any moment burst, and he began to rant about conspiracies against him, the purpose of which was to prevent him from being appointed PC. Everyone was against him, and always had been. Bert's investigation was not about his wife at all, but about himself. Its intent was to derail this final stage of his career.

Tears came to his eyes but he wiped them furiously away. He had been first dep nine years under three different commissioners, and each time one of them resigned, even though first in line for the job, he had been passed over. And the last time by Harry Chapman, a politician. In police terms a nobody, never rose higher than patrolman. A man who had once worked for him, a rookie at a time when Priestly was already a captain and precinct commander. Now was his final chance to be PC, the mayor had indicated that the job was his, the fulfillment of a career whose brilliance other cops could only admire and try to emulate.

Recounting these grievances and others he whined, mewled, and at times shouted. His voice got more and more hoarse, even as a new scenario began to form in Bert's head. It was different from the one he had described to Florence Priestly, and he wondered if this time he had imagined the correct one.

He wondered if it could be Priestly himself who had shot Harry Chapman, not his wife at all.

In this new scenario, instead of the distraught Florence pacing while her husband slept, it was Priestly himself who paced because his wife had not come home, and he thought he knew where she was. Perhaps he had confronted her on some previous occasion: he knew she was carrying on with another man, and he knew who the man was. Now, as Bert visualized it, they had fought again, and she had stormed out. Perhaps she had taunted him first: Harry Chapman was twice the man Priestly was, and he loved her.

Jealousy did not spare people just because they had attained a certain age, a certain high office, and according to Bert's new version, it was the first deputy commissioner who paced all night, who at times talked to himself, or wept. His anguish was the worst of his life, perhaps because he was now sixty-two and so much less time was left to him. This new anguish was worse even than watching his first wife die. He had come back from that experience and married again, and out of despair had come a new happiness, and a joy in his new wife that he had not known could ever exist for him again.

It was this joy that was threatened by Harry Chapman now, and at a certain point he went out into the night. It was snowing, it was cold. He was wearing only a light raincoat (as Bert imagined the scenario) and he began shivering at once. His gun lay loose in his raincoat pocket. He had taken it with him because he always took his gun with him, had done so for more than forty years.

Tramping through the snow he reached Harry Chapman's building. He knew where it was because he had tailed his wife there previously—possibly had got suspicious and started tailing her everywhere she went until he found the truth he had not wanted to find.

He came to the flat and stood in the falling snow peering up. He had started out with no real knowledge of what he intended to do when he got there. Ring the bell. Perhaps remonstrate with Harry in a subservient way, for Priestly had always been a subservient man. Plead with Harry to let him have his wife back.

But now the snow fell on his hair and got in his eyes and mixed with the tears there, and he could not make himself enter Harry's vestibule, much less ring his bell, for Harry was the police commissioner. In fact, perhaps he was mistaken about Harry altogether. Perhaps his wife was as pure as this falling snow, and as faithful as on the first day of their marriage. Perhaps even if she were a weak woman and vulnerable to him, the police commissioner, being more noble than most men, would have refused her and gently sent her away.

If he rang the bell and was wrong, if his wife wasn't there, he would lose his job. Harry would fire him. If she was there, if he actually caught the lovers together, then Harry would certainly fire him.

The indecision that gripped him was a new kind of agony. What should he do? What could he do? Miserable and half frozen, he huddled in a doorway across the street and tried to think it out and couldn't.

He knew which were Harry's windows, and suddenly a light came on in one of them. Figures moved across in front of the curtains, one of them a woman. The woman in the window was Anna Russo, but Priestly didn't know that. His own wife was the one he expected to see there, and so that was who he took Anna to be.

He would have been like an operatic character, Bert decided, a tenor looking up at the palace walls and singing his plaintive aria while his wife in the bridal chamber was being ravished by the prince. The only difference was that Priestly's aria was silent, and he wept real tears.

Perhaps he knew Harry always came out to jog at that hour, perhaps not. Perhaps he was not even aware what time it was. It made no difference to Bert's scenario, which stood up either way.

Harry in his jogging suit and stocking cap came out, danced carefully down the snowy steps, and Priestly called to him, and crossed the street, and began in a disjointed way to speak.

Brushing him off like snow off his shoulders, Harry began to jog toward the corner. Priestly ran after him, not only still begging and pleading, but remembering also the crushing disappointment of only three months ago, being passed over for PC still again in favor of this very man, his last chance ever to get the appointment he had craved for so long, or so it seemed.

Like his wife in Bert's first scenario, Priestly pulled out his gun in an attempt to make Harry stand still, take notice of him, listen to him, agree to stop seeing Florence.

Harry laughed at him.

Priestly might have got so angry he simply shot him. But

Bert preferred to believe, as in the former scenario, that the gun went off almost by itself.

Since any career cop would recognize a corpse the instant he saw it, having seen so many, Priestly did not need the medical examiner to tell him Harry was dead. Like his wife, he had never meant to pull the trigger, or so he told himself. Aghast at what he had done, Priestly ran home and was standing by the phone when the precinct commander called him with the news a few minutes later.

In fact, Bert remembered now, Priestly had been almost the first one at the crime scene—this new scenario also explained how he had got there so quickly.

Gradually the first deputy commissioner's increasingly disjointed monologue tugged Bert back into the real-life present. For forty years, Priestly was saying, he had worked to become PC, forty years of a career as close to perfect as a cop could get. Never a misstep. Never late for work in forty years. No civilian complaints, not one. No corruption investigations, not even an allegation. His uniform, when he had been in uniform, was always pressed, knife edge creases, shoes that glowed. He had passed every promotion exam on the first try at or near the top. He had been an unqualified success at every promotion level. Oh he had heard the whispers as people tried to run him down, run his idea of perfection down, that he was stodgy, a by-the-book officer, unimaginative, not brilliant enough. All untrue, and this time the mayor had seen it as untrue, the culmination of his career was at hand.

Bert watched him. It was painful to listen to. The man had become, as he spoke, increasingly incoherent. His sentences had ceased to track. And more and more often there were tears in his eyes.

"And then this had to happen," the first dep shouted. "You—you—"

His jaws worked, but no sound came forth. He blinked several times, his hands clenched and unclenched, and he bounced up and down as if preparing to step forward and begin punching. And then as suddenly as he had burst into Bert's office, he burst out again. There was no other word to describe it. He turned suddenly on his heel, yanked the door open as if to yank it from its hinges, and strode from the office. He was gone.

In a semi-stunned state Bert moved forward to close his door. His duty sergeant was on his feet at his desk, a bewildered expression on his face, looking from the chief of detectives to the outside corridor, down which Priestly had vanished, and back to the chief of detectives again, looking for an explanation that Bert declined to provide. Closing his door quietly, then returning to his desk, Bert sat down and for a moment put his face in his hands.

Presently he emptied out his in-basket and busied himself with the last of the day's paperwork. His limbs were stiff from the tension of the last several minutes, his face felt like it was sunburned, and he did not hurry, for he wanted to give Priestly all the time in the world to get well away from the building. He did not want to be confronted by the first deputy commissioner—by any of this—anymore tonight.

Finally he went down to the garage and got into his car and Hughie started the engine.

"Where to, Chief?"

"Home," he answered.

Something in his face or voice evoked a further comment from the chauffeur. "Tough day, Chief?"

"Yeah, very tough."

And it wasn't over, but Bert did not know that yet.

They went up the ramp and out into the street and he saw that it was snowing again. The snow was coming down in big wet flakes. It must have been snowing for some time already, for the streets were slushy but the sidewalks were white, and the roofs of the parked cars were puffy and white, and people hurried along with flakes on their shoulders, on their hats.

He settled back in his seat and tried to make his body relax, and to let his mind go, and when the hard thoughts kept coming anyway, he tried to fight them down, to concentrate on nothing. He needed a stiff drink. He needed to sit at his piano and play something soft.

His apartment building was set back from the street with a crescent-shaped driveway in front. There were bushes and other plantings in the cusp of the crescent, plus the white, outreaching ganglia of trees, and more bushes in boxes to either side of the big glass doors in which at this hour, normally, stood two uniformed doormen. The bushes in the crescent were not all that tall, not all that dense, and were inadequate for an ambush, it would seem, though on such a night they were engorged with snow, there was more snow falling, and they would prove sufficient. Bert was not thinking ambush anyway. He did not expect to get shot. He was, after all, almost home.

He got out of his department car in the street because a delivery truck was blocking the driveway. He lifted his head and felt the snow on his face, and he watched Hughie drive away; the brake lights came on at the corner, and then the car turned out into First Avenue. After stepping between two parked cars at the curb, and then crossing the sidewalk, Bert started down the snow-covered flagstone path through the widest part of the crescent. There were bushes and small trees to either side of him. The glass doors and the doormen were hidden from him by the truck, whose cab, he saw, was empty. As he passed between the biggest of the bushes, his eyes half closed against the snow, a man he did not see stepped out from behind one of them and aimed a gun at him and pulled the trigger.

Bert had never been shot before, but he felt the searing pain and started to go down and recognized at once what had happened to him, even before he heard the gun's report. He was used to hearing guns on the practice ranges in station house basements, where they sounded stupendous. The noise of this one did not seem loud at all. Of course he was already dazed by then. A second report followed as he was going down, which he heard, and he hit the flagstones hard, face first it seemed, and then he was nose deep in the still shallow snow, and the pain came, and the terrible weakness that went with it.

During the time he was a uniformed cop on patrol, and then a detective on patrol, Bert had rushed innumerable gunshot victims to hospitals, and now, he realized vaguely, it was going to be his turn. He had leaned over some of the victims for as long as the surgeons would let him, trying to get a description of the shooting, or of the shooter, but if some detective leaned over him now he would not be able to tell him anything. He hadn't seen anything. The detective would want the names of witnesses, would want a feel for what had happened, and would listen for any other word or observation that might help the investigation that was to come, but Bert would not be able to help him there either. Many times he had witnessed bullets being cut out of people, usually by interns, often enough crudely, the victim screaming in pain, because highly paid surgeons did not inhabit emergency rooms, and now he visualized himself on the table and this bullet or bullets that had hit him being cut out, and he feared how much it would hurt, though it seemed inconceivable that it could hurt any more than it hurt already.

Only after all these thoughts came and went did he realize that someone had tried to kill him. This was a profound shock: why would anyone want to kill him? Its corollary was a profound shock too—whoever had shot him was very close, was still there, was possibly moving up to finish him off. A quick shot to the head from six inches away and that would be the end of Bert P. Farber. If he opened his eyes he might see the man looking down on him. Would he recognize him?

He felt so weak and was in so much pain that there was a moment during which a bullet to the brain seemed devoutly to be wished. He didn't care what might happen to him next. Let the man finish him off, if it meant that the pain and weakness would go away.

These thoughts, some less vague than others, did occupy him, but for how much time he never knew, for he felt himself trying to roll over, and then groping for his gun, and then he was sitting up holding it in two hands, trying to steady it. He was aware of people running. Someone seemed to be departing behind the nearest clump of bushes, though the sound was muffled by the snow, and someone else came sprinting around the truck and saw him and ran up and wrenched the gun out of his hand and trained it on him. Bert thought this was the shooter, and that he was about to be executed. The man wore a United Parcel Service uniform, which made him almost above suspicion, and immediately Bert thought: Mafia. How resourceful of them to outfit their assassin in such a uniform, he thought. Where did they get it, he wondered. They'll be outfitting their hit men as priests next. He didn't know who "they" might be. Dominic Russo most likely. The Mafia, who never put out hit contracts on cops, had in his case finally made an exception. It was the most probable explanation he could come to at the moment.

"Freeze, motherfucker," cried the truck driver, holding the gun barrel almost in Bert's face. And then he shouted over his shoulder to one of the doormen, who was cowering behind the truck: "I got the drop on the fuck. Call 911. Tell the cops I'll hold him until they get here."

"It's Mr. Farber," said the doorman, coming closer, peering in the dim light.

"Julio," said Bert, "please tell this man to give me back my gun."

"This man is chief of the police," Julio said, addressing the driver. "He live here. I know him many years."

"Help me up, Julio."

The doorman got his hands under Bert's arms and he was able to stand.

"Now call 911, like the man said. Tell the operator we'll require several units here." As he watched the obedient Julio go back around the truck, Bert was shaking so much he almost fell down. There was blood coursing down over his ear, over his cheek, and down inside his collar, and he wondered how badly hurt he was. His ears were ringing and his head felt like he had been clubbed in the skull by a baseball bat. But the worst pain was in his neck. It was as if someone had taken a blowtorch to his neck.

He steadied himself enough to reach for his gun, and the embarrassed driver handed it to him.

"Thank you," said Bert.

"You okay?" said the driver.

To remain standing took tremendous effort, and he concentrated on it. He had several minutes to wait before the cars got here. Could he remain erect until then, until the investigation was under way, until everything was being done that should be done?

"You don't look so good."

"Did you see anything?" said Bert.

"No."

"Someone running away, maybe?"

"No." Looking over his shoulder, the driver studied his truck. "The fuck not only shot you, he put a bullet through my truck."

"I sure am sorry about your truck," said Bert. He thought he had heard two shots. The bullets would have to be searched for, but one might be in the truck. When men finally got here he would order the truck searched immediately. He would have to stay awake until then or they might not think to do it.

Only when he heard the sirens coming did his eyes close. He was so relieved his knees nearly gave way.

He heard cars pulling up in the street, and cops running toward him. Most, he saw, ran with guns drawn. Some had fanned out, and they came crashing down through the bushes. This meant they were trampling any footprints there, but Bert lacked the will to call out to them to stop.

Soon thirty or more cops and superior officers had gathered. Floodlights were set up. Detectives were inside the truck examining boxes for one with a hole in it; or perhaps the bullet was on the floor. Others examined the bushes, the trees, the walls, hoping to come upon the second bullet; or were canvassing the neighborhood for someone who might have glimpsed the gunman and could give at least a partial description; or ringing the doorbells of every apartment that faced the front, asking if anyone had been at the window and seen something; or taking down the plate numbers of every parked car for blocks around, for although the gunman appeared to have escaped on foot, he might have left his car behind.

Under the building marquee Bert sat on a chair provided by one of the doormen and watched the snow fall, and in his weakness and pain his eyes sometimes closed. Someone had run to get his wife, who had come down at once. Madge had not screamed when she saw him. He was proud of her for that. She had examined his head, his neck, had questioned him, and then had gone back inside for a wet cloth with which she had sponged off some of the blood, making him more presentable. She had wanted him to go to the hospital, the detectives did too, but he wouldn't

Madge stood now at his side, her hand on his shoulder. He

was under the overhang and the snow kept falling on the plantings and on the cops outside, and men reported to him and he tried to tell them what to do next. The chief of patrol had come, and the precinct and borough commanders, and the captain who headed the major case squad. All of them thought that Bert should go to the hospital at once. He'd go soon, he told them, soon. All offered to direct the rest of the investigation, but Bert refused. He was not leaving until this thing was settled, he said. The bleeding seemed to have stopped, but his head throbbed so much it was hard to focus his eyes. He had learned from his fingers, as well as from his wife, that one bullet had taken a gouge out of his skull. The second had seared his neck, not even breaking the skin. The effect was of a terrific burn, as if someone had held a red-hot poker to his neck.

One of the last to arrive was Chief Sternhagen wearing a Russian hat, some sort of furry overcoat, and rubber boots. He said: "I'm ordering you to go to the hospital at once."

"No," said Bert.

Madge still stood with her hand on his shoulder, looking from one to the other.

"That's a direct order."

Bert did not reply, nor did he move to obey. At first Sternhagen did not realize he had been ignored. Finally he said: "Who shot you, Bert? What does all this"—his ineffectual gesture was meant to encompass the many scurrying detectives—"signify?"

"We'll talk about it in the morning," mumbled Bert.

He was closed inside himself, trying to control the pain, the residual shock to his nervous system, the weakness that for some reason made him want to tremble. When he looked up again Sternhagen was gone, and the man standing in front of him was Lieutenant Mosconi.

"I heard you were hurt, Chief. How bad is it?"

"Looks worse than it is," Bert answered, managing a kind of smile. For a moment he watched Sternhagen talking to some detectives out by the street.

Bert's attention returned to the man in front of him. "How are you tonight, Mosconi?"

"The reason I wanted to see you, Chief, was to tell you something that may be important."

Bert waited.

"Willie Boy Benvenuto has met with an accident, Chief."

"The usual kind?"

"Yeah. Three in the back of the head."

Involuntarily Bert's eyes closed. Jesus, he thought, this thing is getting really bad.

"His penis was in his mouth, Chief, which usually indicates he was sticking it where he wasn't supposed to."

"Or someone was. Where'd you find him?"

"They threw him out of a car on Queens Boulevard."

Which meant they wanted him found, Bert reflected. They wanted him found promptly. Who were they trying to teach a lesson to, he asked himself, their own people or us?

"Let me ask you something, Chief. Are you thinking Willie Boy was the one killed the PC?"

In his weakness Bert ached to confide in somebody, but not Mosconi.

"I'm not thinking anything," he muttered.

Mosconi nodded, accepting the rebuke, and for a moment looked away. "Anna Russo met with an accident too, Chief."

Bert cared nothing for Willie Boy Benvenuto, but his feelings about Anna Russo were more complicated.

Just then a detective came running over. "We found the bullet, Chief. It was in the truck."

"Thank you," said Bert. For some reason the news made him woozy, and for a moment he thought he might go to sleep.

Holding the bullet between thumb and forefinger, the detective showed it to him, but Bert had difficulty focusing his eyes.

"It's in good shape, Chief."

To the detective mind this meant it was in one piece and not too badly battered. The striations would show. It could be matched to any other bullet out of the same gun.

"Will you wait over there," asked Bert politely, "while I finish with Lieutenant Mosconi?" To Mosconi he said: "What about Anna? Did he kill her?"

"Somebody beat the shit out of her, Chief. She's got broken

ribs, a shiner, and two teeth knocked out. My men tailed her
to the emergency room. She told us she fell down the stairs."

Mosconi waited, and Bert's eyes closed again. Was Anna's
life in danger? Should he put cops around her close enough
that her husband would see them? Or he could order her
picked up and held. His head and neck hurt so much that his
thoughts would move in no orderly way. To be the instrument
of her destruction was not what he wanted; it was more than
he could bear. He tried to work it out. If her husband had
wanted her killed, wouldn't it be done by now? It would,
wouldn't it? But Russo couldn't afford to have her killed, or
could he? If he had her killed he would have to explain to
his colleagues why: that she was an unfaithful wife. Which,
in the Mafia world, would constitute an enormous loss of
face. Wouldn't this leave him vulnerable to a takeover by
some ambitious underling, or even a rival family? Was it not
more than he would want to risk? Besides which, Anna was
herself the daughter of a Mafia family. Kill her and you might
start a gang war.

He would do nothing, Bert decided finally. Anna did not
need his protection. This beating—of course subsequent beat-
ings were possible—was as far as Russo would go.

Bert thanked Mosconi for coming and sent him home to
bed, called over the detective with the bullet and thanked him
again, and told him to thank the others.

Another hour passed before he allowed himself, along with
his wife, to be driven to Bellevue Hospital in the back of a
police car. In the emergency room part of his hair was shaved
off, and fourteen stitches taken in his scalp. A cooling com-
press was taped to his neck and he was given pain pills, which
he palmed. He would take them, but not yet.

The police car had waited, and in it the Farbers were driven
home. Upstairs, still wearing his bloodstained shirt and ruined
necktie, Bert sat down at the piano and his fingers toyed with
the keys while his wife made him a drink. The pain pills were
still in his pocket. He wanted a drink first, wanted a drink
more.

Madge brought him a scotch and soda and sat down beside
him on the bench, and he put his arms around her, put his
face in her neck, and all the lonely secrets he had been holding

in since the death of Harry came pouring out of him. He had never confided in her before, never confided in anyone as an adult, but once started found he could not stop. He told her every part of the case. He offered her a kind of nakedness that was new to both of them. He had withheld vital physical evidence: the bullet in its plastic envelope in his briefcase, Anna Russo's panties too. He had stolen the little black book out of Harry Chapman's safe, breaking in via the first dep's office, the crime of burglary, trashing the office before and after, the crime of vandalism, in an effort to make the break-in appear what it was not. To his shame he had enjoyed the trashing, the venting of some of his bile against Priestly, whom he had considered pompous and ineffective, the worst type of police official, for more than twenty years.

"I never liked him," he confessed, "but that's no reason to vandalize his office. I didn't know I was going to do it until I did it. Why did I do it? What's wrong with me? Where did such an impulse come from?"

"Hush," said Madge, holding him.

He described his confrontations with Caroline Connolly, with Anna Russo and her husband, with Mary Alice Chapman, with the first dep's wife, and then tonight with the first dep himself. He told her about the death of Willie Boy Benvenuto, his fault also, and how his suspicions had settled first in one direction, then in another. Everything he had touched he had botched, he said. "I was flailing around. I didn't know what I was doing. I just made everything worse."

An assistant DA was in charge of the case, but Bert had never consulted him. He had seized the stained Chanel suit without a warrant, which was illegal, had separated Anna from her lawyer, which was unethical, and probably illegal as well. The police department would denounce him, the courts, the liberal press as well. He would have no reputation left. He would be disgraced, then fired. And then maybe prosecuted.

He didn't even know who the murderer was. In his own mind he had narrowed it down to two people—not good enough—and he had no proof against either of them.

If only some nut had shot Harry, or a stickup man had shot him, or an assassin—an ordinary case, tragic but ordinary, and if Bert had come this far with it, the mayor would certainly have had to consider appointing him PC, might have done it. But an ordinary case was not what this one had turned out to be.

His deepest longings came out then, and this too he had never confessed to Madge before.

From his first day in uniform he had wanted to be police commissioner someday. If he had never told anyone, even her, this was because it had seemed to him too personal to talk about, a need that came from too deep inside him. Harry Chapman, who didn't even care about being PC, had talked about it all the time. For Harry it was only a stepping stone to somewhere else, whereas Bert had nourished this deepest ambition all these years in silence, and this week he had been close, he believed.

"There's still a chance," Madge told him.

This was what he wanted to believe, but he couldn't. "I don't think so," he said.

"Who killed Harry? The Mafia?"

"No," said Bert. "Not the Mafia. Kincaid had that much right."

"Florence Priestly?"

"Or her husband," said Bert. "And that's my problem. I don't know which one."

"Who shot you?"

"Probably Priestly. But Florence knows how to use a gun too. It could have been Florence."

Madge was silent.

The law was specific, he told her. An indictment had to be specific. He could not go into the grand jury and say, hey, it's either one of them or the other. Do me a favor, please, indict them both. And without an indictment the case—the two cases now—remained open. He needed more time, but there was no more time. The mayor had to appoint a new PC, and it might be First Deputy Commissioner Priestly.

How could he stop this? What could he do? If he denounced Priestly, the mayor would demand proof, which Bert didn't have. The mayor would panic. He might appoint Priestly out of obstinacy. Or fire Bert. The mayor was a politician. He was unpredictable. He had a whim of steel. He obeyed different rules from other people.

But suppose Bert did nothing. Pretended the investigation—the two investigations now—led nowhere. If he kept silent the mayor might appoint Bert P. Farber police commissioner. Silence was his chance. But how could he keep silent? He loved the department too much. The stakes were too high.

Bert was trying to think it out, but his head hurt so much that his thoughts would come in no predictable sequence. He began to imagine himself appointed PC: he would make the first dep retire at once, he told Madge. With Priestly gone, there would be time to pursue the case—the two cases—to a careful, logical conclusion. Solid evidence would turn up down the road, something always turned up. The investigation into tonight's shooting that had just started would lead to the breaking of both cases.

But if the mayor chose Priestly, then it would be Bert who would be forced to retire. And the two investigations would end.

No, they wouldn't end, he told Madge feelingly. From outside the department he would keep probing. He would probe until he had whatever evidence he needed. He was a detective. But working outside the department rather than inside would make it harder.

But if he were successful, the man he would bring down would be a sitting PC. Police Commissioner Priestly would claim—and his wife would claim too—that these were trumped-up charges brought by a disgruntled and bitter man, an ex-subordinate named Bert Farber, whom he had been obliged to fire.

The citizenry would believe him.

If only he had more time, Bert told Madge. But he didn't. Time was up. And whatever he did would mean the end of his career.

He stood up, then sat down again. He would have to go to the mayor. No, he would go first to the DA. No, the mayor was better.

One thing was certain. Whoever he went to would call a conference. All the DA's advisers would be consulted; or all the mayor's. Secrecy would end. By tomorrow night twenty or more people would know everything, and even though the case remained unprosecutable the rumors would float. There would be no stopping them. The mess would spill out into the street, provoking one of the biggest scandals ever to strike the city. It would tear the police department apart. Everybody near the case would be destroyed, himself most of all. He would be the messenger who had brought the bad news, and you know what happened to those.

His hand was lying on the piano keys, and Madge took it. "You haven't talked to me like this in ages," she said. "If you wanted to do it more often, I wouldn't mind."

They smiled at each other.

"I wouldn't leak it to the press," Madge said. "Honest."

They held hands over the piano keys.

"Do you want me to fix you something to eat?" said Madge.

"Let's go off someplace together," said Bert.

"Sure."

"Madge—"

The phone rang, and Madge went to answer it.

Already Bert felt immeasurably lighter and better. He had held back nothing except his afternoon in bed with Mary Alice Chapman, and he wished he could have talked to Madge about that as well. I'm free of Mary Alice Chapman, he wanted to tell her. You don't have to worry about that anymore. All I feel for her is pity, he wanted to tell her, the obsession, if it was an obsession, is over, you're the one I want to go on a trip with, you're twice the woman she is, how could I have been so blind?

"It's your duty sergeant," Madge said from the telephone.

He picked up the phone and the voice in his ear said: "Something may have happened to the first dep, Chief. You better get down here right away."

Pursuant to the orders of First Deputy Commissioner Priestly, the office of the late Harry Chapman was still sealed, and the cop on duty there this particular night was Police Officer Wristed. He had been out in the corridor on his way back from the men's room when the elevator doors had opened, disgorging the first dep himself.

Wristed had saluted him, but Priestly's gaze was fixed

straight ahead. Taking no notice of the uniformed cop, he had unlocked his own office suite and gone in and closed the door behind him. It was past eleven o'clock by then, so it was unusual that there should be anyone on the fourteenth floor at all, except for Wristed on guard duty. He had wondered what the first dep wanted up here this late. Also he had noticed that the man's head and shoulders were covered with snow. To Wristed this meant that the snow was still falling heavily outside, and that Priestly, hatless, must have trudged a long way in it. Why hadn't he reached headquarters by car?

Well, it was not Wristed's business, and he went back to the desk he had appropriated outside the PC's office, and watched the small television set up on the wall. But some time later, maybe an hour, maybe two hours, he wasn't sure, he heard a noise. It sounded like a gunshot to him. He knew what gunshots sounded like, and it came from the first dep's area, and he ran down there and pushed the outer door open and went in. He was certainly right about the noise being a gunshot, for once inside he could smell it. In a mild way the place smelled like any of the several police shooting ranges. He sniffed the air again and again as if to be sure. He was already sure. Alarmed too. Gunshot smoke. It was strong enough so that he could almost see it. He was standing in a web of odor that ought not to have been there.

Priestly's outer office was empty, and the door to his private office was closed. Wristed went to it but did not immediately try the handle.

Instead he called out: "Commissioner, are you in there?"

No answer came back.

Wristed called out a second time, then tried the handle. The door was locked.

Already in something of a panic, he ran down to the thirteenth floor to the chief of detectives' office, where he knew there was a sergeant on duty all night who might know what to do.

The two men went back up to Priestly's door.

"Commissioner," the sergeant called out in his turn, "are you in there?" Receiving no answer, he too tried the handle. The door was still locked.

"You smell it, Sarge?"

"Yeah, I smell it," said the sergeant, whose name was O'Grady. He looked around him, and he too was uncertain what to do next. "I better call my boss," he decided, and he did. This was the call that Madge picked up on, handing the phone to Bert.

O'Grady's second call was to the 13th Precinct, which took a car off patrol and sent it to pick up Bert in front of his building.

Upon reaching headquarters the chief of detectives went directly to the fourteenth floor and into Priestly's office, where he listened to what Wristed and O'Grady told him.

"Are you sure what you heard was a shot?"

"He heard it and we both smelled it," said Sergeant O'Grady.

Bert snuffed the air, but by then the odor had dissipated. "Get emergency service on the phone," he ordered O'Grady. "Have them get a battering ram up to the fourteenth floor." He turned to Wristed. "You," he said, "call the chief of the department, the chief of patrol, the chief of personnel, the chief of inspectional services." All these men wore three stars or above. "Call as many deputy commissioners as you can reach. I want a wall of brass in here. This thing needs to be documented."

Three cops from emergency service, one of them a sergeant, were the first to arrive. They wore body armor, were heavily armed, and lumbered in carrying shotguns and other gear. "You want a door bashed in, Chief?" the sergeant said. "Is that all?" He sounded disappointed. "We thought it might be an arrest or hostage situation. Which door?"

Bert told him to set up his battering ram and wait.

The elevator came up again and the deputy commissioners for training and for management and budget got off: two disgruntled men hurrying across the hall and into the office. Bert's bandaged head and neck surprised them. "What happened to you?" one said. "We're administrators," said the other impatiently. "We don't usually get called out in the middle of the night."

Before Bert could brief them, Sternhagen arrived wearing full uniform but looking disheveled. "What is it, Bert?"

So he briefed all three.

"Did you hear this shot personally?" demanded Sternhagen.

"No."

"Did you personally smell anything?"

"No." Bert was trying to figure out what was wrong with Sternhagen's uniform, but his head was not working clearly.

Sternhagen eyed the door. "But you're sure he's in there?"

"I think it's probable."

Sternhagen went over and shook the door handle. "Can you hear me, Commissioner? Open up. Open up, please."

He came back to Bert's side. "He may have done something to himself—that's what you're thinking." It was a statement, not a question.

"That's what you should be thinking too."

The chief of the department hesitated. "If we take his door down and the office is empty—"

Why did Sternhagen's uniform, normally impeccable, hang so badly?

"Could we get a locksmith up here, Bert?"

"It's the middle of the night, Chief."

"You think I don't realize that, for crissake. I was sound asleep. Jesus, twice in one night."

As Sternhagen paced, the bottom of his pajama leg leached out onto his shoe. That's it, Bert thought in a kind of muted triumph, he's pulled his uniform on over his pajamas.

"I don't want to do anything that might seem rash," said Sternhagen.

Not when the mayor still hasn't decided who is to be PC, thought Bert.

"We break the door down, he's not in there," said Sternhagen, "everyone comes to work in the morning—how do we explain it?"

He meant: how do I look? Bert watched him.

"People would say we overreacted," said Sternhagen. "I've known Fred Priestly many years. He's not that kind of man."

Bert said nothing.

"He could have walked out before that officer got down here," said Sternhagen.

"He's been under stress," said Bert, thinking: more stress than you know.

"Or his gun goes off by accident," said Sternhagen. "He's embarrassed. He waits until the first officer goes off to fetch your man, then locks his office and rides the executive elevator down to his car."

"I don't think we can wait for a locksmith," Bert said.

Still Sternhagen hesitated.

"He wouldn't be the first cop ate his gun," said Bert.

Sternhagen knew this too. He eyed the door handle.

"It's a cop's way out," said Bert gently.

The chief of the department made his decision. "You men," he said to the emergency service cops, "take the door down."

Immediately Bert countermanded the order. "I'm as impatient as you are," he told Sternhagen, "but we better wait another few minutes, see who else is coming in."

Finally much of the headquarters brass had assembled: four of the eight deputy commissioners and six high-ranking chiefs all crowded together outside the first dep's office as the battering ram at last went into action. It took only two heavy blows to splinter the frame.

The door swung open.

The first deputy commissioner was seated behind his desk in his swivel armchair. His head was thrown back. His eyes were three quarters closed and he was peering down his nose.

No one spoke, and Priestly did not move. One arm had fallen off the armrest. His gun was in his lap, as was the hand that had used it. The gun had rolled or bounced forward almost as far as his knees.

Bert saw that he had shot himself once in the heart.

There was no mess, and almost no blood.

The note was on his desk, written in ink, presumably with the ballpoint pen that lay beside it. Bert stepped around the desk and read it over the dead man's shoulder. He read it twice, the second time aloud.

"I shot and killed Police Commissioner Chapman after an argument over a personal matter," the first dep had written. "I can no longer live with what I have done." And then: "My wife was not involved in this in any way and is entirely blameless."

"You say he was up here an hour or more?" said Bert to Officer Wristed who, his mouth open, still stared at the corpse.

"I don't know how long it was," mumbled Wristed.

The various deputy commissioners were staring too.

Bert handed the note to Sternhagen.

Beneath Priestly's desk was a wastebasket. Kneeling beside it, Bert began plucking out sheets of paper, which he smoothed on the rug. What he found were other versions of the same note, some of them longer, none shorter, some full of the rantings Bert had heard in his office earlier that night.

As he regained his feet he became momentarily dizzy from his wound, but a jumble of thoughts fought for his attention, and some of them he articulated. "People think we're living in a sexually liberated age," he muttered. "We're not, are we? Deep down, nothing has changed. Nothing will ever change." He stared at the corpse, talking more to himself than anyone else, not caring what anyone thought. "We're poor benighted human beings," he said. "Sex still signifies ownership to us. It always has and it always will. People still kill each other over it, and they kill themselves over it. They always have and they always will."

Then he muttered bitterly: "Jesus, Harry, what a mess you made."

▪15▪

"ACCORDING TO POLICE department records," Bert said, "the gun he killed himself with has been registered to him for thirty years. It's his gun, no question. Test bullets fired from it match the bullet that killed the PC. No question about that either. So if you want to close down the investigation right there, we can."

"You got your answer," said the mayor. "He kills the PC for personal reasons, and a few days later out of remorse he does away with himself. What more do you want?"

"Okay," said Bert.

He had not been to bed. He had stopped off at home long enough to take a careful shower and change his shirt and suit, then had come directly to meet the mayor. As he was driven up the night floodlights still illuminated the City Hall dome, though above it by then the sky was getting toward dawn. The news crews had already begun to coagulate in the corridors. He had hurried in past them, answering no questions.

The mayor's office when he entered it was full of men, but the mayor had shooed them all out, leaving himself alone with Bert. That was an hour ago. They had been talking alone ever since.

"The bullet that killed the PC," said the mayor. "I didn't know you had it. Why wasn't I told?"

"You didn't ask."

"I want to know why."

Bert shrugged.

"Did you imagine it was an unimportant detail, for cris-sake?"

"I didn't think of it one way or the other," Bert lied.

"Another thing," said the mayor. "If the gun was so incrim-inating, why did he keep it?"

"He didn't know about the recovered bullet either."

"He knew enough to get rid of the gun."

"A cop can't just get rid of his gun and not report it. Getting rid of a gun, for a cop, requires explanations, paperwork. I imagine he thought it was safer to keep it."

"Did he ever ask you if the bullet had been recovered?"

"Yeah."

"And?"

Bert shrugged. "I lied to him."

"And now you're lying to me, but about what? That's what I'm trying to figure out."

"I'm holding back nothing," lied Bert. He patted the com-press on his neck to make sure it was still there. "I'm trying to tell you the whole story." He had taken the pain pills, and as a result was feeling half asleep. He warned himself to be very, very careful what he said.

"And the bullets fired at you match Priestly's gun also?"

Bert nodded. "Actually we only have one of them, but it matches."

The mayor picked up a copy of the suicide note that Bert had handed him earlier. "You're sure this is his handwriting?"

Bert nodded. "His fingerprints are on the original."

"An ironclad case?"

"Against Priestly?" said Bert. "Yeah, it's ironclad."

"So it's over."

"Except for picking up the pieces."

"The pieces," the mayor said.

"There are bits and pieces. But we can skip them if you want."

"What are you talking about?"

"Well, just pieces."

"The pieces can be the hardest part," the mayor said, watching Bert carefully.

After a moment he added: "That's what politicians deal

with, pieces. Very important, the pieces. Not too satisfying, at times, though.''

Bert did not reply, and he avoided the mayor's gaze.

"All right," said the mayor finally. "How much of all this do I have to tell the vultures outside?"

"That's up to you."

"Who knows the whole story?" the mayor said. "How many people?"

"No one knows it all."

"John Kincaid?"

"No."

"Sternhagen?"

"No."

"No one else? What about cops? They been working on the case for days. How many of them know everything? A few dozen?"

"Just you and me," lied Bert.

By this time the press had packed itself into the Blue Room. The news conference should have started thirty minutes ago.

The mayor had begun drumming his fingers on his desk. "So how much of it can we contain?"

"Contain?" said Bert. "I'm sorry, I took some pills. I'm not thinking too clearly."

"There must be some things we don't have to announce."

"What did you have in mind?"

"For instance, that this terrific police commissioner my search committee found me was sticking it into every female in the city."

"Well," said Bert, "I don't see where you have to allude to that, no."

"Including he was fucking the wife of a Mafia don."

"She had nothing to do with killing him."

"If she can be linked to him, it can be just as bad. So who knows about her?"

"The fingerprint section processed her fingerprints. They may have an inkling."

"An inkling of what?"

"That she's connected to this in some way. Only an inkling."

"The PC's Mafia connection. That's what I need."

"It may leak out, it may not."

"Let's wait for it to do so," said the mayor. "And hope it won't. And let's not help it along, if you get my meaning."

"I don't quite follow you."

"If it leaks," said the mayor, eyeing Bert, "I think I'll know who leaked it."

He picked up the suicide note and studied it once more. "Do we need to say Chapman was banging the dead man's wife?"

"They may infer it," said Bert.

"Maybe not. It says here 'personal matter.' Which could mean anything. Professional jealousy. Or they hated each other many years. Or Chapman was going to make him retire. The guy's mind snapped, what the hell. Hey, he's dead, his wife's alive, they have no proof, and there are libel laws."

"Okay with me," said Bert, whose head had started to ache again. "Show them the note, tell them about the bullets, and say case closed. Let them infer whatever they want."

"Why did he shoot at you?"

"That's easy. I was getting too close."

"There's something you're not happy about," said the mayor shrewdly.

"Me? Happy? I'm completely happy. Don't I look happy?"

After studying Bert a moment longer, the mayor stood up. "They're waiting for us. When this news conference starts, you stand beside me and you don't open your mouth, got that?"

It occurred to Bert that the mayor still needed him, if only to keep silent. This emboldened him to say: "Can I ask you a question first?"

The mayor looked at him.

"It's the same one the newsmen will ask you. Today is the day you're supposed to announce a new PC."

The mayor gave a dry laugh.

"The city wants to know," said Bert doggedly.

"You mean you want to know." The mayor eyed him thoughtfully. "The city's going to have to wait. You're going to have to wait too."

"The law says ten days."

The mayor scoffed at this remark. "You going to put me in jail?"

He led the way out the door. "Let's get this farce over with," he said.

The press conference started. After making a brief, somber presentation, the mayor accepted questions, recognizing each questioner by name. The mood stayed somber. There were no jokes, no smart remarks. Partly because of the nature of what the mayor called "these sad events," partly because they had a great story already, the newspeople were surprisingly docile. The hard questions, Bert knew, would come beginning tomorrow.

Finally the press conference broke up. Separated from the mayor in the now milling crowd, Bert found himself surrounded by journalists who pressed him for details, explanations, theories, but he answered none of them. Instead he claimed a headache, a loss of memory, and escaped to his car and then home.

His wife prepared breakfast for him, changed the dressing on his neck, then rubbed his back and shoulders with alcohol until he fell asleep.

The mayor, meanwhile, went back to his office, where he sat brooding for some time. At length, without going through his secretary, he picked up his telephone and dialed a number directly, for he wanted no one to know whom he was calling, or why. That would come later, if the call worked out.

When Bert woke up he went out to the living room in a bathrobe and found Madge reading a magazine. It was the first he realized that she had stayed home from work to care for him if he needed anything, and he was grateful.

It was late afternoon by then, getting dark fast, and he went to the phone and called his office. Inspector Potter came on the line, and they talked for a while. First Deputy Commissioner Priestly was being waked at the Frank Conner funeral home on Amsterdam Avenue, Potter said. "Do you know the one I mean?"

It was in the 20th Precinct. "Yeah," said Bert, "I know the one you mean."

The funeral was set for the day after tomorrow in Good

Shepherd Church in Inwood, Potter told him. It was the parish in which the deceased had grown up. Otherwise there had been no new developments and the city was quiet. There had been many phone calls for him, however, from the press and others, and Potter read off a list of them. Bert copied down certain of these.

When he had hung up he said to Madge: "Priestly's wake is starting tonight. I think I should go to it."

"What on earth for?" Madge demanded.

"Respect, I guess. I knew him since the day I got out of the police academy."

"That's no reason."

"Well, I don't think there'll be many people there. His wife is going to need all the support she can get."

"He tried to kill you."

"A crazy man tried to kill me. He wasn't himself."

"What's the real reason?"

"I want to see Florence Priestly."

"Why?"

"There's something I want to talk to her about, something that still bothers me."

"Do you want to tell me what it is?"

He smiled at her with a fondness he hadn't felt in a long time. "You deserve to know," he said. "Just let me talk to her first."

For a moment he looked over the list of phone messages he had copied down, including one that puzzled him. But he resolved to call no one back tonight.

The Frank Conner Memorial Chapel had many rooms, and as he passed along the lugubrious corridor he was able to glance into a number of them: quick glimpses of coffins that were banked with flowers, that were usually open under spotlights. The people standing around were all in black. Priest in black, rabbis in black, mourners in black. You couldn't tell one from the other.

Priestly was laid out in a smaller room at the end of the corridor. The coffin was closed and not banked with flowers. A few large bouquets, one of them sent by Bert, stood in vases widely spaced on the floor. There were no spotlights.

Nor were there many mourners: only five in all. In addition to Florence, Bert recognized two of Priestly's grown sons from his first marriage, men in their thirties, and he shook hands with them. He then went up and stood over the coffin for a moment, but he did not pray. No case was ever open and shut, he brooded. Law enforcement was not an exact science. The degree of a person's wrongdoing was not written on his forehead. Always it was for a jury to decide, and often enough juries were not competent, or got it wrong. In any event, for those particular crimes of which Priestly in his coffin was the final victim, no one would ever stand trial. No jury verdict would ever come down.

As he turned from the coffin Bert was confronted by Florence Priestly.

"Are you happy now?" she said. "Are you satisfied now?"

"I feel almost as badly as you do," he said.

"No you don't."

Dressed in black, with tears beginning to roll down her face, Florence looked small, which she was not, and sixty years old, though she was forty-two. She had always been a big, hefty woman, never particularly attractive, but to protect her a man had just attempted murder, and after that, still protecting her, he had killed himself. This did not surprise Bert. When tragedies of this kind occurred, people always imagined a certain type of woman at the center of them, someone voluptuous, with the face and curves of a film star. They were wrong. The Florence Priestlys of the world were the women at the center of it.

"He didn't kill Harry," said Florence Priestly.

"I know," Bert said.

He didn't know, but he had guessed. For some time he had known that Harry Chapman that tragic night was up in his flat with Anna Russo. What he had not seen until now was what may have been happening down in the street. It seemed to Bert now that both of the Priestlys had been watching the building, not just one, their presence unknown to each other, hiding in separate doorways, or perhaps one was in a car. Both of them would have been miserable and suffering, and cold too, with the snow coming down. The emotion raging in their minds and souls, in their stomachs and their breasts was jealousy, that old standby. It was as if someone, maybe God, maybe the devil, were twanging on a hundred taut strings inside them, and they watched Harry Chapman's lighted windows hoping to be proven wrong. At length Anna Russo moved across in front of the light. It was a ghastly moment for both. My wife, Priestly thought. Harry's other woman, thought Florence. It was the proof both had hoped never to discover.

When Harry came out to jog a short time later, it was Florence Priestly who sprang across the street and accosted him.

It was dark and snowing hard. Seeing this other individual appear, as Bert now imagined the scene, Priestly had jumped back into his doorway or car. But he heard the shot, saw Harry fall, and he ran forward and grappled with the assassin, for he was a cop, was he not, and being a cop took precedence over everything.

After a moment he realized that the woman struggling in his arms was his wife.

At home there must have been tearful confessions. Bert could imagine Florence begging her husband to save her, promising undying love if he would save her. He was first deputy commissioner—acting commissioner now—and perhaps the next PC as well. He could save her, slow the investigation down, derail it—whatever was necessary.

Priestly must have agreed. Certainly he had made every effort to get in Bert's way, in the detectives' way.

He had been a policeman forty years, and was living a lie. Gradually the lie made him crazy—the lie plus the constant imagining of Florence writhing around under Harry Chapman. Finally his demented mind had fixed on ambushing Chief Farber—ambushing the investigation. He was crazed when he tried this, and not so crazed a few hours later when he turned the gun on himself. It was the only way he could prove to Florence how much he had loved her, was it not? It was also a way to hold on to her even after death.

Knowing all this, or imagining he knew it—which, to a cop, was much the same thing—Bert had an automatic reaction. He should arrest Florence Priestly, take her out of here in handcuffs, and charge her with the murder of Harry Chapman.

But in legal terms the murderer of Harry Chapman had already been determined. Priestly's signed confession—a deathbed confession, so to speak—had solved the case.

Bert's theory to the contrary was just that, a theory, on which no jury would ever vote to convict.

Besides which, an arrest, followed by an indictment, followed by the various legal motions, followed by the trial itself, would further traumatize a police department that was already numb and barely functioning, its honor so badly compromised that its ability to keep order would be put at risk. The city would be further traumatized as well.

And what about Bert's own best interests? The mayor had been presented with a nice, pat solution, and would not want to be confronted suddenly by another, whose eventual outcome would be in doubt for months.

To have any hope of being named the next PC, Bert had best leave the present solution in place.

So however much he wanted to work the riddle all the way to the end, to see justice done, he could do nothing. It was too late. The law, which was all human beings had that resembled justice at all, did not care about solving riddles. Often it did not care about justice either. The law was satisfied that Frederick Priestly had killed Harry Chapman.

And how could Bert be so sure that his own final scenario was the correct one? Each of his previous scenarios had pleased him at the time. Maybe one of them was a true picture of what had actually happened. Maybe he had got it right long ago, and was dead wrong now.

Looking into Florence's eyes, his doubts returned. He wondered who had killed Harry Chapman and realized he would never know for sure.

He peered past Florence at the coffin.

There would be no inspector's funeral for Frederick Priestly, who had probably looked forward to one at the end, as all cops did. In a small way this was a tragedy too, for the man had been a cop forty years. "I've been able to arrange a police color guard for the funeral," Bert told Florence. "More than that I can't do."

She nodded through tears. "And the—the investigation?"

"The case," Bert said, "is closed." He left it at that, and left the wake.

In the morning in his office he shuffled through the phone messages that had accumulated, including the one that had puzzled him the day before. It did more than puzzle him now as he stared at it, for he thought he knew what it signified, and he feared the worst.

The message was from a man named Quigley, who was the police commissioner of Detroit. Bert knew him, and had once served under him. A big bald guy with a loud voice and no manners. An authoritarian who shouted at subordinates. Reached the rank of deputy chief in New York, one star, and after that had been passed over by the then commissioner, who did not like him. There was a traditional route for ambitious officers who found their progress blocked, and Bert knew this as well as anybody—they moved out into the hinterlands, took jobs running smaller departments, and hoped to work their way back. Quigley had sent out a hundred or more copies of his resume, and had got only one offer, according to the jokes in the office. In any case, there had been at least one, and he had accepted it: chief of police in Buffalo, a city of about 450,000. Bert had not seen him since, but knew he had stayed there a year, then moved on to San Francisco and now Detroit, bigger departments each time.

Bert had no desire to talk to him, and so slid the message to the bottom of the pile. But he couldn't put it off forever, and an hour later he decided to return the call.

"I understand you got problems there, and no one to solve them," said Quigley.

The brusqueness of the remark reminded Bert of how much he had always disliked and distrusted this man.

"The mayor called me," said Quigley. "He feels he needs an outsider to clean it up. I'm coming in there tomorrow. I'm to be sworn in as PC the next day."

Bert glanced down at the time and date on the message slip in his hand. He must have been hardly out of the mayor's sight yesterday before the mayor phoned his guy and offered him the appointment.

"So what kind of guy is the mayor?" said Quigley.

"Whatever he tells you, you can count on," said Bert. "His word is his bond."

"I'm glad to hear that," commented Quigley. "The mayor is the one a PC works for."

"You're in luck with this guy. He would never do anything behind your back."

"Good," said Quigley.

In silence Bert chastised himself for feeling betrayed. That's what politicians do, he told himself, they betray you.

"As I understand it," said Quigley, "you're in a real mess there. So what can you tell me I don't already know?"

Bert told him what had been in the newspapers.

"I know all that," interrupted Quigley. "What else?"

"When you're PC you have a right to know what else," said Bert. "Until then you don't."

"Don't do anything until I get there."

Bert hung up, and for some time sat with his face in his hands. He was not going to be the next PC, and if he knew anything about human nature Quigley and the mayor were not going to want him around long as chief of detectives. His police career in New York was over, or nearly over.

Quigley was sworn in as PC, and three days later called a press conference at which he named Terrence Sternhagen first deputy commissioner and John Kincaid chief of the department. Bert remained chief of detectives, at least temporarily. They still need my silence, he told himself. For a little while longer. But who knew how long that would be?

The beaming Sternhagen stood in a corner surrounded by reporters. Bert congratulated him, then peered across at Kincaid, who was surrounded by other reporters. Abruptly Kincaid looked up, caught his eye, called out "Bert," and beckoned him over.

"Congratulations, Chief," Bert said to him.

"I'm scheduling meetings with my top subordinates."

Kincaid was wearing a new blue uniform with four stars on each shoulder. "Call my chief of staff," he ordered, "tell him I said to fit you in."

"It won't be right away, I'm afraid."

"Tomorrow," said Kincaid, "will be soon enough."

"I'm taking a few days off, Chief."

"Requests for time off go through my office, I believe. I don't recall approving anything of that nature."

"Doctor's orders." The reporters were listening, and as Bert patted the bandage on his head they crowded closer. "The doctors have advised rest."

Kincaid's jaw muscles tightened.

"We all have to obey the doctors," said Bert. "What can I tell you." Sensing something, the reporters hovered.

"Give this thing a chance to heal," said Bert.

Kincaid glanced at the reporters. "Right you are, Bert," he said. "We want you to take the best possible care of yourself, that's the important thing."

"That's what I'm going to do."

"So how long will you be out?"

"Who knows?" said Bert. Nodding at Kincaid, and then at the reporters, he started out of the room, but after several paces stopped and called back over his shoulder: "And by the way, Chief, congratulations again."

Outside in the city there was another storm. The snow was coming down hard. Bert at his office window could not see Brooklyn.

He went home, picked up his wife and bags, and Hughie drove them to the airport. When the weather caused a delay before takeoff, Bert and Madge sat in the VIP lounge sipping coffee and talked about what the future might hold. Quigley would not be PC forever, Bert said. Sooner or later there would be a new mayor too. Perhaps he could hang on as chief of detectives until then. Provided he stopped baiting John Kincaid, of course.

"Do you think you can stop baiting him?"

"I'm not sure."

"But you admit," said Madge, "that it might be a good idea."

"Oh yes," said Bert. It made Madge smile.

Or perhaps, Bert said, getting serious again, he could find some smaller city that needed a chief or commissioner, and with luck come back to New York some day as Quigley had just done. Or perhaps take a big civilian job. Vice president of security in some conglomerate. For a retired chief of detectives there was always one of those jobs around.

"That's a lot of choices," Madge said.

"What do you think I should do?"

"I'm on your side, Bert. I always have been."

Bert took her hand. "I know."

"I can't imagine you happy anywhere but New York."

"I can get over that."

"I can't imagine you anything but a New York cop."

"I can get over that too."

Madge was silent.

"Maybe I can," Bert said.

"New York is your home. The police department is your home."

It occurred to Farber that perhaps, just perhaps, home for him was wherever this woman happened to be, but he had never been good with words of that kind, and he could not think how to say them now.

"Would you like another cup of coffee?" said Madge. She stood up holding the cups. "You should wait, that's what I think. I think you should hang on as long as you can and see what happens."

Finally they were in the air bound for the Caribbean. The sun coming into the plane was blinding. "I've sometimes thought," Madge said hesitantly, having turned from the porthole, "that whatever problems we've had in our marriage, having children might have helped us."

"Well," said Bert, "we haven't had them."

"No matter how you try, parts of your job—big parts—can't be shared. Children we could have shared."

"Kids would have been nice," said Bert.

"I've often thought you blamed me."

"I certainly hope not. No. Certainly not."

"I've thought it, though."

He looked at her. "That's crazy."

They landed, came out of the airport, and inhaled the super-heated air. Across the street Bert signed for the rented car and they drove around the island to their hotel. They changed to swimsuits, then came downstairs again and Bert went into the store in the lobby and bought a straw hat to wear over his bandaged scalp. Out in the bright hot sun they walked barefoot along the beach holding hands. It was late afternoon now, the sun low but still very hot, and a hot wind blew over the water. They had come very far from the hotel, and Bert peered back at it. When they came to the cliffs at the end they stopped and looked across at other islands.

"I was thinking," Madge said hesitantly, and she touched his arm, "that I'd like to try to get pregnant."

When Bert looked at her, her eyes dropped.

"There are some new procedures," Madge said. She was drawing designs in the sand with her big toe. "I've been reading up on them."

"Yes, I've read some things too."

"What do you think?"

"I'm not against it, if you decide that's what you want to do."

"Maybe that's what I want to do."

"Then I'm for it," Bert said.

"It wouldn't be too pleasant for you. Or for me either, for that matter."

"All right, as soon as we get back to New York that's what we'll do."

As they started back to the hotel, the sand was hot under their feet. Bert was grinning, and he patted her on the rump. "And I say we should make a preliminary try at pregnancy almost immediately. I mean, like, five minutes from now."

She looked very pleased with him as they walked along. "Actually we would be a little old to be having a first baby."

"Old? Who's old?"

"It will be very costly, and it might not work."

"No," said Bert soberly, "that's not the way to approach it. It's going to work." He found himself considering it as he might have done as a young man, and this surprised him: with an extra mouth to feed he would have to work extra hard.

Close to the hotel, they passed among people stretched out in deck chairs on the sand.

"Somehow I can't picture you as a father."

"What do you mean? I'll be a great father."

"The last few days you seem different somehow, you know that?"

"Nothing like getting shot in the head to make one different. It changes one's point of view."

"The new Bert Farber."

"Naw," said Bert. "Not at all."

"I think so," said Madge.

"I don't know," said Bert. "Maybe. We'll have to wait and see."